Neema Shah

KOLOLO HILL

PICADOR

First published 2021 by Picador
an imprint of Pan Macmillan
The Smithson, 6 Briset Street, London EC1M 5NR
Associated companies throughout the world
www.panmacmillan.com

ISBN 978-1-5290-3050-1

Pan Macmillan does not have any control over, or any responsibility for,
any author or third-party websites referred to in or on this book.

1 3 5 7 9 8 6 4 2

A CIP catalogue record for this book is available from the British Library.

Typeset in Bell by Jouve (UK), Milton Keynes
Printed and bound by CPI Group (UK) Ltd, Croydon, CR0 4YY

Visit **www.picador.com** to read more about all our books
and to buy them. You will also find features, author interviews and
news of any author events, and you can sign up for e-newsletters
so that you're always first to hear about our new releases.

For
Nana, Nani
Ba & Bapuji

The time that my journey takes is long and the way of it long.

I came out on the chariot of the first gleam of light, and pursued my voyage through the wildernesses of worlds leaving my track on many a star and planet.

It is the most distant course that comes nearest to thyself, and that training is the most intricate which leads to the utter simplicity of a tune.

The traveler has to knock at every alien door to come to his own, and one has to wander through all the outer worlds to reach the innermost shrine at the end.

'JOURNEY HOME'
BY RABINDRANATH TAGORE

PART ONE

Uganda, 1972

PART ONE

1

Asha

They'd be back before curfew, Asha was sure of it. She got out of the car and looked, far across the water, to where the Nile flowed into Lake Victoria. In the late-afternoon light, the mosquitoes glowed gold, like embers from a fire.

'Be quick, won't you?' Jaya called from the car window, pulling her *sari chundri* tighter over her silver hair. 'And be careful.'

'Hush, Jaya, she's not a child,' said Motichand. 'Besides, we can see her from here.' The car swayed like a rowing boat as Asha's father-in-law hoisted himself into the back seat and lay down for a nap.

Asha slipped off her two *chumpul*, blades of grass tickling her toes, the dragonflies dancing at her feet. She shook her hair free from her ponytail, aware that Jaya was probably looking on (loose hair for loose women).

Jaya had wanted to go straight home, anxious to reach Kampala before the soldiers began their night patrols, but Asha had managed to persuade them to stop off on the way. What harm would it do to get a little fresh air after being cooped up in the car, to steal a few moments in the place she'd visited so many times as a child with her parents? There were more people here in the old days, of course: the sweet, smoky scent of roasting *mogo* carrying across the breeze, tinny transistor

3

radios buzzing in the distance. Now all Asha could see was a few fishing boats, and the crotchety marabou storks with their black feather cloaks gathered in the shallows.

She walked towards the vast water, stretching so far that it looked like an ocean. She'd met Pran for the first time by Lake Victoria, down by Entebbe. She bristled as she thought of him now. She was sure that Pran was keeping something from her, he'd dodged her questions before she'd left for Jinja that morning. Asha wandered further along. It was too beautiful a day to waste it thinking about him.

Something was jutting out at the water's edge: a strange mass that seemed to grow from the banks, blackened in parts, ashen in others. Asha stepped closer. This wasn't the root of a plant, but sinewy muscle, twisting tendon. Upstream, there were more.

Hacked bodies bobbing in the billowing lake.

A crackle of fear.

Asha turned fast, hurrying back towards the others. Slow your pace, she told herself. Don't alarm them.

'What happened, why were you hurrying?' Jaya got out of the car.

Motichand sat up, voice full of sleep. 'What's going on?'

'It's been a long day.' Asha glanced back, trying to sound calm. 'Shall we go?'

'I thought you wanted to spend some time here?'

'I did. I'm just a little tired.' Asha hovered by the back seat. Why wouldn't Motichand hurry up and put his shoes on? She looked towards the road – no sign of soldiers, thank God.

She'd told herself that the rumours must have been embellished, growing as neighbour told friend, told colleague. How could she have been so wrong? The broken limbs flashed through her mind as she climbed into the car. Idi Amin didn't care that those poor people's bodies were bobbing in the water, out on show for all to see. Killing anyone who spoke out against him or threatened his power. He might not stop until the whole river ran red.

*

'Ba mentioned you stopped off at the lake on the way back from Jinja today?' Pran pulled back the bedcover.

'Mmm.' Asha smoothed on face cream, cool against her skin. She was in no mood to pretend everything was OK between them. Their earlier argument hung in the air just as the image of the bodies festered in her mind. But she didn't want to tell him what she'd seen; saying it out loud would only make things worse.

Pran watched as she combed her hair, which was tangled as usual. 'I'm sorry Vijay and I couldn't leave the *dukan*.'

Asha climbed into bed and tucked in the last section of mosquito net, taking in Pran's tobacco-and-soap scent. The short strands of his hair had settled in waves on the pillow. 'I told you before, I understand,' she said. It wasn't the fact that he'd stayed behind at the dukan, their general store, that bothered her, and he knew it. 'Do you want to turn off the light?'

The longer they lay side by side in silence, the louder the electric ring of the crickets seemed to get. Eventually she turned towards him, sheets clammy against her skin. 'I just don't understand why you can't tell me.'

'We went over this, Asha.'

'You and Vijay had to stay at the dukan today because it's so busy. But you're happy to spare him next week to go to London?'

'That's different. Papa will help. It's only for a few days.'

'Your Papa?' Motichand, model businessman – turning up late and giving out credit to friends and strangers alike. 'And what were you whispering about with Vijay yesterday?'

'I told you, the dukan. I'm not allowed to talk to my own brother in private now?' Pran's voice was taut.

Asha knew there was more to their conversation than the business. She'd seen the shadow of guilt on Pran's face, Vijay's wide eyes staring at the parquet floor.

Asha turned her back to him, too tired to push him any further tonight. Sleep – she needed sleep to bury the horrible day. But while Pran's breath grew deep and low, Asha lay awake, the sheets hot beneath her, staring at the sliver of moonlight that cut across the ceiling.

*

The next morning, Asha woke first, her body curved into a question mark next to Pran's as the haze filled the room. Outside, the house had its own rhythm, a secret language that she was still trying to learn: December, their house boy, pounding the washing in the yard; Motichand and his booming sneezes; Jaya humming Gujarati prayer songs as she went about her day.

Pran opened his eyes. 'Don't you ever sleep?' he said gently.

'I'd better get up and help with breakfast.'

'Wait.' He clutched her shoulder. 'Last night . . .'

She gave a heavy sigh. 'I don't want there to be secrets between us, Pran.'

'It's nothing to worry about. I just don't want to bore you with all that dull dukan talk. All you need to know is that I'm working as hard as I can so that I can give you a better life, that's it.'

'But it seemed like you and Vijay—'

Pran moved closer to her. 'Such an active mind for so early in the morning.' His lips brushed against her cheek.

She turned her head aside. This wasn't something that could be kissed away.

'Everything's going to get better, you'll see.'

She looked into his eyes. Perhaps she had got it wrong? The image of the poor souls in the river flashed through her mind, her heart racing, heat blooming across her neck. So naive, going out to the water like that. Perhaps she was wrong about the dukan. 'I don't think the worst of you,' she said.

Pran trailed his thumb across her lips. 'So why don't we both find something else to think about, instead?'

His mouth on hers, his light stubble brushed her cheeks. She tried to ignore that strange pull inside her chest, the faintest of lingering doubts.

2

Vijay

Vijay finished the rest of his *chai*, wondering how late John would be picking him up this time. He looked through the kitchen window, out into the yard. It was framed on either side by the rooms of the house, and on the far side by a wall that adjoined the neighbours' garden. After a moment, Asha emerged from her bedroom, running her fingers through the jasmine shrub, then hurried up onto the veranda and joined him to pour herself a glass of water. Asha always rushed, long dresses swirling around corners, sari chundris brushing over chair tops and door handles.

'Pran and I are watching a film. Want to come?' She stood by the table, painted toes peeping out from beneath her bell-bottom jeans.

'Which one?'

'*Bonnie and Clyde*.' She gulped the water down in one go. He looked at the pool of light that shone on her bare shoulder, imagined a finger tracing along the curve.

Like falling off a cliff.

'Nah.' He smiled.

'Why not?'

'I know what happens at the end.'

Asha rolled her eyes. 'You off to the bar now?'

'Well, the ladies won't talk to themselves . . .'

'You sure about that?' The hint of a smile as she turned towards the door.

Before he could say anything else, Pran walked in and put his arm around his wife.

'*Chaal*, Asha,' he said. 'We'll talk later, Vij.'

*

Two whiskies and a *waragi* and Coke with John later, Vijay only just made it back in time for curfew.

'You left it so late! It's nearly seven o'clock,' said Jaya, stretching to reach the locks on the window shutters.

'There was an accident on Kampala Road, Ba. John drove as fast as he could.' Vijay helped his mother lock up. At least there were no soldiers out in their street tonight, waiting to catch latecomers. Social calls were squeezed into daylight hours now, the days of staying out till dawn long gone. Now you had to be home before the sun had even set across Kololo Hill.

Pran and Asha joined them in the sitting room, followed by Motichand, clutching a glass of whisky. Pran, as usual, was acting the doting husband and son, surprising them all with gifts: a necklace for Asha (even though it was no longer safe to wear jewellery outside the house), silk saris for Jaya, a silk handkerchief for Motichand, and the latest albums, *LA Woman* and *Who's Next*, for Vijay – two copies of each, for when the vinyl inevitably wore out from overplaying. He mustered a look of gratitude, although Pran was too busy basking in everyone else's attention to notice.

'You spent so much!' said Asha. 'You shouldn't have.'

'Oh, it's fine, you know – with the new space in the dukan, we've got more stock, more sales,' said Pran, throwing words into the air and hoping some of them stuck. A tiny wrinkle had appeared between his eyebrows, so small that only Vijay noticed it. The ease with which he lied to his own wife's face . . .

But had Pran noticed the little shadows at the corners of Asha's mouth, the weariness in her eyes?

*

'This way,' said Popatlal, the tailor.

Vijay followed him inside. The heat of the early morning had already seeped into the shop; the smell of hot cotton and stale sweat had filled the air. Three workers hunched over Singer sewing machines that clattered furiously, while a fourth sat by a pile of tattered cloth scraps, sewing buttons onto a shirt. Vijay had heard some rumours about Popatlal: how he'd arrived in Kampala leaving a teenage bride behind in India, promising that he'd send for her when he'd saved enough money. In the meantime, though, he'd made a new home – and a new space in his bed for his housemaid, Mercy.

He led Vijay to the back of the shop, to a small dark room with a desk and a creaky electric fan. Popatlal opened a drawer. His gaze travelled down beyond Vijay's tapered elbow, to the space where his lower left arm should be.

'It's fine, I can put a coat on with this one.' Vijay waved his right hand.

Popatlal looked back at him, confused for a moment, then lowered his eyes. He pulled out a long tan suede coat, showing Vijay the flap of unstitched lining and slotting his hand flat inside it. 'The money's sewn into here.'

'And I'd have to wear this the whole way?' No one wore suede coats in Uganda. Vijay imagined walking down Nile Avenue like Dennis Hopper in *Easy Rider*. But with sweat patches.

'No, take it off if you want, but hold it in a way that looks natural. Anyway, the British are more worried about us staying in their country than some money you've stuffed up your coat.'

Popatlal picked his ear with his little finger and inspected what he found. 'And besides, no one has been caught so far.'

'So far?' How reassuring.

'You'll get plenty of *paisa, neh*?'

'How much cash? Enough for one of those James Bond cars?'

'Yes, yes, enough for one of those spy cars,' Popatlal muttered. 'A second-hand one, anyway. Perhaps after a few trips.' He clapped his hands together. 'So, it's all settled. Give me ten minutes to sew the money inside. Here's the ticket from the family.'

Vijay wasn't told who 'the family' was – safer that way, Popatlal said. But he could guess. One of the wealthy ones, who owned plantations or flour mills or silver mines or factories across the country. They piled their money up like mounds of sugar, living in constant paranoia that the government would take it all away from them. Pran had made the same trip himself, as he often liked to remind Vijay, pouring the cash he got paid straight into getting the dukan back on track. But then he worked out that Vijay, with his younger, unassuming face, would attract less attention. Vijay had gone along with it. A chance to go on a plane, see London, get some money together. If Pran had managed it without getting caught, how hard could it be?

*

A couple of days later, Pran dropped Vijay off outside the airport with a 'good luck' and a pat on the arm, as though he was about to go off and take a maths exam.

Inside the departures area, the soldiers were busy picking on a short, turbaned man, making him open his suitcase and pull out a pair of bobbly trousers and jumpers with elbow patches. Vijay walked past, clutching the folded coat in his hand. He heard a faint rustle from the wads of shillings inside, but no one seemed interested in him, including the woman at the check-in desk, who barely glanced at Vijay. More soldiers hung around at the gate, rifles hanging off their shoulders. A tiny muscle in Vijay's neck twitched as one of them turned to look at him, but the soldier soon wandered away to another part of the airport.

Vijay took in his fellow passengers. Maybe they were hiding secrets too? The blond man in the checked shirt with the gigantic collar – a secret agent, perhaps? A Cold War spy, trying to infiltrate the British government? Probably just a paper pusher with the civil service – but you never really knew, did you?

On board, Vijay stowed the coat in an overhead locker and took his seat by the window. The aeroplane engines thrummed beneath him, the seat vibrating against his back. He'd made it this far. All this metal in the air. Even the in-flight safety video on the overhead TV screen with all the talk of crash-landing didn't worry him, and besides, that inflatable slide didn't look so bad. People flew across the sea all the time. And now, the thrill of taking off, the force of the engines tugging at his belly, leaving the earth behind. He looked out of the window as the plane finished its rickety ascent – though not before a few passengers made use of the paper sick bags in the seat pockets, the sour smell lingering long after the seat belt and no smoking signs were turned off.

The hostess came around with trolleys of food and drink. What were these strange beige mounds, the creamy mush with the yellow chunks? Had they just emptied out the contents of the sick bags onto the trays? Best to stick with the plain bread roll and the plastic cup of water that tasted of, well, plastic.

Then the lights were dimmed, and the only sound was the slow drone of the engines. England awaited. Vijay played out the different scenarios that might lie ahead of him at Heathrow.

Under his breath, he practised what he'd say if he was questioned, deciding that he'd try to storm the customs officers and run out of the airport if things got tricky. In his head, this happened in slow motion with cinematic music playing.

*

When they landed at Heathrow, Vijay stretched his neck from side to side, ignoring the bitter taste on his tongue. He took his bag from the overhead compartment and pulled the suede coat on, the left side hanging empty over his shoulder like a Superman cape.

The cold air was the first thing to greet him as he walked down the steps off the plane. He tugged the coat tighter around his body, wishing he'd worn the jumper tucked away in his suitcase. He followed the other passengers as Pran had told him to do, trying to blend in as best as he could, taking in the lurid lights, mustard-patterned carpet and huge signs that pointed the way to Customs and Passport Control. What would happen if he was caught? Pran hadn't gone into details. Was it because he didn't want to worry Vijay or because he knew he wouldn't go along with it otherwise? Prison was possible, he knew that much. Years, maybe, locked in a cell in a foreign country. Too late now. With each step, his nerves ratcheted up. Waiting.

He watched as others took their turn in front of him. A man in a long white cotton *kanzu* was led away by one of the security guards, disappearing into a windowless office.

It was Vijay's turn.

The man in the cubicle stared at the navy British passport. Like other Ugandan Asians, he'd been given the option of getting one during Uganda's move towards independence a few years back, before the ties to Britain were cut. Ba and Papa had taken the opportunity to secure one for him. A passport for a country he'd never set foot in until now. The official took in Vijay's smiling photo, then looked up at him. Not smiling now.

'How long are you here for?' said the man.

'Just a few days,' said Vijay, hoping the nerves didn't make his voice sound like it had just broken.

'How many days exactly?'

'Five. Five days. Exactly.' Vijay was about to smile but he thought better of it. Best to be serious.

'On your own?'

He nodded. Yes, of course on his own. Not like he was hiding a family of ten under his coat, was it?

'What are you doing here, then?' The official's eyes narrowed. 'On your own.'

Vijay had rehearsed this bit a thousand times, but he still had to say it slowly to make sure the English words came out in the right order. 'Just some sightseeing, maybe a little shopping.'

'No friends or family to visit?'

'Oh, no. My family and friends are all back in Uganda.' Pran had told him beforehand: don't give them any sign that he was going to stick around longer than he was supposed to.

'Unusual to come here by yourself?' The man was spending a lot of time looking at the passport, despite the lack of any stamps inside it, even running his thumb along the crisp blank paper.

Vijay slid his finger into his shirt collar and tugged. Had his neck swollen to twice its size? 'Family business. They couldn't get away, you see.'

'And how much money have you brought into the country?'

'Enough for a place to stay, and some more for food and drink.' He shifted his weight to his other foot and instantly regretted it as money rustled inside the coat. 'Get on the London Underground. That kind of thing.' The kind of thing that involved giving suspicious people all that money that he'd smuggled into England.

The official stared at him.

Now what? Was this the moment the other guards came out and took him away? Everything went quiet. Chest tightening, belly churning. Don't throw up.

'How much is that exactly?'

Vijay said the amount, as Pran had advised him to do. A safe number that wouldn't draw attention.

Another hard stare. 'And I don't need to remind you that we have very strict laws about people staying in this country beyond their welcome. There are clear processes and procedures to follow, do you understand?'

Vijay nodded. Yes, he knew very well – for people like him, there were endless processes and procedures, no matter what passport you had.

'Please wait here.' The official stood up and walked over to a colleague who was standing close by. They discussed something and nodded, each man getting a good look at Vijay while he clutched the frame of the cubicle, hoping the panic hadn't reached his face. A foreign prison, no one to visit him.

After what felt like hours, the official came back over. Vijay hadn't thought it was possible for the man to look any grumpier than he had before, but somehow his brows had furrowed so firmly you could crush peanuts between them.

'Five days then.' A thud and a clink of metal as the man stamped the passport and handed it back.

Vijay gave a watery smile and walked away as calmly as he could. He gulped in the air, as though he'd held his breath the entire time. 'Just stay calm and you'll be fine,' Pran had said. As if it was nothing.

He collected his luggage, then stopped for a split second outside the red zone customs channel where the sign demanded,

'Anything to declare?' He moved past, joining the sea of fellow travellers in the long, brightly lit tunnel of the green zone. A customs official standing behind a Formica table looked directly at him, his grey eyes staring at Vijay's left arm. This was it. Out of luck.

But after a moment, the official's gaze softened. He looked away and continued to scan the crowds. To the man, Vijay was too meek, too fragile to be a threat.

His arm was the perfect disguise.

Out into the Arrivals area. Any minute now, a single hand on his back could still stop him, haul him back when they realized they'd made a mistake. He mustn't run out of the airport, no matter how much he might want to. Had to act like the people around him. He hurried through the families and the taxi drivers with scribbled cards gathered in the terminal.

Outside, the air bristled through his coat; despite the extra insulation of the notes, it felt as thin as chiffon now. Only when he was halfway through the car park did he dare to turn around.

No one followed.

He'd made it. He'd actually got away with it! He looked around. His connection in London, Haribhai, would be waiting in the car park with his brother-in-law. Little islands of grubby snow lined the kerbside; not the sparkling white he'd seen in films. The grey sludge beneath his feet was more like sticky, slippery mashed mogo – cassava. He wandered around the car park, looking past the Fords, Mercedes and Range Rovers, the ordinary people piling their suitcases into their cars, trying to find the beaten-up black Peugeot.

Finally, in the corner of the car park, he saw it.

What now? He stood there, cars swooshing behind him. The Peugeot's doors opened on both sides and two men got out. The driver, skinny as a reed, and his passenger, stocky with heavy jowls and small eyes, not unlike a hippo.

'Get in, then,' said the thin man, as though they'd known each other for years. From Popatlal's description, this must be Haribhai. And Popatlal must have mentioned Vijay's arm; they'd have seen the coat hanging off his shoulder.

Once they'd driven away from the airport and onto the motorway, the hippo asked, 'You got it, neh?'

Vijay nodded. Of course he had it.

'Take it off, then.'

Outside, people were bundled up in hats and scarves. Apart from the jacket he'd handed over, he only had a cotton shirt.

'Relax, there's another coat in the boot,' Haribhai said, glancing at him in the rear-view mirror.

They drove to another car park, quieter this time, a couple of cars dotted here and there. How much electricity did it take to illuminate this gloomy concrete block, he thought, looking at the pockets of light across the building.

They parked in a dark corner, the shadows growing longer across the Peugeot's bonnet. Vijay looked around. These people thought nothing of smuggling money in and out of the country; it occurred to him suddenly that hanging around in a deserted car park with them wasn't the best idea. The man who looked like a hippo took the coat from Vijay and grabbed a small kitchen knife from the glove compartment. Fear pricked at his neck until the man cut into the coat, just enough to check the money was there. He showed it to Haribhai and both men nodded. They gave Vijay a flimsy beige trench coat. The Humphrey Bogart look really wasn't his style, but it was bitter outside.

'What now?'

The men didn't answer. Instead, they carried on driving along broad roads, past fishmongers and butchers and bakers, until they stopped, gave him a brown-paper envelope and told him to count the money inside, just like in the crime movies.

Then they left him at Acton Town underground station. Not quite like in the crime movies.

He took in the clean lines and red bricks of the station. A train rattled in as he reached the platform. The whole carriage smelt of stale smoke; at his feet, fallen cigarettes lay between the wooden slats of the floor. Hanging down from the ceiling were long, pendulous handles. (Had to admire someone who had the guts to design something so public that looked like a penis.)

The woman sitting opposite him wore a tailored jacket and matching skirt. Her grey hair was swept up in a bun, topped with a little navy hat like an upturned dog bowl.

She stared at him, eyes bright blue. It made Vijay think of Jaya, whose eyes had faded from hazel-brown to grey in old age. They made his Ba look sad, even when she was smiling. What would she think of the things he'd done to get here? What would she have done if he'd been caught?

The woman on the Tube continued to look. Where to start? There was his arm. Then his hair, which he'd modelled on Marc Bolan but which looked more like a ball of wool that had lost a fight with a kitten.

The train rolled along the tunnel. Vijay focused on keeping his eyes open until he could get off the Tube, muscles still stiff with tension.

He came out of Ealing Common station and followed the directions Pran had given him. The bed and breakfast was an old house, sandwiched between others just like it, with sandy-coloured bricks and a red-tiled roof. The landlady let him in and he nodded politely as she spoke, knowing that by the morning he'd have forgotten where things were, what time breakfast was served and the cost of the room. Anything to lie down and get some sleep.

After he'd washed up at the little basin in the corner of the bedroom, he climbed into the bed, the chill of the white cotton sheets seeping into his body. He curled his legs up, knees almost touching his belly. When Pran had first asked him to go to London, Vijay had thought it an adventure. Yet now, fear seized him. Pran took his cut, safely tucked away in Uganda, while Vijay took all the risks. It wasn't an easy holiday. And then there was the guilt – lying to everyone, to Ba, to Asha. He looked around the room, the light of the street lamp creeping through a crack in the curtain. The flowery lampshade on the ceiling quivered as someone walked around the attic room above. The last thing he saw before he closed his eyes was a murky yellow patch across the ceiling plaster, like a cloud of piss.

*

By the time he ventured out of the bed and breakfast two days later, the snow had melted. He took in Buckingham Palace, Hyde Park, Leicester Square, where people fed pigeons and a bag of chips lay strewn on the ground, as though they'd made a suicidal leap out of someone's hand. Clutching fish and chips wrapped in newspaper, he ranged further; on to Soho, catching glimpses of posters in the windows. *Non-stop striptease*, silhouettes of buxom women, all in bright colours.

London was nothing like the news reports back home, those pictures of Brigitte Bardot and Michael Caine waving at fans. England had been around Vijay all his life. In the films at the Century Cinema, where 'God Save the Queen' blasted out after each showing; in the stock at the dukan, Lux soap and Heinz baked beans. The British boys at school with their tanned limbs and sun-bleached hair, the children of schoolteachers and civil servants who were sent back 'home' to England during school holidays. English words, too, woven into their Swahili, their

Gujarati and Hindi; into street signs, onto the paper money, into the newspapers that until a few years ago had told them they were British subjects.

But that was an England at the edges of his life. Now that he was here, looking around a country so different from the one he'd imagined, the taste of vinegar prickling on his tongue, he felt further away than ever before.

3

Asha

The snow came down over Tower Bridge, sunlight glinting along the arc of the snow globe.

Asha stood by the kitchen table, watching Jaya as she shook the globe again, delighted by Vijay's gift.

'It's just like grated coconut in there,' said Jaya, the tiny lines gathering in the corners of her eyes in glee. 'You enjoyed yourself then, *beta*?'

'Yes, Ba, it was fun.' He didn't meet her gaze.

'And you didn't have any trouble getting through the airport?' Asha took a shortbread biscuit from the tin. It was covered in a red, white and blue flag with a picture of men dressed in red uniforms with tall fur hats. She passed one to Pran.

Vijay glanced at his brother. 'With Immigration? It was fine. They just like to take their time with their questions. But it was fine, all OK, really.'

'Good, *beta*. And what did you do there?' Jaya perched on the edge of the chair next to Vijay.

'This and that. I went to Leicester Square, walked around a bit. And Tower Bridge, as you can see,' said Vijay.

Jaya tried to ask more questions, about what he'd eaten, what else he'd done, but Vijay's responses were vague. Perhaps he was tired, thought Asha, perhaps he felt bad about leaving Pran at the dukan after all.

'We should talk later,' said Pran.

'Yeah, maybe,' said Vijay, as he walked out of the door.

*

Asha stood with Pran outside their neighbours Naseem and Razia Iqbal's house. The sun had chased the afternoon rains away as quickly as they had started. The earth had turned dark copper, the sunlight catching the tips of the Nandi flame trees. It was good to get out of the house with Pran, these occasions rarer than ever with curfew always looming. He kissed Asha's shoulder, lips warm against her skin, as the house girl opened the door.

'Pranbhai, Ashaben. Come, come,' said Naseem, beckoning them into the house. He was a few years older, a few pounds heavier than Pran. He walked in an unhurried manner, the confidence that came with money.

The Iqbals' house was far larger than others in the street. It was single-storey like many others, but it was made up of two houses extended into one large complex, with a red roof and vast garden. Asha looked around the sitting room filled with European souvenirs, figurines of cherubs and angels and maidens swathed in white fabric, a landscape painting of the English countryside, chiming gold carriage clocks and a large side cabinet filled with fine china. Razia and Naseem lived in the house with their four children and Naseem's youngest brother. His parents, who also lived with them, had gone out to visit relatives, taking the grandchildren with them so that the couple could enjoy some time with their friends. Razia came over, frangipani-yellow silk sari swishing as she walked. A streak of blusher on each cheek made her look like a porcelain doll. '*Kemche?* All well?' she asked, with her usual habit of not meeting Asha's gaze but instead looking past her with her heavy, kohl-lined eyes. Though they'd spent some time together over the past few months, Asha hadn't yet worked out whether it was shyness or snootiness.

'You'll have some food?' Razia headed towards the table, releasing a cloying rose perfume into the air.

There were other young couples milling around, laughing and joking. Pran and Asha said hello to a few of them while they waited for Vijay, who was still getting ready.

'Thought you'd sneak in without saying hello?' Pran's friend Rakesh came over. He slapped Pran's back and greeted Asha, hands together in a salaam.

'What can I say? I thought I'd managed to avoid you,' Pran laughed. Rakesh was Pran's oldest friend; they'd known each other since they were toddlers. His family owned a large fabric shop on Kampala Road.

'You almost did, we're off to a family engagement,' said Rakesh. Asha wondered how much longer they'd be able to go freely to gatherings and celebrations, but she was determined to make the best of it while she could.

After Rakesh had said his goodbyes, she and Pran went over to the buffet. The table was laden with golden slabs of mogo piled up high, along with *kuku paka*, chicken pieces peeping out of a pale-yellow coconut sauce; lamb biryani, plump rounds of *daar na bhajia*; crispy *aloo paratha* and sliced onion scattered with coriander. She helped herself to a fluffy spoonful of *shrikhand*, thick, sweetened yoghurt, saffron-hued and pistachio-studded, knowing better than to put any on Pran's plate; he hated anything with cardamom in it.

As they sat outside in the shaded part of the garden, the strap of Asha's dress fell off her shoulder. Pran hooked it with his little finger.

'Are you planning to put that back on or slip it off?' said Asha. Her eyes settled on his lips.

'I haven't decided yet,' he whispered.

Just then, Vijay arrived and people buzzed around him; his jovial warmth always seemed to draw people closer. He piled his plate with food and joined Pran and Asha.

'Training for a marathon?' said Asha.

Pran laughed. 'Not sure he'd be able to run very far after eating all that.'

'I missed this food in England, that's all,' said Vijay. 'Oh, I forgot the chutney.'

'Missed the food? You were only gone a few days!' said Asha. 'I'll get the chutney, don't want you dropping that huge plate.'

On her way back, she caught the end of the brothers' conversation.

'No, I'm going straight to sleep after this.' A tinge of frustration in Vijay's voice. 'You'll have to wait.'

Pran was about to say something, but when he saw her he decided against it.

Naseem came over and joined them. 'I hope you'll be going back for more, we need to fatten you up,' he said, laughing at Vijay's plate.

Vijay grinned, unable to say anything as he'd just taken another huge mouthful of rice.

'So, how's business?' said Naseem, pressing his glasses back to the bridge of his nose.

'All fine, you know how it is.' Pran and Vijay exchanged a look that Asha couldn't read. 'How about you?'

Naseem ignored the question. 'You're extending the dukan?'

'We've finished. The business is keeping us busy. And how are the exports doing?' Pran took a sip of juice then lowered his voice. 'Government still giving you trouble?' Naseem's family had made a lot of money from their four general stores around Kampala. Things had really stepped up in the past decade after his other brothers opened a sugar plantation near Jinja. The sugar exports changed their fortunes dramatically. But their wealth also brought more scrutiny from those in power.

'It's fine, we'll find a way around it,' said Naseem wearily. 'They love poking their noses in. They've been doing it for a while now.'

'Yeah, remember that ridiculous business conference?' said Vijay. The year before, Idi Amin had made a speech to leading Asian businessmen, under the pretence of supporting commerce.

'Oh, don't talk to me about that,' said Naseem. 'Hours standing there while Amin Dada lectured us for scheming and hoarding all our money, talking all sorts of nonsense. I still thank God I wasn't sitting near the front, those people ended up drenched in his spit!'

'Naseem, you boring everyone with your business talk again?' Razia tottered over.

'Who, me?' Naseem winked at them. 'Never.'

Although their talk turned to new films and cricket scores, the alarm in the streets outside somehow crept back into the conversation. More than once, Asha noticed Razia steering them away, back to lighter matters.

Later, as Asha half listened to Razia's talk about the latest saris she'd brought back from India, she watched Pran and Vijay huddled once again in a corner. Pran tried to grab onto Vijay's arm but he flicked his hand away.

Asha told herself that they were just behaving like siblings. She thought of her own petty squabbles with her brothers back in Jinja and tried to put it out of her mind.

*

The next day, Asha finished helping Jaya in the kitchen and walked out onto the veranda. The shade had retreated to the farthest corners of the yard. As she passed the sitting room, she paused. Pran and Vijay were talking, but the younger brother sounded agitated.

'I had my holiday. A once-in-a-lifetime experience, thank you very much.' His words were terse.

'Come on, Vij. We only need a bit more money for the dukan.'

'You said that last time. Made it sound so easy.'

'But it *was* easy, wasn't it?' The armchair creaked as Pran shifted in his seat.

'Easy for who?' An unfamiliar note of anger in Vijay's words.

'What's the issue?' said her husband.

'What if I'd been caught?'

The breeze in the yard picked up. She couldn't hear what Pran said next, but she didn't need to. She'd been sure something was going on and here was the proof. Asha knew she should walk away or otherwise let them know she was there, but she couldn't move. She had to know the truth.

Vijay's voice was curt. 'We both got paid, but I did all the hard work. Me. All those questions at the airport. I could have ended up in prison.'

'Shhh, Vij. They have better things to worry about than you. Anyway, I thought you wanted to see a bit of England?'

'Not like this.' A shuffling sound. 'Lying to everyone.'

'We're doing this for them.'

'You tell yourself that.'

'Seriously, Vij—'

'Seriously. I'm done.' Her brother-in-law's footsteps got louder; he was coming towards the door.

Asha stepped back. Too late. He paused and stared at her.

Vijay looked as though he was about to say something, but instead, he turned away and headed for his bedroom.

Before she could do anything, Jaya called out to her from her bedroom. 'Asha, can you come here and help me with my sari? We're going to be late for temple.'

Asha looked towards the sitting-room door. 'Coming.'

After she'd finished helping Jaya, Asha hurried back to the bedroom, pulling out a brand-new sari, embroidered birds of paradise soaring through the emerald-green silk. She couldn't pin it in place, her fingers clammy against the metal. How could Pran have kept all this from her?

Heat crept up her neck. She'd find out exactly what Pran had been up to. All the lies he'd told. The gaps between his words.

Her breath ragged, she tried to calm herself as she put on the sari. It had been a part of her bridal trousseau and she couldn't help but think back to her wedding day. They'd come back to Pran's house after the ceremony, along with the groom's guests. The wedding songs were sung in whispers, to avoid drawing the army's attention to the gold hidden under sari blouses. It made the guests' singing sound a little eerie, ghostly even, in the fading light of the day, as though they were trying to cast a spell. Asha, weighed down by the gold thread in her red-and-green *gharchora* sari, and all the earrings, bangles, necklaces, weighed down from the sheer exhaustion of being awake since dawn, anxious about tripping over her hem as she walked slowly into the sitting room.

The wedding games began. There was a steel bowl filled with water, coloured red with food dye, on the table. She sat opposite Pran, face lit up by the little *diva* flames.

'Off you go!' said Vijay.

Pran and Asha had plunged their hands into the red water, cheered on with subdued cries from the onlookers. How strange, after being careful for so long to hide their relationship from prying family members or neighbours, to be able to touch each other in public. The thrill of her skin against his, under the water. The bottom of the steel *sani* slipped and slid beneath her fingertips as she searched for the wedding ring. Pran's brows furrowed in concentration, hunting for the tiny circle of gold in the pool of water.

Too late. Asha felt the cool metal against her fingertip. 'Found it!' she shouted, holding the ring up in triumph.

Pran's eyes narrowed in mock dismay.

'You know what this means?' Asha whispered.

'Looks like Asha will be the one running the marriage, Pranbhai!' said Vijay, slapping his brother on the back.

Pran returned Asha's smile. 'We'll see.'

Luckily, the guests hadn't lingered, wanting to hurry back before it got too late. The rest of the family were tired and they quickly said their goodnights too.

Later, Pran led Asha to the bedroom – now their bedroom – for the first time. She stepped inside and he closed the door behind him.

Unsure what to do next, she fiddled nervously with the rows of thin bangles; the gold glinted, the green and red glass opaque in the light. 'It's going to take me most of the night to get all this off.'

Pran walked towards her and took her wrist in his hands.

Asha looked up, heat blooming on her cheeks.

'Well, we'd better get started then.' He smiled, and brought the inside of her wrist to his lips, his mouth brushing her skin. He slipped off a *bangri* and let it drop onto the bed. He moved his lips further up her wrist and slid another *bangri* off. Now, her palm on his cheek, her fingertips on his neck, the warmth of him, the softness of his skin.

The surprise of him after months of urgent, stolen kisses.

The delicious burn of his skin on hers. The tip of his tongue along her stomach. After all their secret meetings, the thrill of the illicit replaced by the joy of never again having to hide her love for him.

Why did that night feel like a lifetime ago?

She had to focus. They were already running late for the temple. Luckily it didn't take as long as usual; there was no need to put on heavy gold necklaces and earrings as it was no longer safe to wear them anymore. With her finger, she pressed a round green *chandlo* between her eyebrows, then pulled on a few simple green bangri over her wrists, the plastic dragging against hands that were swollen from the heat. Asha tugged at her waves with a comb, brushing her hair into a thick, low bun and spraying it with hairspray. She smoothed on some lipstick, the waxy taste escaping onto her tongue.

She had to speak to Pran, she needed to know everything. But it would have to wait.

*

Long ago, on the land that became Kololo Hill, an Acholi tribal chief was captured by the British. '*Kololo, kololo,*' he'd cried out, 'I'm alone, I'm alone.' His cry echoed through the decades: Kololo Hill. The hill still looked out across the great city of Kampala where, years before, long-limbed impala bounded over the land, surrounded by the other great hills, from Namirembe to Kibuli, Mengo to Kasubi.

Down below, the city centre had sprawled, spurred on by colonial rule. Two broad streets, lined with dukans, bars, restaurants and banks, a vast taxi park, plus the busy markets: Owino, Bwaise and Nakasero, while taller office buildings dotted the skyline. And there, in the middle of it all, the Hindu temple stood proud against the bustle of the city. People went about their daily business, touting their wares at the market or hurrying to and from work, while soldiers looked on from an army truck on the street corner. Asha thought of her own childhood growing up in Jinja, when people went to temple swathed in their finest gold, without a care. Her local *mandir* in Jinja was small but it was always filled with gossip and laughter. She'd join the other children as they stole sweet *barfi* and *jelebi* before running off outside to eat it. But now, people hurried inside as fast as they could.

Jaya led the family into the mandir. Here, the smooth beige walls were dotted with black-and-white photographs of the temple exterior. Bright colours were saved for the front, where the metal and carved stone *murti*s were painted turquoise, scarlet and fuscia to bring out the clothes and the kind eyes of the deities who watched over the worshippers. In front of them, offerings were lined up: fresh fruit and marigold flowers; little pots of milk; pink and mint-green sweetmeats bathed in the glow of the diva.

Asha stayed with Jaya, smiling politely as they spoke to her mother-in-law's many friends. The heat from the mass of bodies swelled around her. She turned towards the back of the temple. Pran greeted his friends before taking his place on the floor next to Motichand and Vijay.

'You newlyweds still can't keep your eyes off each other, *heh*?' said Ramamasi, one of Jaya's friends, nudging her with her elbow. Asha blushed.

Jaya looked equally embarrassed. 'Let's find a place over here, shall we?'

The singing began, the sound bouncing off the marble floor and walls, followed by the chime of the finger cymbals, the clang of the temple bell. Asha's voice joined Jaya's, a ribbon of gentle notes, while others around them half shouted, half squawked the words. Asha admired those who weren't self-conscious in front of God, who sang every word out of tune but sang anyway. It was the ones who had to sing louder than anyone else that she was suspicious of, as though it was a contest: the more forceful the singing, the stronger their faith in God.

The singing was paused for prayers. She stole a glance behind her. Vijay, sitting peacefully; Motichand, legs crossed, head slanted, body swaying as though he might topple over at any minute, softly snoring. Pran's eyes shut tight, flat palms together, the model worshipper. Behaving as though he never lied, had never been dishonest. Behaving that way in front of her, in front of God.

The singing began again, bells ringing, hands clapping, voices louder. The scent of warm ghee and the rose and sandalwood agarbatti swirling in the hot air.

Om Jai Jagdish Hare

She had to cling on to the words, to find comfort in them.

Swami Jaya Jagadeesha Hareh

Her husband kept secrets from her.

Bhakta janonke sankat

Told her that he had nothing to hide.

Kshana mei door kareh

Lying to her face.

Om Jaya Jagadeesha Hareh

What now?

4

Jaya

Outside the dukan, a man rode his bicycle along the long street, balancing a piece of papaya in one hand and manoeuvring the bike with the other. Hitched to the handlebar was a bundle of fabrics so big he had to stretch his neck to see over the top.

Jaya stepped inside. The dust swirled in the low light from the small window guarded by metal rods. Pran had suggested making a quick stop here on the way back from the temple, while Motichand and Vijay stayed behind to help clear up. Nowadays, Jaya made the most of those visits to the temple, one of the few times they could catch up with their friends. For years the family had enjoyed entertaining guests, cooking vast meals of *shaak rotli* and *daar bhaat*, samosa and *bhajia*, languishing for hours in the sitting room or out on the veranda, gossiping and laughing into the long night. But now everyone was eager to get back to their homes in time for curfew.

Jaya took it all in as Pran showed her and Asha around. He had certainly improved it, expanding into the space at the back. New shelves lined the freshly painted walls, filled with tins of Bird's custard powder and ENO fruit salts, stacks of Carnation condensed milk and Ovaltine, jars of gobstoppers, bottles of whisky and gin.

Pran was nothing like his father. Motichand had flitted from business to business the whole time he'd been married to

32

Jaya. In the early days, he ran a small concrete block of a dukan outside the city, where the rain used to rattle like pebbles on the tin roof and the stale air smelt of the spices they kept at the back: cloves and fenugreek and cardamom; not even the many piles of Lux soap could hide the scent. Motichand passed the hours playing cards outside with the neighbouring shopkeepers, until the day stretched into night and the only way he could tell the difference between a heart and a diamond was by waving his cards under the light of the kerosene lamp, the flame flickering as though it too was exhausted by the day's heat. Later he'd owned the auto garage at the bottom of William Street, which he said could service all cars, BMWs to Renaults, Rolls-Royces to Citroens. He painted a sign on a long piece of thick cotton: 'Motichandlal's Motors', but after a few weeks in the sun and a few afternoon showers it was a tattered wreck, leaving only the word '*Moti*', which meant 'fat' in Gujarati, flapping in the wind. The trouble was that Motichand would give his 'customers' – mainly his friends – their own accounts and let them run up tabs as long as the Nile itself. People like Cyrus Mody, who'd been a regular customer since the beginning. Like others, he'd rarely paid his account. Eventually he stopped coming to the dukan at all, and even after Pran cornered him at weddings or outside the temple, Cyrus managed to wriggle out of paying them back, promising to do it very soon, very soon. And of course, the benefit of taking advantage of others was that you had plenty of money for yourself: Cyrus Mody had a huge house looking down on everyone from the top of Kololo Hill, and two sparkling Mercedes-Benzes sitting in the driveway.

No, Motichand had always been too relaxed with the customers. 'Of course, you can pay next week,' he'd tell them, never wanting to disappoint, always wanting to show how generous he was. But a week became a month, a month became two months. Little was written down or recorded and money came and went as often as the customers. The only thing that stopped Motichand going bankrupt was telling everyone he was selling up, which gave him a reason to call in the debts before he sweet-talked someone else into buying whatever business he was trying to flog that time.

For every shilling that slipped through Motichand's fingers, Jaya found a way to catch hold of it again. She'd sewn shirts, made day dresses or an occasional miniskirt (this she wasn't happy about, but they were popular with the girls and at least they were quick to make with so little fabric). Even now that things were better, the habits wouldn't leave her. Asking December to find the cheapest produce at the market, hiding away money in corners of the house where Motichand would never look, just in case, just in case.

'We want to get a fridge, for the Coca-Cola.' Pran pointed to an empty corner at the far end of the shop. Asha didn't bother to turn and carried on looking out of the window.

'It looks very nice, beta,' said Jaya, trailing her hand along the wooden counter, tracing the ridges and dents beneath her fingertips. She sat down on an old chair in the corner to rest her legs.

'And these are all new.' He moved over to the shelves at the back, yet Asha stayed where she was.

Perhaps she couldn't appreciate how much the dukan had changed, how hard Pran and Vijay had worked, but she could at least show some interest. 'What do you think, Asha?' said Jaya.

Asha looked up at Pran, her voice flat. 'It must have cost a lot.'

'Don't worry about the money,' Pran said with a light laugh, as he fiddled with a button on his shirt. 'It's fine.'

'People might talk, all this money being spent,' said Asha. 'Shouldn't we be getting back now?'

In some ways, Jaya was in awe of Asha, the way she'd

arrived at her new marital home, bold as anything. Jaya, on the other hand, in marriage, as with everything else in her life, had made herself fluid. She'd accepted others talking about her while she was still in the same room, as she'd been taught to do since she was a child. Never saying anything out of turn, though she often thought it, of course, screaming thoughts inside her mind, never doing anything to anger her in-laws. Shifting, moulding into new spaces, tucking herself into corners, never getting in the way. Surviving. Which was why it was all the more astonishing for Jaya to see Asha talk to her husband in this way.

'We're doing well, let them talk,' said Pran. 'We've done nothing—'

'Nothing wrong?' Asha said in a brittle tone.

'You don't like it?' said Jaya. Why was she being so rude? 'Pran and Vijay have gone to a lot of trouble to do this.'

'Oh, I know. Tell us how you did it exactly, Pran?' Asha wandered around the dukan, looking along the shelves. 'How you managed to make it such a success.'

'Asha—' Pran's eyes flashed towards his wife.

'It'll bring more money in, I suppose.' Asha shrugged her shoulders. 'And that's all that matters.'

'Let's go home, shall we?' said Pran, before Jaya had a chance to speak.

*

Dusk wrapped itself around the city. The road stretched before them as they drove out of the centre and back up along Kololo Hill. The music on the radio and the rumble of the car through the streets kept conversation at bay.

Up ahead, two army trucks were parked along the road. Four soldiers were standing around, two slouched against the trucks, the others swinging their legs out of the passenger doors, rifles propped against the huge wheels.

Jaya gripped the top of the car seat; the soldiers hadn't been here on the way to the dukan. It used to be police cars in the road dealing with traffic issues. Idi Amin's military police had taken over the official responsibilities now, although the way they hung around never looked official.

Pran brought the car to a halt near the trucks. 'Let me do the talking.'

The soldiers suddenly seemed to spring into action, as though they'd only now remembered they were on duty. They pulled their rifles across their shoulders and adjusted their maroon berets.

'Get out,' shouted one, a stout young man with a voice so deep it seemed to vibrate through Jaya's chest.

Pran spoke through the open car window, his voice surprisingly calm. 'We're just trying to get home before curfew.'

The other soldiers hurried over, staring at them through the windows as though the family were animals in a zoo.

'You *wahindis* think you can ignore us? I said, out.'

They hurried out of the car. Pran stood in front of Asha and Jaya as he squinted at the soldiers through the sunlight. 'I'm sorry, I wasn't—'

'Still talking. Like the sound of your own voice, don't you? Well, you listen to mine now,' said the deep-voiced soldier. 'Get down on your knees.' He shoved the rifle butt against Pran's shoulder.

'We don't want any trouble.' Pran's knees thudded to the ground.

Jaya's breath quickened, her sari blouse tightening against her chest. Please don't hurt him.

'Still going on and on.' The soldiers laughed and circled around the group now, except for the tallest who had stayed by the truck, smoking a cigarette. The low-voiced soldier loomed over Jaya, his eyes on her throat. How could she have been so stupid? She was still wearing her *mangalsutra*, her wedding necklace, a thin gold chain woven through with tiny black beads. She'd forgotten it was there, tucked under the front of her sari; she should have taken it off before she left the house. And here it was, burning against her neck.

The soldier's eyes widened as he pointed at the necklace. 'I think my girlfriend would like that.'

'Girlfriend?' His comrade laughed, revealing the lines in his forehead. He smelt sweet, what was it? One of those sugar-filled fizzy drinks Vijay liked as a boy. 'Which one?'

Jaya knew she should move fast, take it off before they got angry, but it was as though her arms were made of lead.

'What are you waiting for? Is she deaf?' said the deep-voiced soldier, looking at Pran. 'Is she deaf?' he shouted this time, his comrade laughing along with him, so close, his hot breath in her ear.

Asha stepped towards her, fiddling with the clasp until finally it was loose. The gold snaked together in her hand; she dropped it into the soldier's palm.

'Come on, let's go,' the tallest soldier who had hung back by the truck shouted, grinding his cigarette into the door. 'We need to start patrolling for curfew soon.'

'Always spoiling everyone's fun,' the soldier with the necklace called out, but he stayed put. He lifted the gun high and fast into the air, rifle butt pointing towards Pran.

'No, please!' Jaya shouted, hands reaching out. As though she could stop him. The soldier's rifle froze inches above Pran's head. He stared at Jaya to savour her reaction as the other soldiers' laughter rang out behind them.

'At least Mama loves you.' He ruffled Pran's hair and strolled away.

5

Asha

They drove home in silence, too tired to speak. Asha couldn't get the vision of the soldier with the gun out of her head. What if Pran had suffered the same fate as the bodies she'd seen by the river? Fear seized hold of her again, but so did the anger that he'd lied to her.

Jacob, the *askari* who kept watch outside, opened the gate and waved them through. Inside, the house was quiet. Motichand and Vijay were still out.

'How could they do that to us?' Pran shook his head, his outrage awakened by the familiarity of home. 'And we just had to take it.'

Jaya looked at the floor in the hallway. 'The chain. I should have remembered.'

'It's not your fault, Ba,' said Pran. 'It's their fault. Helping themselves to things that don't belong to them.'

Jaya clung to the doorway. 'How is that right?'

Pran laughed, his voice twisting with each word. 'They think they can do whatever they want.'

Asha stared at him. His anger filled the air, trying to force out her own. Not this time. She'd put her feelings aside for long enough. 'Let's not dwell on it,' she said. 'We just have to be more careful in future, that's all.' There was no point going over the details again and again, it would eat them up. Besides, she needed to speak to him alone. Pran started to head towards the sitting room.

'I think I need to – I'm going to rest.' Jaya wouldn't look Asha in the eye; she clutched her hands together, distracted.

'Let me know if you need anything,' Asha said softly, then hurried towards the bedroom. She had to take off this stifling sari, the pins and hooks, the layers of silk and cotton digging into her. She pulled on a cotton *kameez*, undid her hair from its tight bun. She longed to bury her head in her pillow, pull the sheets over her and wait for the haven of sleep, but she needed to speak to Pran now.

Asha headed outside, almost bumping into December on the veranda.

He smiled. 'Is the house on fire? We'd better save the whisky first or your father-in-law will be angry.'

She looked up at him, confused for a moment. 'What? Oh no, sorry.' He held a pile of shirts in his hands. 'I nearly made you drop the washing.' She took in his grey hair – though he was called a house boy as all male servants were in Uganda, he was as old as Jaya. It made Asha think of Florence, the house girl back at her childhood home, who had been with the family for decades, forever holding her tongue when Asha and her brothers touched the flowers in the garden or ruined her newly polished floor, because it wasn't a house girl's place to tell them off. They'd been such brats as children, it made Asha's cheeks flush to think of it. But it also made her long to be back in Jinja, amongst the people she knew the best.

'Is everything all right?' said December.

She blinked, then smiled. She felt shy all of a sudden, trying so hard to hide how she was feeling, but he'd seen right through it. She knew the family was far closer to December than most were with their house boys, but it felt strange to talk openly with him. And most of all, she worried that December's kindness might start tears that she couldn't stop.

'It must be very different to Jinja, yes? I remember feeling the same when I first moved down here from the north,' he said. 'It got easier eventually.'

'Oh yes, of course. I'm fine, really.' She gave him a look of gratitude. 'I was looking for Pran, actually, have you seen him?'

'He's in the sitting room, I think.'

She thanked him and started to walk away.

December called after her, 'And if you – if there's anything you need, let me know.'

She turned briefly and smiled.

In the sitting room, Pran sat in the armchair, resting his head on the seat back. She shut the door behind her, her shoulder blades pressed against the wood. 'I heard you and Vijay earlier. Talking about the money.'

A glint of surprise on Pran's face. 'Money?'

'I heard everything.'

'So that's what that was all about? At the dukan.' Pran rubbed the back of his neck, acting as if this was nothing.

'You lied to me.'

'We needed the cash,' he said. 'We helped some people get their money to some banks in England. That's all.'

'What people?'

'It doesn't matter.'

'That's it? It's OK to lie and smuggle money now? Break laws?'

Pran sighed. 'Are you planning to stand against that door all day or do you want to sit down?'

Asha took a deep breath. She crossed the room and stood over him. 'Is this better?' He'd assured her there was nothing going on before. Looked her in the face, made her feel as though it was all in her head. 'And you made Vijay do all your dirty work.'

'I didn't make anyone do anything. Besides, I couldn't go again.'

'Again? You've done this yourself?' New information unravelled like a frayed rope every time he opened his mouth.

'Papa had left the dukan in such a state. I had no choice.'

'Wait. That trip when we were about to get engaged?' Pran had said it was a holiday with a friend. He'd laughed about how Buckingham Palace seemed on the small side for him, how much he'd missed drinking his daily chai, how much he'd missed her. 'Making out it was just a bit of fun?'

'I did have fun, I just had some business to deal with at the same time, that's all.'

'The things you told me when we first met. Going on about how you'd turned around the dukan, how well it was doing.'

'But that was the truth.' Pran sat forward.

'You made it sound like you'd done it all. The hero who saved the family business,' said Asha.

'I didn't want to worry you, that's all.'

'There must have been another way.'

'I told you, we had to sort out the mess Papa had created.' Pran sounded irritated, as though Asha were the one in the wrong and he shouldn't have to explain himself, least of all to her. His wife.

'You know what people say about us, the way we Asians hide and cheat.' Her voice unsteady. 'And all along I thought, no, that's not fair, we're just trying to get by like everyone else. And now you've given them another reason to hate us.' The stony way the soldiers had stared. The fear in Pran's eyes.

'Come on.' Pran reached for Asha's hands but she pushed him away. 'They're not jealous of a little bit of money. They're jealous of everything that we've built here. Idi Amin wanted someone to blame.'

'And why is it that? Because they think we're leaching their money. You've made us all into money-grabbers.' All the gifts, the updates to the dukan, all of it bought with his tainted cash.

'I was just trying to help my family.' Sweat had seeped in patches onto Pran's shirt. He spoke in a hushed tone, but nevertheless it betrayed his annoyance. 'I want us to have a different life to the one I grew up with.'

'Was it worth the risk?' She shook her head. 'Like earlier, with the soldiers. They could have taken you away, or worse.'

'But they didn't hurt me. And we didn't get caught.' His voice lost its edge. 'I did it for us. For you.'

'There must have been another way to help the business. Perhaps my Papa—' She stopped. Pran stared at her. They both knew he'd never accept money from anyone, least of all her parents.

'You shut me out.' She leant against the wall, the plaster cool against her skin. 'There was no need to keep the debt from me.'

'I was embarrassed. I didn't want you to see that I was failing.'

'Are we just like everyone else? Husbands off doing whatever they want, wives sitting at home, no idea what's going on. What kind of marriage is that? I don't want us to spend our time pretending to be people we're not.' She blinked back the tears. 'What else have you kept from me?'

'Nothing, I swear.' Pran stood up, taking her by the shoulders. 'I should have told you. I'm sorry.'

She shrugged him off. How could she believe anything he told her?

'I'm sorry, Asha. I'm sorry,' he said, as though saying it over and over again might make it right.

*

For decades, the Europeans had lived at the top of Kololo Hill, looking down on the city from their villas and mansions. The scent of jasmine and frangipani wafting in between the houses hidden by mango trees and rose bushes, papaya and hibiscus. After Independence, most of them went home, back to the colder climes of Britain, Ireland, Germany and France. The wealthiest Asians had swiftly moved in to take their place.

Jaya's friend Mrs Goswami lived in one such home, a house with a pink-tiled roof and white walls flanked by proud pillars. Asha decided to join Jaya on one of her afternoon visits: anything to fill the long day that stretched before them. During the drive further up Kololo Hill to Mrs Goswami's house, Asha watched the narrower streets and compact single-storey homes give way to broader roads and vast, gated two-floor houses that looked out across the city centre below. Your place on the hill was directly connected to your wealth, with the richest at the very top. Below them all, the poorest Asians lived in cramped old apartment blocks and crumbling houses, and at the foot of the hill were the cement blocks and corrugated-iron roofs where many of the black Ugandans lived.

Once inside, they were led to a vast reception room filled with statues carved out of soapstone and wood. Asha would much rather have been outside amongst the bright-pink flowers of the bougainvillea and the fluttering monochrome butterflies, but instead, here she was getting a headache from the gaudy knick-knacks in every corner.

'Come in, *besi jaaaowo*.' With each sentence, Mrs Goswami's voice got louder, the vowels more elongated, as though she was in pain. '*Abuja aaaawo*,' she said, gesturing to sit next to her, but Asha swiftly took a place next to a baby elephant (carved, although a real one wouldn't have surprised her). She nearly slipped off the seat as her bottom hit the plastic protector that

Mrs Goswami had wrapped around all the furniture. Jaya sat opposite, feet dangling from a huge velvet armchair.

'Gres!' called out their host. 'Where is that girl?'

Mrs Goswami eased herself onto the seat with her walking stick. Her hair was slick with coconut oil and pulled back so tight into a huge low bun that her hairline had started to recede. That morning, Motichand had joked that he could see his reflection on Mrs Goswami's hair, his face shining back at him in the curve of that black mirror.

'Finally,' she said, watching the house girl, who hummed as she went. A slender girl with almond eyes, she set a tray of food on a table. 'Biscuits for the guests. And a small banana for you, madam, I know you need to watch your weight,' Grace said.

'Yes, yes,' mumbled Mrs Goswami, a look of embarrassment on her face. 'And the chai, Gres!' She gave Grace a thwack on the ankle with her walking stick, interrupting the house girl's flow for a moment, before she hummed louder.

Asha caught Grace rolling her eyes. She gave the house girl a conspiratorial smile.

Mrs Goswami turned back to her guests. '*Kemcho?* Everyone well?' They exchanged pleasantries while Grace left and returned, humming the entire time.

Mrs Goswami must have caught Asha looking at her house girl as she finished serving the tea. 'I know, I know, that humming is so annoying,' Mrs Goswami waved her hand dismissively. 'I tried to hit it out of her a couple of times, didn't I, Jayaben? Give her a *thappat* or two!'

Jaya's gaze remained fixed on her cooling chai.

Mrs Goswami continued, 'But she doesn't clean as well when I tell her to be quiet. If I want floors that glitter like Lake Victoria, I have to let her make that racket, *neyi*? Even if she does sound like a drowning hornet.'

Mrs Goswami thrust a stainless-steel tray under Jaya's

nose, the ginger biscuits slipping and sliding across it. 'Don't be shy now, eat, eaaaaaaaaat.' The biscuits were overbaked and had caught at the edges, but Jaya took one anyway, so aggressive was Mrs Goswami's insistence that she try one. When Asha refused a third time, Jaya gave her a look.

'And how is married life, *beta*?' Mrs Goswami peered at Asha through thick glasses.

'Good,' Asha said, for what else could she say? 'Different, I suppose. I worked in an office for a while, back in Jinja, so I'm trying to get used to the new routine here.'

'Ah, leave the work to the men. Otherwise, what's the point? Why do you girls want to be like them?'

'But it's nice to be able to do things on your own.' Asha shifted in her seat. 'Earn money.'

'*Bapre*, did someone put ghee in your ears or what? That's why you put up with a husband. To provide for you, neh?'

Asha stared back. What did Mrs Goswami know? She was a widow with four sons who kept her in the lavish lifestyle she was used to. She didn't know what it was like to have a husband who couldn't be trusted. Asha had barely spoken to Pran in the days since she'd found out the truth, though he'd tried to reach out to her. She couldn't bring herself to forgive everything.

Before Asha had a chance to respond, her mother-in-law piped up, 'Well, it's not safe to go out to work nowadays, so there's no point talking about jobs.' She gave Asha a look, a warning not to get into a debate. Jaya changed the subject, telling Mrs Goswami about the soldiers that had stopped them on the way back from the dukan.

'*Eh bhagvan!* This country has gone mad – again. But it will pass, it always passes,' Mrs Goswami said. 'Idi Amin got power from Obote and someone else will get power from him in time.'

'But it was never this dangerous before,' said Asha.

'It's true,' said Jaya. 'We used to be able to go out, never worrying. We used to visit all sorts of places when the children were younger. Murchison Falls. The gardens at Entebbe. You know, we stopped somewhere one day when they were little, for a picnic lunch. We always had to pack jelebi, or Vijay said he wouldn't go. We were dozing in the shade afterwards but Pran went missing, we couldn't find him anywhere. Motichand walked a mile looking in the trees and shrubs, calling out for him.' She shook her head. 'Even Vijay started to worry, poor thing.'

'What happened?' Mrs Goswami said.

'He'd been sleeping on the back seat the whole time. No one had thought to look in the car.' Jaya laughed. 'He had no idea we'd all been looking for him.'

Asha thought of Pran, how carefree he must have been as a boy. She couldn't imagine him like that now. 'I remember times like that,' she said. 'I'd go out with my brothers too, around the neighbourhood. We wouldn't come home until nightfall, playing outside. My Ba would call out for us.'

Mrs Goswami shook her head. 'You're too young to remember – you're both too young.' She twirled her thick gold bangle around her wrist. 'Those first years after I came here from India. We used to live near the border, did I tell you, Jayaben?'

Jaya nodded but Mrs Goswami was oblivious. She turned to face Asha.

'We lived on a small farm looking out over the grasslands. A few miles away, we had a dukan that sold everything, *kitenge* fabric, bicycle pumps, tinned fish: we sold it all, things you didn't even know you needed. No competition. Lots of money to be made. That's why we stayed. But our house was far away from the dukan, and by that time I had a baby to look after, my eldest, Dipesh. We lived with another family who were distant relatives of my husband, but they'd gone away for a few days and I was alone with the baby all day. Anyway, there'd been reports of animals getting over the fences of the neighbouring farms and attacking the livestock, so my husband bought a gun. We'd sit out on the veranda in the evenings, the baby dozing in my arms. Imagine that, look at the size of Dipesh now, he used to fit in my arms back then, barely fits through the door now. And my husband's rifle always rested by his feet, always ready.'

Asha couldn't imagine such a solitary life. Jinja wasn't as big as Kampala, but there were always people around that they could call on.

'So he showed me how to use the gun, just in case,' said Mrs Goswami. 'But it was so heavy in my arms. The rifle butt left bruises where I held it against my shoulder. The gunfire rattled through me. Made the birds flee, they'd scatter across the sky.' She waved her hand in the air. 'I hated it. Hated it!'

She sat forward in her chair. 'And then one morning, when I was sweeping the veranda, I spotted a lioness, slinking through the grass. She looked straight at me, then moved towards the house.

'Well, I was shaking by this time but I knew I couldn't make any sudden movements. I pulled the rifle up slowly as the lioness moved closer to the chicken coop nearby and I slotted my finger against the trigger. You know, I remember my skin slipping against the steel. I couldn't press it. And by now, the chickens were frantic, clucking and flapping.' Mrs Goswami paused, relishing the look of surprise on Asha's face.

'But I was too late. The lioness sloped off. I watched her clutching two chicken carcasses between her teeth, leaving a trail of blood as she went. And that night – in those days I was too timid for my own good – when my husband came back, I told him that the lioness had been too fast, that there hadn't been time to run and fetch the rifle. He'd simply nodded, too tired to do anything but sit down and eat his dinner.'

Asha opened her mouth to speak but Mrs Goswami got there first.

'And then a few days later, after I'd finally got the baby to settle for a nap one afternoon, I was sitting inside the house, looking out through the window. I could see three men approaching, armed with *pangas*. I remember the curve of the metal flashing white in the sun, that's how I saw them from so far away, you see. They walked right up to the steps of the house, chatting amongst themselves. They even commented on how nice the wooden chairs were, how much they might have cost, as though they were picking out furniture in a shop. Imagine! I didn't know what to do,' she said. Squinting with one eye, she put her arm out straight as though it was a gun. 'The rifle practice with my husband had always been from the top of the veranda pointing out across the grassland. I'd practised scaring off wild animals from afar, but never shooting at close range. Not at a group of armed men.'

Asha put her teacup and saucer down.

'I pulled out the rifle and called out through the mosquito screen. Told them I'd call the master if they didn't stop. The men stopped talking and looked up towards the house. I knew they wouldn't be able to see through the mesh of the mosquito screen because the house was dark inside. But still they climbed onto the first step of the stairs and one of the men shouted, "There's no master here."'

Jaya must have known what was coming next, but even she raised her head, waiting to hear the next part of the story.

Mrs Goswami continued, 'My hands were so sweaty I could barely hold the rifle by then. Still, I rushed to the door and pointed it at them. The gun was heavy but it was the fear that made my arms shake. I tried to steady myself as best I could. "The master will be back in a minute. Can you go now?" I was so stupid then. Imagine asking them! Politely requesting they go away when I'm pointing a gun at them. Now I would tell them to leave, *gandas*!' Mrs Goswami slapped the armrest. 'They stood on the stairs and looked at each other, then back at me. But they didn't turn. The baby had begun to cry inside the house. I raised the gun and pulled the trigger, praying I'd aimed correctly. The bullet shot over the heads of the men and skimmed across the grass. The men stepped back, stunned, and one of them tripped on the bottom step.' Mrs Goswami giggled, like a naughty girl who'd been caught eating sweets.

Jaya leant forward.

'Then I told them I'd use it again. And they moved faster, somewhere in between a run and a walk.' Mrs Goswami chuckled. 'The way they hurried away, trying to act like they weren't scared. What do you think of that?'

Asha looked Mrs Goswami in the eye, taking in the cool but triumphant look on the old woman's face. Her brittle manner was her way of surviving, Asha could almost respect her for that. And Mrs Goswami had looked after herself, taken control, protected her baby. Asha thought of Pran's lies, but the talk of the gun reminded her of the way the soldier had held the rifle over Pran's head. Her heart pulled in different directions.

'That's why we shouldn't worry. No matter how bad it seems, all this *bakwas*, this nonsense with Amin, it'll pass too,' said Mrs Goswami. 'It's hard now, but things will get better. They always do.'

6

Jaya

Jaya placed a glass of papaya juice on the little table next to the folding bed in the storeroom.

'You have better access to the snacks now, *bwana*,' joked Motichand, slapping December on the back and eyeing up the steel containers that stored *gathiya* and *sev mumbra*, piled next to bags of grains. No one laughed.

December smiled out of politeness. Jaya looked on as he put a book, his comb and some letters on the table, the light bringing out the traces of silver in his hair. The room was stuffy but there was little they could do with only a narrow window above the door.

For decades, December had left his home outside the city at dawn each morning, worked all day and headed back to his house each night. But with more of Amin's soldiers roaming the streets looking for people to pick on – or worse – it was now too dangerous to make the trips back and forth. And so he did what other house boys and girls now did, and stayed in the family home.

If she could have, Jaya would have comforted December with a hand on his shoulder; instead, she settled for a kind smile. Motichand went off for a nap but Jaya remained in the doorway. 'Did you hear from your family?'

December sat down on the bed, arms flexed to either side

of him. 'I got news from my village a few days ago, they were trying to get out. But I haven't heard from them since.'

Jaya knew that Idi Amin had set his sights on entire tribes. Those like the Acholi – December's tribe.

'It's difficult to get word out with the army interfering,' said Jaya. 'Try not to worry.' December knew everything about her own family: the sound of Motichand's voice, gruff and low, in the morning; the way Vijay liked to eat *choparya* when he thought no one was looking (rolled up with the sweet-sour chutney in the middle); the reason Pran had a scar the size of a matchstick on his right arm (an ambitious attempt to jump down from the tree in the yard as a child). Yet they knew so little about December's family.

She'd picked up everything she knew about them in snippets, a life compiled by patchwork. He didn't talk about his family often. Jaya recalled a time, a year or so after she had arrived in Uganda, back when both of them could still run fast across the yard when it rained and when they both had luxurious heads of thick dark hair. He'd come to the house one morning beaming as he clutched a box of *mandazi*, the sweet globes of fried dough eaten with strong black tea in the traditional way, to celebrate the birth of his daughter, Aber. He'd talked once or twice about a woman, Mary, but he never mentioned her after that. Jaya asked him to bring Aber to the house one day, told him how she'd love to meet his daughter, but they'd never had the chance.

'How can they do this?' Jaya shook her head, shaking off the anger she felt at Idi Amin, his army, at all the people that allowed it to happen. 'Picking on ordinary people who have done nothing wrong.'

'This is the way of things. Obote picked off his rivals before, Amin's picking off his rivals now,' said December. 'These men in power prey on people who are losing hope. People who think their lives will be different, that they'll be given a little piece of that power themselves. Of course, it never happens. They're lucky if they have a life to live at all.'

'I wish they'd leave us all in peace,' said Jaya.

'I should have gone back north when I had the chance.' December's voice sounded unfamiliar, filled with uncertainty. He'd planned to go a few months back, leave for good so that he could keep Aber safe, even though it meant he'd have to leave his job with the family. He looked down at the storeroom floor. 'They say they're going through entire villages.'

'It's probably just a rumour,' Jaya said.

Later, as the sound of distant gunfire punctured the night air, the family ate dinner and tried to work out what to do. December smoked and sat in a dark corner of the yard where he wouldn't be seen by the neighbours.

'He can't stay here forever,' Pran whispered.

'It's not forever, beta,' said Jaya.

'We have to get him out,' said Pran.

'Out where?' said Motichand, bundling another forkful of rice into his mouth.

'I don't know, but things don't look like they'll get better,' said Pran. Amin had already got rid of the Langi and Acholi soldiers during his coup, and now there'd been stories about the Acholi men and boys upcountry. So many slaughtered that their blood had pooled in the red earth at the bottom of ditches. All that was left were women and girls.

'You know how it is with these *kara* dictators, he'll be over-thrown like the others.' Motichand belched and then sighed, looking pleased with himself. Jaya remembered the days after Amin's coup, the elation that rang out across Kampala. But then the cheers and the drums stopped and all that was left was the broken cracks in the kerbs from the ferocious army tanks, Acholi and Langi faces disappearing from the streets.

'It's worse than before,' said Pran. 'And it affects us too, Papa.'

Jaya put down the jug of *chaas*. 'December's looked after us all these years. It's our turn to look after him now.'

'But we need to be more careful. What if someone sees him?' said Pran, shaking his head. Anyone could tell the army if they thought it would keep their own family safe.

'We will take care, beta,' said Jaya.

'Perhaps things will die down soon,' said Asha.

Vijay took another *rotli* from the pile and folded the flat round in half on his plate. 'Exactly. Let's wait and see what happens.'

'Don't you get it?' Pran looked at his younger brother. 'This isn't a game. What if the soldiers come to the house and find him?'

'They wouldn't come to our house without good reason,' said Jaya. Of course, there was a risk, but they couldn't leave him out there.

Pran huffed. 'They don't need a reason.'

'We will make sure no one sees him, beta.'

'But Ba,' said Pran, 'it's not safe for any of us.'

'How many times? He is staying!' Jaya slammed down her cup. 'We're helping him. There's nothing else to be said.'

Pran stared at her. Everyone's eyes were on her.

They had to help him. They owed him that much.

*

The afternoon was so warm it felt as if the air would burst open from the heat. Jaya shifted in her seat, trying to catch a whisper of breeze. She and Asha sat out on the veranda, each with a round steel sani in their laps, half filled with rice. Jaya flicked the rice from one side of the *sani* to the other, looking for small grit and stones and putting them aside. As far as house chores went, it was one of the few that she liked doing, along with getting a new bowl of rice out of the gunny sack in the storeroom. She took her time over that; she loved sinking her hand into the grains, the silky rice sucking her fingers in.

Jaya checked in case the neighbours were out in their own yards, and though she could see no one around, she whispered. 'I should take December some more water soon.'

'Yes, it must get so hot in that room. I've been thinking,' Asha turned her head towards Jaya, 'do you think that there's another way to help him?'

'What do you mean?' said Jaya.

'Hiding December. It's not easy for him, cooped up in that storeroom. And . . .' Asha paused, though she carried on moving the grains of rice across her sani.

'And?'

'Well, is it safe?'

'We have no choice.'

'But if the army find out, we could all be arrested.' She looked like she was about to say something else but thought better of it. But Jaya could guess. Asha didn't want to say it out loud, but they could all be taken away, tortured even.

Jaya looked up. 'What's Pran been saying to you?'

Asha's eyes narrowed. 'Nothing. We've not spoken . . . about any of this. But I was thinking about what he said at dinner. I know December's been working here for a long time, but is it worth putting the family at risk for a house boy?'

Jaya sighed. 'We can't throw him out on the street. Yes, he's been with us a long time, but it's a lot more than that. December helped us, in a lot of ways. He isn't just another house boy, Asha.'

'He helped you? With the house, you mean.'

'You just have to trust me, Asha.'

Asha put the sani down between them on the bench and shifted her body towards Jaya. 'But what would happen if the soldiers came here?'

'We would hide him. We agreed he could hide away well enough in the storeroom.' Jaya's voice was trembling now.

'Look, I'm not trying to upset you, it's just—'

'Stop now, Asha.'

'Perhaps you should talk to Pran yourself. He probably just wants to be sure you've thought this through, that's all. Things have changed so much these past months; it must be a strain, I know, what with the army stopping us like that and everything, things have changed so much.' Asha was rambling now, almost too fast for Jaya to understand.

Jaya stood up, shoving her sani onto the bench behind her, the rice grains that she'd so meticulously separated now a jumbled mess. 'You stupid girl. You are supposed to respect me, not question every decision I make in this house. *My* house.'

Asha looked at her in shock.

Why couldn't the girl understand?

'I'm sorry. I didn't mean to—'

'Leave the rice, Asha.' Jaya turned and walked away. 'We have more important things to worry about.'

*

The sun watched over Jaya as she crossed the yard, carrying a bowl of *posho* and beans. Silence. No swoosh of the *fugyo* sweeping away the dust, no thwack of wet clothes being beaten against the washing board. She missed the sound of December's voice as they talked through the day.

Jaya knocked on the storeroom door. She heard the sigh and groan of the metal folding bed as December got up to let her in, as though it too was carrying the weight of his worries. Fat bags of lentils and chapati flour lay slumped in corners, three folded newspapers and a book were neatly piled on one of the nearby shelves.

Jaya had hoped that the sunshine-yellow posho might cheer

him, a taste of home, but it was clear that she didn't know what she was doing; up until a few weeks ago she'd never made it before, never even tasted the food that was eaten all over Uganda. She'd imagined him, each day after she left the store-room, frowning as he jabbed at the poorly cooked cornmeal with a spoon and lifted up the lumpy mass like a giant lollipop. But today December didn't even look at it; instead he eked the corners of his mouth into a smile and set it down on a shelf. The soft fold where his head and neck met deepened.

'Perhaps you can eat it later,' said Jaya, standing in the door-way. 'You need to keep your strength up.'

'I thought I'd be here, working in this house, until my body gave up, or until the day I died. It looks like that will come true sooner than I thought.'

'Don't talk like that.' She turned towards him, her tone tender. 'We'll get you out.'

'I just wish I knew that Aber was all right,' he said. His daughter must be in her teens by now, eighteen or nineteen. Still there'd been no news. 'I should have got her out of the country somehow.'

'None of us could have known how bad things would get,' said Jaya.

'At least she was blessed enough to be born a girl, so they will spare her,' he said.

But even as Jaya nodded, she remembered the stories she'd heard in hushed whispers outside the temple, how the soldiers had gone to the campus at Makerere University and picked out women. That one glimmer of hope that for once it might have been a blessing to be born female disappeared.

Jaya looked around the room, at the bowl of magnolia and frangipani flowers that had been placed in the corner to hide the musty smell. The edges of the petals were already frayed and curled, wilting in the heat.

'Try to think of good things,' she said, telling herself the same thing.

Telling herself the same, December mustered a smile.

'I'd better get back to the cooking,' she said. A lizard flickered into the shadows as she closed the door behind her.

*

She hurried to the kitchen, taking out a knife to chop the *bhinda* then piling the chunks of okra into a bowl. The more she cut, the more the anger swelled inside her chest. How dare Amin do this to innocent people. Why should December suffer like this? And all the while, Pran and Asha were questioning why they needed to protect him. It must seem odd to them, she knew that, but she had her reasons.

He'd been there from the very beginning. She'd stepped off the steamer at the port in Mombasa, still dazed from her trip on the ocean, long weeks at sea from India to the Kenyan coast, a year apart from her husband while he'd got things settled.

Motichand took her suitcase by way of greeting. She'd known her husband for such a short time before he'd left India that she had little way of telling whether he'd changed much. He was chubbier than she remembered, his face full of curves, his shirt straining at his belly.

The memory of the ship, rocking in the water, had not yet left Jaya's body. Despite the sand beneath her feet, creeping in between her chumpul, she continued to sway. The air, sea salt and sweat stuck to her skin. Motichand led her through narrow streets, past compact white buildings where women watched them from dark wooden balconies; shopkeepers shouted as they sold their wares below; street hawkers sold roasted corn and cashew nuts scattered with chilli powder, and Motichand stopped to buy some. Her husband seemed quite at home speaking Swahili, already fluent in this new language she'd never heard, with its concise yet melodic tones.

Motichand bought tickets at the station and they boarded the train. Jaya wriggled in the leather seat, sari clinging to her skin, the air stuffy. He pointed things out on the journey: the hilltops layered in thick forest, the green fields of sugar cane shot through with red earth. Farmers, schoolchildren and stall traders went about their daily business. As in Gujarat, where the mix of people ranged from fair-skinned children with copper hair and grey eyes to dark-skinned men with wavy hair, the people of Uganda were equally diverse: from deep-brown skin that gleamed in the sun to russet-toned faces with high cheekbones. As they passed people tilling the land and strolling along the roadsides in patterned cottons, Motichand told her about the dukan he now ran.

'And in the marketplace, you can buy anything you want,' he said. 'It is so fine. *Mircha, buteta, tumeta.*'

'*Chiku?*' asked Jaya. Chiku was her favourite fruit, dense and sugary.

'Well, no, not chiku. But anything else you want. They will have that.' Motichand turned to the window and mopped his moustache with his handkerchief.

Outside the train station in Kampala, the roads were three times as wide as those in her village. They stopped briefly at Motichand's dukan, which did indeed seem to have anything you could ever need and many things you'd never want, but she couldn't take it all in. How far away her father was, her brothers, her home. Everything was different, strange, the buildings, the air. Her husband.

The house was centred around an open yard. The single-storey building was painted pale green like the inside of a pea pod. Running along three sides of the yard were a kitchen, a walk-in storeroom, a sitting room with two wooden armchairs, three bedrooms and a small enclosed space with a tap for morning ablutions. It was a larger house than the one that she'd lived in for the past year back in Gujarat, crammed in with Motichand's brothers and mother. This home was bigger than any she'd ever seen. All that space for two people.

'And this is December,' announced Motichand proudly, waving his hand towards the man in the corner of the courtyard, as though he was another feature of the house, like a brand-new radio or a stove. 'Everyone has house boys here.'

December was tall and slim, with a head of thick hair like unspun cotton. He was already too old to be considered a boy by a good few years, closer to her own age in fact, but Motichand had explained on the train that the name 'house boy' was the label for all male servants here. December glanced over at Jaya. His rigid brows made him look as though he was annoyed but then he flashed a brief smile, his eyes narrowing into crescents. Jaya pulled her chundri tighter around her face and turned her head away, as she'd been taught to do with all men for the sake of propriety. But she regretted it immediately. It must have made her look stuck-up.

Jaya unpacked a few items in the bedroom she'd share with Motichand, a simple square with two large beds. Separate beds. She didn't linger, going back outside onto the veranda.

'Here, I have translated the main things you'll need, so you can get December to help you with anything you want.' Motichand thrust a scrap of paper into her hand.

Jaya looked at the paper, a mess of scribbled words written in Gujarati with notes for the Swahili translation.

'I am going back to the dukan now,' said Motichand.

'You are leaving?' Jaya looked up.

Motichand called out something in Swahili to December, who was sweeping the veranda. He waved his hand in response.

'Do not worry. He used to look after an English widow for

a while, she lived on her own, nothing to worry about. He is most helpful. Most reliable. Back soon,' Motichand called out, leaving a spare set of keys on a hook and slamming the door behind him.

Panic ran along her spine. He'd left her there with a stranger roaming the house. A Ugandan man. Could she trust him? In Gujarat, she'd never been alone with a male who wasn't a relative; no respectable woman would be left alone with a man she wasn't married or related to. What would her father say if he heard about it? What would the other Asians who lived nearby think of her and Motichand? But if there was one thing she'd learnt about her husband in the few weeks she'd spent with him in India, it was that he was oblivious when it suited him.

She turned towards December, who was crouching on the far side of the veranda, sweeping. He looked up: an awkward smile, shy even.

The day passed in a muddle. Either Motichand's translations or her pronunciation were wrong. When she asked for a saucepan to make chai, December poured water from the copper pot into a saucepan and made the tea himself. When she asked for matches to light the outdoor fire for dinner, he lit the fire himself and beckoned her over when it was ready.

She wanted to shout at him, to make him stop. She couldn't get used to someone else serving her. Certainly not a man. '*Revah deh*,' she said to him, the Gujarati words sounding strange in this new setting, and of course December looked at her in confusion. He got up and poured another cup of water, raising his eyebrows in the hope that he'd got it right.

Jaya drank the water, even though she wasn't thirsty.

*

Each day, December brought home food from the market, using the money Motichand gave him. Some measly *tumeta*, a paler red than she was used to, along with a few stringy pieces of chicken and a gunny sack of millet that he'd cradled in the crook of his neck all the way home. She looked at the food but lacked the words to ask December why the money provided so little. Now she realized she lacked the words to ask Motichand either; her mother had made it clear: you couldn't involve men in household matters, nor question them when things went wrong.

She longed to speak to someone she knew, to ask their advice. At least when she was in Gujarat, Jaya had been able to see her own family once or twice, even though she'd moved to another village after her marriage. It was the tiny details about each of them she missed the most. Her youngest brother gleefully pulling their Kaki's little pigtail and running away; the string of soft sighs her father made when he fell asleep, as though the very act of sleep itself was exhausting. She even missed the people that were on the periphery of her life in the village. The people she'd never worried about leaving, people she'd assumed would always be there, their lives intertwined forever.

*

In the evenings after dinner, Jaya joined Motichand in the sitting room. He knocked back a glass or two of whisky while they listened to the BBC World Service. Even though she couldn't understand the announcers, Jaya found the muted, crackling English words a comfort, a voice to cut through the loneliness. She asked Motichand about December's life, where he came from, whether he had a family to support, but her husband had never bothered to ask. Meanwhile, Motichand's occasional visits to her bed at the end of the evening were as awkward and bumbling as their wedding night had been, but thankfully infrequent.

Motichand's brothers were supposed to follow him across the black water, the *kara pani*, as it was known, because the people in their villages said the sea would pollute and wash away your caste. They were supposed to help grow the business, but their letters were full of vague promises to join him, arriving months after they were written, only adding to the confusion. Looking back, Jaya wondered if they knew what she'd later learnt for herself: Motichand couldn't be trusted with money – it seemed to flutter in and out of his hands like a bird.

Most days, Jaya was stuck at home until Motichand finally returned. The cricket call was often the only thing to keep her company as dusk fell. Wanting to take more control of the household and converse in Swahili, she encouraged Motichand to teach her words whenever he was around. Sometimes, when they went to the newly built temple, Mrs Goswami would teach her a few words, though Jaya learnt to ignore her sly digs about a husband who left his wife alone with a Ugandan man all day. Jaya picked up the names of different foods – *mchungwa*, *ndizi* – and found out how many shillings they cost. Her Gujarati was infused with the softness and timidity expected of a woman, an echo of the women she'd left behind in India, but in Swahili she was emphatic and assertive, her vowels rounder, diction stronger, rhythm bolder. She became someone else.

*

'What does your name mean?' Jaya asked December. They were in the yard, turning over the chillies they'd left to dry out on her tattered old saris. As the day had gone on, the bright scarlet chillies had shrivelled and darkened, as though they had soaked up the terracotta colour of the earth beneath.

December looked up at her in surprise; their conversations tended to focus on housework. His eyes were streaming; the heat of the sun brought out the fire of the chillies. They scorched the air, burning Jaya's throat.

'December. It's the name of a month, in English.'

'And it is a common name for people in your village?' Jaya had assumed it was a traditional tribal name, similar to the way that Indian names were given, according to caste and religion. Yet perhaps it was usual to take the names of the English?

December laughed and wiped his eyes with the back of his arm. 'It's not my name, not really. One of the families I used to work for before was English. The little girl said December was her favourite month and they struggled to pronounce my name. Adenya.'

'A-den-ya.' Jaya thought it much easier to pronounce than December. 'Well, we will call you Adenya from now on.'

'No,' he said. 'Call me December, it's my name at work. Adenya is my family name.'

*

'*Kupata maiji*,' she called out to December one morning. He paused and smiled at her; she'd probably pronounced something wrong again. He nodded and went to fetch the bucket of water anyway. Despite the many months in Uganda and all her efforts, she still struggled with some basic words.

Jaya turned to go into the kitchen. A sharp pain. She reached out, her body doubling over as she fell. December ran to her, bucket of water spilling across the yard, the trace of tobacco and washing soap as he picked her up. The shame of a man that wasn't her husband touching her was overtaken by the pain searing through her stomach. She glanced over his shoulder. Two tiny moons, darker than the red earth, on the ground where she'd been standing.

December laid her on her bed. He shouted something she didn't understand in Swahili, eyes frantic, words fraught with alarm. A word she understood. Doctor.

'No,' she managed to say. 'Please. Let me rest. Nothing's wrong.'

'You need help.' His voice was firm. 'Now.'

'No. I told you.' Who did he think he was? He had to listen to her. Nothing was wrong. It couldn't be wrong. She strained to say the words. 'If you leave, don't come back to work tomorrow.'

He shook his head. 'I have to go.' He started moving away from the bed.

'No!'

December ran out of the room.

Dampness across her legs, seeping into her sari, bright blood spreading along the length of the lilac cotton, like the streak of vermilion sindoor in the parting of her hair. She fell into darkness.

*

When Jaya awoke, the curtains were drawn and the fierce smell of the kerosene lamp filled the room.

'Eh bhagvan! I was so worried, Jaya.' Motichand got up from the chair in the corner of the room. As he came closer, darkness crept into the crevices of his face, filling every sag and droop, turning him into an old man in moments. 'I spoke to the doctor. He says you'll be fine. He said that if December hadn't been here and gone straight to him instead of me . . . They don't know what might have happened.' He shook his head, his voice wavering. 'Why didn't you tell me?'

Jaya's mouth was too dry to speak so Motichand filled the silence.

'Don't worry, the doctor says we may have more . . . chances.' He rested his hand on her arm for a moment, then took it away. 'You shouldn't do so much. Let December help you more.'

Jaya nodded her head. He still had no idea how much December did around the house. She felt a pang of guilt as she remembered what she'd said, threatening to fire him for trying to help her.

'There is some water here. You rest now.' Motichand stood up. 'The doctor said I could pay him next week,' he said, more to himself than to Jaya.

She must have fallen asleep soon after Motichand left. When Jaya opened her eyes again, the muffled morning light came through the curtains. Her body ached, her stomach and legs were so heavy it was as though something was holding her down. She hadn't been able to stop it happening: yet another thing she had no control over. Tears crept into her eyes, a new longing filled her, but this time it wasn't for her old life in Gujarat.

Her grief was the only proof that the baby had ever existed.

She brushed her tears away as Motichand came into the room, smiling. He left some water and a paratha by her bed, then took out the money he kept hooked under the bedside table to pay December.

Jaya eased herself up. A crackle of pain shot across her stomach, but she called out to Motichand as he opened the door to leave, 'Wait, I wanted to ask you something.'

Motichand turned around.

She whispered to him, 'Why don't I save you the effort? I can deal with December's money from now on.'

'It's fine, Jaya. You must rest, go back to bed now.'

She put her hand on Motichand's arm. 'No, really. I can help make sure we're spending the money on the right things for the house, buy some decent food.'

'The food is first class, Jaya. First class. Now please, rest.'

Jaya took Motichand's hand and unwrapped the thin wad of money from his sweaty fingers. Three notes. So little?

'I'm waiting for a few accounts to be settled, you see.'

Motichand's eyes stayed on the money. 'Harilal is a little behind, but he'll pay next week. I'll buy you anything you want then.'

So that was why December had looked at her like that each time he came back from the market. It was her husband's guilt that she'd seen in the house boy's eyes, not his own.

After Motichand left, she went over to the window and looked out into the yard. December was sweeping the veranda. She looked over to where she had been standing the day before, but the spots of blood were no longer there, fresh earth swept over them. In the far corner, her clean lilac sari fluttered on the clothes line in the morning breeze.

For days after, he left food out for her, making sure she ate while Motichand busied himself at the dukan until nightfall. When she was well enough to sit up, he waited outside the door, pretending to sweep or tidy, keeping her company for a while. Keeping her dark thoughts at bay.

Jaya had never forgotten what he'd done. If he'd listened to her and done nothing, she might not have survived. Even if she had, she wouldn't have been able to have Pran and Vijay. What kind of life would that have been? Without a family of her own? How could she forget that? Of course, she couldn't talk about such things with Pran, it was impossible to discuss these things with any man, even her own family.

7

Vijay

Vijay looked into Pran's bloodshot eyes.

'Go on, pass me another,' said Pran.

'You're really trying to catch up with Papa over there?' said Vijay. Motichand was snoring in his favourite chair, legs splayed, arms hanging down either side, mouth open so wide he could catch grasshoppers.

'Come on.' Pran beckoned for the whisky in Vijay's hand.

Vijay poured two glasses, far more generous than any bartender in town. If they couldn't go out like they used to, why shouldn't they make the most of it now? He got up and flicked off the light, casting the room into darkness. Outside in the yard, fruit bats flitted in the gloom.

'So, is Asha still angry with you?' asked Vijay. The seat fabric was warm beneath his skin as he sat back down. 'With us?' He couldn't ignore it, that way she looked at them both now, occasionally accompanied by a beautifully arched eyebrow.

Pran slumped further into his chair, resting his head on the seat back. 'She'll be fine.'

Vijay laughed. 'Yes, that's definitely what fine looks like.'

'I've explained everything. She just needs more time to cool off.'

'Cool off? The only place cold enough is the North Pole.'

Vijay gulped the whisky too fast; it seared the back of his throat. 'You just got married and you're already in her bad books.'

Pran laughed. 'Such an expert, hey? Maybe you should have married her.'

Vijay shifted in his seat, hoping his face didn't betray how he felt.

'I told her I didn't mean to hurt her,' said his brother.

'But you have hurt her, haven't you? We both have.'

'It's too late to feel guilty now. You played your part. It's not like I forced you.'

Vijay glanced at Motichand. He was still sleeping, but he jolted, as though some invisible hand had tried to shake him, then settled again. Vijay turned back towards Pran. 'I know, but—'

'Asha'll come around. Or maybe I'll find another way to make it up to her,' he grinned.

'Spare me the details.' Vijay watched his elder brother as he knocked back the rest of his drink.

'Pour me another,' said Pran, batting away a fly that had landed on his glass.

Vijay served him some more. 'I might go and see if December wants some.'

'Leave him, it's late.'

'I just want to see if he's up. He must get lonely in there.'

'Why is everyone suddenly treating him like he's some long-lost uncle come to stay?' Pran was starting to slur his words, or maybe Vijay had drunk too much. 'Always trying to muscle into this family. He's found a way now, hasn't he?'

'I think that has something to do with working here and having to wash your smelly clothes!'

Pran shook his head. 'All this special treatment. We have enough to deal with, getting the dukan back on track.'

Vijay downed the rest of his glass. 'What's your problem? The dukan? We could be talking about his life.'

'But why risk all this when he's just a—'

'Just a what? A servant?'

Pran put his glass down on the armrest. 'Well, he is.'

Vijay got up, the floor rolling beneath him.

'Where are you going? Sit down and have another drink,' said Pran in a wayward voice.

Vijay snatched the bottle of whisky from the table, bottleneck hanging down from his fingers. 'You really think we should throw him out on the street?'

'No. But the sooner he's out of here, the sooner we can all sleep at night.'

'Well, get on with it. You've been saying it for ages. Help him get out of here.'

'Trust me, I'm doing everything I can.'

'What is that exactly? What are these hotly guarded plans of yours?'

'It's under control.'

'Sure it is.' Vijay walked to the doorway. He didn't need to hear any more.

'Vij, wait.'

Vijay waved his hand dismissively. 'Forget it. I'm off to find another drinking partner.'

*

Out into the humid night air. Vijay felt his way along the outside of the house with the tip of his left arm, around the veranda.

He knocked on the storeroom door softly, or at least he hoped he had.

'Come in,' December whispered.

'Sorry. Did I wake you?' said Vijay.

'No, I couldn't sleep anyway.'

'I thought you could do with some company.' Vijay raised the bottle.

December laughed. 'That's my kind of company.'

Vijay put the whisky down on the table. He slid his body onto the floor, back resting on the shelf behind. 'You'll need to catch up with me, though.'

December poured some into a glass on his table. He lay back, propping himself up on his elbow, feet hovering off the bed.

'Forgot my glass, this'll have to do,' said Vijay, taking the bottle back and gulping the buttery liquid, hot down his throat.

They talked a while, thinking about the old days, remembering Jennifer, the lady who'd come around selling fruit and vegetables each morning, who'd taken a shine to December a few years back.

'She kept flirting with you,' said Vijay. 'Remember?'

'No, she didn't, she did that with everyone.'

'Oh, come on, you remember, don't you?' Vijay put on a high-pitched voice, fluttering his eyelashes. 'Look at these tomatoes, Mr December, very fresh, very fresh, Mr December.'

'Stop that.' December waved a hand in dismissal, stifling a laugh. 'Anyway, what's your father up to? Gone to bed?'

'Papa's probably on the floor of the sitting room by now,' Vijay grinned. 'Pran's there with him.'

'He didn't want to join you?' December looked away, a wrinkle forming between his brows.

'Tired, I guess,' said Vijay.

'Because of the dukan? I'm not helping matters staying here.'

'We're all pulling together, he's not doing it alone.' Vijay poured a triple into December's glass. 'Here, have another.'

'Might as well. It's not as though I have anything to do in the morning.'

They sat in silence for a while. The electricity generator from a nearby house hummed outside.

December glanced at the books and papers Jaya had brought him to read piled up on the table. 'You read the *Argus* today?'

'I skimmed through it. But it's more of the same. Whatever crazy law Amin's come up with this time. They keep the real news out because they're scared of him. And everyone believes his propaganda.'

'Not everyone,' December said, his tone soft. 'But some people want to believe the headlines. If you were promised a better life, wouldn't you want to believe it was true?'

'But why don't they see what's behind his lies?'

'When you're left to rot in the slums and no one seems to care, wouldn't you believe it? Rifles give them power, the army treats them well. Of course the soldiers swallow the lies that give them hope.' December stared at him.

Vijay nodded. All he'd thought about was the fear he felt, his problems.

'And there are people who don't think the Asians have been fair,' December said.

Vijay knew what people said about them, how they spoke in Gujarati and Hindi about their workers, kept others down while they grew rich. 'Some Asians have behaved badly, I know that. But those people, those headlines that say we're bad. Amin eats the flesh of his enemies, that's what the rumours say. We're not like him.'

'He is crazy, no doubt about that. But remember that who-ever writes those stories has their own agenda.'

'But either way, Amin's eliminating everyone who gets in the way. Like you, hiding away like this.'

December sighed. 'I'm sorry you all have to deal with it.'

Vijay lifted his head, trying to hold it steady. 'That's not what I meant. We're fine. Anyway, it's not for long. Pran's nearly—'

'I am not stupid.' December sat up. 'Pran doesn't want me here.'

Vijay thought of the best way to answer.

'I don't blame him,' December looked down, tracing the rim of the glass with his finger.

'Come on, don't talk like that.' Vijay ran his hand through his hair, tugging at the tangles. It was a risk for all of them, he knew that, but what was the alternative?

'Sat around like a useless piece of mutton, slowly rotting in the heat. Waiting, always waiting.' December's voice rose with each word. 'I need to find Aber.'

'Please . . .' said Vijay. The words wouldn't come, all jumbled up.

December looked up. 'You know, when I was younger, all I wanted to do was earn enough money to chase women and drink waragi. I wasted all that time when I should have been with my little girl. I wasted so much time.'

'You were young, it's what we do,' said Vijay, trying to muster a smile.

'But working so hard, just to make money. And for what? I don't even know what's happened to my daughter. Don't make the same mistakes as me.'

Vijay stared at him, felt the guilt burning in his chest, thinking of the money he and Pran had chased together, all the way across an ocean. 'Just wait, Pran will—'

'Your brother wants me to leave, can't you see?' December slammed his hand down on the table. He froze for a moment. 'I – I didn't mean it.'

Vijay tried to put the whisky bottle aside but instead he knocked it over, brown liquid spreading across the concrete floor. He pulled the bottle up again, managing to save some. As he tried to scoop the liquid with his hand he quickly realized how futile it was. 'Why won't you accept our help?'

'I'm sorry. I can't just sit around here.' December stood up, pulling out his bag from under the bed, shoving his spare clothes inside.

'What are you doing?' Vijay tried to pull himself up, but his head was spinning.

'I have to go.' December hoisted his bag onto his shoulder.

'No, wait, hear me out.' Vijay clung to the shelf. 'What you said about Pran, it's not true.'

December paused.

'No, I mean, of course he's never forgiven you for that time when we were kids, at the market.' Vijay's tone was playful. He waited to see if December would take the bait. December had taken Vijay and Pran shopping. Pran had gone missing, running off to talk to an old woman who sold vegetables at one of the far stalls. He had tried to find his way back to the others and worked himself into a state. By the time December and Vijay found him, Pran was shouting and all the people in the market had turned to stare.

'How could you do that?' Pran had cried, hitting December's chest as people pushed their way past them. 'You're supposed to look after us.'

'You shouldn't have run off,' said December.

'You're paid to look after us!' Pran yelled.

December held his wrists gently, letting the little boy shout and cry until he was exhausted. After a few minutes, December crouched down and looked at him.

Pran stared, then raised his hand. Surely he wouldn't hit December?

But instead, he shyly held his hand out in front of him.

December took his cue and shook it. 'Good, now let's go get a soda *baridi*.'

'Do you remember that day?' Vijay said. 'Pran was furious!'

December gave a small laugh.

'Look, don't do anything rash,' Vijay said. 'Promise me. For Ba, if no one else?'

December nodded, lowering his bag to the floor.

'I better go and get some sleep.'

'Vijay?'

'Yes,' he said, turning around.

'Leave the whisky.'

8

Asha

Asha opened the bedroom door, keen to change after her trip to temple with Jaya. Hopefully, Pran would be in the sitting room and she wouldn't have to bump into him. He'd spent the past weeks trying to reconcile with her, ever since she'd found out about the smuggling, but she couldn't get over his lying.

Inside, Pran stood at the far wall, a nervous look on his face. There were plates of food covered with lace doilies on the little table and a vase filled with white flowers, the petals fringed in pink.

Asha frowned with confusion.

'I'm sorry,' said Pran, walking towards her and taking her hands.

'What's all this?' she said.

'We're going on a picnic.'

'What? It's nearly dark, curfew will start soon.'

'We don't have to go anywhere.' He uncovered the plates of food. She surveyed them: samosa, *kachori*, gathiya, all her favourites.

'I don't know, Pran . . .' She stayed by the door.

'Just give me a chance. Eat a little food and then you can leave, if that's what you want.'

She had to admit that even she was tired of keeping her

distance. 'We're going to attract the ants. Your mother won't be happy.'

He led her to the bed, where he'd spread out a picnic blanket. 'But you'll stay?'

'It's my bedroom, where else can I go?' She sat down on the edge of the bed. 'What's that?' She pointed at a messy pencil drawing on a piece of paper propped up against the wall.

'It's a monkey, of course!' Pran laughed.

'Oh,' Asha said. 'Could have sworn it was a hyena.'

He looked at her with mock indignation, then took a plate and piled it up with food for her. 'It's like the monkeys at Entebbe, remember?'

The first time they'd met. That day, Asha's friend Sahar had decided to gather all her friends for a picnic at the Botanical Gardens. Sahar's idea of 'nothing big' was thirty people armed with bags of food, a portable Primus stove and a huge steel pot filled with bottles of Coca-Cola and beer that had to be carried by three people. They'd wound their way through that prehistoric world with the swathes of green: lime, fern, moss. Liana vines hung down like ropes from the colossal trees, squirrels flitted from branch to branch, vervet monkeys with biscuit fur and shy brown faces peeked out from the foliage.

They arrived at a stretch of grass along the banks of Lake Victoria where the men had gathered for a game of cricket while the women stood and watched. 'Make sure that the ball doesn't hit you over there,' one of the men called out, far too pleased with himself.

'You too,' Asha said, then muttered, 'I'd hate for it to knock some sense into your head.'

Sahar's long curls made waves along her back as she laughed. They passed the time catching up on their news, talking about films and music, not paying much attention to the cricket match until there was a shout. The ball flew through the air, hurtling towards them.

Asha ran, the thrill of muscles being stretched and flexed, the breeze in her hair, that feeling she'd had many times as a child, climbing trees with her cousins, making herself dizzy from cartwheels.

The ball was close. Asha leapt for it, nearly knocking over one of the other fielders. She caught it in her hands, the leather ragged beneath her fingers, staggering to steady herself. She held her hand in the air, triumphant.

'Where'd you learn to catch like that?' A man walked over to her. The sun glittered in his dark hair, picking up the bronze and gold hues.

'Same place you did, probably,' Asha said. Tiny dimples appeared in his cheeks when he smiled. Like upside-down tears.

'I hear you're visiting from Jinja?'

'You heard that from all the way over on the other side of the field?'

'Well, have you seen the size of these ears?' He flicked his earlobe. The others were shouting for him to get back to the game, but he stayed where he was. 'I'm Pran.'

She glanced across at Sahar, who muttered something about needing to check the food and took her cue to wander off.

Growing up, the boys had always been busy trailing after Sahar. Charming, delicate-featured Sahar. Asha, on the other hand, was treated like a sister, no need for pretence, no reason to impress her, too clumsy, too loud. Later, though she was the same person, something seemed to change. Boys suddenly sweetened their tone, some too shy to approach, while others prowled around her like a leopard after prey. So fickle.

But not Pran. He walked straight up to her, looked her in the eye and listened to her when she told him about her life in Jinja, her family, her job as a secretary working for a chaotic boss. And as she talked to him, she couldn't help but wonder what his mouth tasted like.

They saw each other again but always as part of a group, flirting but no more. She told herself nothing could come of it, that she'd accept an arranged marriage like all her friends. She went on dates with the boys she was introduced to, trying to piece together what kind of husband they'd make after a handful of conversations: if they were polite to the waiter did it mean they'd be kind to her? If they brought her flowers or a gift, did it mean they'd always be romantic? But Pran, there was always Pran. After years of seeing each other as friends, forever surrounded by other people, she couldn't fight her feelings any more. The pull of him was too strong.

'Here you go.' Pran handed her the plate of food and sat down on the bed next to her. He put his plate down on his lap. 'I should have told you everything.'

'But why did you do it? There must have been easier ways to help the business.'

His words unsteady: 'The dukan was in a worse state than I thought. After going through the books, I realized I couldn't easily turn things around. I didn't want to get into more debt. We wouldn't even have been able to get a loan with the business in such a state. I had to do it.'

'And if you'd been caught? What would have happened to the dukan? To us?'

'It was a risk. But I'd heard of a couple of others who'd got away with it,' he said. 'The way I grew up, never feeling secure. I didn't want my children to live like that one day.'

Asha looked down at her plate. Pran mentioned children now and again. She always thought of it as something vague and far off in the future, *one day*.

'You know I could have gone to university,' he said. They also both knew that the firstborn was expected to follow in the father's footsteps. 'And if being a *dukanwara* was my future, I wanted to make it the best it could be.'

Asha didn't agree with what he'd done, but at least she could start to understand why he did it. 'You didn't have to lie to me.'

He paused, he wouldn't look her in the eye. 'I should have been able to do this on my own.'

'No. I'm proud of you, no matter what,' she said.

'I didn't want to bother you with all this. You understand that, right?' He waited for an answer.

Asha wanted to forget everything that had happened. He'd told her all there was to tell and they could put it behind them now. 'Don't lie to me again. Promise me.'

He nodded.

She took a bite of her kachori, crisp pastry giving way to the spiced pea filling inside. 'So, if you'd had your way, you'd have become a science graduate?' He'd told her before that it was his favourite subject. He loved atoms and molecules, minerals and organisms, was fascinated by the fact that it could take centuries for some starlight to reach earth and that the shooting stars they watched together were rocks hurtling through the sky. 'What would you be doing now?'

'I don't know. Researching cures for cancer maybe? Or a meteorologist?' His face lit up.

He carried on talking about the other life he could have had. It dawned on her that the man she loved hadn't been able to make the life he wanted, that perhaps the life they'd have together would in some way always be a disappointment.

After they'd finished eating and washed their hands, they lay side by side in bed.

'So what did you want to be when you were younger, then?' said Pran, turning towards her.

The question took her by surprise. Her parents, her extended family, schoolteachers, everyone knew the path set out for women like her. Finish your education, work for a few years, get married and have a family. What *had* she wanted to be when she was a child? 'I wanted to travel. See the world, learn about other cultures.' Her dreams seemed ridiculous now, she could barely bring herself to say them out loud.

'Travel?' Pran paused. 'So you could have been an air hostess?'

Asha gave him a sharp look. She was capable of far more.

'No, I wanted to work in government.' Her words firm, expecting him to laugh at her, ready for another argument. 'A diplomat, even.'

'In politics? Wow, you'd be a force to reckon with.' He stroked her cheek. 'Though you'd probably have to keep that temper under wraps.'

She tugged the front of his hair playfully. 'You'll see that temper again in a moment if you're not careful.'

He pulled her close and as he unwrapped her from her sari, all she could think about was his kisses falling like petals on her skin, his hands along her spine, her thighs tight around his.

*

A few weeks passed. One night, Asha joined the others in the sitting room after dinner. 'Vijay's gone to his room?'

'He wanted to get away from all this racket,' said Jaya. The new TV set buzzed with music while Motichand chatted with his friend in Mbale on the telephone.

'It happened at the wedding, apparently,' said Motichand, voice booming so loud his friend could probably hear him all the way over in Mbale without the aid of the phone.

'No, it was an engagement,' Jaya told him.

'An engagement. It was an engagement. And it happened in Rasangpur—'

'Rajkot,' said Jaya.

Motichand finally finished his conversation, then picked up his chai. The surface rippled as he blew across it.

Asha looked over at Pran, who sat in the armchair browsing a newspaper. Her heart filled with relief again, glad they'd reconciled.

'Everyone in Mbale is well? Premchandbhai is back on his feet?' said Jaya.

Motichand poured his tea into the saucer and slurped from it.

'Listen.' Pran stood and turned the volume up on the TV.

Idi Amin was on the screen again, military shirt hugging his belly. His speeches were so frequent that most of the time they paid little attention; he obviously thought that these were things great leaders did, giving long, dull sermons about whatever had entered their head that day. He addressed the viewers: 'The Asians came to Uganda to build the railway; the railway is finished – they must leave now. I will give them ninety days to pack up and go. Asians have milked the cow but did not feed it.'

Motichand leant forward, giving a phlegmy cough. 'What's he talking about?'

Amin continued, 'Africans are poor. Asians are rich. Asians are sabotaging the economy of Uganda. They have refused to allow their daughters to marry Africans. They have been here for seventy years.'

'Did he say leave? In ninety days?' Motichand laughed, a chai-coloured spray showering across his white shirt.

'He's lost his mind this time.' Asha shook her head. 'What will it be tomorrow? People whose names end in "k" must only walk on the right side of the street?'

'He wants us to leave everything and never come back?' said Jaya.

'He makes these rules up as he goes along,' said Asha. Amin

changed his mind from one day – or hour – to another. All the more reason not to take him seriously.

'"Sabotaging the economy" – we helped *build* the economy,' said Pran.

'He'll change his mind tomorrow.' Motichand waved his hand in the air. 'No point worrying.'

'Let's turn it off. Idi's given us enough entertainment for tonight.'

Pran walked up to the set. The screen went black.

*

But by the next evening, they wondered if they should have dismissed it so easily.

'He's still going on about it.' Motichand walked into the kitchen, back from the dukan. He pinched a tomato slice from the bowl of *kachumber*. Jaya moved the bowl away.

'You mean Amin?' Asha lowered the heat on the stove and turned to face them.

'Whisper, will you?' said Pran in a low voice.

'Why? You think he suddenly understands Gujarati? You think he's hiding under the table?' Vijay ducked down to look. 'Amin Dada, where are you?' He sang it like a nursery rhyme, with the term of endearment that many in Uganda used. 'He's so big he would have got stuck between the table legs. He'd be crawling around the kitchen like a tortoise!'

Motichand let out a belly laugh that showed his back teeth.

'What has he been saying?' Jaya asked.

'He's saying that the Asians who aren't Ugandan citizens must leave, but others can stay,' Pran whispered, which made the news sound like a child making up stories.

'He's saying some of us should go? He's serious about this?' Asha's head spun. How could they tell what was rumour and what was true? She carried the bowl of coconut mogo, the pieces of creamy cassava wobbling in the pot as she set it down on the table.

'He knows the money would roll out with us, so now he's backtracking,' said Vijay.

'Well, perhaps the Ugandans feel we've already been rolling the money out of this country for years. Perhaps that's one of the reasons we're in this mess now.' Asha couldn't hold the words back. She stared at Vijay and Pran. Both looked away.

'That's only the wealthy families.' Motichand pulled out a chair and squeezed himself into it. 'Hiding cash in foreign banks. As if the rest of us have that kind of money.'

'The rest of us are only trying to get by,' Jaya said, sitting down next to him.

'It's the same old story, the same one they told when we first arrived here, remember, Jaya?' Motichand turned to his wife. 'Then they said the British favoured Asians because they trusted us to oversee the railway construction. There's always someone else holding them back.'

'But it did hold the Ugandans back,' said Asha. 'Not everyone treats them well.'

'We didn't have it easy back in India. Why else would we have travelled so far?' Motichand sighed. 'Why are they acting like it's all our fault?'

Asha caught Pran's eye.

He looked away. 'Obote used to blame us too, but even he would never have done this. It's Amin who's to blame. Anyway, we need to decide what to do. The other dukanwara are saying he's serious.'

'He's done it before. When he sent the Israelis away,' said Vijay.

'That was a few hundred people.' Motichand shook his head. 'This time there's thousands and thousands of us.'

'But the point is, he did it,' said Pran.

'Remember that census of his? Makes sense now,' said Vijay. The surprise census that Amin had ordered had seemed odd at the time, but everyone had put it down to yet another of his whims.

'Counting us Asians up like he counts up his money,' said Pran. 'Making sure he has us exactly where he wants us. And he'll have seen what his friends across the border are doing in Kenya and Tanzania too. Squeezing Asian businesses until they choke.'

'Harassing us. Telling us we're all corrupt and greedy ever since he first got into power, while we tried to run our businesses,' said Motichand. 'We should have seen it coming.'

Asha stared at him. It seemed a bit rich, Motichand complaining about how difficult he was finding it to run his dukan when his sons were struggling with his mess.

'They can keep on clashing amongst their tribes if they want to, but why don't they keep us out of it?' Motichand shook his head.

That's when it dawned on Asha: they'd all told themselves that it was nothing to do with them, even when it became obvious that things were getting harder. They'd all lived up there on Kololo Hill as though they were immune.

'Well, it's OK for you, Pran, you'll be able to stay here with your Ugandan passport. We're the ones who'll be going for a nice, long holiday.' Though Vijay tried to make light of it, no one laughed.

'But Pran can't stay here on his own,' Jaya said.

Asha looked at him. They couldn't be apart. Surely no one would do that to them? It was all such a mess. Asha, Vijay and Jaya had the British passports that they'd secured before Ugandan Independence, while Motichand had kept his Indian passport. Like so many other families, they'd hedged their bets, collecting passports between them like stamps, trying to tie themselves to different countries. They never expected to have to rely on any of it.

'Where'll we go?' Vijay rubbed his temples.

'India will let us in,' said Motichand. 'Of course they will.'

'All of us?' Vijay said.

'Are we not Indian?' Motichand threw his hand in the air.

Asha had never even left Uganda, let alone visited India. She'd sometimes wondered what her life might have been like there, tucked away in a small town, stuck in the house all day doing nothing but chores. And what about her parents, her brothers? What would happen to them?

'This is crazy.' Pran shook his head. 'I'm going to do something.'

'Like what?' said Asha.

'I'm going to fight it. I'm not going to let them just take everything.'

'Let's think about it tomorrow, it has been a long day,' said Motichand, helping himself to a kachori and dipping it into the *ambli*, tiny drips of tamarind sauce falling onto the table. 'He might have changed his mind by then.' But even Motichand didn't sound certain any more.

'And what about December? What's going to happen to him?' Jaya said, running her thumb along the side of her plate, over and over.

But no one had an answer.

*

Days passed as the family tried to gather information about the expulsion. The newspaper headline that confronted Asha as she sat in the kitchen made it clear. Idi Amin said that it was up to the British government to take responsibility for Asians who left Uganda, while the British government tried to persuade

India to take them. Everyone passed the buck, no one wanted them.

Pran walked in, opened up a steel container and piled a spoonful of *chevro* into his hand. He knocked it back in one.

'What are we going to do?' Asha's life had become a jumble of calls and conversations with her parents and brothers, aunts and uncles, cousins and friends, all trying to work out where to go. A few people they knew had already left, not wanting to take any chances. She thought of Sahar and her husband. They'd emigrated to Pakistan months back, worried about the growing violence and curfews, while others tried to convince themselves it would all pass.

'We're not going anywhere,' said Pran.

'What do you mean? You've heard what they're saying.' She showed him the newspaper; perhaps the thick black letters would jolt him back to reality. There'd been a letter in the *Argus* that week, wishing the Asians 'a long, cold winter'.

'We'll stay. I'm working it all out.'

'What are you saying?' Had Pran already forgotten that the government was led by a man who changed his mind, his wives, his right-hand men, all on an impulse? Shouldn't they be pre-pared, even if Amin did change his mind?

'They can't just throw us out of the country we were born in.'

'But you've seen what happened to Naseem.' The week before, she and Jaya had gone to visit his parents and Razia. The family were beside themselves. They'd spent a long night waiting up for him but he hadn't come home. The next day, Naseem's abandoned car was found on a roadside just outside Kampala. His glasses and jacket were on the front seat.

'He never goes anywhere without his glasses,' Razia had cried, eyeliner running in black rivers down her cheeks. 'They've taken him, I know it. They won't tell us anything.'

Though Jaya and Asha had tried to console them, Razia was convinced that the army was responsible. She was still trying to find out what happened.

'It's not the same. Naseem was mixed up with government officials. You think he made that money all on his own?' said Pran.

'You want to stay in a country that can just take people like that?' She recalled the anguish in Razia's face, how she'd clutched her handkerchief so tightly as she sobbed. Asha took his hand. 'I'm angry too. But we'll be safer if we leave.'

'Don't give up so easily. That's not like you,' said Pran. 'I'll find a way to stay here, trust me.'

'OK, fine, you're staying,' she said, unable to hide her annoyance any longer. 'Nothing's going to change. What about December, is he just going to stay in that storeroom forever?'

'I'm working on it.' He washed his hands, then turned back towards her.

'How?'

'It's not that easy, Asha. Anyway, we have enough to worry about.'

'What happened to telling me everything? This isn't what married life is supposed to be like.'

'How do you know, have you been married before?'

Still he cracked jokes. Asha put her palms against the table, tiny wooden ridges beneath her skin. 'You said you'd be honest with me.'

Pran's smile faded. He pulled up a chair next to her, a hand on her shoulder, the heat from his skin meeting hers. 'I'm sorry. I didn't want you to worry about December on top of everything else.'

'I'm not a china doll that needs protecting. Are you speaking to the same people? The ones you . . .' she thought of the right words to use, 'worked with before?'

'I'm going to ask them, yes. I don't know if it'll work, though.'

'You really have to go back to them?'

'This is different. I'm not hiding money this time.'

She still didn't like it. If people could cheat the authorities, hiding their money all over the world and getting others to do their dirty work, how could you trust them? Asha looked up at him.

'I'll work it out, I promise. The last thing we should be doing is arguing, right?' He put his hand on her shoulder; his familiar scent, musk and a hint of cigarette smoke. And there were the tiny dimples in each cheek.

Asha stared into his eyes, black in the afternoon shade of the kitchen, and nodded.

9

Vijay

'Record player, Vijay!' Motichand sat forward in the armchair, rescuing the glass from his wobbling belly just in time.

'Shhh, everyone's asleep.' Vijay rubbed his eyes. They were in the sitting room with Motichand's best whisky for company. His father poured some into a third glass for December to drink the next day, as he'd often done over the years, though Motichand had drunkenly forgotten that December could now no longer come out into the kitchen to get it.

'Sorry.' Motichand rested his index finger on his lips. 'Record player, Vijay!' His volume remained the same.

'We can't put a record on at this time of night, Papa.' He didn't say the rest, but they both knew it. They couldn't let patrolling soldiers hear.

'Fine!' Motichand jumped to his feet. 'I make my own music.'

Vijay followed his father as he wandered outside into the yard, lifting his arms into the air and clicking his fingers in a rhythm that Vijay couldn't place.

'How about some more whisky?' Motichand held his hand up, showing Vijay a tiny gap between his thumb and index fingertip. 'Just a little one?'

'Come on, Papa, let's go to bed.'

Motichand started dancing around the frangipani tree. 'This song, this is my song, Vijay!'

Vijay followed him as he sang his favourite song, pretending to be happy-go-lucky Raj Kapoor, his Papa's favourite silver screen actor.

'*Meraa juuta hai Japani.*' Motichand sang the Hindi song. Badly.

'Shhhh, Papa, you'll wake everyone up,' Vijay said. 'And I'm pretty sure your shoes were made at the shoemakers on Jinja Road, not in Japan.'

The fruit bats scattered away into the night to escape the singing. '*Yeh patluun Englishstani.*'

Vijay laughed in response to the lyrics and whispered, '*Englishstani*? The trousers were from Manaklal's Fancy Stores in town, not from England.'

'*Sar pe laal topii Ruusi.*' Motichand tapped a toe with each step forward.

'You don't wear a hat,' said Vijay, 'not even one from Russia.'

'*Phir bhi dil hai Hindustanii.*' Motichand's voice fell to a whisper. '*Phir bhi dil hai Hindustanii.*' A shadow of sadness in the way he sang the words, now.

'Now that is true. Your heart is truly Indian,' Vijay said, taking a sip of whisky. He looked out across the yard, hearing the cricket call humming in the air, suddenly tired. 'What's going to happen to all of us, Papa? When we leave, I mean?'

'What do you mean?' Motichand had sprung back to life, clapping his hands in the air. 'This is an opportunity, Vijay!'

'An opportunity?'

'We can finally all go back to Gujarat.' Motichand grinned.

Vijay stepped towards him. 'Papa, some of us were never there in the first place, how can we go back? Back to what?'

'I was there. And your hearts are also *Hindustani*, no?' Motichand ruffled Vijay's hair.

But Vijay had no answer. To leave your friends, your city, everything you'd ever known? His father made it sound so easy, to just up and leave. To go to a place he didn't know at all, never even visited? So he spoke Gujarati, could hold a conversation in Hindi, ate daar bhaat and shaak rotli. You couldn't know a country from afar, from films and news reports and what other people told you. That wasn't home.

For a moment, Vijay wished he was a child again, that Papa would brush away his tears or soothe him with a hug as he'd done when Vijay had fallen and hurt himself. He wished Papa would tell him that everything would be OK, even if both of them knew it was no longer true. He watched Motichand as he carried on wandering around the tree, dancing to the imaginary music that only he could hear. Vijay rested his head against the back wall and closed his eyes, hoping it would make his head stop spinning. Swallowing hard, the bitter tang of whisky on his tongue, his belly churning. So much to think about, leaving everything behind, three months. Too much to take in. He heard a crackling sound and opened his eyes.

Motichand was pissing against the tree trunk.

*

'That's all? *Etlooj?* said Nileshbhai the barber, holding his index finger and thumb in the air and frowning at the space between them.

'That's all,' Vijay said apologetically. Swaddled in a white cotton cloth as he sat in the barber's chair, he looked at Nileshbhai through the reflection in the mirror.

'What sort of fashion-bashion is this?' Nileshbhai looked at Motichand, who was sitting in the chair next to them, waiting his turn.

On the other side of the barbershop, a worker was busy sweeping the floor and wiping mirrors. The air smelt of herby hair oil and hair cream. The walls were lined with framed photos of various white men with neat, short hair directing their most winsome grins at some happy scene in the distance. Vijay was pretty sure a white man had never even entered the barber's; it was usually filled with Asians and a few Ugandans. But it was difficult to find magazines filled with pictures of Asian men – at least those with decent haircuts – so Nileshbhai used these instead. There was also a photo of Queen Elizabeth, but as far as he knew, none of the men asked to look like her.

Outside, the street was quieter than usual. Some shops had their shutters closed; a few had a cluster of people outside, hoping to take over a business that had already been vacated. The same people who might have queued to pay for their goods were now waiting to take the dukan itself. Through the government lists that reallocated the businesses, no money even needed to change hands, except bribes for the officials, of course.

Opposite the barber stood Lalji General Store, where years ago Vinodbhai had given young Vijay a free bag of sweets or shooed him away to get some peace, depending on his mood. The dukan had already been taken over by a man whom Vijay had never seen before. Now it was this man who swept the floor, pulled open the metal gates on the door each morning, who stared out into the street waiting for customers in the same place that Vinodbhai had done a couple of weeks before.

'Don't leave your hair so long. Let me cut a little more off.' Nileshbhai waved his scissors around in the air.

'No, honestly, that's all I want.'

A pause, a sigh. A begrudging snip. A sliver of hair on the floor.

Vijay and Motichand had decided to get their hair cut while they could, knowing there'd be more important things to think about after they left Uganda. Motichand browsed the newspaper, licking his finger to turn each page, shaking his head at the headlines that affronted him.

Nileshbhai lowered his voice. 'You're all making plans?' He was referring to the expulsion, but by calling them 'plans', the barber made it sound more like they were booking a short trip away.

Vijay nodded as Nileshbhai ran his black plastic comb through his hair, never an easy business as it snagged on endless tangles. No point telling Nileshbhai everything. Best not to go into too many details: you didn't know for sure who you could trust. And if the army knew when you were leaving, they'd descend like locusts before you'd slammed the car door shut. 'How about you?'

'We are sorting it all out now. Paperwork, passports and more paperwork. What good is it though, Motichandbhai? What good is paper? You can tear it up, you can burn it in a flame—'

'You can wipe it on your arse!' Motichand put out his hand and Nileshbhai slapped it in amusement.

'Exactly, no one cares what your passports say! We are being shoved out of this country but where will we go? You, Vijaybhai, what does your passport say?'

'British.'

'Good luck, my friend, they don't want you either. They've conveniently forgotten everything us Asians did to bring them wealth in the first place.' Nileshbhai gestured with his hand. 'And you, Motichandbhai?'

'Indian, what else?'

'I am the luckiest one then,' said Nileshbhai. 'I have one of this fine country's passports. What use is it now? They said I could stay, then they said I couldn't.' He waved his head from side to side as he said it. 'As if I'd stay in this place anyway, without my family.'

'It's terrible, Nileshbhai, terrible.' Motichand shook his head.

Nileshbhai's thick moustache twitched, followed by his equally thick eyebrows. 'And we still have to get out of this country in one piece.' Nileshbhai raised his chubby hand to his forehead as though he was taking his own temperature. 'All these money-grabbing karas with their guns.' Nileshbhai's worker looked up from the sweeping when he said the word '*kara*'. He probably couldn't have understood most Gujarati, but he likely knew the derogatory word for black people that Nileshbhai had used.

'They have been stopping the buses at the checkpoints,' said Motichand. 'Three or four checkpoints, at each one they make them stop. Make them all get off—'

'And rob them.' Nileshbhai's scissor-waving was more animated than ever. Vijay leant forward a little in his chair in case he caught a particularly energetic swerve of steel. 'Wait a minute, they've taken everything from me at the first checkpoint, what am I supposed to give you at the next checkpoint? The stupid *sala*s. And he tells us we can leave with one thousand shillings – what's that, fifty pounds sterling? What does it matter? Guns are the currency, weapons are the government now. Money means nothing. You know, we should have fought back when that sala president first said it. The Punjabis, they fought alongside the British during both the world wars. They know how to go to battle.'

'But they were trained for generations, Nileshbhai,' said Motichand. 'We don't know how to fight.'

Vijay decided not to remind them that those Punjabis were older than any of them now. They'd never stand a chance against Amin's soldiers.

'And even if we did, how many of us are there?' said Motichand. 'Seventy, eighty thousand maybe?'

Vijay shifted in his seat, thinking of Pran still insisting that he was going to find a way to stay in the country, as though he could somehow fend off an entire army on his own. 'We're a minority. We'd have no chance.'

Nileshbhai's face puffed up more the angrier he got. 'We were a minority all these years and we controlled most of this country. Me, I'm closing the barbershop this week. And once I sort our papers out, I'm taking all the family out for the biggest meal, the best meal. We will order a bottle of imported whisky and the most expensive things on the menu.'

Motichand chuckled along and Nileshbhai played up to the attention. 'If we can't take it with us, well, I'll show their precious president. I'll rub the money I earned all these years into their faces.'

The barber poured hair oil on his hands and rubbed them together, making a slippery whick-whick sound, then smoothed it through Vijay's hair before he had a chance to stop him. 'In fact, Motichandbhai, why don't you all come along? It's on me. No, wait, it's on Amin Dada. After all, it is his money now.'

10
Jaya

Across the sky, a wash of pink faded away, giving in to the rising sun. Jaya paused in the driveway while Motichand locked up the house and the children made their way to the car. Over the road, the ornate iron gate that led to their neighbour Jaswinder Singh's house was wide open. Jaya moved a few steps closer. The mint-green front door was also wide open.

'Come on, Jaya, let's go,' Motichand called out, raising his voice over the fuzzy car radio as he tried to find his station.

'They've gone.' Jaya climbed into the back seat. 'They've all left.'

Everyone looked over towards the house. It was difficult to tell whether Jaswinder had simply decided that there was no point in locking the door on the way out for the last time, or whether looters had broken in and helped themselves, taking their chance before the government association had a chance to reallocate the home to a Ugandan family.

'They didn't even say goodbye,' Jaya said, her tone sombre.

Pran started the car. 'People are terrified, Ba, it's not their fault.'

'Did Kushwant say anything?' Jaya turned to Vijay. For years, her boys had played together with Jaswinder's son Kushwant, running up and down the street all day till long after dark. Motichand and Jaswinder had often reminisced about the good old days in India over an evening whisky, and Jaya whiled away long afternoons with Jaswinder's wife, Nimrat, sitting on the veranda drinking chai.

'Not seen him in a while.' Vijay shook his head. 'Not sure where they were going.'

'Canada, didn't he say?' Motichand continued to fiddle with the radio.

'I thought it was England?' said Pran.

'I was going to go and see them, I wanted to give them all some of the *dhokra* I made,' Jaya said, looking down at her hands.

'Perhaps one of the other neighbours knows,' Asha said. 'We'll go and ask later.'

This is how it went now, houses abandoned in the night, cars left by the kerb, keys still in the ignition, turning the area into a ghost town. All these tiny losses, day after day, piling up inside Jaya's heart, filling it with sorrow. How long before it burst?

They fell silent. Even Motichand had given up trying to find a radio station and turned it off. As the car progressed slowly towards the city centre, they watched a tall man with a tight-cropped Afro trying to start a car by the roadside. It made a sickly noise, coughing and spluttering, but the man persisted in trying to drive it as it juddered down the street.

'Why's he trying to drive it?' Asha asked. 'It's clearly broken.'

'Someone must have put sugar in the engine,' said Vijay. 'Nileshbhai was telling me about it. "If these gandas want my car after I've left, they can have it, but they won't be driving it far!"'

They watched the man with the struggling car until he got to the corner of the road. He got out, kicking the wheels before wandering off.

When they arrived at the British High Commission there was already a long queue. All were expected to leave the country, but no one was making it easy for them.

'Where's the British efficiency now?' Motichand muttered. 'We should try India, like I said.'

'They won't let us in, Papa, you know that,' Vijay said. 'Our best chance together is England. We have three passports between us.'

'That's if they let you in,' Pran sneered. 'And there won't be much of a welcome when you get there, you saw the paper the other day.' There had been advertisements that an English council had put in the *Ugandan Argus*, telling people not to come to Leicester, where many had gone because they already had family there.

Motichand had laughed when he'd seen it: 'Imagine, this Leicester place has so much money they can put these advertisements in the paper! There must be lots of jobs there if they can afford this.'

Pran shook his head. 'We helped them build this country up, made Britain wealthy too, but they've forgotten all that Commonwealth business now.'

'But if they only let those of us with British passports in, what's going to happen to you and Papa?' said Jaya, looking at Pran.

'They wouldn't split up a family.' Vijay shook his head.

'I've not even decided if I'm going yet,' said Pran.

'How are you going to fight them?' said Vijay.

'I'm working on it.'

Asha whispered. 'They're talking about rounding up anyone who doesn't leave and putting them in the old army barracks. You can't stay.'

Jaya stared at Pran. There was no way she'd let him stay in this country. Who knew what would happen to him?

They carried on waiting, wilting in the heat.

Hours passed. She tried to catch the faint breeze on her face, felt the sweat pooling on her chest and in her armpits. There was nothing to do but stay as still as possible and watch people go by. It had been a while since Jaya had come to the city centre. It was too dangerous to leave the house after dark, and even during the day there was a new edge, a volatility that cut through the air, a feeling that at any minute someone could do or say anything to you, emboldened by Idi Amin's decree. She watched two women hurrying along the wide street, past the bakery, the tailors, the fabric shops and the *pili pili* bazaar with the piles of spices, *hurdur, chutni* and *jeeroo*. The women were wrapped in ten kitenges each, their bodies swathed in a mass of patterned cotton, walking as fast as they could with their newly acquired haul. Motichand had come home with stories of the looters; some of them had been friendly with the old owners of the dukans for years. It was not uncommon, Motichand told her, to see people walking down the street, arms piled up with goods so high they couldn't see in front of them. Jaya took it all in, but reminded herself that for every dishonest person, there were the ordinary Ugandans, many of Motichand's customers and people like December, who faced despair just like them.

Across the street, she saw two children playing. They were putting little pebbles into holes in a wall. It was only when she looked again that Jaya realized: it was a rainbow of bullet holes. She quickly turned away, looking further down the broad road, where she and Motichand had strolled for hours with the children on Sunday afternoons, for festivals, Divari, Eid, Vaisakhi and Ugandan Independence a few years back. They'd stop for snacks of sliced green mango scattered with chilli powder, saying hello to friends while firecrackers and fireworks went off around them. Hindus, Jains, Sikhs, Muslims, Parsis,

Christian Asians together; sometimes it felt like being back in India, even though, in truth, India had never been like that. This was a dreamlike version of what India might have been like for her. She had to admit that however bad Motichand had been with money, her life in Kampala was far easier than it could ever have been in Gujarat. Uganda offered more opportunities to improve their lives – that was why he'd left in the first place. And now here she was on the same street, saying goodbye to yet another life.

Dusk began to settle over the city. They were close to the front of the line, but when a security man with a green uniform came outside, they all knew what he was going to say. They'd have to start all over again the next day. They decided that Pran and Vijay would keep their place until the morning. The army seemed too busy harassing people on their way to the airport or looting recently abandoned homes to worry about anyone else.

That evening, as Jaya walked across the veranda towards her bedroom, the questions whirred in her head. Where would they all go? Could they get out safely? Would they see December again? And now, images of the house flooded her mind, as she remembered when the boys were little.

Pran and Vijay had come home from school but they wouldn't listen to her, buzzing with energy like little wind-up toys. They'd been on a school trip to Entebbe zoo that week and Vijay kept doing impressions of a snake, slithering around the floor, covering his school clothes in red earth. Meanwhile, Pran jumped around and roared like a lion.

'*Chup!* Quiet now!' said Jaya. She had a mountain of sewing to do and her eyes were still streaming from a morning spent pounding green chillies. Vijay stood and wrapped his arms around her yellow cotton sari, leaving a fine pink film across the fabric. 'Vijay!'

He grinned and ran away before she could catch him, getting back down on the floor and slithering off to the shade of a mango tree.

'*Raaaauw,*' Pran roared again, hanging off the edge of the veranda. 'Look, Vijay. *Raauw!*'

'*Ssss,*' said Vijay. 'I'm going to bite you! *Ssssss.*'

Pran, louder now: '*Raaaauw! Raaauw! Raaaauw!*'

'*Ssssssssssssssssssssss.*'

'Stop that. Go and sit quietly and read your books!' The boys ignored her. Her voice withering in the heat, arms swelling, cotton blouse digging into her skin. She longed to take it all off and lie down. Why couldn't she have one minute on her own? A single minute, no grasping little hands, no irritating noise, no incessant questions. A moment to think about no one but herself? Just one. 'Please stop now,' she said. The exhaustion frayed her voice but still they would not stop.

'Boys, come here, tell me what you saw at the zoo.' December walked over from the sitting room where he'd been tidying.

A roar. A slither, a trail of red earth. The boys carried on.

'Boys!' said Jaya. No response.

December looked at Jaya and smiled. A look that told her he understood. 'What are you supposed to be? Is it a gazelle?' he said, pointing at Pran.

'No! I'm a lion. Not a gazelle!' Pran pouted.

'And you're a . . .' December rubbed his chin, pretending to think, 'a hippo?'

Vijay looked up. 'I'm a snake. A snake!'

'You tell me what you saw at the zoo,' December said. 'And then I will tell you about some other animals. Ones you might not even have heard of before.' He beckoned the children over to the corner of the veranda. 'Let's leave your mother in peace.'

She watched them. They kept running around, but every so

often they would stop to listen to December and his stories as he tidied the yard. She went back to the kitchen.

By the time Motichand came home that evening, the children had eaten dinner, still enthralled by December's stories. He'd told them about hyenas and crocodiles and buffaloes with horns that dipped in the middle of their heads like centre partings. He'd told them about creatures he'd never seen himself because he'd never seen the sea: octopuses and whales and sharks.

'What's for dinner?' Motichand boomed, pulling out boiled sweets from his pocket like a magician.

'Papa!' the boys shouted, running up to him and snatching at the sweets. Motichand picked up Vijay and flung the boy across his shoulders. Pran laughed and jumped, trying to tap Vijay on the head. Jaya exchanged a look with December. Between the sugar and the excitement, they both knew how long it would take to settle the children again.

'There's *ringra nu shaak*,' said Jaya, putting the aubergine curry on the table. 'And the *bundhi* I made yesterday.'

'No chicken?' he said, still prancing around with the boys.

'No chicken,' Jaya said quietly.

'Sit with me,' said Motichand, after he'd washed his hands. Pran sat to one side, Vijay to the other, each unwrapping sweets and stuffing them into their mouths.

'They must go to bed soon,' said Jaya.

'They have their whole lives to sleep.' Motichand burped. 'You too, Jaya, sit with me.'

Jaya sat down. December finished his work in the kitchen and called out, 'Goodbye, I will see you tomorrow.'

But Jaya was the only one who noticed, nodding as he slipped away into the night.

Now, in the evening light, Jaya sat down on her bed. She thought ahead to another day waiting at the High Commission, wondering how she'd be able to say goodbye to all those memories, the life, the good and the bad, that she'd lived for so many years.

*

The next day, they left the house before sunrise. They took their places in the line again. As Vijay and Pran unwrapped and ate the paratha she'd made for breakfast, she passed the time watching people go by. A woman with a baby swaddled in kitenge fabric across her back, followed by another who walked as regally as a queen, balancing a basket on her head without once looking down. Jaya knew she'd have to leave these sights behind.

At five o'clock, woozy from the heat, they were finally told to go inside. The interior of the High Commission was pristine, with white walls and a pale-grey tiled floor. The only colour in the room came from the Union Jack, hanging forlornly in ripples of red, white and navy. The ceiling fans churned hot air over the people waiting to speak to officials in the cubicles. A mere handful of people were on hand to deal with all these crowds.

Another hour passed, and one of the officials called out to say that unfortunately the office would be closing and they'd have to come back tomorrow. Murmurs of confusion turned into louder grumbling.

'They have to be joking?' Pran said. Motichand sighed and turned towards the door.

Asha walked up to the cubicle, peering through the window at a young man with a comb-over. 'You expect us to come back. We've had two days of this.'

'Asha.' Pran looked uncomfortable. 'Don't.'

'*Revah deh.* I'm fed up of other people deciding what we can and can't do,' Asha whispered in Gujarati.

The guard who stood near the flag eyed Asha. 'Your demands won't work here. The days of you wahindis clicking your fingers are gone.'

Asha ignored him and focused on the official, oblivious to the stares of the people in the queue. Causing a scene with no thought for anyone else.

'Let them wait, Jacob.' At the next cubicle, an older white man with a fuzz of red hair peered over the top of his glasses. 'I'll see them in a moment.'

'Next time leave these things to me, Asha,' said Pran.

'It worked, didn't it?' Asha said. For once, Jaya was grateful for Asha's temper.

The man with the glasses mopped his brow. 'Could I have your papers please?' The soft Swahili words conflicted with his stiff English accent.

Pran passed over the passports but he responded in English. 'Good afternoon.' It was one of the few phrases Jaya understood. He said something else about the papers that Jaya didn't understand.

The man looked up, surprised by Pran's shift in language, but he continued in a prickly Swahili. 'So you all have British passports?'

'No, *bwana*.' Pran switched to Swahili, knuckles tense as he gripped the edge of the counter.

'Why did he switch back to Swahili?' Jaya murmured.

'He's trying to suggest Pran can't speak English properly,' Asha whispered. 'We were taught it for years.'

'So.' The man lit a cigarette.

'So?' said Pran.

'Only some of you have British passports?'

No wonder there was such a long queue outside if the officials took this long to work out basic facts. Surely it was clear from the passports?

'Yes, but we're a family so we want to stay together,' Pran said.

'Now you must know, the British government can only admit those with suitable passports.' He showed the passports to Pran, in case he'd forgotten what they'd looked like in the few seconds since he'd handed them over. The little hairs on the man's lower arms quivered as he shifted in his seat. 'Your father would need to go to India. And you have a Ugandan passport, so you'd need to—'

'We want to stay together,' said Pran.

'As a family.' Vijay leant forward.

'My father and I need to look after the others,' said Pran. Vijay's brow furrowed, annoyed at the implication that he couldn't look after anyone.

'There is nothing I can do. The rules are clear. You don't have the correct paperwork to comply with—'

Pran moved closer to the counter. 'They're taking everything from us, can't you see that?'

Motichand tried to pull him back. 'Pran.'

Anxiety flared in Jaya's chest. It was all falling apart, all of it.

'I realize this is very upsetting.' The man glanced towards the guard behind them. 'But you're not the first family—'

'The first family you've split up?' Pran stared at the man as he made a big show of shuffling the papers.

Jaya placed her hand on his arm. If they annoyed the official, it might mean that none of them would be allowed into England. 'Beta, let him do his job.' She took a long breath, trying to calm herself, hoping it would somehow settle Pran.

By the time the official had processed Jaya, Asha and Vijay's passports and they'd come outside, it was growing dark.

'If England doesn't want me then I don't want England,'

said Motichand, his voice breathless. 'But I can't just let you go alone.'

'Are you all right?' Jaya climbed into the car. The colour in his cheeks had faded.

Motichand sucked hard at the air. He mopped his upper lip with his handkerchief.

'You need to rest, Papa, it's been a long day.' Pran stared through the windscreen, out into the dark street. 'We'll have to try to get you to England somehow.'

'You've seen the reports,' said Asha. 'They're sending people back to the countries that issued their passports.'

He turned to face her. 'But don't you see? Even if I leave, they can't send me back here.' A bitter current ran through Pran's laugh. 'Uganda doesn't want me either.'

*

Later that evening, Jaya sat at the table in the corner of the bedroom, slowly taking the pins from her bun, letting the hair fall loose across her shoulders. A beetle scuttled across the floor by her feet and escaped through a crack in the wall, out into the night.

How could this have happened? The fear she'd felt when she left India for Uganda came back to her now.

Back then, many people had already moved away from the small Gujarati villages to bigger cities, to Mumbai or Amdavad, where they could make a better living. Motichand had decided to go even further afield, bewitched by the tales of riches that others had made in East Africa, running dukans, factories, plantations. He told her he wanted to have a business, to buy a new house and drive a brand-new car, a Rolls-Royce like the local maharaja drove around in. Jaya understood his desire for money and for security, never having to worry about droughts or hunger, but why make huge sacrifices, leaving family behind, to go to a land so different to their own?

They'd only been married a few weeks when Motichand set off on his journey. He left before dawn. He'd dropped to his mother's feet and she cried as she pulled him back up in an embrace. She told him to be careful, superstitious about defying the taboo of the kara pani that could wash away his caste. He got on Laljibhai's bullock cart, saying goodbye to Jaya with a smile, a wave and an 'I'll send for you soon.' She watched as he disappeared into the darkness along the road to the port.

They waited for Motichand to get in touch. Word was sent via other people's letters, those who had made the same journey as Motichand and had settled in Uganda already. His first letter consisted of a few lines, telling them that he'd arrived in Mombasa. Later, another airmail from him said he'd made it to the Ugandan border. Other specifics, names and towns and cities, were absent, and Jaya started to wonder how she could be certain that any of it was true. How could they know? An entire country. They were separated from Motichand by a mass of water, and not just any water, but the kara pani. How did they know, with the hundreds of miles that lay between them, that the story hadn't got mixed up, that the letters from acquaintances in Uganda weren't talking about someone else? After all, there was an added complication. Motichand no longer carried his family name, 'Motichand Meghji'. After the end of the relaxed immigration rules of the British – desperate for reliable Indian men to help them build the Kenyan-Ugandan railway – they tightened up the law. New arrivals from India had to rely on sponsorship from an already-established family member. And if there were no relatives in Uganda, the ever resourceful Gujaratis found ways to create new ones.

'Two husbands for the price of one, Jaya!' Motichand had told her. He changed his name from Motichand Meghji to

Motichand Zaverchand, taking the name of an older man he'd never met before. This Zaverchandbhai had already set up his business in Uganda and agreed to 'give' Motichand his name, in return for the young man's help in his dukan.

There was no word from Motichand for ages. Jaya's usually amenable mother-in-law had been getting angry with her for no apparent reason other than the fact that Jaya was in her house and her son was not. Many weeks after Motichand had left India, he finally sent word again. He told them that he'd saved plenty of money, enough to take part-ownership in a business. It would only be a matter of months before he could branch out on his own and she could join him in Uganda.

And so Jaya prepared for her own journey. She'd never seen the sea before. She imagined that it was as black as the bottom of a well, a ferocious body of water, an angrier version of the spindly little river in her own village.

One of Jaya's distant relatives, Vidhyaben, and her husband were also making the journey to Uganda and they'd agreed to collect her from the village on their way to Porbandar. The breeze picked up as they approached the port town, the salt sea air crackling on her lips. The kara pani was nothing like Jaya had imagined. There was no sign of black; it was pale blue, like one of her blue cotton saris that had been washed in the river too many times, with ribbons of colour along it: turquoise, emerald, mud-brown in parts, like the earth.

The steamship was bigger than any house, any building, in fact, that she'd ever seen. The pointed tip gave it a proud, haughty look and the sides were dotted with little windows, which she'd been told were for the first- and second-class passengers. The water brushed against the side of the steamer, teasing, playful, frothy rolls of water, which reminded her of boiling chai in a pot.

She forced herself to step onto the boat. How could it

possibly stay afloat? How could wood and metal be the only thing that separated them from all that water? They were shown below deck, to the belly of the ship. The ceiling was as low as those in the house she'd left behind. She could see no windows; the only light came from the stairwell, making shadows in corners. The tight, hot air filled her throat.

The women and children were separated from the men in different sections of the steamer. Jaya laid out the shawl that she would sleep on next to Vidhyaben and settled her things. After a few moments, the boat began to judder and rumble. Everyone hurried back onto deck.

She watched Porbandar recede into the distance, fishing boats and harbour shacks getting smaller and smaller until they looked like children's toys. The way that the light hit the water, sea became sky, sky became sea, swallowing her whole, drowning in blue.

'Can't go back now, heh, Jayaben?' Vidhyaben nudged her arm, her fingers sticky on Jaya's skin. They reminded her of her husband, a man she'd only known for a short time, waiting for her on the other side of the ocean, in a country she'd never seen before.

Jaya felt that same dread now; from the top of her throat to the pit of her stomach, she felt it all again. She put her comb on the bedroom table and looked out into the night, but her thoughts were disturbed by the distant crackle of gunfire.

As she oiled her hair, Motichand walked in and sank down on his bed.

'I really thought they might let us all go to England, Jaya. How stupid I was.'

She could see him in the reflection of the mirror. 'What will we do now?'

'We can't go to India together, they won't let you in either.' He propped up one of his legs, rubbing his chubby foot with his hand. 'I will have to go to India with Pran, work out a way for us all to be together.'

'As if we didn't have enough to worry about.' She ran the comb through her hair; the coconut oil made it shimmer silver in the lamplight.

He shook his head, face full of sorrow. 'They'll split us apart, Jaya, and there's nothing I can do.'

She went over and sat opposite him on her own bed. The scent of sweet-spicy betel nut lingered, his lips pale pink from the *paan* he'd eaten earlier. They'd sometimes sat the same way when they were younger, facing each other as they got ready for bed.

'How much more are we supposed to take?' said Motichand. Jaya didn't have the words for him. She'd seen that look on his face only once before, when the children were young and he'd received a telegram telling him his mother had died back in India. He'd kept going all day, making arrangements for a small memorial service for her, even smiling as he told Pran and Vijay stories of the many times his Ba had told him off as a child. The children were confused about the death, they couldn't understand how a grandmother they'd never met could die in a far-off land. Motichand carried on trying to make them laugh, telling Jaya he was fine and didn't need to rest, that the children were a welcome distraction. He played the role expected of him, to be jovial at all times. It was only later, after they'd both gone to bed, that Jaya heard him across the room, softly sobbing. The following morning, she'd gone to him as he buttoned his shirt and she pretended that he had an eyelash on his cheek. She stroked his face, then pulled him towards her. Though he was almost twice her height, he crumpled in her arms like a child. They held each other until she was no longer sure which tears were his, and which were hers.

'I don't know what to do.' Motichand shifted on the bed

now. His voice, usually so cheery, sounded empty. He was the one who usually buoyed her; he looked on the bright side, even when there was no light ahead.

'We will be all right,' she said, swallowing down the uncertainty she felt. 'I'll be with Vijay and Asha, you'll have Pran. The main thing is that we get out of here alive.'

'And what then? I haven't been back to India in thirty years.'

'Thirty-five.'

'Thirty-five years. And I'm supposed to start again? At my age?'

'But you wanted to go back?' She tried to keep her tone light, but she knew what he meant. Over the years, Jaya had pored over pictures of India in the newspapers. Behind the well-known faces in power – Gandhiji, Nehru, Jinnah, smiling or solemn – were the ordinary people, standing aside and looking on from the corners of the photographs, their features blurred, broken by cracks in the film or by the wrinkles in the paper breaking up black ink. The women in the pictures looked like Jaya, they dressed like her in saris, wore small, round chandlas between their eyebrows and wrapped their hair in tight buns just like her. But Jaya wasn't like them. The people who'd crossed the black water to Africa were in a whole new caste of their own, with their own language, their own food, their own ways of life. 'You will have Pran,' she said. 'You know he'll work hard like a real Indian countryman.'

'He will work hard, yes. But he knows nothing about Indian business,' said Motichand. 'They do things differently there.'

'You'll both get by. You speak the language, we have family who'll help.' Jaya tried to reassure him, reassure herself, even as she remembered Mrs Goswami, who had visited India a few years back. She'd complained to Jaya that nothing was the same: she'd got sick, the food tasted different, the people she knew had grown up, moved away, died – in some cases, all three.

'I was a tourist in my own country. Imagine!' she'd said. Even the way she spoke stood out; the words had changed, modernized over the years, while the Gujarati she spoke in Uganda remained the same, frozen in time. They teased Mrs Goswami, told her that she sounded like the elders of the village, long gone now, an echo of a forgotten past.

'And we don't know if we'll be able to get you to India. All these passports. What was the point, Jaya?'

'So that we could be safe. So that if they tried to throw us out, we would be safe.' Passports were supposed to give them some options, their fates written onto paper.

'We've only got a few weeks left before the deadline is up. There's still so much to think about.' Motichand rubbed between his eyebrows and sighed.

She watched him, taken aback by his despair. 'We will find a way,' she whispered. 'God will look after us.'

Motichand eased himself up from the bed, smiling as he moved towards her. He took a strand of her hair, brushing his thumb across the tips, the way he'd done when they'd first married. 'Perhaps, Jaya. Perhaps.' He walked over to the light switch and turned it off, leaving nothing but the night.

11

Vijay

'Sorry I'm late.' Vijay walked into the flat and greeted John. 'There were some soldiers hanging around on the street. Had to wait until they'd gone.'

'Don't worry, come in. Steven had to go out, he said he'll come and see you before you go.'

They'd been friends since their schooldays, after the Asians-only rule was relaxed at Vijay's school and John had been one of the first black Ugandans to join. The flat was owned by Steven, a friend they'd both met on a night out. Steven was American, an ex-Peace Corps volunteer who'd fallen in love with Uganda and its beautiful women. He'd stayed on to live with his local girlfriend after most other foreigners had left, scared off by the political tension. It was too dangerous for Ugandans like John to be seen with Asians, the lines of separation carved even stronger than before, so Steven had suggested they meet at his place.

Vijay took in the framed film posters that lined the far wall of the compact sitting room. He tried to catch his breath; he'd bounded up the stairs to the flat as fast as he could, making sure none of the neighbours were around. He was glad to see that the window blinds were pulled down, to stop prying eyes from looking in and to keep the sun out.

'I definitely need this,' Vijay said, opening a bottle of whisky he'd brought with him and pouring it into the tumbler glasses that Steven had left out for them. Vijay hoped the soldiers outside didn't come back; he had to sneak out before curfew started.

'Vijay, there's no need for that,' said John, leaving a faint scent of fresh cotton in the air as he moved. 'I'm happy with waragi.'

'Why save it?' Vijay shrugged, pouring them both a generous measure. He knocked it back in one, hoping it would settle his nerves.

'How are you doing?' said John, quietly. It was the first time they'd seen each other since the expulsion announcement.

'All right,' said Vijay. 'I just can't believe we have to leave so quickly.'

'I can't believe any of this.' John took a sip.

'Doesn't look like I'll be joining you at Makerere now.' He'd hoped that after the trip to London and with the dukan back on track, he'd be able to join John at university.

'Thank God for that, and all it took was Amin Dada making you leave the country.' John smiled. 'But I hear they have one or two universities in England too.'

'Yes, just a couple!' Vijay humoured his friend; they both knew he'd have bigger preoccupations like finding a job and somewhere to live. 'What's going on with you? Your family OK?'

'What is OK nowadays?' John looked down at the floor. 'My neighbour at the university halls was taken by the army last night. We're still waiting to hear what happened. They've been hounding the lecturers too.'

'Amin's frightened of anything that he doesn't understand,' said Vijay. 'Perhaps it will get back to normal once we wahindis have left?'

'Nothing will change, you know that. Amin Dada is after blood. He doesn't care whose it is.'

Vijay remembered December's words, how ordinary people

felt that their troubles had been ignored. 'He really feels the country will be better without the Asians here.'

'But he's acting like every single one of you is at fault.' John shook his head.

Vijay shifted in his seat, the guilt burning his throat as much as the whisky. What would John think, if he knew what he'd done, smuggling money out of the country? Blindly going along with Pran's plans. 'Let's forget all that, we're going, whatever the reason.'

The sound of men shouting outside. Vijay put down his glass and hurried over to the window. He pulled the edge of the blind back an inch. Bright light pierced his sight. Once his eyes had adjusted, he looked down towards the street.

'Are the soldiers back?' said John, starting to get out of his seat.

'No, it's a couple of locals, maybe they're drunk. I should probably head back soon though, while the coast is clear.'

'OK, after this one.' John poured more whisky.

'Have you heard what people are saying?' said Vijay, sitting back down. 'That the reason our dear president wants us to leave is because he tried to get a Hindu girl to marry him. But her father sent her out of the country before Amin had a chance to get his hands on her. He got so angry he took it out on all us Asians.'

'That sounds so crazy . . . it could actually be true,' John laughed. 'But imagine if you started holding grudges against every girl who said no to you?'

'I know—'

'There'd be no girls left!'

'It's not like you had much luck with the girls, remember?' Vijay thought of Jaspreet, the prettiest girl at school. Both boys had spent their entire time trying to impress her, and she'd milked it for all it was worth, getting them to do her homework, carry her books, bring her gifts. Not that she'd ever really been interested in either of them. Still, Jaspreet was only a girl. Asha, on the other hand, knew her own mind, hadn't been afraid to confront Pran when she found out about the smuggling, and fought to make sure they got their time at the High Commission.

For a moment Vijay forgot why he was there, as though they'd see each other next week, next month; the alcohol mellowing his thoughts, smoothing away the horror.

'OK, OK, no need to remind me. You're the heartthrob around here, right? I suppose you'd give yourself a ten out of ten then, such a catch?'

Vijay didn't miss a beat. 'Nine and a half.'

'What have you taken the half off for?'

'I'm also modest,' said Vijay.

They laughed and clinked their glasses together. 'OK, you try out your wonderful luck with the ladies the next time we go out—' John stopped laughing, realizing what he'd said.

'Next time we go out. It's OK. We'll go out again soon enough. I'll hold you to it,' smiled Vijay, but they fell into silence, the sound of shouting in the street cutting through the quiet.

John lifted his head. 'You'll keep in touch, won't you?'

'Of course.' Vijay swallowed his whisky in one gulp. 'And we'll go out when I come back. I promise.' But as soon as he said it, he wondered whether the words were already a lie. Would it really be Idi Amin that stopped him returning, or would it be his own bad memories of the place that he'd once called home?

*

Vijay leant against the countertop, willing someone to come into the dukan, anything to fill the time. Since the expulsion announcement last month, fewer and fewer people came to the shop. This week, the family had only opened to say goodbye to a few loyal customers. It wasn't as though they could take any money they earned with them when they left Uganda.

'Right, I'd better go,' Pran said, an endless afternoon of goodbyes stretching ahead for him too, driving Jaya around to visit the few friends that were still left in the country.

'Wait, Pran,' Vijay called out. 'Ba's been talking about December again, she'll probably ask you about it today. She's really worried.'

'I've got it under control, I just need to pick the right time.'

Vijay came out from behind the counter. 'Are Popatlal and that rich family going to help? They're still in the country?'

'Leave it, Vijay. It's not like you to worry so much.'

'Things have changed, in case you hadn't noticed.' Vijay didn't bother hiding the annoyance in his voice.

Pran opened the door. 'I'll see you tonight.'

Motichand came out from the storeroom at the back.

They stood behind the counter, watching people go by, not bothering to come inside. What need was there to spend money elsewhere when they could simply take what they wanted from their own newly acquired businesses? An hour passed and just as Vijay was about to suggest that they close up, the door opened.

'Motichandbhai!' Sardarji's familiar silver beard glinted as he came inside.

'Hello!' Motichand beamed, slapping Sardarji's hand.

'Vijaybhai, you're well?' Sardarji shook Vijay's hand vigorously.

'What a mess we find ourselves in, Motichandbhai!' Sardarji leant forward against the countertop, ruffling Vijay's hair as though he was still a kid. Vijay tried to straighten it out again discreetly while the older men spoke. In the old days, Sardarji would ease his way onto the wooden platform at the back of the dukan, legs creaking as he sat down. He brought his own soundtrack: the cricking of his neck, the rusty sigh that punctuated his sentences, whiling away the hours with Motichand.

'Have you made plans? Where will you go?' His Papa put his hand on Sardarji's shoulder.

'I'll be fine, Motichandbhai, I'll be fine.'

Vague answers were common with Sardarji. No one even knew where he lived. 'Over there, past the road to Namirembe,' he'd say whenever he was asked, waving his hand in the general direction, although Vijay noticed that sometimes the location seemed to have moved further south or north. Long before expulsion, he could often be seen walking along the streets, off to visit one of his many friends, and at mealtimes he'd head to one of the places that the community gathered. Sardarji could breakfast on paratha at the gurudwara, lunch on biriyani at the mosque and have a dinner of shaak rotli at the mandir; he had many friends who would feed him, yet no family to speak of.

When Vijay was a boy, he would sometimes stay inside the dukan and listen to Sardarji's stories rather than play outside in the street with Pran and the other kids.

'I came here before your father was even born, you know that?' Sardarji would tell him, as he stuck his finger under his huge white turban and scratched, while young Vijay sat next to him on the platform with his legs folded. Sardarji's silver hair was wrapped up in cloth but Vijay imagined it was so long it tickled his ankles, trailing down his back like a waterfall.

'They said we could go to Africa and make some money, that's what they said. Big ships, big sails, big stories! But you know, these ships, they were made of wood, just like this,' Sardarji said, giving a hollow knock on the platform. 'Made of trees. How do they float, we said, how do they stay on the water with all of us inside? But then they promised us money, and the promise of money can silence all fears, all doubts.'

Sardarji stared at Vijay, his eyes grey-blue like the sea. 'We travelled for many days, all the way down, across the belly of Gujarat, to Porbandar. And the poor salas by the port, they were starving. Ribs on show,' he said, moving his fingers across his own chest, 'dark shadows, like zebra stripes across their skin. We were told we could just go up the coast and make some money. Sail on the kala pani. Go on the black water, they said. Easy, they said. But only for a day or so, they said, so short, so short. And all we had to do was dip our fingers in the ink, place them on the white pages of their big leather books.'

'Like criminals?' Vijay had jumped up. 'Fingerprints, like in the films?'

'Not like criminals,' Motichand laughed, bringing over cups of chai. 'To sign their names.'

'That's right,' said Sardarji. Flecks of spittle flew through the air as he blew on the tea. 'Couldn't write, couldn't read anything. We climbed onto the dhows, watched the land disappear. I cried and cried, I was not much older than you, boy, imagine? It made grown men cry too, when we realized how long we were going to be at sea, when we found out where we were really going. But there was nothing we could do, the black ink on our fingers tied us to the black water. They took us away from the coast, all the way from Mombasa, through the jungle, to build the railways of the British.'

'And some men were eaten by lions!'

'Your father told you that?' Sardarji's eyes narrowed, he'd forgotten that he'd told Vijay the story before. 'Yes, in Tsavo, the lions were as hungry as we were and some men disappeared into the night.'

Sardarji put down his tea and lowered his voice. 'And then we finally got to Uganda, and the railway was finished. Most went back. But I stayed.'

'But the other week, didn't you say you were taken from your home in the night, Sardarji?' Motichand called out from behind the dukan counter.

'What? I'll tell you what happened to me if you let me.' Sardarji lifted his eyes to the ceiling, raised his palm and let out a long, luxurious fart, punctuated with a sigh. '*Bhai*, don't you think I'd know whether I ran away from my family or not? Now listen.'

And this was how it went: every afternoon, a different story. Vijay loved all the tales, but wondered whether any of them were true. Perhaps they were Sardarji's memories, or perhaps he'd gathered them together from the people he knew over the years, and woven them into his own.

'And all these men,' Sardarji continued, 'when they came here, they'd not spoken to a woman for months, you know, let alone touched one. So some of those men started putting their *dandiya* in all those *basuti* skirts.' Sardarji would giggle and nudge Vijay with his bony elbow.

Vijay had been completely confused by this point. His childish mind couldn't work out why men would put dandiya – the smooth wooden sticks that were used for dancing at the Navaratri festival – underneath the gathered skirts of the Ugandan ladies' basutis?

Papa seemed flustered, 'Let's not talk of such things now, Sardarji.' His father had busied himself wiping an already clean shelf.

Sardarji put his finger to his lips, bowing conspiratorially towards Vijay. 'You see, no one ever wants to talk about it. But you'll see them out there, those children with their curly hair and that cane-sugar skin.'

Vijay hadn't understood any of it as a boy, but he knew what it meant now. The clear lines of separation between Ugandan and Asian were forgotten in those earliest days before the

Asian women came over. Yet years later, even though Asians and Ugandans lived in the same country, shopped at the same markets, went to school together, worked together, drank and ate together, the rules were clear: that was where it ended. An invisible line divided them. But no matter how much the Asians tried to stop it, there were people like his friend Silver, with his rounded nose and almond eyes, many people called them *chotara*, with a Baganda mother and an anonymous Punjabi father who pretended Silver didn't exist. And now Silver and hundreds of others like him would have to choose: leave with the Asians or stay with the Ugandans. Like placing a bet where you lose either way.

Vijay thought of all the things he'd learnt from Sardarji, not quite sure what was true and what wasn't. When Vijay had asked him sometimes to clarify a date or a detail, Sardarji had told him that even those few people who could write were too busy trying to survive to bother with putting pen to paper and indulging in thoughts and feelings, no time to think about what year they'd arrived or what day someone was born.

'How will you get out? Do you want some help with your plane ticket?' Motichand said.

Sardarji moved away from the counter, looking around. 'The dukan is looking very good.' He wandered around, hands clutched behind his back, admiring the renovations.

Did he even have a valid Indian passport or paperwork after so many years in Uganda? Who knew? But the old man ducked all their questions, and when it came time for Sardarji to leave the dukan, they all took part in the pretence, saying goodbye to each other as though it was an ordinary day, as though nothing at all had changed.

By four o'clock, the yawns were catching. Mr Kagwa, another regular customer, came in, his long cotton kanzu rippling at his feet as he walked. He always moved with swaying shoulders, as though he was walking to music that no one else could hear.

'How are you, bwana?' said Motichand.

'All fine.' Mr Kagwa put up his palm and smiled. 'And you, I suppose you've been busy making plans to go? Such a sorry business.' At least there were a few people who didn't want them to leave.

Motichand nodded and they continued to chat for a few minutes. As Vijay finished packing up Mr Kagwa's groceries, two young men stormed in, laughing as they leant over the counter.

'You wahindis still here?' said the shorter of the two men. He wore a bright-red T-shirt. 'Sitting around taking our money?'

His friend held back, staring at Motichand and Vijay.

Vijay stepped closer to the counter. 'Look, we don't want any trouble. We'll be gone soon enough. What can I get you?'

Mr Kagwa edged towards the window.

'Give me that.' T-Shirt Man pointed towards the shelf.

The quieter of the two spoke. 'Let's go, Michael, I'm bored.' He didn't look bored, he looked anxious. He met Vijay's eyes and turned away.

Motichand looked behind him, sweat gleaming in the light. A single shaving kit on the wooden shelf. 'That's all you want?'

'Come on, Michael. Leave them alone. Let's just get out of here,' the quieter friend said, looking out of the window.

Mr Kagwa tried to appeal to them. '*Bwana*, they don't want any trouble.'

'Shut up, no one asked you!' the man with the red T-shirt shouted. 'Just give it to me or I'll come behind there and help myself. Hurry up, old man.'

Motichand's fingers stiffened as he stretched his arm out. Body twisted, face contorted. His hand tried to reach for the shelf but he fell short, grasping a bar of soap, his other hand clutching at his chest. He fell onto the floor behind the counter.

Vijay rushed over. 'Papa?'

Motichand's cheeks flushed.

'What have you done?' Vijay shouted at the men, but they were already out of the door.

'I'll get help.' Mr Kagwa rushed out into the street.

Vijay leant over Motichand. His father's eyes were closed. White crescents of Lux curved along Motichand's fingernails; the cake of soap lay nearby. Vijay pulled back Motichand's tweed jacket, shirt damp with sweat. 'Papa? Can you hear me?'

Vijay put his head against his father's chest, struggling to listen for a heartbeat. Papa had been fine just a moment ago. He'd get up soon. 'Please answer me. Please get up.'

More people shuffled around behind the counter, shouting a string of instructions in Gujarati and Swahili: get some water, give him air, move him, don't move him, call for a doctor, drive him to a hospital: a sea of voices who all thought they knew best.

Vijay put his hand to Motichand's face, his cheeks clammy, his eyes full of anguish.

Was it minutes or hours later that a doctor arrived, wading through the crowd? Vijay looked around the dukan for the first time since Motichand had fallen. Groups of people were talking, pointing, shaking their heads. A street hawker had even set up outside, selling peanuts in a bag.

The doctor asked for space and told people to leave.

Vijay stepped back, clinging to the counter. Helplessly watching the medic loosen Motichand's shirt. He willed him to get up; one of his silly jokes, it had to be, yes, just a joke, that must be it. Please, Papa, get up. Get up now.

12
Jaya

Jaya heard the front door close, footsteps across the floor.

She called out from her room. 'You're back early?' She hurried to tuck her sari into place, bangri tinkling against each other on her wrist. Vijay was standing in the kitchen. 'You shut the dukan for the day already, beta?'

Vijay stared at the floor. Body still.

'Where's Papa?'

He didn't move. Usually by now, the space around him would be filled with Motichand bounding around the kitchen, crunching his teeth into a *chakri* or glugging a glass of water or asking what was for dinner.

'Vijay?'

'Papa . . .' Vijay's face showed his distress.

'Where is he?' Jaya hurried over to him, grabbing his hand. 'Was it the soldiers? Vijay, tell me what's happened.'

He stared at her. 'Papa – he's gone. I'm sorry, I tried to help him, the doctor tried to save him, but he's . . .' His voice fractured before he could finish his sentence.

Jaya grasped a chair. She must have started crying because he gave her a handkerchief, she must have sat down because she could feel the wood beneath her. It must have grown dark because someone turned the light on.

*

They brought Motichand home from the embalmers the following day. The room was filled with the scent of the mourners' white cotton and the burning divas. There were only a few guests, Mrs Goswami plus the few neighbours who hadn't yet left the country. The many friends Motichand had made during his life were already scattered across the world like ashes. Others had called with condolences over the phone, the same repeated exclamations: 'so sudden', 'so young', 'what a burden for you', all mingling into one until the words lost their meaning. Jaya had stood by the sideboard for hours, holding the telephone a little away from her ear, still not used to the tinny sounds that came from it, until finally Pran fetched her a chair and she sat with her legs hovering above the floor until the calls stopped.

Vijay and Pran brought the coffin into the sitting room with help from Mrs Goswami's sons, but there was such a difference in height between them that it swayed and tilted like a ship in a stormy sea.

Jaya wanted to hurry through the ceremony, knowing that December was hidden away in the stuffy storeroom. At least people wouldn't want to linger, too busy making their preparations to leave and wanting to get back before curfew.

The coffin was opened to reveal Motichand's body. A thick pain spread across Jaya's chest, the tears in her eyes blurring the image before her. She looked up at Vijay, his white kameez now grey near the collar where she'd hugged him, wet with her tears. His eyes seemed to say, 'That's not my father.' And it was true, he didn't look like Motichand in a way: he wore a cream cotton kameez which he'd once tried on briefly, a gift from a distant relative that he'd never worn in public.

'I look so plain, Jaya,' he'd said, glumly. No matter the weather, he preferred a tweed jacket that made clouds of sweat bloom on the shirt beneath. In the muddle of her grief she hadn't had time to think about what he should wear for the very last time.

Now, his skin was yellow and waxy like cold ghee; the life had seeped out of his cheeks; the laughter lines smothered away by death; thick lashes, once fluttering moth wings, now still.

Vijay was flanked by Pran, still and calm, gaze steady, but then he'd always tended to hold things in. Sadness swept across her body as she realized she'd never see Motichand's face again, that he'd never be able to cheer up their sons with his silly jokes. Anger swelled in her chest; she was on her own now, she'd have to look after them all. She watched Pran perform the rituals, applying sandalwood paste to Motichand's skin and circling the body with Vijay and Asha following behind. Even in his death, she was left on the sidelines.

Later that evening, after they'd taken Motichand's body to the temple and the guests had gone, she went to check on December, taking a fresh newspaper and a plate of leftover food. In the candlelit room, he looked even more exhausted; the hours of sitting in the storeroom with only a tiny vent for fresh air had taken their toll.

He looked up at her. 'It's all finished?' He asked the question as if, even now, there might still be a hope that somehow it had been a mistake, that Motichand was still alive.

Jaya nodded.

'I still . . .' December looked down at the floor. 'I know it was hard for him, for all of you. But he was never the sort to let the stress get to him.'

'I thought so too.' Jaya took a big gulp of air. She looked back, thinking of that evening she and Motichand had last spoken about leaving, the unfamiliar worry in his eyes. If only she'd known how much he worried, perhaps she might have been able to help him. She put her hand over her mouth, trying to bury the grief. 'I was so busy with everything else, I didn't realize.'

December pulled at the corner of his pillow. 'There's nothing you could have done. You have to keep your strength up now.'

They fell silent. Though Jaya knew she should get back to the family, something kept her there.

'I'll ask Pran about the plans again,' she said. 'He's been distracted these past few days, but we haven't forgotten.'

December shook his head. 'I shouldn't be here, adding to your problems.'

'Don't be silly.' Jaya stepped a little closer. She needed something good to happen after all this hurt. 'We're all going to get out of this country, you too.'

'I just wish I knew what happened to Aber,' he said, in a hushed tone.

There were no comforting words. Who knew where December's daughter was, or any of the hundreds of people who'd not been heard from in months? At least, with Motichand, there was some comfort. At least he was at peace now. There was no peace for those who remained.

'Try not to think about that now. You need to get yourself to safety, then you can find a way to help her.' Her voice light, though she didn't feel it. 'Are you scared?'

In the gloom of the storeroom, December's face looked haunted. 'Are you?'

Jaya thought about the best way to answer. 'We're all together. There's no reason to be scared.'

'I'm sorry, I shouldn't be talking about this.' He rubbed his face with his hands. 'Not today. You must be tired, why don't you go and rest?'

As he said the words, a wave of fatigue swept through her bones. She should check on the children. She told December she'd come back in the morning, as he lay down on the bed and blew out the candle.

Jaya was glad to see that the others were still in the sitting room, their white clothes beacons in the dim light. She wasn't ready to be alone yet. Vijay was resting his head against the back of the armchair and he opened his eyes as Jaya came into the room. Pran and Asha sat opposite, staring into space, empty cups and saucers on the table in front of them.

'Shall I get you some chai?' Asha looked up at Jaya.

'No, you rest.' Jaya sat down on a chair. 'It's been a long day.'

'There were a lot of people today, considering,' said Asha. Jaya was grateful for her attempt at making conversation, keeping the silence at bay.

'Yes, it was good of them to come.' Jaya pulled her chundri off her head, smoothing her hair with her hand. They talked about the day, the stories people told about Motichand. Whatever his faults, people liked him: his energy, his enthusiasm for life, a whirlwind that rushed in and out of their lives, brightening their days.

'He'd still be here if it hadn't been for the expulsion.' Pran shook his head, hard, as though he was trying to shake the anger away. 'This country keeps taking and taking from us.'

'Don't talk like that, beta,' said Jaya. What was the use of letting it eat them up inside?

'It's true, though.' Pran sat up. 'Don't you think he'd still be here?'

'Shh, Pran, it's late.' Asha put her hand on his arm.

'Whisper, please,' said Jaya. Soldiers might be prowling the streets outside and they wouldn't take pity on a house in mourning.

'He's been taken from us because those people thought it was OK to bully old men. And they're led by a madman who is stealing everything we ever had. You think that's right?'

'Leave it, Pran,' said Vijay.

'Doesn't it bother any of you? They've taken our father and you just accept it!'

Jaya clutched the armrest and leant towards him. 'It was your Papa's funeral today and you are flaunting your anger in our faces? He's gone, think about that, not about how you're going to get back at the world. Not today. Stop now.' As soon as she'd finished, she regretted it. She saw his distress, felt his torment as deeply as her own as he sank back into his chair. Harsh words wouldn't bring Motichand back.

Later, after the others had gone to sleep, Jaya sat at the kitchen table in the darkness, mustering the courage to go to bed. There had been so much pain lately that the grief she felt for Motichand and the sadness she felt for her home and friends were all mixed up inside her. She understood Pran's anger, but it seemed to be growing, black roots twining around his heart. She couldn't think about any of it tonight, eyes blurry, the hours of crying and her tiredness wearing her down.

Night shrouded Kololo Hill in darkness. Jaya walked through the house, turning off the remaining lights one by one. In the bedroom, she took off her sari, a white pool in the middle of the floor, and climbed into Motichand's bed, the familiar tang of tobacco and betel nut still lingering on his pillow. In the early days of their marriage, he'd talked in his sleep. She used to pretend that he whispered to her all the things he never said when he was awake, too busy impressing the rest of the world and worrying about what they thought. He'd died like he'd lived, no warning, no plan. Now she reached out, finger-tips on cold sheets, her hand on his body.

No, in the space where he'd once been and would never be again.

*

They brought Motichand's ashes back from the temple the following day. She thought of the musky charcoal smoke of the funeral pyres back in India, burning fiercely all day and fading away into the black night, the ashes later scattered in the Ganga river. The Nile, once a substitute in their adopted home, could no longer be used, polluted as it was now with so many murdered bodies. She scattered his ashes in the yard by the magnolia tree. Later, she watched them wash away in the heavy afternoon rain, no trace left behind.

*

The raindrops fell thick and heavy, pelting the windscreen. From the refuge of the car, Jaya watched people making their way through the city, caught short without umbrellas, hurrying along the streets. As they wound their way a boy ran past, sheltering his head with a hollow green coconut shell, while other people huddled under corrugated-iron awnings, twisting their bodies to avoid the leaks that found their way between the cracks. The rivers of rain weaved across the road, gathering red soil along the way, copper rivulets breaking off here and there.

Jaya peered over the front seat at Pran. He clutched the steering wheel tight, staring ahead intensely. He'd been so quiet since the night of the funeral, she was starting to worry. At least Vijay seemed better; he'd taken to his bed the day after the funeral, but he was up and about again, trying to make gentle jokes and take everyone's minds off what had happened. She had Motichand to thank for that side of him. In a way, Jaya was glad that the expulsion had given her something to focus on. There was too much to do for her to dwell on her grief right now.

'What do you have planned for today, beta?' said Jaya.

'A few things,' said Pran.

'Pran and Vijay are preparing to hand the keys for the

dukan over in a couple of days, aren't you?' Asha had also been trying to coax him back to his old self.

'I know it's difficult, but it will be one less thing to worry about,' said Jaya.

'One less thing to worry about?' Pran glanced back at her. 'How can I not worry?'

'I didn't mean that, beta.'

'Watch the road, Pran,' said Asha, pointing out a pothole so wide it almost stretched from one side of the road to the other.

'We have other things to think about, that's all. Like December.' But as soon as she said the words aloud, Jaya knew it was a mistake.

'I can't think about that right now!' He slammed his hand against the steering wheel.

'Calm down, Pran, please,' said Asha.

'I'm not going to listen to this bakwas today. I owe it to Papa to fight. That's all I'm going to think about.'

'I'm sorry,' Jaya said, lowering her voice in the hope that it would calm him, 'I shouldn't have brought it up.' As they continued on their way up Kololo Hill, the only sound in the car was the rhythmic swish of the windscreen wipers, back and forth.

*

The rain had cleared up by the time they arrived at Mrs Goswami's. Jaya and Asha said goodbye to Pran, watching the car drive away from the gates. Jaya gathered up her sari and slowly made her way towards the house, but Asha was too late to save her grey bell-bottoms; a dirty terracotta trim ran along the hems.

'Come, coooome in,' Mrs Goswami greeted them, sari pleats swaying in front of her as she led them inside the house. The walls were bare, the carved Masai statues had been packed away and boxes were piled in the corners of the hallway.

'Can you believe these gandas have driven us to this,

Jayaben?' Mrs Goswami led them into the sitting room, the ornaments that had once adorned every wall and shelf now gone.

'Sit down. It is a mess, I know, there's still so much to do. We've sent some things on to my cousin in Canada already, but who knows if they'll arrive? And we have given other items to the temple too, for the people who are staying behind.'

'Do you think they will be safe there?' Jaya sat down in the chair next to Mrs Goswami.

'Well, they'll get a bit of wear and tear, I suppose, some scratches on the wood.'

'Not the furniture, I meant the people who are staying behind, at the temple?' Jaya said, ignoring Asha's raised eyebrow.

'I don't know.' Mrs Goswami pursed her lips. 'But I do know that if it was me, I would not stay even if they paid me.'

'But the people staying behind are getting paid,' said Asha. 'Now that the government's finally realized they need Asian civil servants to keep the country going.'

'Yes, well,' said Mrs Goswami, flicking a hand in dismissal.

'I don't understand why they'd stay?' said Jaya. Whatever lay ahead in another country, could it be worse than what they'd already been through in their own home?

'Do they have a choice? Would Idi Amin have given them an option? I suppose they aren't seen as a threat any more, there's only a few hundred of them,' said Asha. 'I hear most are going to live together at the temple and the gurudwara. At least they'll be able to look out for each other that way.'

'But not everyone?' said Jaya.

'I don't know, perhaps the others will find a way to lie low in their homes,' Asha shrugged.

'What do expect from a *jungloh* like him?' said Mrs Goswami.

She called for Grace, who was in the kitchen. But today, there was no singing or humming; instead her walk was slow, stiff and her eyes downcast. When she came closer Jaya saw the swollen bruise across the side of her face. Surely Mrs Goswami hadn't done that?

'What?' Grace glared at Jaya.

'I—' Jaya didn't know what to say, surprised by Grace's response.

Mrs Goswami's voice mellowed. 'Gres, can you bring us some *chai nasto*?' She even finished with a 'thank you'.

'What's happened?' Jaya whispered when Grace had shuffled out of the room. She'd never heard Mrs Goswami talk so kindly to her servants before.

'They took her. She was walking in the street and the soldiers took Gres, drove her somewhere, four men, imagine. What was she supposed to do?' Mrs Goswami shook her head, clutching the armrest as she spoke. 'They dumped her in the street the next morning.'

'They just grabbed her?' Asha's eyes widened. 'When?'

'Last week. She was kept in hospital overnight. I told her to stay home. But she wanted to come here, she's sleeping in the servants' quarters. And you know what she said to me? I feel safer here.' Mrs Goswami gave a bitter laugh. 'Think about that. Safer with us, who are being thrown out of the country.'

'How could they do that to her?' said Jaya. There'd been rumours of other girls, servants and shop workers, as well as the young Asian women who travelled with their families to the airport. They were considered lucky if they came out of it alive.

'Poor girl. And the house is so quiet. You know, I even miss her ridiculous humming!'

They fell silent as Grace came in with a tray of food and cups of chai. Mrs Goswami twisted her gold bangri around her wrist, round and round as she served them.

Grace began to leave but stopped at the doorway. She turned to stare at them. 'You can carry on gossiping about me now.'

Mrs Goswami's mouth dropped open. It took her a moment to compose herself. 'Gres—'

'I know you were talking about me,' said Grace. 'I can see it on your faces.'

'It wasn't like that,' Asha said gently.

'Perhaps if you'd all spent a little more time worrying about other people before, they wouldn't hate you so much that they want you gone.' Her voice was sharp.

'No, Gres, it—'

'Enjoy your tea!' she said, and left before they could say anything else.

Mrs Goswami stared at the space where Grace had been standing for a long while, then turned back to her guests. 'I don't know . . . what do I say to her?'

'The poor girl. She's been through so much,' said Jaya. 'Don't take it to heart.' How could men do these things? She stared at the floor, searching for some more words of comfort, but what was left to say? And Jaya couldn't shake the words from her mind, the sliver of truth within them. *People wouldn't hate you so much they want you gone.*

They sat in silence for a while; no mundane news to share, no festivals or weddings to plan for, no good news to cheer them. After finishing their chai, they listed all the families they knew that had left for India, Pakistan, England, Canada, Australia, the United States, Kenya and Tanzania, some even going to places like Sweden and Germany.

'And how are you all coping?' Mrs Goswami said. 'I'm sorry we couldn't stay longer after the funeral.'

'We are keeping busy, at least,' said Jaya, thinking of Pran, how angry he'd been in the car.

'And Motichandbhai, so close to leaving and going back to India,' Mrs Goswami said, her voice mournful. 'It feels like yesterday that he first arrived in Uganda.' They'd known each other for decades. How lonely Jaya had been when she'd first arrived in Kampala, waiting for Motichand to come home each night, counting the days until they'd be able to go to temple. Apart from Motichand's piecemeal efforts and support from December, Mrs Goswami was the only person who'd tried to help Jaya settle into life in Kampala in the early years. She'd helped her to understand how to adjust to a life in this un-familiar country, how to haggle down prices for *matoke* and *buteta*, teaching her useful Swahili phrases to use when speak-ing to house boys and house girls, although Jaya ignored Mrs Goswami's stronger rebukes ('Make sure my washing's clean or I'll throw you into the Nile and scrub you raw myself'). Mrs Goswami had shown her the way. Who would show her now?

'Here, my husband's cousin moved to Birmingham years ago. This is her address.' Mrs Goswami went over to a drawer, leaning on her walking stick as she went, and thrust a piece of paper into Jaya's hand. 'When we're settled, I'll write to them from Canada and let them know my address. You do the same, Jayaben, when you have your own house.' Jaya admired her friend's optimism, that she'd have her own home in England and that they'd somehow manage to stay in touch through their letters. 'And you can come visit me in Canada one day.'

Jaya nodded her head and hugged Mrs Goswami goodbye, even though she already knew they'd never see each other again.

*

Evening in Kampala. No telltale signs, no slices of light under doors or window shutters; no murmuring from radios; no crackling from the TV or record players playing out across the streets and weaving through the trees, across walls and through open windows; no yelling for children to come indoors after roaming the streets all day; no laughter laced with whisky or beer; no scent of roasting rotlis carrying across the breeze. Nothing. Instead, the sound of gunfire smothered the sound of the crickets.

Screams if the victims were lucky enough to be alive, silence if they weren't.

Jaya finished lighting the last of the divas, usually saved for celebrations, weddings or Divari, in the sitting room. She checked for a third time that the tape around the windows was secure (no need to worry about the damage it might do to the plasterwork when she'd be leaving soon), making sure that no cracks of light could escape and betray them to soldiers on the hunt.

None of them could focus. Asha picked up her chai, forgot to take a sip and put it down again. Pran, lost in thought, stared out into the darkness. Vijay had escaped to his bedroom, his record player on low. What would Motichand have been doing now? Slurping his tea, telling a funny story.

Tonight, the gunfire outside was louder, the shouts and screams ringing through the air, loud enough that they could make out some of the words: *'Hapana!'*, 'Please, no!', 'Stand over there now!' On and on it went, the soldiers making sure they got their riches before the government seized it.

Jaya left the others and went to check on December, hurrying in the darkness to the storeroom, clutching a copy of the *Ugandan Argus* for him to read.

'Have you heard any more?' said December, the bed creaking underneath him. 'Can you go to England together now?'

Jaya shook her head. They'd hoped that they might let Pran go to England so that he wouldn't be separated from all of his family. But the stories from those who'd already left confirmed that only people with British passports would be allowed in.

She explained that Pran would try his luck in India as a state-less refugee instead. She didn't tell December that Pran was still talking about staying behind. It sounded so ridiculous.

'The British still pull the strings. We shouldn't be surprised,' said December.

'What do you mean?'

'They were happy to support Amin into power. Obote was an inconvenience, they hated his policies.'

'They must have realized their mistake by now,' said Jaya.

December's voice sounded strange, tinged with anger. 'They were the ones who invited him for tea with the Queen at Buckingham Palace, inflating his ego.'

'I don't know about all that, but I know that he's the man who has caused us all so much hurt,' said Jaya, thinking of Motichand. Her grief weighed heavy in her throat. She still expected to hear him call out for her any moment, but instead silence smothered her.

'What a life we find ourselves in,' December whispered, staring at her. 'But I don't deserve your help.'

'Don't talk like that, please.'

December sighed. 'You might not be so willing to let me stay if you knew what I did.'

'What do you mean?'

'For years, I didn't see Aber.'

'But you had to stay here and work. It wasn't your fault that you had to be apart.'

'Yes, it was,' he said. 'I looked after her and her mother for a while when Aber was a baby, sending them money like I told you. But they were so far away. I wanted to go out and have fun with my friends. All I could see were the pretty girls around me.'

Jaya felt her cheeks flush. These weren't the kind of things they usually spoke about.

December continued, 'And so, I stopped going back to see Aber. The money stopped too.'

'When was this?' Jaya thought back to that time, remembering the way December used to split the wages she gave him into two, folding one set of notes around the other, half to send back home, half for himself. When had he stopped doing that? She had been too wrapped up in her own family to notice.

'A few years after Aber was born.'

Jaya looked at his face, full of sorrow. 'I don't understand.'

'I went back home, about eight years ago, to try and make it right. I knew I'd been stupid. I tried to get in touch with her again, but she wouldn't see me. Her mother kept her away. But I went back, every chance I got. Finally, Aber agreed to see me.'

'You should have told me.'

'Would you tell people that you'd abandoned your own family?'

She couldn't imagine leaving Pran and Vijay, not talking to them for years. She wouldn't be able to trust anyone else to raise her children. 'But you are talking to her again now?'

'God gave me a second chance. It took a long time before Aber could forgive me. Her mother will never forgive me.'

Jaya looked at him. Her life was so different to December's, separated from his loved ones, working long hours. Who was she to judge? 'People make mistakes. And you are trying to make up for it now.' He'd saved her life so that she could have her own children. She couldn't ignore that. She thought of the people at temple, people like Mrs Goswami. They'd say that December was in danger now because of those bad deeds, paying for it all, God had chosen to punish him. But no, she would look at it another way. God had put him in this house so that he could help them all these years, and make her feel less alone. And now she could help him.

'I'm going to leave tomorrow.'

'Be strong, you can't go on your own. It's not safe. Just get some rest and you'll feel differently in the morning.' She held her chundri in place as she turned to leave. She hesitated. Still facing the door, she said, 'I know it's difficult. But if you love Aber, you owe it to her to stay safe to help her. Please, December.'

'Adenya,' he said softly.

Jaya turned towards him, looking into his eyes.

'Call me Adenya. Only family would help me like this.'

In a hushed voice Jaya said, 'Adenya.'

*

In that moment, as she closed the door of the storeroom behind her, the gunfire ringing in the air, Jaya knew she was ready to leave, whatever England might hold. Even if her family would be scattered across the world, at least she knew they'd all be safe. Alive.

Some people talked about coming back one day; they hadn't even left yet but already they talked about coming back to Uganda. But Jaya was old enough to know that it would take many years for the pain to go away, if it ever did. Years she didn't have.

She'd had enough. She never wanted to see this house again, never wanted to feel that prickle of fear running through her muscles that stayed with her from the moment she woke up to the second she fell asleep, never wanted to be told what to do by strangers, never wanted to have the things she'd worked hard for taken away from her, never again wanted the threat of being parted from those that she loved the most.

No, in that moment, Jaya was ready to leave.

13

Vijay

It was the first time Vijay had been back to the dukan since Papa died. He opened the door, and the heavy, stale air that had been trapped inside for over a week escaped into the street. Pran followed behind and went to check if there was anything worth taking from the storeroom.

Vijay walked over to the counter, remembering how he'd sat on top of it when he visited as a child, his legs dangling in the air, while Papa joked: 'Don't sit there too long, a customer might decide to buy you and take you home with their ENO salts!'

There wasn't much to do; they couldn't take the stock with them, but they needed to check that they hadn't left anything important behind. Anything important apart from the dukan, the stock and the money, of course. He took a step towards the space where he'd last seen Papa alive, on the floor behind the counter. He pulled out one of the heavy ledger books and turned the musty pages. Here was Papa's scrawled handwriting, surrounded by islands of white space where he'd forgotten to write things down. For Papa, the books were something that showed you were a proper businessman; it didn't much matter if you actually filled them in or if the accounts made sense. Later pages were filled with Pran's terse, neat handwriting; not a single credit for a pleading customer in sight.

He looked out of the window into the quiet street, remembering Motichand, up late most mornings, arriving like a celebrity, waving at fellow dukanwara across the street, handing out bottles of pop to the customers' children.

Who would the government give the dukan to now? Or worse still, which looters would demolish it first? At businesses down the street, floors were covered with footprints in the scattered flour, glossy sauces spilt like blood, tin cans that had fallen off the shelves and rolled to the other side of the shop, as though they too were trying to get away.

Vijay leant against the counter. Who would remember them once they'd gone? At school, Vijay had taken in all the bookshelves filled with Africa's history. But it was the history of the English and Germans and French in Africa – the shelves were full: no space for Indians, nor Africans. How could you disappear from history books you'd never been inside in the first place? And no one had ever bothered to write it down on paper; their history had been told by one person to another, words changed, parts left out, or added. What did it matter now anyway? Their history in Uganda was over. Who would remember this dukan or Papa?

'Ready?' said Pran, coming out of the back room with a small cardboard box. 'There's not much worth keeping.'

Vijay nodded, taking one of the ledgers, a tiny memento of Papa. Before he closed the front door for the final time, he looked across the dukan, Papa's voice echoing in his ears, the place behind the counter where he'd once stood now empty.

14

Asha

'At least he's home now,' said Asha.

'He's sleeping. All Naseem wants to do is sleep,' said Razia, staring at the floor.

'Rest is good,' said Pran. They were visiting Razia and Naseem, who'd finally made it home after his disappearance.

'Here, let me put this away.' Asha took the bowl of mogo and samosa that she and Jaya had made for the family to the kitchen. The house was silent; she didn't ask where the children and their grandparents were. Probably best that Naseem had some peace.

When Asha came back into the sitting room, Razia was telling Pran what happened. 'We kept going back. We went every single day to ask the army where he was but they wouldn't tell us. Then yesterday, an army truck just left him at the side of our road. Naseem just had this strange look on his face, wouldn't say anything at first.' She brought her hand to her mouth. 'We've been trying to piece it all together.'

'And now?' said Pran, the concern on his face clear to see.

'They stopped him in his car, but we knew that already, that's how we knew he'd been taken,' said Razia. 'They told him they were arresting him and grabbed him. Naseem kept talking about the cell they kept him in. It was dark, there were dozens of other prisoners. He talked about the water at his feet, the stench.'

'Oh, Razia,' said Asha. She'd heard the rumours of the squalid conditions in which prisoners were kept, but she didn't know the details. 'How is he now?'

'You should see him, he can't stand up straight.' Razia's voice cracked. 'His hands . . . his legs . . .' She didn't go on. She didn't need to. The horror of what they'd done to him was written on her face.

'And do you know why they took him?' said Asha, putting her hand on Razia's.

'We heard they found his contacts in the government.' Razia couldn't look at them. 'Their bodies, I mean.'

Pran gave Asha a look, warning her that it was best not to pry further. There was no need. The contacts must have done something to upset Amin, taking their own cut most likely. They'd paid the price for it.

'Naseem?' Razia called out. In the far corner of the vast room, Naseem appeared swathed in a thick blanket, head bowed. His steps were small and awkward, his broad frame shrunken. 'I'd better go and check on him.' She got up, talking to him in a tender tone, the way she usually spoke to her youngest child.

Asha whispered to Pran, 'Do you understand now why you can't even think about staying behind?'

'It's not the same,' said Pran. They watched as Razia led Naseem back to the bedroom.

Asha leant forward. 'Would you really do that to me? Did you see the look on poor Razia's face?' Anger burned in Asha's veins so strongly Naseem could have been her own husband. How dare they treat people like that?

'What's happened to Naseem is terrible. But I've never got involved with the government like that.'

'They don't care. They could take you away merely for driving your car too fast. Or too slow. For anything at all. I couldn't bear it. If they did that to you . . .' Asha was surprised by the tears forming in the corners of her eyes.

'They wouldn't.' But his voice betrayed him. Asha could see Naseem's ordeal weighed heavily on him.

'You're really going to stay here alone? There'd be no one left to help you if you got into trouble.'

Pran looked down at his hands. 'I can't believe what they've done to Naseem.' Had he finally admitted defeat?

'I can't believe that he even came back. Not when you think what happened to the others.' The bodies in the Nile flashed into Asha's head, but there was no point trying to work out the logic of Idi Amin and his army.

'At least their family can go to India together now,' said Pran.

'Pranbhai!' Razia's panicked voice carried across the house.

Pran stood up. 'I think she's out front.' Asha followed him towards the door.

They heard the fire before they saw it, crackling in the metal *sigri* that the watchmen used to keep warm at night. Naseem was throwing something in.

Razia's hands were red. She tried to stop him. 'Naseem!'

As they stepped closer, smoke filling the air, they saw that he was burning money.

Pran tried to pull Naseem back, but though he flinched, it was as though he was made of lead. He carried on flinging piles of notes into the flames, ash floating in the air like black moths.

'Stop it!' Razia cried out. 'We could have given it to the servants at least!'

'Why should anyone else have what we worked so hard for?' said Naseem. 'Besides, it's only paper. It has no value for us Asians any more, does it? It can't keep us safe.'

'Naseem, *chaal*, come away,' Pran said, putting his hand on his friend's arm. 'We shouldn't draw attention to ourselves.'

Asha looked around; luckily no one else was nearby to see the money. Many neighbours had already packed up and gone, with the expulsion deadline only three weeks away.

'Please stop,' said Razia, tears running down her face, clinging to her husband.

But Naseem carried on, flames reflecting in his eyes as though they too were on fire.

*

Later that week, Asha was hurrying back from the storeroom when she saw a movement in the corner of the yard. She stopped. A chill travelled up her neck despite the warm evening air.

A figure was crouching on the ground, digging.

A soldier? She gasped so loudly that the figure turned around.

Moonlight revealed their face. Pran.

'What are you doing?' she said. 'You scared me.'

'Nothing.' He tried to hide something behind him.

'Let me see, Pran. Are you keeping things from me again?'

Pran hesitated, then showed her what he was doing. 'We'll need this again one day.' He was wrapping a cloth around a metal box, ready to place it in a small hole in the ground.

'What do you mean?' She recognized the box as the same one Motichand had kept valuables in. They kept it hidden in the sitting room behind a bronze clock cut into the shape of Africa. Had the stress pushed Pran over the edge, burying things in the ground under cover of darkness?

'We'll come back for this.' Pran didn't look up at her. 'I'm just keeping our money safe.'

'What are you talking about? The government will give

this house to other people to live here.' It still angered her to say it out loud. Strangers living in their home.

'It's all temporary.' Pran finished patting the earth down and stood up. She'd felt such relief when he'd given up his talk of staying, realizing that it was far too dangerous. But the things he said still concerned her. 'We'll get this house back. They're not taking my Papa's home, nor my business. I'm going to fight for it one day.'

'Pran, what are you saying?' She didn't bother to hide her annoyance, or her wariness. The idea of coming back to this nightmare. Pran was sapping everyone's energy with his anger. She put her hand on his shoulder. 'You want to come back here, after everything?'

Pran turned and looked at her. 'Don't you?'

*

Later, they ate dinner by candlelight and kerosene lamp, breaking the diamond-shaped *dhebra* with their hands and using it to scoop up the lentils in the *mugh ni daar*. Asha sipped the last of her bland chai, craving a teaspoonful of sugar. It was difficult to come by now that the plantations were in such a mess.

At least the gunfire hadn't started yet. Some nights, it seemed to get louder and louder, as though the soldiers were in a ridiculous battle with the crickets. She knew it was important to listen for the sound, measuring the distance by how loudly it rattled through the air. But the moments to watch out for were those brief times when she realized she'd tuned the noise out in her head. That was far worse: to become so used to the terrible sounds that they blended into ordinary life.

When they'd finished eating, Asha and Jaya went to check on December. The storeroom door was ajar, but out of courtesy, Jaya knocked as she always did.

Inside, December was lying down on the bed, the plate of

matoke and beans that Jaya had made especially for him sitting untouched beside him. It was strange to see him so subdued, so different from the first days after Asha had arrived, when he bounded around the yard, sweeping the veranda, painting the walls and tending to the shrubs in the garden. In the dimness, his skin looked ashy, the weeks without sunshine taking their toll.

Recently, he'd spoken to Asha about Jinja, where he had a few friends. They recalled the places they both knew, the local market, the nearby waterfalls, close to the source of the Nile. Old times, when you could make conversation about everyday life, without care or worry.

'Adenya, you've not eaten?' Jaya asked.

'I'm sorry, I'm not hungry,' he said.

'Why not eat something, keep your strength up for your journey?' Asha said, picking up the plate. Pran had confirmed that he'd found a way out for December, he could leave in a couple of days' time, making a trip to the border, getting out through Kenya. Yet sorrow had replaced hope in his eyes.

'Have you heard anything?' December asked Jaya.

She shook her head. He asked the same thing every time any of them came to the storeroom. But the answer never changed. No news about the northern territories, no word from his daughter, nothing to cheer him.

'Pran said we'll be able to get you to the border in a few days,' Asha said, in a vain attempt to make him feel better.

Outside, there was a loud rattle of the gate, followed by a shout in Swahili to let them in. Jacob, who used to keep watch outside each night, had long gone, taking up one of the Asian businesses. This voice didn't sound familiar.

'Why would anyone come to the house now? Curfew's started,' said Jaya, clutching her sari chundri at her neck.

December got up. 'I could still try and get out, over the back wall?'

'No,' said Asha, heart drumming. Even if he escaped, soldiers would find him in the streets in no time. 'You need to hide, we'll go and find out what's going on. Perhaps it's nothing.' Asha and Jaya hurried back to the others in the sitting room.

'Perhaps it's Naseem and Razia, or one of the other neighbours needing help?' said Jaya.

Pran's breath was shallow. 'No. It must be soldiers.'

They'd talked many times about what they'd do if the army came, as they heard more and more stories about other houses in the neighbourhood, looted while the families were inside, the men beaten, the women shoved into bedrooms. But the closer the family got to leaving, the more Asha told herself that they'd get away with it and leave Uganda before the army got their chance.

'Let's just stay here like we agreed,' whispered Vijay, his tone filled with impossible hope. 'They won't be able to see any lights at the front of the house. They might just be trying their luck.'

No one moved.

Another knock, another shout, this time more demanding than the last. 'We know you're in there,' they said, then laughed.

'We'll have to let them in,' said Vijay. 'They might try and shoot their way in otherwise.' How ridiculous it sounded, like something from a film, but there was a strong possibility that they'd actually do it.

Pran took Asha's hands. 'Hide in the bedroom, both of you. Lock the door and don't come out, no matter what. Vijay, go and tell December to hide in the storeroom while I go and get them.'

'Be careful, beta,' Jaya whispered.

They made their way across the yard and into the bedroom.

Asha's fingers slipped against the metal as she hurried to lock the bedroom door behind them. While Jaya stood close behind her, Asha peeked through a crack between the door and the frame. It smelt of old wood and oil. She looked out across the yard. Vijay had turned on the kitchen light so that it didn't look like they'd been hiding in the dark. The light threw shapes across the yard, as though the frangipani tree, branches cast in dark shadow, was cowering in the corner. Asha strained to listen for voices beyond the thrum of the crickets. Thank God there was no gunfire in the neighbourhood tonight.

Nothing, no movement, no sounds from the kitchen.

'What's going on?' said Jaya in a hushed voice.

'I can't tell. There's no sign of anyone, not even Pran and Vijay.' What if they'd already been attacked, lying on the floor? How long before the soldiers found the rest of them?

Behind her, Jaya whispered a prayer under her breath. Asha listened for a sound, a sign.

Four figures came out from the kitchen. Pran's slim frame and Vijay's stockier mass were flanked on either side by larger silhouettes with lopsided heads and jutting shoulders: the soldiers' berets and upended rifles.

Asha held onto the door frame, her heartbeat pulsing through her. She couldn't make out what they were saying. The soldiers didn't have loud, demanding voices. Instead, they spoke in subdued tones, almost as though they were house guests, stepping outside to enjoy the fresh air after dinner.

The taller soldier turned to look towards the bedroom. Asha flinched, stopping herself from jumping back from the door. There was no way he could see her, but it was as though he was looking through the darkness, beyond the thick mahogany door, straight at her.

'What happened?' said Jaya.

Asha waved her hand to hush her. Laughter came from across the yard, but she didn't recognize it. It must have been the soldiers. Perhaps that was a good sign. They weren't angry, at least. She stepped towards the door again and peeked through the crack, no longer able to see Pran, Vijay or the soldiers. What was going on? She edged her face as far to the right as she could but it was impossible to see the sitting room or the storeroom.

The room grew stuffy; the only sounds were the ringing insects outside and the heave of Jaya's short breaths. Asha kept close to the door, alert to footsteps or voices. She turned and surveyed the room. If it came to it, they'd have to slip under the bed and hide.

What could they be doing? Pran was supposed to show the soldiers the valuables to get rid of them. And if they were with December, there'd surely be noise by now. Shouting?

Gunfire?

15
Vijay

Vijay ran and helped December hide the folding bed.

'It's the army, isn't it?' December whispered, hiding himself behind the gunny sacks as best he could.

Vijay looked at him. He didn't want to say it out loud, lacked the words to comfort him, the danger right outside their door.

'Be careful, don't put yourself at risk for me,' said December. 'I mean it.'

'We'll be fine,' Vijay said, smoothing out any signs of panic in his tone. 'Don't worry, they won't get anywhere near here.' He quickly shut the door before December could reply and rushed back to the kitchen, heart swelling with every beat, pulsing through every vein. Should he stand right by the door? No, too aggressive. Rest his hand here against the table? No, too relaxed. There was no right way to behave in a situation like this. So he stood with his back against the wall. Like waiting in front of a firing squad.

Pran's voice, grave and low, along with two others that didn't belong. The slow thud of footsteps, the familiar creak of the door in the hallway.

The first thing he saw was the rifles, standing to attention along the soldiers' backs. The tips of the guns glinting in the light like cold eyes. Pran seemed to have shrunk as he stood next to the two men with their badly fitted khaki and their slanted berets. The strangers filled the space; it was Pran and Vijay who didn't belong now.

The first soldier stared at Vijay with heavy-lidded eyes. He wasn't much older than Pran but his close-cropped hair was flecked with grey, and he moved his neck slowly, like a tortoise, as he looked around the room. The other soldier, younger, broad-faced with hazel eyes, came closer.

Shoulders proud, head high, Vijay told himself.

The broad-faced soldier spoke, his breath laced with the sharp, chemical smell of waragi. 'You want to show us around.' It wasn't a question but a command.

'Look, we've got some cash in the other room, thousands of shillings,' said Pran. 'Please take it.'

But the soldiers were already walking out into the yard. The younger soldier tried to light a cigarette, but his fingers kept slipping from the expensive-looking silver lighter. 'Eh, there's something wrong with this lighter,' he said.

'No, there's something wrong with your head, David,' said the grey-flecked soldier. He slumped his body when he moved, curled shoulders, hips low. He had a go at lighting it too, but still it didn't work.

Pran took a matchbox from his pocket and lit a match for them, the flame lighting up every worry line on his forehead. David, the younger soldier, nearly burnt his hand, unsteady on his feet as he held the cigarette close to the flame. The two comrades talked amongst themselves, the younger soldier muttering about the stars, pointing out the Southern Cross with his finger. For a moment, December's words rang in Vijay's ears. Young soldiers with little money, little choice. What would that soldier have been in another life? A teacher, a map-maker?

Vijay and Pran exchanged a look. What now? Did the

soldiers know what they were doing either? The stench of alcohol gave them the answer.

'This is the sitting room.' Pran pointed, trying to direct them towards the money in the hope that they'd leave soon.

But the older soldier turned his slow neck from the kitchen towards the storeroom. 'Eh, you got any whisky, anything to drink?'

'I'll get some.' Vijay hurried to the sitting room, decided against taking a whole bottle outside and poured it into two glasses instead. The last thing they needed was the army utterly drunk on the veranda. Even if they passed out, the idea of them slumped like gunny sacks in their house for hours didn't appeal either. He rushed back outside with the drinks, drops of whisky spilling as he went.

'How many rooms do you have?' said David, looking around the yard.

'Six.' Pran answered quickly, omitting the storeroom that would have made seven.

'Show us.' The soldiers started walking towards the sitting room.

They wandered about, laughing at the soapstone knick-knacks that Jaya had gathered in her glass cabinet, picking things up, throwing them in the air a couple of times. Vijay stayed by the door. Pran stood against one of the walls, back flat, as though he was trying to disappear into it.

The soldier picked up a gilded photo frame from the side cabinet. 'Eh, where are they?' He was tracing his finger over Asha's face, a photo from her wedding day.

'They've already gone, they left ahead of us. We're sorting out the last of the paperwork before we join them,' said Vijay.

'Got rid of the women. Having fun without them, I'll bet.' The young soldier giggled like a schoolboy.

Growing bored of the room, the two army men walked

outside. Vijay's room didn't seem to interest them much but his heart sank when the younger soldier said he'd take the record player on his way out.

The only place left on this side was the storeroom, the door hidden in the gloom. From where they stood on the veranda, there was a chance they hadn't seen it at all.

'There's not much else, to be honest.' Pran tried to say it lightly but Vijay knew him too well, his voice tinged with tension.

David lit another cigarette. He inhaled, then stepped towards the storeroom.

'Aren't you going to leave now?' The words burst out of Vijay's mouth before his mind had a chance to catch up.

Pran stared at him. The soldiers too.

'What?' said David, turning towards him.

'Did you come here for something in particular?' Vijay's breath quickened. Whatever happened, he wouldn't let them reach the storeroom.

David threw his cigarette down and rushed towards him, grabbing Vijay by the shirt, the seam of the collar cutting into his neck.

The soldier's face was inches from his. 'What did you say?'

'Please, he didn't mean it. He's been drinking too.' Pran tried to get closer to them but David's comrade shoved him back.

'Eh, you have a big mouth to make up for the rest of your cripple body.' His breath sour, his voice low.

'Like I said, when are you going to leave?' They wouldn't find December, nor Jaya and Asha. There was no way.

The soldier clutched the back of Vijay's shirt, dragging him back towards the veranda, earth scattering under Vijay's feet, dust flying into his eyes.

The last thing Vijay saw was the wall hurtling towards him.

16

Asha

Asha stood at the door, struggling to swallow, mouth dry. She turned to Jaya. 'How long do you think it's been since we heard anything? Forty minutes?' She'd stopped wearing a watch months ago and there was no clock in the room.

'Maybe an hour?' Jaya whispered, as she sat down on the bed. 'Can you see anything?'

Asha shook her head, then gestured with her hand for her mother-in-law to stay where she was. She looked through the crack. Still nothing. She opened the door a fraction. Did it creak when you opened it? No noise, luckily. Even the crickets seemed to have quietened down, the breeze still. She held it ajar, waiting to see if the movement had alerted anyone. She bristled with fear, trying to steady her hands before she stepped out. She took a deep breath – even that seemed impossibly loud, as though she might wake the whole of Kololo Hill and send all the soldiers in the area running towards them.

Asha smelt the cigarette smoke before she saw it; the trails twisting themselves around Pran as he leant against a wall.

'What happened?' She hurried over to him. 'Pran?'

He sucked hard on the cigarette, looking out into the black.

'Why didn't you come to get us?' Asha placed her hand on his arm, warm to the touch. She scanned his face for any sign of injury. 'Are you OK? Where's Vijay?'

Pran turned towards her, as though he had woken up from a dream. 'Vijay. He's still in the kitchen.'

She rushed to find Vijay. He was slumped against the wall, blood dripping from his forehead.

'What happened, Pran? He needs help.' Asha grabbed a clean cloth and soaked it with water. She put it against Vijay's forehead. 'Vijay, can you hear me?'

Vijay opened his eyes and moved his hand towards the wound. 'They've gone?'

Asha nodded. 'Don't touch it, it's still bleeding.'

'They hit me.' A sleepy smile appeared on his face.

'Yes, I can see that. Don't move. We won't be able to go to the doctor until the morning.' Too dangerous. Another thing they could thank the army for.

'Bapre! Vijay, what did they do?' Jaya hurried into the kitchen and went to Vijay's side. His shirt was blotched with blood and he moved his body awkwardly as he tried to sit up.

Asha turned towards Pran, who stood in the corner. Alarm turned to confusion as she grabbed his hands in hers. 'Look at me. How did this happen?'

'They were heading for the storeroom and Vijay said something, some smart comment. They threw him against a wall and then hit him. Asha, they were so drunk, they could barely speak.' Pran clenched his hair with his hands. 'I didn't know what to do. I didn't know how to stop them.'

'It's OK, beta.' Jaya's voice wavered as she held the cloth to Vijay's forehead.

'They were moving towards the storeroom,' said Pran. 'I ran to get the money from the sitting room but by that time . . .' He looked down at his shoes. 'I told them we had no idea December was hiding there. They were so drunk, they believed me.'

'What do you mean? December?' Jaya stood up.

'I didn't know what to do, Ba.' Pran closed his eyes, holding the tears back.

Asha ran, the door to the storeroom obscured by darkness. The door was wide open.

December. Did she call out or did she merely think it? She said it again, but her voice faded along with her hope. Even as she said it once more, Asha knew there'd be no answer.

She stared at the room, willing December to appear, to jump out, even though it was ridiculous. Impossible.

Jaya came up behind her and stopped. Hand clinging to the door frame as she took in the empty space.

*

Asha climbed into bed next to Pran. His eyes were closed.

'Are you awake?' Asha whispered, turning to him.

'No, I can't sleep.' He opened his eyes. There was a whisky tang on his breath.

'Your Ba, I think she's in shock.' Asha had helped Jaya to bed; she'd lain there, looking up at the ceiling. After Motichand, after everything, this was the last thing she needed.

'The rest will do her good.'

'That's if she can sleep,' said Asha. If any of them could sleep. 'At least Vijay seems to be OK now. All that blood when we came into the kitchen . . .'

'I'll take him to the doctor in the morning.'

'And then you'll go to the station, see if you can find out what's happened to December?'

He sighed. 'We'll go. But I don't think it's going to help.'

'We have to try. For your Ba's sake if nothing else.' She blinked. 'Are you all right?'

'I'll be fine, I was the lucky one apparently,' he said. At least he wasn't hurt, she was so grateful that they hadn't touched him.

She put her hand on his chest, felt the tiny hairs tickling her fingers, the rise and fall of his breath. 'I don't understand what happened, Pran.'

'What do you mean? I told you.' The pillow rustled beneath Pran's head as he turned.

'When I came outside, you were just standing there, even though Vijay was lying on the kitchen floor.'

Pran sighed. 'It was probably shock, just like Ba. I wasn't thinking straight.'

Asha stared into the darkness. She tried to imagine what it must have been like for Pran and Vijay. Facing the soldiers in their own house, knowing how much was at stake.

'You saw them take December?'

'I – I guess so. It's all a bit of a blur.'

She heard the high-pitched buzz of a mosquito near her ear and flicked it away. 'And they didn't get angry with you, for hiding December?'

'I told you, Asha, they were drunk.' His voice louder now. 'They didn't know what they were doing.'

Silence. She knew she should let him sleep. Ask him again when things were calmer. Whenever that might be.

Pran edged closer, his warm breath on her face, his tears falling onto her cheek. 'I'm sorry.'

'It's not your fault. You must have been terrified.' She put her hand on his jaw, light stubble prickling against her skin.

'I should have done something. I'm sorry, Asha. I'm sorry.' He said it over and over again, long after she'd pulled him close to her.

17

Jaya

Jaya woke up surrounded by a cloud of mosquito net. She looked at the alarm clock. Ten o'clock. She jolted upright. Maybe Pran and Vijay had come back from the doctor or from the police station with December, they might be sitting in the kitchen right now? No. They would have rushed straight in to wake her. She'd lain awake for hours last night. Why hadn't she done something, tried to stop it all somehow?

What might have happened to December? There were hundreds, maybe thousands, who'd been murdered across the country. They still didn't know if December's family were amongst them.

And then there were those who had come back. People like Grace. She'd returned, but the damage was done. And those who'd been tortured by the army, like Naseem. They were all supposed to be grateful when their loved ones returned, no matter how many scars, seen and unseen, they might have to carry for the rest of their lives.

And then there was the third option, the in-between world of not knowing what had happened to someone. *Disappeared*, that was how people described it, when somebody vanished, as though it was some kind of magic rather than brutal murderers that had taken them away. At least when Motichand had died she could take comfort in knowing that he'd escaped life's hardships. But not knowing what had happened to December, whether he was alive or dead, what they were doing to him. That was worse.

She'd spoken to him the morning before, when she'd taken him a cup of pomegranate juice. His mood low, he gave her a weak smile, barely looking up at her to take the cup from the tray. It should have cheered them all, knowing that Pran had made the final plans to get December out, that he would leave in a few days, but it also meant that the family would never see him again. Jaya had felt a little sorry for herself: how shameful, looking back on it, how selfish. If they'd only been ready a couple of days earlier, December might have been safe now.

She'd tried to raise his spirits with stories about Vijay and Pran when they were little, reminding him how *tofani* they'd been, how naughty. 'Remember that time Vijay mixed up all the guests' shoes?' They'd had one of their many gatherings one Sunday, somehow squeezing dozens of adults and children into the house, roasting chicken and corn on the cob on the sigri in the yard. There'd been thirty pairs of shoes laid outside the hallway and Vijay had spent the afternoon muddling them all up, hiding half of them around the house. 'Do you remember how long it took us to find them because Vijay had forgotten where he'd put them?'

December stayed silent.

'Look, I know it must be hard for you,' Jaya whispered. 'But you'll be safe very soon.'

And that was one of the last things they'd said to each other. Jaya thought that she had more time. After everything that had happened in Uganda, how foolish she was to believe that there would always be another chance.

She heard the familiar clang of the outer gate, the thunk of the front door. No voices.

Jaya hurried, battling to push the layers of mosquito net

aside, opening the bedroom door and slipping her leather chumpul back on her feet. As she moved from the veranda to the hallway she realized she was still wearing the sari she'd slept in, but it was too late to pull on a *saal*, she needed to know if December was all right. She strained to hear his voice, anyone's voice. Three figures stood in front of her. Pran and Vijay by the door. Asha across the hall.

No December.

'Well?' Jaya asked, unable to hide the impatience in her voice.

They looked at each other, but would not meet her gaze, as though they'd betray what she knew already. She needed to hear it for herself, out loud.

'We tried—' Vijay's eyes were bloodshot. A bandage covered the cut on his head.

'They won't tell us anything, Ba,' Pran said, voice so quiet she had to watch his lips to be sure of what he said.

'So there is a chance?' Jaya looked from one son to the other. A fragment of hope.

'They told us not to bother coming back,' said Vijay.

'We tried, Ba, but they were getting angry with us. Told us not to waste their time.' Pran clutched the back of his neck, then looked down at the floor.

Jaya's cheeks flushed. 'They can't. They have made a mistake. They must have.'

'We could try again tomorrow,' Asha said, glancing from Pran to Jaya.

'Yes, might be someone else on duty tomorrow,' said Vijay. Jaya had seen that look before, full of anguish, when he'd told her Motichand was dead.

Silence. The boys had already put themselves in danger by going anywhere near the army, taking huge risks with their own lives. But what about December? She had to do something, there must be something left. 'Who can we speak to? Who is still here in Uganda, with contacts in government?' Jaya walked towards the kitchen, palm flat against the wall, guiding her way.

'Ba—'

'What about that boy you were friends with at school, Pran?'

'Ba, this won't help—'

She ignored Pran. 'Come here.' She kept her voice steady, ignoring the fear pulsing through her body. Thank God Motichand had doled out so much credit all over Kampala. She could call in favours from those people now, at least those that were still in the country. 'Let's make a list. Vijay, get a pen and paper.'

Vijay didn't move, nor did Pran, staring at Jaya as though they were scared of her. Asha opened her mouth, then closed it, thinking better of it. Instead, she took a step forward and put her hand on Jaya's shoulder. But she didn't need special treatment, least of all from Asha; she certainly didn't need to be treated like a child. December was all that mattered right now.

She clutched the sides of the table as she sat down, trying to steady her shaking hands. 'Vijay, I told you to get me a pen and paper.'

Asha sat down next to her.

'There's no one left to help us, Ba,' Vijay said. 'And even if there is, they won't take the risk. I'm sorry. I'm so sorry, Ba.'

'There's nothing more we can do,' said Pran, casting a shadow across the kitchen. 'I'm sorry.'

December might be alive, they might have beaten him up, but he could still be alive. Yet all the while, in her heart she knew: he was Acholi. It didn't matter, he was Acholi and they could kill him for no other reason than that. She looked around the room. She wanted to pull out saucepans and throw them, shove the chairs and watch them fall onto the floor, to shout and scream.

But she wasn't that person.

She got up, walked out of the kitchen and pulled her chundri over her shoulders, so that no one would see her tears.

*

Sleep hadn't dulled the pain of December's disappearance. Exhausted, despite spending all day and night in bed, Jaya walked into the kitchen the following morning. The smell of paratha made her stomach churn.

'Here, I'll get you some chai.' Asha's voice was kinder than she'd ever known it to be.

Vijay briefly rested his hand on his mother's shoulder as she sat down next to him.

She'd had time to think about how close the family came to danger. Vijay was lucky to escape with his injuries. She and Asha, especially Asha, were lucky to have escaped the soldiers' attention. Jaya had risked all their lives to try and save December and now she had to live with the consequences.

'About December—' Pran began.

Jaya put up her hand. 'Let's stop talking about things we cannot change.'

The family watched her sip her tea. She couldn't face eating.

'I can help you pack later, if you like?' said Asha.

'I will be fine, there's not much to pack anyway,' Jaya replied.

'It's probably best, the checkpoints are getting worse.' Vijay tore a piece of paratha with his right hand and scooped up some *katki keri*, the tiny cubes of green mango glistening in the thick chutney syrup.

'You'll have to look after everyone, you know.' Pran looked

at Vijay. Pran would stay behind at the house and finish the last of the paperwork before he went to stay with Jaya's brother in India. It was too dangerous for him to take the family to Entebbe airport and come back on his own.

'And what will Vijay do that I can't?' Asha turned from the stove and faced Pran. 'In front of a soldier with a gun, we're all equal.'

'You all need to be careful. And I still think you should take the knife.'

'You honestly want me to keep that in my handbag?' Asha shook her head. Jaya agreed; even if it didn't provoke the army, it was more than likely that Asha would forget it was there and cut herself on it.

'And what about at the airport, in England? When they ask if there's anything to declare?' said Vijay. 'Yes, sir, just this gold watch and, oh yes, I nearly forgot, this huge knife!'

Pran's eyes darkened. 'Stop it. This is serious. You could throw it away when you get to the airport.'

'It might make things worse, beta,' said Jaya. She could see how much it bothered Pran not to be able to keep them safe, although he'd forgotten that Jaya had made a similar journey, while the world was at war. Anyway, the thing that she was most worried about was Pran staying in Uganda, even if it was just a few more days, with the mood growing ever darker. The more Asians that left Uganda, the worse the feeling grew towards those who remained. A cold and cruel goodbye.

*

After breakfast, Jaya packed her belongings into Motichand's battered leather suitcase, covered in travel stickers for places that neither of them had ever been to: Japan, Spain, Brazil, stickers from a friend of Motichand's, none from Uganda or India.

Motichand had always talked about saving just enough money to return to India and live comfortably. He said it so many times that Jaya had started to believe it too, making plans to see her family again, thinking of all the stories she'd be able to tell them, truly believing that one day they'd be reunited. But after his many business ventures started on a whim and ended with a whimper, going back to India was always out of their reach. And just as Jaya had made her peace with the idea of never going back, Pran and Vijay had begun to put money back into the dukan and her hope returned. The chance to see her brothers and their families after thirty-five years apart, too late to see her father, whose death she'd mourned from afar years ago. After all that, here she was, moving even further away from India, doing it all over again, leaving Uganda for England. She wondered what her next life would be, what would happen to her soul after they'd burnt her body on a funeral pyre. Didn't she deserve a rest, after so many lives lived already? She knew she should be grateful, count herself lucky to be able to leave Uganda for a country that was safe, if not familiar or welcoming. But she'd wanted to see how this life, right here, was going to carry on, surrounded by her loved ones and her memories of Motichand and December, to see it out to the end in her own home.

Home. How could she have ever called Uganda that? She should have learnt after she got married, home didn't exist for her. Other people decided where she could stay, where her home would be.

How could they tell you? Home wasn't something you had to think about. You didn't think about it as you strolled around Kololo Hill, waving at Mrs Walji, whose children had played with yours for years, the same children you'd told off when they'd found your fresh *talpindi* cooling in the storeroom and gorged on it until they'd thrown up; you didn't think about it when you avoided the *khadoh*, the little pothole at the bottom of your road, out of habit. You didn't think about any of it. As soon as you had to be told, or it had to be written down, or you were forced out of the country where you'd lived most of your life, that's when you thought about home.

'Here you go.' Asha came into the bedroom and handed Jaya a thick black cardigan, one of the few items of warm clothing they'd managed to buy in town before they had been snapped up by others leaving for the colder climes of Europe, Canada and the United States. Asha checked the suitcase, putting her hand against the false lining that Pran's tailor friend had helped sew into place, feeling the thin layers of Ugandan shillings slotted inside. Idi Amin had decided that they could only take a small amount of money with them, claiming that the sneaky Asians had spent years stashing their wealth in Europe. As though most of them had those kinds of riches to spare.

They had to invent clever ways to smuggle out whatever they could now. Mrs Goswami had shipped pots and pans out of the country, rolling up notes and sliding them into hollowed-out handles. That was still a gamble; there was no telling whether the pots would arrive in Canada at all, let alone with the money stuffed inside. Later that day, Jaya and Asha would spend a couple of hours frying *bhajia* with gold stud earrings inside, packed away in containers as a 'snack' for the plane.

Asha looked at Jaya's belongings, laid out on the bed. 'You're taking all those things?'

What was it Motichand used to say, when she tried to urge him to spend less? 'You can't take it into the next life.' Unlike him, Jaya didn't have many belongings. Why shouldn't she take the few things she had? They were all gifts: a small figurine carved out of soapstone from a trip her husband took to Mombasa years ago; from Pran, a set of small notecards with bonded paper envelopes, the fronts decorated with watercolour flowers, hibiscus, jasmine, poinsettia, still in its original cellophane packaging and kept for a special occasion that never came. There were a few ornate saris, silks and brocades, *baranasi* and *bandhni* in sea green, royal blue and scarlet. She'd never had a chance to wear most of them and now she never would, resigned to the simple pale cotton saris of widowhood.

Asha tapped a piece of yellow Tupperware, a treasured gift from her friend Sonaben after a trip to Europe. 'They must have these in England?'

Jaya peeled open the lid and showed her the Lux soaps inside. 'Look, I'm making use of all the space.' Jaya couldn't stand the waste, all the things they'd worked for.

'I think they have soap in England.' Asha patted her on the shoulder. 'I'll leave you to it.'

*

The last day arrived. The sun still high, thin shadows slicing across the yard. Jaya had fought the urge to pack the housewares away, not bothering to fold bedsheets, nor wrap glasses in newspaper so that they were all protected and cared for. What was the point? Those things were no longer hers to protect; why look after them when they'd be in someone else's hands soon enough? Now the sideboard stood empty in the sitting room, the storeroom bare, the picture frames in the bedroom taken down. She stared at the crack in the window, a lightning bolt that Motichand had promised to get fixed for years, but the day never came.

She couldn't imagine someone else walking around the house – her house – pulling open drawers, banging cupboard doors, gathering as a family around the kitchen table for breakfast, entertaining friends with chai and ginger biscuits in the sitting room, shelling peas out on the veranda. She walked through the bedrooms, where Vijay and Pran had pretended to be ghosts, draping the mosquito nets over their heads, through to the sitting room, where years before she'd often found Motichand dozing in front of the rickety gramophone, the rippling crackles on the records and the soft, echoing songs of Lata Mangeshkar a long-distance call home to India.

She moved her fingertips along the walls and doors of each room, trying to commit the feel of them to memory. She made her way to the front door, lingering on the threshold, telling herself to leave her home for the final time.

Outside, the others were gathered by the car. They were going to travel to the airport with Motichand's old customer, Cyrus Mody. As soon as Jaya and the others had started making plans for the airport and they had heard that Cyrus was on the same flight as them, Jaya knew exactly what to do. She'd gone straight to Cyrus's grand villa up at the top of Kololo Hill, reminding him of the long-standing friendship between him and her husband, how Cyrus had been such a loyal customer, how Motichand had looked after him all those years and what did it matter now about the unpaid bills when all their lives were at stake, how surely it made sense for them to stick together, as she, a widow, had no idea how she'd get the rest of her family to the airport safely otherwise? And that was how, after all those years, it was Jaya who had finally managed to get Cyrus Mody to repay his debt to her husband.

18

Asha

Asha was dizzy with goodbyes. Dozens of people, old friends and new, cousins and uncles and aunts. She should have been well practised by now, ready for her parents and two younger brothers, Raju and Sailesh, who made a hurried stop at the house on the way from Jinja to Entebbe airport the week before Asha was due to leave.

'You'll come to India soon, I'm sure,' Asha's Ba said. 'Or we'll come to England. It won't be long, beta.' Asha humoured her mother, knowing that nothing in their lives could be locked down with certainty. She hugged them tight, felt sorry for all the times she and her brothers had argued, wishing instead she'd spent more time creating good memories before she'd left for her marital home. And for a moment, she wished she could leave with them.

Her Papa was distracted, worrying about the checkpoints, the airport, the flight out, the new life that awaited them. He'd only known India as a baby, before his parents had settled in Uganda. 'We're too old to learn our lives all over again, aren't we, Jayaben?' he'd said, before hugging Asha so tightly and for so long that her Ba had to gently prise them apart.

And now, the final goodbye, as Asha and the family left their home for the last time.

'We'll see each other soon, Ba,' Pran assured Jaya, but they all knew it would be a long journey for him from Uganda to India, let alone joining them in England without a British passport. Jaya held him tight, lingering in his arms and leaving specks of tears on his shirt pocket.

Vijay ruffled Pran's hair with a 'Take care, bhai, see you soon,' trying to keep it light, though he fooled no one.

Asha gave Pran the briefest hug, leaving it at that for the sake of propriety. She took him in, trying to commit him to memory, trying to pretend she hadn't seen the glimmer of anxiety, the shadow of fear across his face. Instead, she focused on the hint of aftershave on his skin, the way his hair brushed against her forehead. She stepped back. The feel of him, the warmth of his body quickly disappearing from her own.

Cyrus climbed into the driver's seat. His hair was a dirty copper colour from his henna dye. He'd battered the Mercedes with a hammer that morning, smashing one of the tail lights and shattering a headlight. 'Who wants a car that looks like it's been beaten up by a lorry?' he'd said. The cream paintwork had also been ruined, covered in scuffs and scratches. 'You don't expect someone driving a car like this to have any money, do you?'

Asha, Jaya and Cyrus's wife Aruna were crammed into the back of the car, the air stuffy with the scent of petrol and warm leather. Vijay climbed into the front.

As the car pulled out of the driveway and down the street, Asha watched Pran's figure fade away.

The night before, Pran had moved across the bed and kissed Asha on each eyelid. 'At least you won't be alone,' he said. 'I know you sometimes struggle with Ba, but you'll watch out for each other, won't you?'

'Of course,' Asha said. She gently pushed away a strand of Pran's hair from his eye. 'But you've got to be careful too.'

'Don't worry about me. Just remember I love you and stay safe.'

But as the thought of the journey ahead made her throat tight with worry, she already struggled to recall last night's whispered goodbyes, his lips on her shoulders, his fingers along her back.

As they drove through the neighbourhood, Asha watched other families preparing to leave, strapping luggage to car roofs or making their way to the buses the government had laid on to try and stop the soldiers' looting, for all the good that did. Abandoned cars had been left at the side of the road, some with the doors still open, as though the drivers had been spooked and simply run away. They reached a part of the road where the tarmac wasn't finished and the car rumbled and rocked over the uneven ground. Asha wound her window up to keep out the red dust that turned the air pink and caught in her throat, shutting out the petrol fumes and the smells of the smoking meat on the stalls outside.

As they left the city, the road cut through layer upon layer of green trees and shrubs. The colours seemed too lurid today, too celebratory. All those things she'd taken for granted. Along the road to Entebbe, they passed smaller shacks with rusty metal roofs, lined with shelves of goods and rows of clothing; barbers, and butchers with carcasses of meat hanging in front. A few fruit stalls were dotted near the roadside, selling papaya, jackfruit and tiny yellow bananas, the sorts of places her family might once have stopped at, taking their hoard of treasures home for dessert.

'We just have to get to the airport, that's all. Get to the airport,' Jaya said, repeating it over and over like a mantra, in between the real prayers that she murmured under her breath. 'Just get to the airport.' She clutched her handbag so tightly, pressed her fingers so hard, that it made the tips white, finger-nails leaving tiny waves in the leather.

Asha thought of the stories they'd heard of looting and violence. Of Mrs Goswami's house girl, Grace. What would she do if that happened to her? She'd fight back, wouldn't she? Yet the spectre of the soldiers' guns always loomed above her. She'd been wrong about what she said to Pran earlier: they weren't equal.

On the road ahead, there was a checkpoint with two soldiers standing next to a truck. As they got closer, she saw that one was female, her hair close-cropped like all the others, but with a delicate jaw and full cheeks.

'Remember what we agreed,' Cyrus said. They'd decided that it was best for him to do the talking. He owned a restaur-ant that all the army officials used to go to and he'd made a few acquaintances over the years. He was used to dealing with soldiers and thought it better that they make their own way to the airport, rather than be sitting ducks on the government buses.

The female soldier approached the car. Cyrus wound his window down. Her face was so close that her nose almost touched his. The soldier's round eyes took each of them in, one by one. Jaya kept her head down. Asha glanced at the soldier but decided against looking her in the eye; this was not the time to show defiance.

'Where are you going?' said the soldier in Swahili. It was obvious where they were going, unless this idiot had somehow missed the news that all Asians had to leave the country.

Before Cyrus had a chance to reply, the other soldier who stood at the roadside started shouting for everyone to get out. Vijay began to open the door on his side. Asha followed suit.

'Wait, not yet,' said Cyrus. He took money out of his trouser pocket and showed it to the female soldier.

She snatched the money from Cyrus's hand, flashing it at her friend, who'd also approached the car. Cyrus got out but gestured with his hand for the rest to stay inside.

They sprang into action, just as they'd agreed. Vijay pulled out some notes from his shirt pocket, Asha took off the single gold bangle she wore on her arm, having decided earlier that it was best to have some jewellery on show, to stop prying eyes and hands searching anywhere else. Please let it be enough, she thought, let them be satisfied.

Cyrus piled it together and handed it to the two soldiers. They took the crumpled heap as though it was worthless rubbish and stuffed it into their pockets, telling them to move on.

They drove away, as fast as the car would go.

'That was lucky. Didn't even bother to look in the boot,' said Vijay. To think yourself lucky after being robbed, was this what things had come to?

'God is looking down on us.' The relief in Cyrus's voice broke through.

Once they were out of sight of the checkpoint and the road was clear, Cyrus pulled the car over. He reached down towards his feet and pulled out another stash of notes that they'd gathered together before the trip. He handed out the money and gave his wife a gold necklace.

At the next checkpoint, there was a pristine navy BMW parked up near the army truck. Cyrus pulled in behind and a soldier came towards their car. He was so young that his face had not yet hardened into the clean edges and sharp lines of an adult, hadn't lost the softness of childhood, as though his features were still trying to work out how to settle under his skin. He stared through the windows with milky brown eyes. Sweat pooled on Asha's forehead, but she didn't dare move. Jaya's arm was resting against hers; she felt the rise and fall of her breath.

'Get out,' said the soldier, his voice hovering between man and boy.

'Here, please, this is all we have.' Through the car window, Cyrus handed him the valuables they'd collected. The soldier paused, eyes narrowing, then walked away to speak to his comrade, glancing back at the BMW behind them.

No one in the car dared speak.

The young soldier came back to the car and stared at Cyrus, then at his wife, Aruna, eyeing her gold chain. Not waiting to be asked, fiddling with the clasp, she hurried to take it off.

The soldier looked down and then waved Cyrus on, sending them off with a hard thump of his fist on the car bonnet. Asha could barely look at the family who stood at the roadside, waiting alongside their gleaming BMW, waiting to surrender the last remaining fragments of their lives, as the trashed Mercedes trundled past them.

'What happened?' said Cyrus's wife, covering her mouth with her hand. 'They didn't make us get out.'

'I told you before, *mere jaan*, why bother with tin and copper when you can have gold and platinum?' Cyrus said wearily. 'They see this heap of rubbish and they look for their treasure elsewhere.'

But a few miles later, another checkpoint loomed ahead. An army jeep was parked in the middle of the road. To the left, three soldiers were slumped against a tree trunk, shaded by a swathe of thick foliage. If it hadn't been for the khaki uniforms, the rifles at their sides, the berets the colour of dried blood, they might have been three ordinary young men, bored and looking for something to do. When the car approached, the soldiers perked up, backs straightened, guns raised. They moved swiftly to the middle of the road and surrounded the Mercedes.

'Out, now.' The first soldier was skinny and tall, the eldest of the three. He walked with his shoulders hunched and looked like the sort of boy who might be picked on at school for being lanky and awkward, but here he was, the bully pointing a gun at others. Asha's lips parted, her cheeks bloomed with heat. Was this when their luck ran out?

'We're just trying, well, we wanted to get to the airport, you see . . .' Cyrus seemed to have lost his earlier bravado. The exhausting rounds of talking to the soldiers were taking their toll. He stuttered like a toddler learning to speak. His softly spoken manner, which had helped to build rapport with the army at the previous checkpoints, now made him sound child-like and vulnerable.

'Shut up,' said the skinny soldier. 'You're boring me. Get out now.'

This time, they all climbed out. The sun was fierce. Usually at this time of day they'd be inside, perhaps taking a nap in a shaded bedroom.

'Open the boot,' he said.

The other soldiers watched as the thin one, apparently the leader, gave the order to put their suitcases on the ground and open them. He seemed to blink fast, as though he constantly had dust in his eyes. Another one, the smallest of the three, who had a light gait and a torn collar on his shirt, came forward, kicking at the clothes in the suitcases with his foot. Asha watched as the rusty dirt from his boot smeared the clothes inside.

'You know Sergeant Hawar? A friend of mine, in the army?' Cyrus said quietly. It was unlikely that anyone he knew in the army was a friend, but he'd probably figured that, at this point, anything was worth a shot.

'Never heard of him,' said the soldier with the easy gait. 'Have you?' He looked towards the tall leader.

'No, us lieutenants don't pay much attention to the ranks below us,' he replied, blinking hard.

'Now, take it all out.' The shorter soldier moved closer to Asha.

Asha's hands shook as she pulled the clothes out on the ground, while the male passengers were told to empty their pockets. She looked up from the suitcase. The soldier was no longer staring at the clothes. He was staring at her.

He lifted his rifle and pointed it at Asha. He placed the barrel of the gun, cool despite the heat, against her neck. Her body tensed. The soldier moved it down towards her chest. Everyone was still, watching them.

'Asha—' Jaya called out.

'Who told you to speak?' The lieutenant moved towards Jaya.

The other soldier still had his eyes on Asha. She willed him to stop, hoping that Jaya had broken the spell. But instead he carried on, tracing the shape of her breast with the tip of the gun. He glared at her, waiting for Asha to react. She held her breath, swallowed her fear. She wouldn't give him the satisfaction.

'People like you hide things,' the soldier said. 'In places that people like me can't see.'

She forced herself to look him in the eye, to appeal to him, showing him the clothes from the bag to prove she wasn't keeping anything from him. 'I'm not hiding anything.'

'But there's plenty more to hide.' He nudged her blouse open with the gun tip. He gestured with his head towards a parting in the nearby trees and shoved her shoulder with the rifle.

'Please, here, we have more money, take what you want,' Vijay called out. He moved forward, the earth scattering under his feet.

The tall, skinny soldier held him back. 'Look at this. What's wrong with you?' He prodded Vijay's left arm.

'That's not the hand that keeps him company at night, so why feel sorry for him?' said the soldier standing near Asha.

'Eh? What do you need a hand for when you have a woman?' the lieutenant replied, blinking fast again.

'Don't you know? You need *two* hands to hold her down.' The soldier dug the gun into Asha's skin and grinned, eyes lit up with contempt. 'Let's go.' He pushed Asha.

'Wait, let's just take what we can and send them on their way.' The third soldier, who'd stayed quiet until then, spoke, his gaze shifting from Asha to his comrades. He looked at them all with wide eyes; his cheeks were covered in pimples. Eighteen years old at most. 'There'll be more coming soon.'

'I don't have any more money, I swear,' said Asha, wishing her voice had come out louder than a whisper.

'I don't want money, Joseph.' The soldier prodded her with the gun again, digging into her breastbone.

'Look, we haven't seen what else is in the suitcases,' said Joseph, dropping quickly to his knees to look at the contents. He wiped his forehead. 'They've probably got some gold in there, let's have a look and send them on their way.'

Hope.

'I'm sick of you going on, Joseph. One more time and I may have to shut you up myself.' The small soldier shoved Asha; she glanced once more at Joseph as he remained on the ground, silent. A chance of escape taken away as quickly as it appeared.

Now, the soldier pushed her along, away from the roadside to the undergrowth, the bark scratching her arm as she reached out to steady herself. They arrived at a small clearing, the air thick and humid.

He said nothing, leering at her blouse.

Asha knew what he wanted but she couldn't bring herself to do it. 'Please don't do this.'

He lowered his gun and stepped forward. 'Fine, I'll do it myself.'

Asha pushed him away as hard as she could. 'Stop!' The soldier stumbled backwards and looked up at her.

'Bitch,' he said in English, then smacked her across the face.

There was a call from the roadside. 'What are you doing down there, can't get it up?' The booming voice of his tall comrade.

The soldier dropped his rifle and rushed towards her, as though he had to prove himself before he went back. She glanced over his shoulder at the abandoned gun, wondering for a split second if she could push him aside and reach it. But what would be the point? There were more soldiers waiting. Always more soldiers.

Now his fleshy fingers fumbled at the buttons of Asha's shirt. She willed herself to move, to stop him, but her muscles tensed, the panic running through her body like wildfire. He gave up and ripped her shirt open, the buttons hitting the tree trunk like bullets. His breath stank of alcohol.

He stepped back, eyes crawling all over her. 'Show me, now.'

'Hurry up, William,' the soldier at the roadside called out. A roll of dry earth as another car pulled up.

The soldier unzipped his trousers.

This couldn't be happening.

His fingers fumbled at the zip of her bell-bottoms, struggling to pull them down. Salty tears stung her skin. No way out now. How dare he? How dare he do this?

A gunshot.

The soldier stepped back, as though Asha had slapped his cheek. Had she? She scanned his body for blood, a wound. Nothing.

Asha looked down. Bruises were already forming on her arms where the soldier had grabbed her, but no sign of blood.

Another shout from the roadside. 'Hurry up, William. Take your little gun out of those dirty places. We have more guests.'

The lieutenant must have fired the rifle to hurry him up.

The soldier looked at Asha as she tried to cover her chest, then up at the roadside. He muttered something under his breath as he grabbed her arm and dragged her along.

Asha felt the others' eyes on her, her hands clutching her torn shirt across her bra. She was almost glad that the soldier was pulling her along; she lacked the strength to move one foot in front of the other.

The soldier pushed Asha. She fell onto Cyrus. He steadied her with his hand on her shoulder. Though he did it as gently as possible, she recoiled, the memory of the soldier still fresh.

'Get rid of them,' the tall soldier told the others.

Jaya put her arm around Asha, but she couldn't help but flinch. They got into the car. In the rear-view mirror Asha could see the sparkling blue BMW from the previous checkpoint slowed down by the army truck. She could see the passengers as they climbed out of the car. There were two tall men with matching maroon turbans and, next to them, three women, all a similar age to Asha, with the same look of dread. As the Mercedes drove off at full speed, she saw the soldier who'd attacked her walking towards them.

No one spoke. Everyone was still except for Cyrus, who edged the steering wheel back and forth.

Asha felt herself shrinking into the seat, her skin sticking to the leather. Because of the hurry to get away, Vijay was now sitting in the back. He seemed to move as close against the car door as he could, doing everything possible to create a safe distance between them, not wanting to unsettle her further.

To her left, Jaya lifted a hand. It hovered over Asha's leg

before settling on her knee. It gave Asha something to focus on, and it gave Jaya the courage to speak.

'We'll get some water at the airport,' Jaya said. 'To clean it up.'

Asha looked over to her. Only then did she feel the salt on her tongue, the sting on her cheek. She put her fingertips to her face, then looked down at her hand. Not tears but blood, already turning from scarlet to rust.

'I'm so sorry, Asha,' whispered Jaya.

Cyrus caught her eye in the rear-view mirror. He looked away swiftly. Guilt, as though he had done it himself. As though it was somehow his fault.

Night loomed as they approached Entebbe airport. The car followed the bend of the road along the banks of Lake Victoria, the water disappearing over the horizon.

Asha climbed out of the car with the others. The airport car park was cluttered with badly parked cars: Citroëns, Peugeots, Mercedes Benzes, Morris Minors. At the far end, soldiers were already driving some of them away. People pulled suitcases off the tops of their vehicles and found their bags as they came off government buses, crying, praying and saying goodbye to one another.

'Come on, let's get through this *fujo* and onto the plane as quickly as possible,' said Cyrus.

They walked into the squat, flat-roofed airport, to be greeted by stale air and chaos. Frantic parents tried to quieten their crying children, afraid of angering the soldiers. In the corner, an older woman stared into empty space, her earlobes smeared with blood: a soldier must have torn her earrings off without waiting for her to take them out. Other people waited in line to be searched by yet more soldiers.

'What else could there possibly be left to take?' said Jaya.

Asha clutched Jaya's saal around her despite the heat, the

only way to keep herself covered now that her clothes were in tatters, but she had no energy left to respond. Haven't you had enough, Asha screamed inside her head, so close to shouting it out loud it scared her, haven't you taken all you can from us? She jumped every time a soldier walked by, as though they were charged with electricity. Their voices grated, their arrogant laughter rang in her ears. The soldier at the roadside was touching her, holding her down all over again.

But they'd never touch her again. They'd taken all they'd ever take.

'Here, have some water.' Vijay walked over, a shyness in his voice. He handed her the thermos.

Vijay. Pran. The money they'd smuggled. The anger that had spread across Uganda against the 'greedy' Asians. Amin had stoked the resentment until it burned bright with hate. Yes, Vijay had played his part, but it was Pran who planned it all, made it possible in the first place. Hadn't Pran helped light the touchpaper?

She gulped the water down, tried to wash away the bitter taste in her mouth.

'There's a bathroom there. Do you want me to come with you?' said Jaya.

'He didn't—The gunshot stopped him,' Asha whispered. She needed to say it out loud, not for Jaya, but for herself. The words gave her comfort, reminding her that it could have been worse.

Jaya patted Asha's arm, with a look that said she understood.

Asha changed into another blouse in the toilets, her muscles sore as she lifted her arms, her fingers tender as she did up the buttons. She washed her hands and dabbed the cut on her cheek with a damp tissue, although she longed to scour her entire body clean of the soldier's touch.

Outside, the others were already in the queue to leave. The British Caledonian airline officials rushed through the ticket checks. All the passengers were hurried along the baking tarmac, past the grass and palm trees that lined the runway, the grey airport seeming so out of place in this lush landscape. Climbing the stairs onto the plane, her legs felt stiff with each step.

No need to turn around and say goodbye to her home. It was already gone.

*

On the plane, Jaya sat by the window while Asha took the aisle seat. They looked around at the hundreds of tons of metal and plastic, at all the people crammed in. Cyrus and his wife found seats at the back. Some of the younger men like Vijay had to sit on the aisle floor, no more seats left. Rules bent so that lives could be saved.

She helped Jaya with her seat belt, then looked around. A man up ahead was praying, or perhaps talking to himself as he found a space. He lit a cigarette and sat down. The swirls of smoke rose up and over his scarlet turban, as though he'd been set alight himself.

The plane was a jumble of Gujarati, Hindi, Punjabi, Urdu, broken with cries of anger and grief. Swahili was no longer needed, already cast away with their homes and belongings. The tannoy boomed, the pilot spoke in a tight English accent about their journey: Entebbe, London Stansted.

She turned to Jaya, who clutched her handbag tight, looking out of the window at a group of soldiers standing under the airport lights. Their guns stabbed down into the red earth, some soldiers slouched against their rifle butts, while others joked around. Jaya stared at one of them. His cheeks were filled with the chubby fat of youth. The soldier stared back at Jaya.

Asha expected her to pull her sari chundri over her head and look away. And yet she kept staring. Even now, there was little to stop the boy boarding the plane and pointing his gun at them. But still Asha willed her to keep looking. Why should Jaya feel intimidated by him? He was not too old to be taken by the ear, and she was not too old to make it hurt. Jaya held his gaze until the soldier's comrade flicked his arm. He turned away and laughed, as though they were fooling around in a playground.

The plane began to wheeze and rumble down the runway. The cabin went quiet as people prayed for a safe journey; next to Asha, Jaya's eyes were closed as she whispered under her breath. Asha considered praying too, but what good would it do now? What help had it been so far?

Outside, the wings seemed to flap like cardboard in the night sky but Asha felt no fear. They were in the air, the sky black, as Uganda disappeared beneath them.

PART TWO

England, 1972

PART TWO

19

Asha

Asha stepped off the plane. A wisp of her breath escaped into the icy air, as though the life was seeping out of her. In front, Jaya clutched her cardigan close, flimsy sari rustling around her ankles in the wind. Vijay followed behind, joining the lines of people as they hurried towards the terminal. The chill clung to Asha's clothes as she looked at the trees beyond the runway. The bare branches were like ancient fossils, the sky above a wash of blotchy grey.

Inside Stansted airport, Asha was surprised to see the bright lights were on even though it was the middle of the day. They were ushered into cordoned-off lines by airport officials in white shirts. Compartmentalized, told where to go, led along like children. Still being bossed around, even now.

Cyrus and his wife joined another queue nearby. The waiting people spoke in whispers, through exhaustion and the angst of not knowing what would happen next. In the farthest line, a young family with a baby and a toddler approached the booth at the front. The official inside looked at the man's blue passport, then paused at the woman's, which was maroon. He pointed at it. The couple glanced at each other, then back at the official, speaking in low tones.

The woman shook her head frantically, then said, 'No.' She

sat down in front of the booth with the baby. 'Not moving,' she said in English.

'You can't split us up. Two young children, you not see?' said the father.

The official shook his head, looking embarrassed as he turned towards his colleague. A security guard approached and tried to help the woman up but she shook her head. The baby started crying, which set the toddler off.

'What's going on?' said Jaya.

'The woman doesn't have a British passport,' Vijay whispered.

'How did they get here, then?' said Jaya.

'They must have bribed their way out somehow,' he said.

Had Jaya already forgotten the rules of the place they'd called home? Asha rubbed her eyes; the bright light was giving her a headache.

The official and the security guard stood near the family, glancing at the crowds of people who stared. Both men seemed to have decided to leave the woman alone for the time being while they guided more people from the queues to the booth.

'Maybe we should have tried the same thing with Pran?' said Jaya.

'I don't think it's that easy, Ba.' Vijay shifted his weight from one foot to the other. 'They have young children, it's different.'

They watched and waited as more nervous and weary people took their turn. Finally, they were called to come forward.

The man in the booth wore thick, black-framed glasses. He picked up the three navy British 'D' passports, curving his gnarled knuckles around them. 'We're going to check the passports, yes?' He looked through the photos. 'And we're going to check them against the papers, yes?' Everything he said seemed to be in the form of questions, as though he wasn't sure what he should be doing and wanted them to guide him along.

Vijay and Asha glanced at each other and found themselves responding with a 'Yes' too.

He wrote some details down and observed the passports again, 'You're all related, yes?' Eventually, even Jaya nodded along, though she didn't understand what he was saying.

Asha wished he'd just hurry up. They had no idea where they were going to sleep that night, why couldn't she have one moment of peace?

To their right, they watched as the official returned to the young family who'd been left in the corner. The woman rocked the baby, trying to calm her down. But the relief on the father's face spread to the mother as the man said something to them. Smiles appeared on their faces. They must have been told that they could stay.

Asha watched the official in front of her as he stamped the passports and handed them back to Vijay.

After passport control, they were led to an area with floor-to-ceiling windows, overlooking the wet runway. A plane took off in the distance, determined nose lifted in the air. Trestle tables and chairs had been set up in rows on one side of the room. They were guided to the other side, where racks of clothing lined the walls.

'You can each help yourself to a coat,' said a young woman who stood in front of a table, waving her hand at the mismatched clothes behind her as though she were selling luxury items in a shop. She wore a navy-blue uniform and a matching hat, and though the clothes reminded Asha of the Ugandan army, she felt comforted by the badge that said *St John Ambulance.*

'You must be ever so chilly.' The woman's voice was full of cheer.

Asha couldn't help but raise an eyebrow. Chilly was an understatement. Even in the warmth of the airport Arrivals area, the cold lingered on her skin like the sting after a slap. Jaya shivered; her bare toes were grey-blue where they peeped out from beneath her sari.

'Well, you carry on, just let me know which items you've picked and I'll write them in my little book.' The woman pointed at a huge black ledger.

Asha wondered who the items had belonged to, the lives they'd lived, whether any of them had been through anything like this. The smell lingered, musty yet medicinal, but at least it was warm amongst the fabric, the heat caught between the layers of wool and leather, suede and velvet.

'They are giving us brand-new clothes?' said Jaya.

'They're donated, people didn't want them any more.' Asha pulled out one of the wool coats with a rash of tiny bobbles along the sleeves.

Jaya looked horrified. To her, donated clothes were what you gave to the poor, not people like them. 'But what if they haven't washed them?'

'Don't think about it, Ba.' Vijay browsed the rail for things that might fit his mother.

Eventually, Jaya settled on a navy coat, intended to sit on the knee, which reached mid-calf on her tiny frame. Asha helped roll up the sleeves before they swallowed Jaya's arms. She also picked out a black wool hat, but Jaya decided to pull her sari chundri over the top of it, leaving her with a lollipop head.

Asha pulled on a long maroon coat and natty black scarf. What did it matter now what they wore?

Vijay wanted a black biker jacket, like the one that he'd seen Steve McQueen wearing in one of his films, but Jaya insisted that it wasn't warm enough. Instead, he chose a black wool coat.

It was not just the unfamiliar things they wore, but the way their bodies tensed to keep the cold out, their heads bowed, dark circles around their eyes from lack of sleep. It made them all look like different people now, with different lives, as though they'd left Kampala behind many years ago, not hours before.

After they'd finished at the clothing racks, they were invited to join other families and sit down at the trestle tables. More volunteers, mainly women in identical uniforms, came around with drinks. They poured tea from china teapots, which everyone drank because it was hot and free.

'This isn't at all what I expected,' Jaya said, looking around at this strange world where white people served brown, where you were given free food and clothes.

None of them had known what to expect, despite stories that had found their way back to Uganda about help that the British had given new arrivals, not after seeing those news reports with British protestors telling people to go back to their own countries. And yet here they were, surrounded by people who were willing to give up their day to look after a group of strangers in an airport.

Asha looked over to the end of their table, where a couple sat with their daughter. The girl couldn't have been more than five or six years old, oblivious to the weary look on her parents' faces, immersed in her own delightful adventure: pointing out the gigantic planes on the tarmac; gleefully devouring orange squash and Marie biscuits; twirling around and around in her new – or almost new – red coat. Many of those who'd come over on the plane were families, but in the far corner Asha spotted a young Punjabi man with a black turban, who seemed to have no one else, sitting with a pack of playing cards in front of him. He'd taken one of the cards, staring down at it as he tore off tiny pieces and made a little pile on the Formica table.

She thought of Pran, making it out of Uganda, running the treacherous gauntlet of army roadblocks to reach India and find a way to England. She felt guilty for the anger she'd felt at Entebbe, somehow blaming him for what the soldier had done to her. She at least had Vijay and Jaya. Pran was alone. The sadness weighed heavy in her throat, like a teardrop about to fall.

*

Outside the airport, they said goodbye to Cyrus and Aruna, who had been allocated places in a different resettlement centre, hours away in Somerset. They all made polite but empty promises to stay in touch. Asha was glad: one less reminder of her last hours back home.

By the time the family boarded their coach, it was already dark. Someone called from the back, asking what time it was. No one had a watch, all hidden away or stolen back in Kampala. So Asha asked the bus driver the time in English.

'Four o'clock,' he said.

'*Chaar vayga che,*' she called out to the whole bus.

'How can they afford all this electricity?' said Jaya, as they wound their way through roads lit by street lamps, a far cry from the dim suburbs of Kampala. The dark outlines of trees dotted the horizon but it was difficult to see beyond the road, out into the dark.

The army barracks, empty for years and repurposed for new arrivals, were a cluster of long, flat-roofed buildings with one larger building at the centre. As far as Asha could tell, they were surrounded by fields. They got out of the bus, hurrying to collect their luggage. Inside, a familiar photograph of the Queen, resplendent in her coronation gown, hung on one wall.

She had gazed down on them from framed pictures like these for decades, followed them around while they bought condensed milk or Vimto in the dukans; seen them off on their rail journeys in the station hall; turned her head aside on ten-shilling notes as they paid for their goods; greeted them on stamps before they'd had a chance to open the envelopes. But in later years, the Queen had faded away; as Uganda decided she wanted independence from Her Majesty's great country, most of the photographs of her were put away or replaced with those of Milton Obote and, later, Idi Amin. On the opposite wall were a row of black-and-white photographs of young soldiers, as though they were lined up and ready for royal inspection.

Underneath each photo, there were neat handwritten notes about each man: 'Richard Markham. Parachute Regiment, 1st battalion. 1944.' The uniforms were different from those the Ugandan soldiers wore, thick formal jackets instead of short-sleeved green shirts, but Asha was back there, in those last terrible hours in Uganda. The gun tip tracing her neck, the soldier's eyes watching her every move.

'Hello,' said a plump woman with fleshy arms and a froth of curls, as though someone had taken an eraser and softened all her edges away. Her heels clicked on the parquet floor. 'Come in, welcome, welcome. I'm Mrs Boswell.'

She shook hands, and as she came close, Asha caught the slight scent of cigarette smoke and talcum powder. Five more women stood in line ready to greet them, taking everyone's details, checking them against their clipboards and allocating dormitory numbers.

The new arrivals were shown around the barracks: first, the mess hall, with high ceilings, dark wood panels and long tables set up in rows. The sulphurous smell of boiled vegetables and onions hung heavy in the air.

'Tea's served every night from six o'clock to seven o'clock,' said Mrs Boswell.

'Tea? They only serve chai for dinner?' mumbled one of the men behind Asha in Gujarati.

A younger man translated back into English. 'Excuse me. You only serve tea in the evening? There will be no food?'

'Tea?' Mrs Boswell's look of confusion dissolved into a smile. 'Oh no. What I mean is dinner. We use the word tea for dinner, you see. And we use the word tea for, well, tea. That you drink, with milk. Does that make sense, cherry?'

'So there'll be both tea *and* tea. One to eat and one to drink, no need to worry,' said another of the ladies in the welcome party, pleased that she'd been able to clarify things further.

The young man paused for a moment, deciding the best way to translate it back into Gujarati. 'Yes, there'll be dinner.'

They moved on to the dormitories, where metal beds with blankets were lined up along the long walls. A few were already occupied by those who had arrived on previous flights from Uganda; they stared at the newcomers as they came in.

'Here is one of the women's rooms.' Mrs Boswell paused, waiting for one of the party to translate from English into Gujarati and Hindi.

'We have to sleep with other people in the room? With strangers?' Jaya whispered.

'It's only temporary, Ba,' Asha said.

'We only have space for a few families to stay together, I'm afraid, those with babies and young children. Some of the other barracks have lots of family rooms but we just don't have the space. I'm very sorry.' Mrs Boswell led them out of the room, trying to ignore the murmurs of discontent.

Next, they were taken to the shower and bathroom areas, which were stark but clean. 'There's hot water each morning. I'm afraid we can't keep it on all day.'

'This is like being back at school,' a man behind them huffed.

No, it's like being in the army, Asha thought. But she didn't care. They were safe, they had food and a bed, with no chance of being robbed or worse.

'We've boiled some water over there for tonight, though, so you can have a wash before tea. I mean, dinner,' said Mrs Boswell.

They were too exhausted to eat. Vijay left for his own dormitory down the hallway. Asha helped Jaya, who had wanted to change into her indoor chumpul, the ones she usually wore inside the house. 'I can't wear the same shoes at home that I wear outside,' Jaya said.

'Don't worry about all that here,' said Asha. The floor was a dusty mix of brown English earth and the Ugandan red dirt they'd brought with them. This wasn't a home, so why pretend?

Jaya put the little carved wooden *murti* of Ganesha and a prayer book on a wooden chair that would serve as a bedside table.

Asha went to the bathroom, desperately wanting to scrub all trace of the soldier from her skin, but as soon as she felt the icy flow from the basin tap, she knew it was too cold to stand under a shower. She washed herself as best she could with a cup of the boiled hot water – already tepid – that the welcoming party had provided, then went into a toilet cubicle to change into a *salwar kameez* and cardigan.

Back in the room, Jaya was sitting on her bed, anxiously glancing around her new surroundings. 'Do you need anything?' she asked softly.

Asha shook her head, too tired to speak. In the relative safety of the domitory, she realized how stiff her body had been since they'd left home. Her arms and hips still ached in the places the soldier had grabbed her; her shoulders hunched from the many weeks of worry and stress before the attack. She got into bed and pulled the coarse blanket over her body, tucking her head under the freezing white sheets. She closed her eyes tight, trying to shut out the voices that bounced around the room, the ghosts of Uganda.

Sleep was fitful, flashes of a life abandoned and a strange new country, all tangled together.

20

Jaya

'Ewe Uganda, the land of freedom.'
  A whispered song, soft Swahili.
  'Our love and labour we give.'
  Sounds of home, left behind.
  'And with neighbours all.'
  Grace, always humming. A memory slipping away.

*

Jaya opened her eyes. There was no mosquito net above her, no warm sunlight breaking through curtains. Instead, she woke to the murmured conversations of other women in the room, to the frigid air.

She turned to see where the song had come from. Across the other side of the dormitory, a little girl sat on a chair, swinging her legs and singing the national anthem of Uganda. Her mother, dressed in a blue salwar kameez with embroidered flowers that traced the line of her collar, made the bed.

The exhaustion weighed on Jaya's body. The metal bed frame had squeaked whenever she'd turned in the night; the blanket, barely wide enough for the mattress, had slipped off. She slid out of bed. Despite the little electric heater by the wall that glowed bright orange, her bones were frozen. She scratched a mosquito bite on her shoulder, a furious red reminder of her old home.

In the next bed, Asha was still sleeping, her body sunk into itself, curled up like a child, blanket pulled up to her chin.

Jaya looked around the room. She was used to living with a large family, sharing homes as a child with aunts, uncles, cousins, brothers and in-laws. Even though those around her now were strangers, she found it comforting to be around people. Anything to keep the silence out, the painful thoughts away.

She took her wash bag into the bathroom, where two women were huddled in the corner. The older woman sobbed while the other, perhaps her daughter, slim with long curls of hair draped down her back, spoke in Hindi: 'You're safe now, put it out of your mind.'

'I can't stay here. I want to go back.' The woman wiped her eyes. 'Anything's got to be better than this.'

Jaya considered intervening but what good would it do? What could she say to comfort the woman when Jaya had no idea what lay ahead either? The daughter helped her mother out of the bathroom.

The thought of Pran all on his own came back to her. December's disappearance. No, this wouldn't help. Thinking about them, giving in to all the loss. She would find out whether they could call Pran at home and then get through the day, that was all that mattered.

Jaya braced herself for the challenge of the toilets, which were upright, like the ones at the airport. Used to squatting and hovering over the ground, she found these English toilets too high for her, even though they were the same height as an ordinary chair. Perhaps she could stand on top of them? No, she was twenty years too late to attempt that, and besides, it wouldn't be fair to those who had to put their bottoms on the seat after her. She tugged at the thick green toilet paper that seemed to have the coarse texture of bricks, placed two long pieces of the paper around the sides of the seat and gingerly sat down.

Next, she tackled bathing. Concrete cubicles stood side by side, each with a fixed overhead shower. All her life, she'd filled a metal *dhol* and then used a cup to pour the water over her, the air cooling her damp skin each time she reached for another cupful, a brief and refreshing respite from the heat. After undressing in the cubicle, she turned the tap on the way Mrs Boswell had shown them all; the shower spluttered and icy water shot out over her head. Jaya gasped as she stepped back, pulling down the clean sari that she'd hung up over the door. She rushed to pick it up but half of it was already soaked. Shivering, she waited for the water to heat up, but it stubbornly remained tepid.

She went back to the dormitory to find a clean sari and put on her petticoat. She tightened the cord around her waist – body thinned by grief and worry – and began to say her morning prayers. The little girl Jaya had heard singing early that morning was now talking to her mother on the other side of the barracks dormitory.

'Alia,' the mother called out. '*Aaja*, come, let me plait your hair.'

The girl sat in a little camp she'd set up in the corner of the bedroom, a grey blanket draped over two wooden chairs to make a canopy. She was making funny faces, moving her feathery eyebrows up and down, filling her cheeks with air and then blowing it out in a raspberry. Too young to mourn her home, yet young enough to create a new life in a new country, to let her memories fade away.

When she'd finished getting ready, Jaya went to wake Asha for breakfast.

'Please, leave me to sleep,' she whispered. A purple bruise

and a crooked cut had formed on her cheek where the soldier had hit her.

'You must eat, Asha.'

No answer.

'Is there anything I can do?' she said, but again there was no response.

Vijay came to the dormitory and they agreed it would be best to let Asha sleep a little longer. They queued for the telephone but when they tried to call Pran, the line was disconnected.

'We'll try again later. The lines are in chaos at the moment,' said Vijay, reading the worry on Jaya's face. 'Let's go eat something.'

The mess hall was filled with the smell of cooked meat and toasting bread. The English volunteers waited at the counter with large metal trays of food in front of them.

Vijay explained that the pink, shrivelled food drowning in fat was bacon. Jaya settled for toast, which was set out furthest away from the strange meat. She took a bowl of small crisps that were the colour of chickpeas, deciding they were safe because they looked like one of the ingredients that she usually mixed into chevro, her favourite fried snack.

Jaya sat down opposite Vijay and crunched a little yellow crisp between her teeth. 'There's not enough salt on this,' she said.

'Ba, those are supposed to be eaten with milk,' Vijay said.

Jaya looked down at the bowl. 'Is it not like chevro?'

'No, they're made of corn, Ba. Cornflakes.'

Jaya resolved to stick to the toast.

They spoke about their first night in the barracks, interrupted sleep and lukewarm showers. Vijay seemed to be coping well under the circumstances; at least he hadn't lost his appetite. Like Jaya, he was more worried about Asha.

'We can take her some food later, after she wakes up,' said Vijay.

'Yes, she needs to rest,' said Jaya. 'Not dwell on . . . what's happened.'

Vijay nodded, looking down at his plate. 'I should have done something.'

'Beta, there was nothing you could do.'

'I suppose so,' he said. 'What d'you think happens now?' He sipped his tea.

Jaya looked around the room at the other people, tentatively navigating their way around things they weren't used to: queuing up to eat, picking out unfamiliar foods, sharing their lives with strangers.

'Hopefully they will tell us soon enough,' said Jaya. 'Try to make the most of all this free food while you can, Vijay.'

There was so much to take in: where would they live, how would they earn money? And even the smaller things: what was beyond the barracks walls? Jaya had no idea where they were. How would she start all over again? Her life was like the lines on her hand: new paths, some that faded to nothing, others that were forged hard into her palm. Perhaps it was her destiny never to live one life through to the end, to keep beginning new ones, never belonging anywhere.

Jaya tried to keep her mind off Pran. She told herself they'd get through on the phone later. Across from her, Vijay ate his food as though it was just another Kampala morning, sun streaming through the kitchen window, leaves of the banana trees rustling in the breeze outside. Jaya tried to ignore the unease in her chest. Getting a job was going to be difficult for everyone, but for Vijay, it would be even tougher. She couldn't help but think of those first few moments after his birth in the hospital, the brief silence that fell across the room as the doctor and nurse whispered to each other. Jaya had been too exhausted to take it all in properly, grateful that the baby's lungs were full of air, full of life as he cried. The baby was fine, that was all that mattered.

Later, when she and Motichand had spoken to the doctor, Motichand had skirted around the questions, not daring to meet Jaya's gaze. 'And is there any . . . reason? I mean, why might this have . . . ?'

'No one's quite sure,' said Doctor Shashtri. 'These things happen sometimes,' he said, as though they'd split some milk that needed mopping up.

In those early days, even though Motichand never spoke of it with her again, Jaya worried too, wondering if it had somehow been her fault. Was it something she'd done, had she worked too hard? Should she have done something differently? Yet those concerns soon slipped away, for Jaya and for Motichand, as Vijay's wide eyes gazed up at them, as his tiny fingers wrapped themselves around her finger, clutching on to her, clinging to life as tightly as he could. Jaya's heart brimmed with love instead of worry.

As Vijay grew older, Jaya knew he would face difficulties that others didn't. She heard it in the occasional comments from children – and sometimes adults – in the street, and the times when Vijay came home crying because someone had teased him about his arm. She knew it was up to them to ensure he lived an independent life. Luckily, Vijay was the sort of child who threw himself into living, not wanting to miss out on a second of it, wanting to do everything that Pran did, including the times when Jaya or December had to pull him down from the tree in the yard that he'd climbed just like his older brother. As he reached his teens, Jaya felt certain that Vijay would make his own way in Uganda. But what now?

'Don't think much of these British holiday camps, Ba, do you?' Vijay grinned.

'What? Oh yes,' she said. There was so much to work out, but as he smiled back at her, the only sounds around them the weary chatter and the clinking of plates and cutlery, Jaya was happy to sit with her son in peace for the first time in months.

As they finished their breakfast, Alia came into the mess hall with her parents. The little girl stretched up onto her tip-toes, peeking to see the array of foods set out for service. Her eyes shone as she took in all the new and exciting things on offer. Once she'd taken some kind of chocolatey cereal and milk as well as jam and toast, her mother let her go and sit with some of the other children. Shy for a moment, she soon joined in their conversation.

They went back to the admin office to use the telephone. This time Pran answered, his tone as anxious as her own.

'You made it out safely?' he said.

'Yes, we are all here in England, beta.' She blotted her tears with her handkerchief.

'And Asha, can I speak to her?' His voice was so full of hope Jaya could hardly speak. Now wasn't the time to tell him about his wife's ordeal.

'She's fine, she's sleeping now. Your brother is well too,' she said, trying to change the subject.

'We're all OK, don't worry.' Vijay moved towards the receiver and called out.

But with the poor line and the high cost, they couldn't talk for long. Jaya hurriedly gave Pran the camp address and wished him a safe journey to India. Then he was gone.

A wave of fatigue hit her and when Vijay suggested that they should go back to bed and rest, she agreed. She put a plate of buttered toast next to Asha's bed, then pulled her own covers over her head, praying that God would take care of her son.

*

As the days passed, more weary new arrivals joined them at the barracks. Jaya wanted to comfort them and help them settle in, but it meant enduring their stories, whispered in the dormitories and mess hall, of desperate, scavenging soldiers, wise to all the money-hiding tricks, who knew that their haul of Asian treasure would soon come to an end as the expulsion deadline approached. She heard the tales of those who'd left it late to buy tickets, spurred on by sheer optimism that Amin Dada might yet change his mind as he had about so many other of his decisions. They'd faced a scramble for the last overcrowded flights out of the country, in the last days and hours before the deadline.

Yet there were others, those who'd arrived well before Jaya, who were already refusing to talk about Uganda, turning away, going silent at the mere mention of the curfews, the army, the looting, as though they'd never been there at all.

She wanted to forget too, but she had to know everything that was going on in Uganda. Pran should have left the country by now, yet she caught hold of every bit of news, in case it provided a clue to her son's journey out. They couldn't be sure how long it would take for the Indian authorities to process Pran as a refugee or give him permission to stay with Jaya's brother, but right now all she cared about was that he'd made it out safely.

Jaya crouched by Asha's bed. 'Why don't you get up now? Eat something.' Days of this, watching her picking at the food that Jaya brought her and then closing her eyes again.

'I'm fine here.' Asha stirred, pulling the cover back over her head. 'I'll eat later.'

'Later never comes, though. Please eat something.'

Asha shook her head.

'I know this is hard, Asha,' Jaya whispered. 'All of it. But please, eat something. We need to get ourselves out of here and to do that, you need to get your strength back.'

'I don't want to stay here.' Asha's voice was strained, as though it took all her effort to talk.

'But we can't go back.'

'That's just it.' Asha lifted her head briefly, looking at her. 'I don't want to go back; I don't want to stay here either. Wherever I am, there's pain.'

Jaya patted her arm. 'You cannot escape your mind.' Jaya knew that all too well. She wished she could take away Asha's hurt, take all their pain away. 'But you'll feel better if you try to focus on something else.'

'Please, just go.'

'I know it is difficult, but you have to focus on the future, not dwell—'

Asha turned fast towards Jaya. 'I'm not dwelling! I'm exhausted.'

'I'm sorry. But that's because you won't look after yourself. We need to stick together now. For me, for Vijay, for Pran, if nothing else, please eat something.'

No answer. Eyes closed.

'Asha, think of Pran. We need to start rebuilding our lives and then he can join us. Don't you want that?' Still no response. Why was there was always so much to deal with? They'd never be free, always struggling, the ghosts of their old life haunting them forever. Jaya moved closer, putting her hand upon the rough blanket. 'You can't let Idi Amin win,' she said, kindly. 'I didn't think you'd let him win.'

Asha remained still, rolled up in a ball, face pale.

Jaya left the room and went to join Vijay in the mess hall.

'No Asha?' he asked.

Jaya shook her head, once again, and ate her lunch: a jacket potato with butter and lots of black pepper. She played cards with some of the other ladies, her mind still on Asha. Perhaps she'd been too harsh, but she'd hoped that giving her daughter-in-law other things to focus on might help. Jaya needed her to be strong, for her sake as much as anything. She couldn't do it alone.

Later, Jaya stopped by the dormitory doorway. In the corner, Asha's bed was made, the plate empty, her bedclothes neatly folded away.

21

Vijay

'Of course, we know you have all been through quite an ordeal.' Mr Hutchinson's eyes darted around the mess hall, looking everywhere except at the people in front of him.

Vijay sat with the others, watching the barracks' head administrator address the room. Mrs Boswell and the other volunteers looked on. Outside, the sky was a startling blue – as bright as any afternoon in Uganda – striped with feathery white aeroplane trails.

'But it is best to look forward,' said Mr Hutchinson, now turning his attention to the double doors. 'With that in mind, we would like to give you some information so you can leave as soon—'

Mrs Boswell coughed.

'That is,' Mr Hutchinson continued, tugging at his blue tie, 'information on how you can move on from the barracks and quickly settle into your own homes. There will be new jobs posted on the noticeboard outside. We'll also have copies of the local newspapers so you can look for opportunities there. And I am sure there will be something for you, as long as you are willing to work hard. There is a wide variety of work to match the skills and education of people like yourselves.' Mr Hutchinson's eyes moved to the light fitting. 'We've also arranged a trip to the jobcentre on Tuesday. And a representative from the local council will join us later to explain the process for applying for a council house and welfare benefits for the infirm. For those of you who have the means, you may want to consider private rental. Please do speak to Mrs Boswell if you have any questions. And until the English lessons begin, I hope that those of you who can translate what I have just said into your various dialects will do so privately.'

Just as Vijay was sure the speech was about to end, Mr Hutchinson continued, gaze flitting to the far window. 'The main thing is that you've gone through a lot but you'll all come out the other side.'

'Like shit?' muttered a teenager behind Vijay in Hindi. Sniggers spread along the back of the room as Mr Hutchinson left.

'All this help they're giving us,' said Ramniklal, the little black hairs in his nose quivering like spider legs as he spoke. He and his sons had owned a dukan in Mbarara. While he and his wife Hiraben had made it to England, his family were now scattered across the world, in India, the United States and Canada.

'Yes, all this help for, how did he describe it?' Asha switched from Gujarati to the taut English vowels Mr Hutchinson used, 'People like yourselves.'

'Forget him, we'll be out of here soon,' said Vijay.

Asha leant forward. 'But in the meantime, we have to put up with him behaving like we're beneath him? We had jobs and homes, just like him.'

Vijay had to admit she had a point. He watched her as she spoke. He'd felt the guilt well in his stomach every time he thought back to the army at the roadside. If only he'd been able to stop the soldier. He was pleased that she was up and about again; these past few days she'd been so unlike the Asha he knew. Today, she wore no make-up, a plain mustard polo neck and denim bell-bottoms. She was as beautiful as ever.

'No, he shouldn't behave that way. But his life is not like ours,' said Jaya. 'He has never had to worry about soldiers coming to his house or people around him disappearing.'

'Well, let's just forget Mr Hutchinson and focus on getting out of here,' said Vijay, standing up. He couldn't help but wonder about Pran. What was he doing, had he made it out safely? He pushed the worries to the back of his mind.

He walked out into the hallway and surveyed the noticeboard, alongside others. He hadn't expected anything particularly exciting; those who'd been at the barracks a while had warned him that the jobs were basic. People who'd once managed hundreds in Ugandan factories and plantations were now themselves looking at jobs packing in factories. Others who had degrees in medicine or law were in the same position; their qualifications meant little in England. But there might at least be some jobs working in shops, anything to get away from the same four walls of the barracks, cooped up all day with little to do and no money of their own. There was only so much poker and snap any man could take.

'These jobs are all local.' Ramniklal came and stood next to Vijay. 'And the problem is, if you get a job around here, you'll be stuck around here.'

Asha flicked a curl away from her eyebrow. 'Perhaps we should find jobs closer to London?'

Vijay looked at her. 'Right now, I'd just be happy with any job, anywhere.'

＊

One evening after dinner, Mrs Boswell asked everyone to remain seated at the tables in the mess hall. Vijay took a seat next to Jaya. Asha sat with Ramniklal and Hiraben.

Mrs Boswell set up a cardboard box at the front and handed out pieces of paper with grids of random numbers on them.

'Now, I thought this evening we could play bingo!' she said, clapping her hands together. 'Here's some pens. But I'll need them back, Mr Hutchinson will go spare if I don't keep a hold of them.'

As they sat and waited for the game to start, Jaya's friend Madhuben, who'd been at the centre for over a month, told them about the letter she'd received from her brother. The British government used their lists of refugee names and locations to ensure post reached them. 'They made it to Canada,' she said, clutching the folded blue letter in her hand. 'He said it's freezing, snow everywhere, they can't go outside for more than a few minutes even with coats on or their hands and toes go numb. But he got out, they all did.' She brought the letter to her chest. After a pause she turned to Jaya. 'I'm sorry, I'm sure you'll hear from your son soon too, Jayaben.'

Jaya patted Madhuben's hand and gave her a weary smile. Vijay took in the now familiar sight of his Ba blinking back tears.

'It's probably too early,' said Vijay. It could take weeks for a letter to arrive from India. 'And then there's the post; there's so much coming into England at this time of year. I'm sure a letter will be on its way soon.' Right now, it was the only hope they could cling to.

Jaya looked at him with gratitude, tugging at the neck of her cream cardigan as she listened to Madhuben going on about her family.

Vijay looked over to the table of girls, all in their late teens and early twenties, chatting amongst themselves. He thought of his nights trying to meet girls in Kampala with John. He missed his friend, wondered if he was safe, hoped he was living in peace. It wasn't the same here, of course, but he'd flirted with one or two of the girls when their parents weren't looking and made friends with a group of rowdy boys who sat at a nearby table. Usually, he'd have joined them, but today something told him he should stay close to Jaya.

Mrs Boswell explained that to win the game, you had to match the numbers as they were called out. She told them that many also had rhymes or nicknames linked to them. 'So number 88 is two fat ladies,' she said, looking around the room.

'Two fat ladies doesn't rhyme with 88,' said a boy with a topknot wrapped in white cotton.

'No, but it looks like, well, they look like ladies, you see.' She swirled 88 onto the back of some paper and showed it to them all. The boy looked confused but the elder Sikh gentleman in the seat next to him gave a knowing smile; the feminine form obvious. 'It'll all make sense once we get on with it,' said Mrs Boswell.

'But not everyone speaks English, Mrs Boswell,' said the boy with the topknot.

'I thought that those that do could translate. How's that sound?'

'Translate the rhymes as well? That will take some time,' called out someone at the back of the room.

'Well, no, just the numbers if you want. Anyway, it'll still be fun, you'll see.' She held her pink lipstick smile, though her voice tightened. 'Let's just get started, shall we?'

She started to call out the numbers, but by the time they were translated into Gujarati, Hindi and Punjabi, depending on who was at each table, the point of the game – to find numbers as quickly as possible on your piece of paper – was lost.

'There'll be a winner soon, I'm sure of it,' Mrs Boswell called out, as brightly as she could manage.

Vijay watched his mother, her shoulders relaxed as she swiftly found the numbers. For once, she was enjoying herself, instead of worrying and fretting about everyone.

After a few more numbers, a woman with her hair in a tight

bun waddled shyly up to Mrs Boswell with her completed pages.

'Bingo!' Mrs Boswell called out on the woman's behalf. 'Well done, Mrs Patel. Oh, wait, you've gone onto your third page.' Mrs Patel hadn't realized that you were supposed to shout out 'Bingo!' when the page was complete; rather than fill out as many pages as possible.

They carried on and played another two disjointed rounds before Ramniklal wrested control, persuading Mrs Boswell that it made more sense for him to call out the numbers in Gujarati and Hindi, as these were the languages spoken by the vast majority of people in the room. Soon he'd created his own names for the numbers instead: '22, two flamingos,' he shouted out. 'Number 3. *Trun Jun*' – three people. Eventually the group spent more time coming up with the names than marking the papers. Mrs Boswell wandered off, presumably to make herself a strong cup of tea and have a smoke.

*

Vijay and Asha piled off the coach with others from the barracks and went into the jobcentre. There were rows of felt-covered boards with little handwritten cards pinned to them and, at the far end, a line of desks occupied by men in grey suits. A few people turned around to stare at the new arrivals. A whole coachload of Asians arriving at once wasn't exactly easy to miss.

'Right, have a look around at the boards, but you're best off getting in the queue quickly, as it'll be a while before you're seen,' said Mrs Troughton, one of the volunteers from the barracks.

'I'll get in the queue,' said Vijay, smiling at Asha. 'Why don't you have a look around? Remember, boss of a record company for me, it's that or nothing. Thanks.'

'Yes, sir, of course, sir,' Asha said in a mocking tone.

Vijay watched the two men at the front of the queue. At the desk, a younger man with blond hair was sitting talking to a middle-aged man with a bald head and thick-framed glasses, as if they were in some kind of competition to see who could look more bored.

'Still waiting?' Asha came and stood next to him. 'Can't trust you with anything.'

'Found me a job that pays at least a million a year, I hope?' said Vijay.

'There was a job as a comedian but I don't think you're qualified,' she said, raising a brow. 'There's a couple of things at a nearby factory, and a job at a solicitor's firm. Some kind of clerk's job you might like?' Asha gave him the cards.

'I'll be sure to ask the friendly assistant.' He looked back over at the adviser at the desk, who was now readjusting his zigzag tie while he waited for the next person in line to sit down. 'What about you?' Vijay said.

Asha told him there were a couple of things she was interested in too, secretarial jobs similar to the work she'd done in Jinja before she'd got married. They compared roles but Vijay trailed off as he overheard two young men by the job boards, chatting and staring at some of the older Asian men nearby. Asha followed Vijay's gaze.

'They said, didn't they, Rob, they'd be over here taking our jobs,' laughed the first man, with a broad accent that Vijay didn't recognize. His glasses flashed in the light.

'And now here they are, literally taking our jobs from under our noses,' said the second. He had a haze of thin fair hair.

They laughed and shook their heads.

Asha glared. 'What's the matter with these people?' She started to head towards the two men.

'Wait, Asha,' said Vijay.

Her voice hardened in anger. 'Who do they think they are? We were part of their Great Britain until a few years ago. It's not our fault we've lost everything.'

What was the point in confronting them? He remembered December's words about people with little hope. It wasn't so different now, people would look for others to blame when they felt that choices were taken from them. 'Forget them, we need to make a good impression here,' said Vijay gently. 'Anyway, I think there's some jobs going at the boxing gym. The sign said they needed punchbags. Those two would be perfect.'

Asha's lips curled into a smile.

After a few more minutes' waiting, Vijay sat down at the desk with the middle-aged man.

'So, have you reviewed the positions on offer?' The man at the desk was too busy lighting a Camel cigarette to look up.

'There's a clerk's job.'

The adviser sucked on the cigarette and peered at him, eyes landing on Vijay's left arm. 'A clerk?'

Vijay handed over the card.

'You really think you'd be suitable?' The man blinked heavily, as though he was trying to catch flies between his lashes.

'Well, I've got my O levels and I dealt with customers back in Uganda.'

'Yes, but what about that?' The man frowned, staring at his arm.

Vijay wouldn't rise to the bait. 'What, this?'

'Look, Mr—'

'Vijay. You can call me Vijay.'

'Look Veejay, I'm not sure what things were like in Africa but there's enough demand for jobs as it is.'

'I'm willing to work. I'll do whatever it takes.' Vijay's voice was firm.

The man stubbed his cigarette out in a red ashtray. 'I'm not sure we have any job that would be suitable.'

'I helped run the family business back in Uganda.'

'Well, families have to look after their own, don't they?'

Vijay stared at him, anger coursing through him now. He just wanted a chance, couldn't the man see that?

The man started rummaging around in his desk for something. 'There might be some monetary assistance available, but you've not been in the country long, so . . . Here's some literature, have a look through that. You're staying at the barracks, aren't you? They'll also be able to advise on welfare benefits for people like you. Now if you'll excuse me.' The adviser was already looking past Vijay to the next person in line.

Vijay got up and waited for Asha.

'How did it go?' Vijay asked as she walked over to him clutching a wad of papers.

'Not bad.' She showed him an application form. 'How about you?'

Vijay looked at her, unsure how to answer.

'What about the clerk's job?' she said.

'He said it wasn't suitable for me,' he said quietly.

'Why not?' Asha frowned. 'What's the—' She stopped, looking over at the man then back at Vijay, eyes travelling down to his left arm.

'Shall we get back on the coach?' he said. No point standing around in a place he wasn't wanted.

'Oh, Vijay. I'm sorry. There'll be other jobs,' she sighed, glaring at the man. 'Don't listen to idiots like him.'

'Let's just get out of here.' Vijay hurried past the walls of jobs and out into the cold air.

22
Jaya

Jaya looked down at the blue airmail letter. On the front, English words she couldn't understand. It didn't matter, she recognized the lines and curls of the writing. Looking across to the row of stamps in the corner, tiny illustrated people waving the Indian flag, she put on her reading glasses and walked across the dormitory.

'Wake up,' she said, turning towards Asha's bed.

'What is it?' Asha sat up. 'Is it from Pran?'

'It's my brother's writing.' Jaya opened the letter carefully with a butter knife that she'd snuck out from the mess hall, not wanting to tear a single word inside.

'What does it say?' Asha came over to her.

Jaya finished reading and scrunched the letter in her hand.

'What's happened?'

'They've not heard from him.' Jaya shook her head. 'They don't know where he is.'

'But it's been weeks. No, it's not possible, let me see.' Asha scanned the neat Gujarati script inside. 'Maybe the Indian government have detained him? It's probably something to do with paperwork. He can't still be in Uganda. It's past the expulsion deadline.'

Jaya looked up at her, the letter rustling in her hand. 'Of

course he could still be in Uganda, just like December.' Bitterness seeped into Jaya's words. Uganda still hung over them.

'Don't think like that, please.' Asha placed her hand on Jaya's arm.

'He might have been taken to those camps they talked about.' Jaya thought back. Idi Amin had warned them all that if anyone dared to stay behind, they'd be rounded up and forced to live in internment camps under army rule. He never said what would happen next.

Asha stared at her. 'Pran got out. He must have. It was chaos back there. But he's safe. He has to be.'

*

Everyone was getting tired of their surroundings, even Alia, the little girl in the dormitory. Jaya watched her complaining to her mother one lunchtime in the mess hall. Even though Alia attended classes each morning with the new friends she'd made, she wanted her old bed, and to play out in the sunshine with those she'd left behind. 'Where are they?' she demanded. Arm stretched out, Alia curled her body onto her mother's lap with the grace of a dancer. Why was everything so different, why couldn't they could go home?

'Look.' Her mother pointed out of the window at the sky. 'Not everything's different. Look at the *akash*, that's still blue, just like Jinja, remember?'

Alia raised her head for a moment, then flopped back down again. The mother stroked the girl's hair but there was little she could say to comfort her daughter. After all, nothing would bring back the home they'd lost.

'We are going to stay with a Mr and Mrs Thompson of Bedfordshire,' said Ramniklal, taking a fat chip between his fingers and inspecting it. 'They have a room for us. And they even have a garden. We'll leave in a couple of weeks and stay until we can get back on our feet, that's what they called it in the letter.'

Jaya found it perplexing. Ordinary British people were giving up rooms in their own homes to ease the burden on the barracks and help families settle across the country. 'The Europeans', as the Asians had called them, those who had tended to keep a polite distance in Uganda, were now opening up their homes to them.

'I can't believe they'll send you to live with English people,' said Madhuben. She'd left behind a fleet of cars, a sugar plantation, and a vast house, which Jaya felt she knew intimately, from the pristine lawns to the marble floors, because Madhuben never stopped going on about them.

'They don't know our customs or our ways.' Madhuben shook her head. Her grey-brown eyes appeared faded, as though the weeks of tears had drained them of colour. 'And what if they serve us beef?'

'Or pork,' said Mrs Khan, who'd left behind a small-town dukan near the Ugandan border. 'Idi Amin still haunts us, even now. Here we are freezing away, worrying about what we'll be given to eat by strangers, and he's lazing about over there with that army of his.'

What would Jaya give to have Pran here, freezing along with them right now? She kept him close in her heart and her prayers, but she had to focus on getting the rest of them out of the barracks.

Asha's voice was curt. 'I'm sure if you ask politely they'll not serve it while you're there.' She paused, her tone mellowing as she said, 'They're taking complete strangers from another country into their homes. How many of us would have done that?'

The silence said it all.

'Anyway, if I were you,' Mrs Khan took a spoonful of baked

beans and looked at them disdainfully as they slopped back into her plate, 'I would be more worried about them serving you these.'

'Yes, the food is certainly . . . different,' said Ramniklal, smiling. He had cheerful eyes, eyebrows slanting upwards in the middle, as if trying to greet each other. He also had an unfortunate habit of speaking with his mouth full, and although he covered it when he spoke, tiny bits of spittle broke away and made their escape, landing on the table in a final dash for glory.

Food at the camp was a minefield: the beef that was served with large mounds of baked dough put off the Hindus and Jains, and the pork sausages served with mushy potato put off the Muslims (as well as the vegetarian Hindus and all of the Jains).

'At least we can use the kitchen a little,' said Jaya, taking a chip, which she'd done her best to liven up with salt and plenty of pepper.

They'd persuaded Mr Hutchinson to let them use the kitchen now and then, headed up by Kamlaben, who had catered every wedding and festival in the Mbarara area, cooking huge quantities of food in huge *sufarya*, the steel pots hand beaten in the local market. They commandeered a section of the kitchen to make vegetable shaak and rotli.

Asha had made friends with Jack, who travelled up from Wembley every couple of weeks. He wore a navy turban and had changed his name from Jaswinder because it was easier for people he met at the pub to pronounce. Jack was hazy about how long he'd been in England but the melody of his Punjabi mother tongue was tinged with the broad vowels of a born Londoner: 'I'll get you anythin' you need.' Jack sold them the fried snacks they'd taken for granted in Uganda, along with all manner of illicit spices, traces of cumin and cardamom contraband drifting through the air despite being packed away in plastic bags.

'Yes, but they still expect us to clean our own toilets. *Chi!*' Madhuben pursed her lips.

'Of course they expect us to clean our own toilets,' said Asha. 'Anyway, we've spent far too long letting other people decide our lives already.'

Jaya watched her. Despite the dark shadows around Asha's eyes, they sparkled again with life. And with no word from Pran, that was more important than ever.

23

Asha

Raindrops ran in rivers down the windowpanes, and a grey haze settled across the mess hall. Asha looked along the metal trays of free food. Of course she was grateful, but what she would have given to eat *thepla*, to tear off the warm flatbread with swirls of fenugreek and dip each piece into a little butter.

Jaya joined her in the queue and picked up a cheese and tomato sandwich, one of the few foods she was happy to eat (though she took out the slabs of cheese, complaining that they tasted like soured milk).

'What time do you think Vijay will be back?' Jaya asked. He'd gone with some of his friends from the barracks to look around the local shops but she wasn't keen on him going out alone. There'd been stories about some of the young men being harassed and called names. Perhaps it would be better when they moved to London. They'd started making plans to move out of the camp, but they needed to save up some money first.

'He didn't say, but there's a group of them, he'll be fine.' After months of rushing home for curfew, was it any wonder he wasn't in a hurry to rush back now? Asha was spending more time than ever before with Jaya, but she didn't mind, not with her own family so far away in India, sporadic letters her only connection to them.

'As long as he doesn't forget about getting a job.'

Asha didn't have the heart to tell Jaya how her son had been treated at the jobcentre. She didn't want to dampen her hopes yet again.

'Both my children are giving me too much cause to worry.' Jaya tried to make light of it, but she couldn't hide the concern in her voice. 'But perhaps we will hear from Pran this week,' she said, so quietly that Asha had to move closer to hear her.

What could Asha say? It had been two weeks since Jaya's brother's letter. They'd have heard by now if for some reason the Indian government had detained him. Panic gripped her once again as she remembered the haunted look in Naseem's eyes while he threw his money into the fire, the empty storeroom after December disappeared. Pran must have made it to India, he must have. She wouldn't let herself think about the alternatives.

They moved to the front of the queue, putting food on their plates as they went. As Asha waited for Jaya to pour some water, she overheard a group of three women talking in hushed voices at a nearby table. Snippets of chatter carried across the mess hall bustle: 'nasty soldiers', 'she might not be able to marry'.

Asha glanced over to Jaya, who was engaged in conversation with an elderly gentleman.

One of the women at the table, who wore a green salwar kameez with a cardigan buttoned over the top, carried on talking. 'And then they dragged her away, two soldiers, her father screaming.' She shook her head. 'But there was nothing he could do.'

Nothing he could do. The girl who'd been taken by the soldier could do nothing either, but it was the men they focused on: the soldiers who attacked her, the father left behind. A silent space for the girl, except for how it related to her 'ruined honour'.

'They've wrecked her life,' said the woman opposite her.

Asha put down her plate at the women's table, her hands flat against the wood. She looked each of them in the eye. 'All you can think about is how these women are tainted? That's the worst part of all of this? Not what happened to them?'

'That's not—' The woman in the green salwar began to speak, but her voice faded. Her gaze darted across the room. Everyone was staring.

'Asha,' Jaya called gently.

'Gossiping like this?' said Asha, thinking of the soldier's hand on her. Thinking of Grace and the fury in her eyes when she guessed they'd all been talking about her at Mrs Goswami's house. They'd never be free of the memories. A wound that never heals.

The women bowed their heads down at their plates. Was this how people thought about her?

'Asha,' Jaya said again, coming over and taking her arm. 'Come.'

She stayed where she was, staring at the women. She wouldn't move until they'd looked her in the eye.

Jaya led her to another table in silence. It would never leave her, Asha thought, the attack, haunting her. The thoughts and comments of others, following her like spectres wherever she went.

Asha and Jaya sat down, staring at the plates of food as they grew cold in front of them.

*

The next morning, Asha joined Jaya and Vijay on a large blanket on the mess hall floor. The bright blue sky and the crisp sunlight that filled the room still surprised her, playing tricks on her, making her think it was warm enough out there to go outside in a cotton blouse and skirt.

Jaya and a few of the others from the barracks had set up a makeshift temple in the mess hall after breakfast. They'd draped a table with a *bandhani* sari; intricate tie-dyed yellow dots swirled across the red cotton. On top, there was a collection of metal and wooden-carved deities that they'd managed to cobble together between them.

Asha marvelled at the way Jaya had coped. Every day, she was up by seven o'clock, braving the chilly mornings to get ready and say her prayers. She'd got to know the other women in the dormitories, their names, where they used to live, what kinds of business their families had left behind. Jaya still talked about her old life, but she focused on the good memories: the trips to temple, the funny things Mrs Goswami used to say, family outings to Entebbe. It was almost as though she was trying to rewrite their history and pretend that the bad things had never happened, that the life she'd enjoyed for many years was perfectly preserved, untainted by the horror.

Asha tried not to look back; she needed to make new memories as quickly as possible. Bury the old ones forever, hoping that the noise around her, the cacophony of languages, the daily sounds of life, could drown out the past.

Once everyone was settled, one of the men began the prayer songs. Asha joined in, as she always did. She'd been brought up on trips to the temple every Sunday morning, not to mention for festivals and weddings. There were even trips to the gurudwara during Vaisakhi and congregations outside the mosque during Eid. Like everyone she knew, Asha had been wrapped up in this medley of religion all her life: a part of her as familiar as the magnolia trees in her family home or the sound of the street sellers hawking their wares. But had she really thought about the reasons for all the rituals? She'd gone along with the rules, never questioning any of it. Your deeds came back to you, that's what she'd been taught. But then, if that was true, after everything that had happened, why wasn't Idi Amin's body bobbing in the Nile along with those of his victims?

Jaya, on the other hand, held onto her faith as tightly as she clung to her *mara*. There was certainty in her prayer beads, never faltering. Each morning in the barracks dormitory, Jaya lit *agarbatti*, despite the fact that Mr Hutchinson had told them all that lighting matches or candles was forbidden. Even Jaya could rebel when it suited her.

And then there was Vijay, like so many men Asha knew, dutifully attending temple as often as necessary, sitting peacefully and praying, eyes shut tight. What did Vijay really think? Their religion told them that misdeeds in your past lives led to hardship in the present one. No one said it out loud, but it could only mean that they believed that Vijay's arm was a kind of punishment.

Asha took in the rhythmic chanting of temple hymns, the chime of the finger cymbals: a comfort, a constant. But as she said the words, whispering the prayers her mother had taught her when Asha could barely write her own name, it was the sound, the familiar beat, the memory of saying them hundreds of times that she clung to. The words themselves had lost their meaning.

When the group stopped, in the quiet moment for silent prayers, she could no longer fight the thoughts, couldn't fight the reminder of the army barracks, forcing her mind back to those last days in Uganda. She thought of Pran, trying to conjure his smiling face, the small hollow of his dimples beneath her fingers, but all she saw was that dull look in his eyes the night that December had disappeared. How he'd stood there, frozen, while Vijay lay on the floor of the kitchen. Shock, fear perhaps? Pran, the one who usually took charge.

She kept her eyes shut tight, grasping for another memory of her husband, the musky yet sweet scent of him. But all that came to her was the image of the soldier. Fingernails digging into her arms. Her thoughts of Pran, tainted.

24

Jaya

Outside the barracks, frost coated the blades of grass and the pearly-white leaves shivered in the wind. Inside, ice crystals had gathered along the window frames and pockets of cold air lingered in corners where the electric heaters couldn't reach. Jaya wrapped herself in her thickest saal and joined Vijay in the hallway, following the other residents to the mess hall.

Mrs Boswell stood at the entrance to the dining area, pink cheeks glowing. She opened the doors to the hall, calling out a cheerful greeting that Jaya didn't understand.

Every possible surface, tables, walls, even the ceiling, was covered in red, green and gold. Glossy leaves and red berries, paper and foil garlands looped across the walls, although one garland that had intricate shapes cut into it was now lying piti-fully on the floor. Mrs Boswell picked it up, expanding it out like an accordion and hammering the end back onto the wall with her fist.

'This reminds me of Saila's wedding,' muttered Jaya, look-ing around.

'But with worse singing,' Vijay grinned.

'What is all this?' Jaya pulled out a hankie from the cuff of her cardigan and blew her nose.

'It's Christmas, do you remember?' Vijay helped himself to

some dark cake with white icing, the clove and cinnamon scent reminding her of her own childhood sweets.

Jaya nodded, recalling the days off that December took each year, along with some of the other neighbourhood workers, to visit family or attend church. Her throat burned at the memory of him. She blinked back her tears. 'But we're not Christian?'

'No, but Mrs Boswell said she thought it would be nice for us to celebrate with them, the way we included them in ours.' A sultana fell to the floor as he took another bite of the cake.

Jaya looked around and now recognized the fairy lights draped across a window, and the red candles that had been lined up on one of the tables that Mrs Boswell had put out in November so that they could celebrate Divari.

The barracks volunteers stood in a line, proudly singing songs from paper booklets. She wondered what they sang about. Like the temple songs, some of the music was gentle, almost melancholy, while others were jolly and upbeat. The younger children, faces lit up with glee, chattered around the dark-green tree in the corner, wooden decorations hanging from its branches, presents sparkling underneath.

Asha rushed into the mess hall, stuffing an airmail letter into Jaya's hands. She looked down, her eyes filling with tears as she took in the words, the handwriting.

Pran's handwriting.

They hurried out into the hallway. 'You didn't open it?' said Vijay.

'I wanted to wait until we were together,' Asha said. And delay the bad news? Jaya wondered.

'At least it shows he's OK.' Vijay ran his hand through his hair. 'I mean, he wrote the letter.'

The hope in his voice made Jaya hopeful too. She looked over at Asha, whose face was pale.

Jaya stared at the patchy charcoal postmark in the corner,

something she didn't recognize, definitely not India. She opened the letter, heart soaring at the sight of the familiar neat loops and lines of Pran's handwriting.

'I've left my reading glasses in the room,' said Jaya, the words blurry in front of her.

Asha took the letter from her.

Jaya struggled to breathe, as though the air had suddenly thinned. She watched Asha's eyes move from left to right.

'He's in Austria,' said Asha.

'What's he doing there?' Vijay took the letter from Asha.

That didn't make sense. Why wasn't Pran in India? Jaya put her hand on Vijay's arm. 'What does it say?'

'The Red Cross helped him to get out, he's in one of the transit camps there.'

'Why, he was safe with my family in India?' said Jaya. A maze of questions, none of them leading to answers.

Asha shook her head. 'It doesn't say why, maybe he wanted to be careful about what he wrote in the letter? But he's a stateless refugee. There was always a chance India wouldn't take him either.'

'So he'll have to get to England somehow?' Vijay reread the letter as though it would reveal something new.

'I don't know,' said Asha. 'They won't let him come here. Even if he could afford the airfare to England.'

'He must have hidden some money,' said Jaya. 'He must have got some out of the country?'

Asha caught Vijay's eye, but he looked away.

'He's not hurt, is he?' said Jaya.

'He doesn't say much, just wanted to tell us he was safe. He got out, that's the main thing.' Vijay's words were a ribbon of hope, as he leant back against the hallway wall to let a couple of people pass. He was too young to understand, thought Jaya.

Pran was alone with little money. He didn't speak German. What would he do now?

'He hasn't given an address where we can contact him,' said Asha, scanning the letter again.

Jaya put her hand to her mouth. After all this time, every second of silence, she couldn't stand waiting to hear from him again.

'I'm sure he'll write soon.' Asha briefly rested her hand on Jaya's arm. 'He was able to write to your brother and get the barracks' address, wasn't he?'

She stared at the letter in Asha's hands. There was nothing to do but wait.

25

Jaya

Jaya walked past Arnos Grove Underground station, taking in the circular facade, the strange flat roof. Why anyone would build something that looked like one of the spaceships from Vijay's childhood comic books was beyond her. Though she'd passed by it for weeks since they'd moved out of barracks, she still couldn't get used to it. At the bus stop, a man with long hair waited, his neck covered in flowery writing: a tattoo, though it looked as if someone had decided to write their shopping list on him instead of finding a piece of paper.

Jaya waited to cross the street, the hem of her sari gathered at the top of her lace-up shoes. The glowing green man told her to walk across the road, but as usual she panicked as the symbol started to flash, skip-jogging the rest of the way to make it across before the red man appeared.

Inside the shop, she wandered around looking at the tomatoes, giving them a sly squeeze for ripeness when Mr Johnson the grocer wasn't looking. The handwritten prices on the signs above the fruit and vegetables were just about decipherable: some of the corners and lines of English numbers were similar enough to the loops and slants of Gujarati, and she'd been taught the rest by Asha and Vijay. But like a tourist, she found herself converting the money back to Ugandan shillings. Jaya picked up the other goods she needed, having memorized the cobalt blue and bright orange of the washing powder; the familiar teal of the tins of beans; the red, yellow and green cockerel on Vijay's breakfast cereal. She had to look around and above and below the letters to understand this new world, looking at the pictures, colours and shapes as though she was a child again. It made her think of Gayuri, her friend in her parents' village, who'd taught her to read when she was a little girl.

Gayuri was usually busy, helping her forever-pregnant mother until she was ready to have the latest baby. Gayuri could be found wandering the narrow lanes of the village, bony hip jutting out to hold the weight of a young sibling, while she shouted at her younger brothers to behave.

And yet, even with all the new children in her family, she was able to go to school for three years longer than Jaya. Gayuri's father was a successful farmer who had money for educating his ever-growing brood – even the girls – while the younger children were looked after by the large extended family.

Jaya filled the hours until Gayuri's return by doing her daily chores. Sometimes she spent time grinding and pounding the millet, using the stone *ghunt*, which Jaya thought the perfect name, just like the sound it made, heavy and tough. Other times she helped her family harvest the millet, placing her feet flat on the ground, leaning back and pulling the ragged yellow pokers out. Some of the other girls used their feet to kick off the earth but Jaya liked the feel of it in her fingers, shaking off the soil, revealing the twisted roots beneath. Day after day she worked, as the sun burned across the sky and the skin on her hands and feet grew rough.

The best part of her day was when she sat down with Gayuri, who taught Jaya how to read the letters of the Gujarati alphabet, '*Kuh Khuh Ghuh*'.

A few years later, a stranger came from the village across

the river to meet her father. Jaya had sneaked into the court-yard with her younger brothers, listening to their conversation from outside the window.

'She's strong, works hard,' her father told the stranger. 'And she can read and write.'

'We have no need for that,' said the stranger.

But it didn't matter. Jaya had a need for it, even after she was married. Through those stolen moments with Gayuri, Jaya had learnt to do something that, for the first time in her life, was hers alone.

When had she become someone so different from the girl she'd once been in a tiny village in India? Someone who had crossed seas and oceans and now found herself in a corner of London. A lifetime away.

She handed over the money to Mr Johnson, a smile her only means of conversation. Even though she'd had to learn Swahili from scratch when she'd arrived in Uganda, her mind couldn't absorb English as quickly, her tongue wouldn't fold itself into the sounds she needed. Forcing English words into her head was far more difficult, as though there were too many other words crammed in there already. She tried to form simple sentences but couldn't find the right words; instead, her mind pulled out a jumbled mass of the Swahili, Gujarati and Hindi words she already knew. Vijay had taught her some phrases: 'One adult to Stanmore, please,' 'thank you,' and 'I'm sorry, I do not speak English,' but she'd learnt them without fully understanding the meaning of each word, and so remained without the ability to express her own thoughts and feelings in this strange new language. She knew she sounded like a child: broken sentences, fractured vowels.

She envied Asha, going out to work, talking to Mrs Houghton who lived next door, moving with ease in their new world. Jaya had to make do with a series of polite smiles and nods, standing back while the women chatted about . . . well, she was never quite sure exactly what they were talking about. That morning, she'd watched Asha as she spoke to their neighbour about the tree at the end of the road. Jaya could tell from the smiles and the tone of their voices and their laughter that they were saying something positive, how big it had grown, perhaps; but without English, she had to construct her own conversations in her head, or wait until she heard them second-hand.

Once she'd finished her shopping, Jaya hurried along the street, shopping bags rustling at her ankles. In Uganda and in India she'd walked slowly, calmly, not wanting to get sweaty and hot. But here in England there was no choice but to try and outrun the cold, to hurry, sticking her neck out, rushing as fast as she could, like a bird about to take flight. She felt the chill in her bones, felt as though the blood in her veins was shrinking.

Their house was sandwiched in a long terrace, with crumbling white window frames and a patchwork roof where the terracotta tiles had fallen off. Jaya opened the door and looked down at the mat the same way she did every day, just in case there had been another letter from Pran while she was out. Nothing. Who knew exactly where he was?

Weeks after they'd found out he was in Austria, they'd finally received a long letter from him, forwarded by the Ugandan Resettlement Board. He explained that when he'd been expelled he'd decided to go to Austria instead of India, believing that there was more chance for them to be reunited if he went to Europe.

'It's so typical of him,' Asha had said, in a sour tone. 'Making decisions on everyone's behalf.'

'He just wanted to be closer to us,' said Jaya.

'We've been so worried about him. And we can't even write back.' Asha's voice faltered. Pran's letter said that he would soon be moving to another camp, so they should wait until he'd confirmed a new address.

Asha had eventually calmed down, trying to focus on contacting the Resettlement Board and their local MP in case they could help. After all, there were other families just like them, separated by passports and circumstances. It was even being debated in parliament.

Jaya took the shopping through to the kitchen. They'd refused the house the council wanted to give them, instead teaming up with Vikash, an acquaintance of someone they knew from the barracks, who lived in the room upstairs and shared the burden of the bills. Vikash worked night shifts at a factory. 'Moonlight pays better than sunlight,' he liked to say. Usually, though, he was upstairs sleeping or out with friends. Jaya rarely saw him, although sometimes she could hear him shuffling around the kitchen in the twilight hours like a giant mouse. It was inevitable: in these tightly packed houses, you were reminded of the people all around, eating, washing, living nearby. The walls on either side were thin and it startled her when the little girls next door giggled or the man sneezed violently, ghostly sounds, as though people were trapped inside the walls.

They'd set to work to make the house as homely as they could, cleaning each room, hands gloved in yellow rubber and armed with Vim and Domestos, scrubbing the mantel that framed a grumpy electric heater, mopping the patterned kitchen linoleum, until the whole house was filled with a chemical tang that lingered for days. Better that, though, than the must and the damp.

In Uganda, like many other people Jaya had kept the plastic on all the new furniture, even the mattresses, so that when you turned in bed you could hear it crinkle and squeak under you. She'd even wrapped plastic around the sides of Vijay's record player and over the top of the radio (though he'd ripped it off straight away). But what was the point now? Why bother saving anything when it could be taken away from you?

She missed the space of the old house. The family made the best of it in their terraced home: Asha and Jaya shared a small double bed in the second bedroom and Vijay took the sofa in the sitting room downstairs. The kitchen doubled as a dining room and led straight through to the bathroom, which had an enamel bath and matching sink in avocado green. Outside the kitchen, there was a small brick enclosure housing a toilet with a pull flush, which, despite Jaya's efforts to clean it, seemed to be regularly draped in cobwebs and bits of dead leaf from the garden shrubs. And the worst thing was going out there, the icy slap of the toilet seat on her bottom, and washing her hands in water so cold it made her fingers ache.

She'd never got used to the showers at the army barracks but now she had to adjust again. A bathroom right next to the kitchen meant that once you were clean, you had to step out to the waft of chai or rotli, depending on the time of day, or alternatively step from the smell and warmth of the kitchen into the icy bathroom.

She unpacked the shopping, lining the shelves with tins and packets. The day seemed endless. She looked at the clock on the wall: half past eleven, quarter past twelve, willing the hands to turn faster. She'd already ironed all the shirts, rearranged the crockery and gathered the clothes to take to the launderette at the weekend. Sliding the leftover rotli under the grill, she left the heat low so it would take longer to cook, and watched it crisp and brown. She ate it with a lime pickle they'd picked up in Southall; it was one of the few places where they could reliably buy Indian goods.

What would December have made of all this? He'd probably have looked in horror at the carpet sweeper, for a start ('You roll some metal over it and expect it to be clean?'). Many chores were faster here, designed to save time, so you could do other things, but what if there was nothing else with which to fill your time?

After she'd finished washing the dishes and cutting the vegetables for dinner, she poured some chai and went into the sitting room. She hadn't thought it possible, but the house was colder than the barracks. Here there were no warm bodies to fill the air, and the conversation had been replaced by silence. She'd spent her life being chased by the sun, moving inside the house in Kampala when the shade crept away, going back out to the veranda when the shade grew longer. But now, with the tiny fragments of winter light seeping through the clouds, she craved the warmth that she had taken for granted for so many years. When it was time for bed, Jaya buried her whole body under the blanket, making a little fold to create a gap, like a whale's blowhole, so that she could breathe.

Night loomed. Though it was only three o'clock, the time she might wake up after an afternoon nap in Kampala, in England the darkness was already creeping in. Gone were the days of afternoon visits to neighbours, daily trips to the temples, wedding invitations to gather and celebrate with friends. Gone were the days of Motichand heralding the end of a meal, downing his large glass of chaas in one, slamming the glass on the table, tugging his shirt over his belly, the buttons lowering their faces in dismay. Gone were the days of gathering in the sitting room, listening to the World Service or trying to watch the news despite the running commentary from Motichand.

Here in England, when the chores were done but it was too early to turn on the heater or to start dinner, all she had was her memories.

*

The latch. The front door slammed shut. Relief, someone else in the house. Jaya waited for Asha to come through from the hallway to the kitchen. 'How was work?' Asha had fortunately found a secretarial job after answering an ad in the newspaper.

'Good, thanks.' Asha's cream blouse set off the caramel tones of her skin. She asked where Vijay was and Jaya explained that he'd gone out with friends.

Asha washed her hands. 'I'll go and change in a minute, then I can help with dinner. What did you do today?'

Jaya wondered if there was any way to make her day sound more interesting than it had been. 'I went to the shops, made a start on dinner, not much. I thought perhaps we might have heard from Pran.'

'No letter, then?'

Jaya shook her head. 'It's so difficult, not being able to write back to him.'

'It won't be for long.' Asha looked down. Jaya couldn't tell whether Asha truly believed this.

Jaya sank into a chair. 'There's always something else. Why can't we just get on, together?'

Asha leant against the worktop.

'We can't even tell him we're OK,' said Jaya. 'He must be worried about us.'

Asha didn't say anything.

'What is it?' Jaya leant forward.

'He could have gone to India like we talked about. You'd be able to write to him, he'd know we were all right.'

'But he thought there was more chance he'd be able to join us if he went to Austria, you know that.'

Asha shrugged. 'I suppose. But what difference did it make where he went? India or Austria, he's still not here with us.'

She paused, looking at her red fingernails. 'It doesn't bother you, all that time we waited for news about him?'

'What's the point going over all that again? Doesn't it bother you that's he's all alone? That he has no idea when he'll see his family again?'

'Yes, it bothers me.' Asha stood straight, her tone resentful. 'But it also bothers me that he's caused us all more stress. He could have told us before he left. Why keep his plans from us?'

Jaya knew she was right. But the anger she felt, the injustice of being separated from her son, was stronger. 'There'll be time to talk about all that when he's here. But what will we do now? We will keep going. We'll write to the Home Office again.'

'Yes, but—'

'But what?' Jaya stood up, hand firm on the table. 'Nothing else matters, we need to get him to England. He's lost enough. We all have.'

26

Asha

A few days later, Asha had barely closed the front door before Jaya called out to her.

'You're back.' Jaya pushed a letter into her hand.

'From Pran?' It had been weeks since they'd last heard from him.

'No, I think it's something official.'

The envelope was made of silky cream paper, addressed to her. She tore it open.

'What does it say?' said Jaya. If she'd been taller, Jaya would no doubt have stood and read the letter over Asha's shoulder.

Asha scanned the information from their MP. 'The Home Office says that "my husband and I can be reunited".'

'That's good news.' Jaya's voice was joyful. 'When? What else do they say?'

'Reunited in another country. Back in India. That's what they're saying.'

Jaya dropped her smile. 'India won't let you in either, you're not a citizen. I don't understand.'

'It's the same as the High Commission in Kampala. Just because I have a British passport, doesn't mean they'll let my husband come here. All those news reports, saying we're "burdens on the state"?' said Asha. 'If we want to be together, it won't be here.'

Jaya gripped the end of her sari chundri, the cotton curling and wrinkling in her hands. 'One person. Why's it so difficult for them?'

'But there are others, aren't there? I'm not sure what else we can do.' There were dozens of men classified as stateless citizens. They had families in England too, some with young children. Asha walked through to the kitchen and poured herself a glass of water, trying to take it all in. What could they possibly do now? And could she really go to India, start all over again, even if they did let her into the country?

'We have to keep trying.' Jaya clung to the back of a dining chair.

'And hear the same thing again?' Asha took a sip from the glass, then looked up at her mother-in-law.

'You want to give up, then?' said Jaya, voice growing louder.

'I just need to think about this.' Asha tugged at the neck of her jumper. The constant struggle to be together exhausted her.

'But what are we going to do, Asha?'

'I don't know!' She slammed the glass down on the table and ran up the stairs, calling behind her. 'I told you, I don't have all the answers.'

*

Asha opened her eyes. The bedroom was dark, the street light casting shapes across the room. She looked at the clock: 9 p.m. She must have fallen asleep after her argument with Jaya.

After changing out of her work clothes into an old pair of jeans and a cobalt-blue kameez, she went downstairs. The buzz of the radio came from the sitting room. Jaya was curled up on the sofa, asleep. Asha headed to the kitchen, where Vijay was eating dinner with the portable radio on low volume.

'There you are,' said Vijay. He took a piece of rotli and dipped it into the chicken curry.

'I fell asleep,' said Asha, wondering if Jaya had told him about their argument. She shouldn't have stormed off like that, Asha knew; she'd taken out her frustration on someone who didn't deserve it. She took a plate and sat down next to him.

'We knocked on your door earlier, but you didn't answer. Ba told me,' he said, 'about the letter.'

'I'm off to Gujarat, apparently,' Asha said bitterly.

'It won't come to that.'

She looked at him. 'It *has* come to that, although they might not let me in either.'

'It's not like you to give up so easily. You're not going to keep writing, keep trying?'

'It's the government. What magical power do you think I have?'

Vijay took a sip of chaas. 'We're starting to get settled here. You've got a job, I'll get one soon, hopefully. Shouldn't we try one more time, at least?'

'Why are we bothering? Scrabbling for rent money, separated from all the people we grew up with?' Frustration began to bubble inside her. Why did everything make her so angry? 'I'm so tired.'

'But you're not doing this alone,' he said. 'OK, you're the one picking up that fountain pen, writing the letter, but you're not on your own.'

'All this effort, instead of just accepting our fate? All these letters back and forth, instead of getting on with a normal life. I don't know, it's just that . . .' Asha trailed away. How could she tell him?

'What is it?' Vijay stopped eating.

'Somehow they all remind me of Uganda. Everything that

happened there,' she said, looking down at the table. 'Those last months.'

Vijay didn't say anything for a moment. 'Uganda was more than just those last months.'

'I know that. But I can't seem to leave those memories behind.'

'Well, we need to crowd them out with the good ones then,' he said, his low voice reminding her of Pran's.

'What do you mean?' She raised her head.

'Tell me one good memory of Uganda.'

'I don't know.' Did she really want to go back there? She'd told herself to try and focus on the future.

'All right, I'll go first,' he said. 'Playing hide and seek with Pran when we were little. He was terrible at it. Always hid in the same spot behind Ba's bed.'

Asha thought of her own brothers. 'We could never play hide and seek. My brother Sailesh always cheated. Never counted to ten.'

'Brothers, hey?' said Vijay, grinning. 'OK, now another one.'

Asha thought hard, conjuring up the Jinja of her childhood. 'Walking to temple, trying to dodge the sun. We always had to duck under the trees so we didn't end up dripping with sweat by the time we got there.'

'See, wasn't so difficult, was it?' said Vijay. 'I've got one. Putting records on, Rolling Stones playing on a Sunday afternoon.'

Asha shook her head. 'Lata Mangeshkar was more my thing.'

'Very good taste,' said Vijay. 'Another one?'

Asha thought of all the times Pran had woken her up, kissing her forehead, the tiny hairs on his arms tickling her stomach as he moved closer. She longed for him, would give anything to feel that kiss again, just once. 'My wedding day,' she said, cheeks flushing.

Vijay looked down at his plate. 'Diwari, fireworks in the streets.'

They took it in turns to come up with the things they'd loved as they finished their dinner. Even though the bad memories wouldn't completely leave her, at least she'd had Vijay and Jaya through it all. At least, when the soldier had grabbed her and the gun fired, her hands trembling for hours afterwards, at least through all that, they'd shared her suffering.

No, she'd been selfish. Whatever she was going through, it was worse for Pran, who was on his own. She had to keep going for him. For Jaya and Vijay.

27
Vijay

At the jobcentre, Vijay walked past the boards with dozens of handwritten cards on them, past the men and women who stood staring at them. All those cards, promising so much. He knew how it went now, months of the same. Ignoring the advisers and turning up to apply for jobs even though they made it pretty clear there'd be nothing for him. Even when he somehow managed to get an interview through an advertisement in a local paper, the employers usually took one look at him – and his arm – and told him not to bother.

But what else was there to do? He stood in the queue but let others go in front of him. It was Marie in particular that he wanted to speak to. Nothing to do with her playful laugh or those dark lashes of hers.

'I think I've found you a job,' Marie said as he sat down at the desk.

'Oh? What is it this time, managing director of Ford Motors? Prime minister?' Vijay gave a little laugh.

'No, really.'

'What's it involve?'

'Customer service.' She looked down at the desk, lining up her pen with the edge of her notebook. 'But it's varied, too, no two days will be exactly the same and you get to spend some time outside.'

'Sounds OK.' Vijay wasn't so sure about the outdoor bit but at least it sounded like a reasonable job. And besides, it would be a bit warmer with summer approaching. 'What is it?'

Marie leant forward across the desk. Vijay did the same. She smelt of patchouli oil and vanilla. 'Well, it's not strictly official,' she whispered, and for a moment he wondered if it was too optimistic to think that Marie might have something very different in mind. 'It's my uncle,' she said. 'He's got this petrol station, you see, down Turnpike Lane way. And he needs an extra pair of hands. Oh God, sorry. I mean, he needs some help and I thought of you.'

'And you've spoken to him about it? Told him about . . . me?'

'Well, I told him how hard you'd worked before, all the hours you put in. He was very impressed.'

Just then a man in a brown suit came over and stood behind Marie. 'The queue's getting longer, Marie. Can you hurry up?'

'Sorry, Mr Clarkson,' Marie said, without looking around at him. She rolled her eyes.

'What are you talking about, anyway?' he said, looking at the papers on the desk. Did he really have to stand so close and stare at her like that?

'We're discussing various options at the moment.'

'Like what, exactly?' Mr Clarkson glared at Vijay's arm.

Marie looked up at him. 'I really should get on, Mr Clarkson. We don't want that line getting any longer, do we?'

Just then, the door opened and a couple of men walked in, the smell of greasy bacon wafting in with them. Mr Clarkson's eyes darted between Vijay and the queue.

'Fine, but be quick,' said Mr Clarkson.

Vijay watched him walk away. 'So what would I have to do?'

'You know, fill up cars with petrol. They fix vehicles sometimes too, and you can help with that, maybe.'

'But why would he want to take me on?'

Marie looked at him, the light catching a sliver of a scar across her forehead. 'Don't you worry about that, it's all sorted. So, you in?'

'I could go and talk to him and then decide?' Vijay wasn't sure any of it was quite as Marie said it was, but he'd give it a try. Wasn't like he had anything to lose.

'I guess so.'

Marie handed him a piece of paper with all the details.

'Thanks.' Vijay stood up. 'I'll have to find a way to make it up to you.'

'Yes, I think you will,' she said, returning his smile.

*

The next morning, Vijay walked onto the garage forecourt. It was lined with pumps, the thick smell of petrol hanging heavy in the air. He headed to a little building to the right with a sign above the door. Inside, a tall man with a bald head stood in the corner behind the till reading a newspaper.

'Excuse me, are you Frank?' said Vijay.

'Yeah.' A single thick brown hair in his eyebrow poked out like an antenna.

'I'm here about the job. Marie sent me.'

The man wandered towards him. 'And where's the rest of you?'

'Rest of us? No, it's just me.' Vijay knew what Frank meant.

'No,' the man sighed, 'I mean that.' He pointed at Vijay's arm. 'Misplaced it, have you?' He grinned, pleased with his little joke.

'Didn't Marie mention it?'

'Yeah, she mentioned it, I just didn't realize you'd be missing quite so much of it.'

'No need to worry, I'll work hard.'

'And how are you going to manage the pumps with that?'

said Frank. They went outside. Vijay picked up the nozzle from the petrol pump with his right hand and showed Frank how we could still manoeuvre the hose with the tip of his upper left arm.

Frank sighed. 'OK, we'll see, shall we? At least your English seems all right. Where d'you learn to speak like that, anyway?'

Vijay opened his mouth but Frank got in there first.

'Actually, spare me the life history.' Frank crossed his arms over his chest and cocked his head. 'Main thing is that you understand this: you'll be paid less. As there's less of you.'

This time Frank wasn't joking.

They talked over Vijay's tasks. He had to look out for cars to serve at the petrol station and help the mechanics the rest of the time. His boss confirmed when and how he'd be paid; not that there was much choice, any cash was better than nothing.

'And I can work seven days a week.'

'Seven? Sunday is a day of religious rest here, mate.' Frank walked back behind the counter. Vijay suspected Frank took more interest in the rest part than the religion. 'Right, you can start by making me a cup of tea. Kettle's over there. Three sugars, whisper of milk. And squeeze that teabag till it's begging for mercy.'

Frank showed him how to fill a car with petrol and how he wanted cars cleaned, then introduced him to the two mechanics. Gary was tall and had a scattering of acne across his chin. He smiled and nodded before getting back to his work. Woolfy was a broad man who stared at him from under a swathe of thick hair brushed forward across his forehead.

'Right,' said Woolfy, not bothering to alter his bored expression.

Frank told Vijay to get started, then wandered off to spend more time with his newspaper.

'Where you from?' said Woolfy, leaning against the bonnet of a Vauxhall Viva.

'Uganda. Africa.' Vijay took a broom and began to sweep.

'I was reading about that in the paper. Chucked you all out, didn't they?' said Gary.

'Yeah,' said Vijay, amused at the idea of being chucked out of a country like a child throws away an unwanted teddy.

'That Idi Amin bloke.' Gary rolled back under a beige Ford Fiesta.

'What happened to you, then?' said Woolfy.

'This?' Vijay waved his arm at him. He briefly toyed with the idea of giving them some exciting tale, how he'd lost it to a man-eating lion, or in an epic car chase across a desert. People always expected a story. But what was the point? No need to make up stories after everything he'd been through recently. 'Born this way,' he said, and carried on sweeping. Woolfy's grey eyes were still on him.

'What's Uganda like, then?' Gary said cheerfully. 'I was reading about the gorillas there a while back.'

'A forest full,' said Vijay, impressed at Gary's knowledge – most people just saw Africa as one large piece of land and had no idea where anything was.

Woolfy watched him, arms folded.

'Not had it bloody easy.' Gary's voice echoed across the bottom of the car. 'How d'you manage to wangle this job?'

Wangle. Another new word that might come in handy. 'Frank's giving me a trial.'

'Woolfy!' Frank shouted from inside the service area.

Woolfy stopped staring at Vijay and picked up a wrench, waving it in the air to show how hard he was working.

'Where did you live over there?' said Woolfy.

'In a house with my family. We had a shop.'

'And what about the Africans?' Woolfy put the wrench down; it clinked against the concrete floor. He peered inside the bonnet of the car.

Vijay checked outside. No cars waiting for petrol, but it was still early. 'Yeah, some of them worked with us. Helped in the house, too.'

'What, like servants?' Gary rolled back out from beneath the car and looked at him.

'Very posh.' Woolfy didn't bother to hide his smirk.

Vijay didn't really think of December as a servant, but that's what he was, what all the house boy and girls were. 'No, not really.' He shrugged his shoulders. 'We weren't posh. Most people had help around the house. It's not like the Queen or anything. No one served us smoked salmon in bed. We didn't have those butlers who look they've got sticks up their arses all the time.'

Woolfy let out a loud laugh and turned towards him. 'You know what, Veejay? You're all right. For a Paki.'

*

Vijay turned up the radio on the mantelpiece; it crackled and buzzed with the sounds of the football. The springs in the sofa squealed with surprise as he sat down.

Jaya got up and turned it down again. She settled herself into the wooden chair in the corner.

'Right, I've found a pen.' Asha walked in. She was wearing a tan A-line skirt, the lowest button undone where her knee met her thigh – particularly bold with Jaya around. She sat down, placing a folded newspaper across her leg so she could lean on it.

'What will you say this time?' said Jaya, hands clasped together, her grey sari draped in waves across her lap.

Asha took the lid off the fountain pen and placed it on the

bottom. 'Keep on reminding them that they've split up a family. If that doesn't work, I'll go and see them myself.' Her fire stronger than ever.

'I hope it works this time,' said Jaya, face full of doubt.

'It'll work, Ba.' Vijay leant forward. 'With all our letters we'll wear them down. Or bury them in paper, if nothing else.'

'Anyway, at least they seem to be taking it seriously now,' said Asha. Despite the letter refusing Pran entry to the UK, politicians in parliament had been discussing whether they had a duty to reunite families with their heads. Some had already been brought back together, especially those with dependants who relied on the men of the household to provide for them. But every time an official letter arrived at the house, all it said was that each case was reviewed on an individual basis. How could you possibly know what the rules were?

'We'll get him back, won't we?' Jaya looked from Asha to Vijay. He'd felt disappointment swell in his chest too many times; he felt hers too.

'Of course we will,' said Asha, as she began to write.

'I'll go and make us some chai.' Jaya headed to the kitchen.

When she'd finished writing, Asha waved the letter in the air, waiting for the ink to dry. 'Here, what do you think?'

Vijay read the letter. 'It looks good. Let's see what happens.'

Asha blew on the paper, making sure the last of the ink was dry. Her fingers were covered in blue from the leaky pen. 'I hate fountain pens.'

'I can see that.'

'Always hated practising penmanship at school. I'd much rather have been outside.'

'Me too. Forever being told not to climb the trees in case our heads split open like coconut shells.'

'That's one way to get children to behave, I suppose.' Asha

folded the letter and slipped it into an envelope. Her smile faded. 'This has to work. I'm not sure what's left otherwise,' she said.

Vijay remembered what she'd said before, how their struggle to get Pran into the country reminded her of all the terrible things in Uganda.

'Hey, you owe me,' he said, turning the radio to a music station. Susi Quatro rang out.

'Owe you what?'

'Something you love about Uganda.'

'Do I really? Well, OK.' Asha sat back and thought for a moment. 'My Ba's ginger biscuits.'

'No, *my* Ba's ginger biscuits, best in the world,' Vijay laughed.

'The scent of magnolia trees at dusk.'

'The scent of Papa's whisky at dusk.' His voice went quiet. 'He'd pour a little into the glass, always intending to sip it slowly. Never did, of course. Downed it one. Every single time.' The burnt-sugar scent of the alcohol came back to Vijay and sadness welled in his heart.

'Aren't we lucky to have shared all those memories with people we love?' said Asha, gently. She must have seen the look on Vijay's face and he was grateful to her for trying to make him feel better. 'My Papa liked beer. Didn't care which kind,' she said.

As Vijay was about to speak, Jaya came back with a tray of cups. 'We'll need to let it cool.'

'Another one,' said Vijay, catching Asha's eye again. 'Chai, any time of day, in the sunshine, made with the freshest milk.'

'And eaten with paratha and chutney,' added Asha.

'What are you both talking about? You want paratha in the middle of the afternoon?' Jaya turned to look at them.

'No, it's fine,' said Asha.

'Don't worry, Ba,' said Vijay, placing his cup on the mantelpiece. 'It's nothing.'

Asha took her chai, smiling at him briefly as she picked up her cup.

28

Asha

The letter looked like all the others: smooth bonded paper, crisp and white, address neatly typed on the front. Asha tore it open, sure that it would be the same as the rest, always the same: that they were reviewing her husband's case and asking for her continued patience. But the words inside seemed so bland and official: 'Leave to enter,' it said, 'documents processed.' A few simple sentences typed in black ink that told her that her husband could finally join his family.

Jaya sank into a chair in the kitchen when she heard the news, eyes filled with tears. Vijay couldn't speak, shaking his head in disbelief, over and over again. And Asha looked at them both, waiting for the surprise to subside. She'd spent so much time battling to get him back, she hadn't dared to imagine what it would be like when they saw each other again.

That weekend, they decided to go out and celebrate with a picnic in the local park. The sun peeked out from skies scuffed with clouds, and the light glinted between the leaves of the trees.

They laid out a blanket and spread their food across it: margarine tubs repurposed for fried golden twists of gathiya, Wall's tubs filled with samosa and dark-brown diamonds of dhebra. Once they'd eaten, Vijay bought them ice cream: a Fab lolly for Asha, a Choc Ice for himself and Jaya's favourite, a 99 with an extra flake.

'And it will only be a month now?' said Jaya, face bright as she poured water from the thermos.

'That's what they say.' Vijay smiled at her.

'All that time, writing those letters,' said Asha. 'I can't believe it worked.' What would it feel like to hold Pran in her arms? What would he think of their new life?

'We were lucky that the government took it seriously. Those debates in parliament helped,' said Vijay.

They finished their ice creams, listening to Jaya talk about all the food she'd cook for Pran and making plans to collect him from the airport together. They cleared away the containers and Jaya lay down to rest on the blanket.

'Shall we go for a walk? I need to work off the dhebra!' whispered Vijay. 'Ba will be fine over here.'

Asha nodded. There were a few young families picnicking nearby but no one noisy around to wake Jaya up. She looked like a child, her knees tucked into her chest, her head resting on her curled arm, the years of worry disappearing from her face as sleep settled in. Through the squeals of the kids in the playground, the creak of the swings going back and forth, the barking dogs and laughing teenagers, somehow, Jaya slept on. The breeze had picked up and the citrus scent of geraniums drifted through the air. They carried on their Uganda game as they walked up the hill.

'Falling into a pothole on Jinja Road,' Vijay laughed.

Asha gave him a look. 'That's your idea of a good memory?'

'It was kind of funny, you can't deny it.'

'That's true.' Asha paused. 'OK, snoozing on the grass at Entebbe.'

'My friend Rahim's kuku paka that he'd cook for us after school.'

'Ice-cold Coca-Cola, straight from the bottle.'

'The well-stocked bar at the Apollo hotel.'

'Of course, trust you!' said Asha, shaking her head. 'Sleepy afternoons in Mr Das's English class reading *Pride and Prejudice*.'

'Eating freshly chopped sugar cane at the side of the road. I used to chew and chew and chew that stuff until it was as soggy as wet straw.'

'Watching *Dr Zhivago* while throwing peanuts from the back seats at the Odeon cinema.'

Vijay pretended to cough. 'That's not what the back seats are for.'

Asha rolled her eyes. But as they carried on walking, the light shining across the top of the hill, she stumbled on a stone and lost her balance, briefly nudging the arm of a man who was walking in the opposite direction. He had a tapered face and stiff hair that made him look like a hedgehog. He muttered something under his breath.

'I'm sorry,' she said.

This time she caught his words.

'Always getting in the way, you lot. Just go back to your own country,' he said.

Asha stared at him. She was too tired to be angry and fed up of ignoring the comments as she usually did. These people who threw words at them. They were the ones who were scared, she'd heard enough to know that. And no one was going to spoil her mood today.

Asha put her hand on her hip, mustering a brightness in her voice. 'You know, I was wondering what was wrong, thank you so much for reminding me. I seem to have misplaced my country. Now, where *did* I put it?'

The man stared at her.

'I just can't think,' she said, laying her hand on her forehead. 'So forgetful.'

'Oh, how careless of you,' Vijay smiled, catching on. 'I wonder if they sell new countries down at Londis?'

Asha cocked her head, the man's face wrinkled in confusion. 'Yes. But are they stocked next to the sugar or the cornflakes?'

'Tough one,' said Vijay, trying to stifle a smile. 'Personally I would have said next to the Ovaltine.'

The hedgehog man looked from Asha to Vijay and back again. He was about to say something but decided against it, scurrying off as fast as he could.

Asha felt the laughter bubbling up inside her as they watched him shrinking into the distance, but Vijay beat her to it.

He threw his head back, laughter spilling out. 'Did you see his face though?' he said. She watched the deep curve of his throat, just like Pran's.

'And the stuff about Londis.' Asha smiled. 'The way he ran off like that.'

'Silly little man!'

'Stocked near the Ovaltine!' She shook her head.

She moved closer, but they were no longer laughing. They stared at each other. Her hands on his arms, his warm breath brushing her cheek.

Her heart lurched. What was she doing?

She stepped away quickly, glancing down the hill at the spot where Jaya rested. Still fast asleep.

Asha turned towards Vijay, guilt welling in her chest. And yet the look on his face wasn't the one she'd expected.

As though he wasn't surprised at all.

*

Asha ran up the stairs and hurried to the bedroom. She stood with her back against the door, trying to catch her breath and calm her thoughts. She'd made a vague excuse, telling Vijay she felt unwell and that she'd see him and Jaya back at home.

What had just happened? Her muscles tensed with guilt or . . . No, it had to be guilt. It couldn't be . . . she didn't feel anything for Vijay. It wasn't possible. Perhaps she'd just imagined the look on his face?

She focused on thinking about Pran. Yet every time she tried to bring to mind his face, his kind brown eyes, the tickle of his hair against her cheek, they were jumbled up with Vijay's. What was the matter with her?

Asha perched on the end of the bed, running her hand through her hair. It had been so long since she'd seen Pran, that was all. They'd all been under a lot of pressure. She and Vijay had spent more time together purely out of necessity. It would all be fine when her husband joined them. All she needed was to see him again and everything would be fine. Pran was the one she wanted, had always wanted. All she had to do was hold on until then, pretend nothing had happened. Nothing *had* happened, after all.

A look meant nothing.

*

Every morning that week, Asha sneaked out of the bedroom like a naughty schoolchild, hoping she wouldn't bump into Vijay. Luckily, he'd taken to waking up and leaving earlier, and he'd stayed out late most nights. On the evenings that he was around, they engaged in small talk in front of Jaya as though nothing had changed. Asha lingered in the kitchen cleaning up for as long as she could and then went up to bed to read her library books.

This morning, Asha shut the front door behind her and waved at their neighbour, Mr Theodorou, who was tending to the small patch of earth in his front garden. He nodded in response, then peered over the top of his brown-rimmed glasses at the flowers, a mix of daisies and something more flamboyant that Asha couldn't identify. He had a thick moustache, and hair peppered with grey. His stomach stuck out far in front of him and he bent over slowly, so slowly that it was almost theatrical. It was hard to tell when he was in a good mood, as most of the time his responses were the same whether he was happy or sad. A brief wave or a few sparse words, 'Nice day today,' delivered in a tone that sounded more like he'd announced the death of the Queen. Jaya joked that he was one of the few people she could have a conversation with in her broken English, each of them stingy with their words.

Sunshine streamed through the newly budded branches of the trees, forming intricate lattices on the pavement below. Usually, she enjoyed her commute. She liked the rattle of the Tube through the tunnels, liked joining the throng of people on their way to work, in their mackintoshes and suits, smart pinafore dresses and tweed skirts, but today, as she walked to her office, the memory of the park jolted through her mind. A strand of Vijay's hair caressing her cheek. The hint of desire in his eyes. She had to pull herself together. How could she have let this happen? She'd told herself that she needed to bond with Jaya and Vijay so that they could get Pran back, but somewhere it had all gone wrong.

She put her thoughts aside as she arrived at work, walking into the stately four-storey house. Asha sat down at her walnut desk, covered in a patina of dents and scratches. A pile of smooth paper was neatly placed in one corner, plus a notepad and a typewriter taking pride of place in the middle. Her office was a spacious rectangular room with ornate details on the ceiling and large sash windows. The eight secretaries' desks were positioned in two rows along the room, with doors leading off to the solicitors' offices behind them.

'Good morning, Penny,' Asha said, putting down her handbag in the corner.

'Morning, Asha.' Penny bit her lip and looked up.

'Are you all right?'

'We're not getting the Thompson files until the afternoon.'

'Don't fret about that,' said their colleague Sinead, coming out of one of the offices. Her moss-green sweater brought out the hazel in her eyes. 'The other clients' records are in now, so they'll crack on with them.'

Penny frowned all the same and got up, the backs of her heels twisting inwards with each step as she went to over to the kettle.

Mrs Walters arrived, hanging her coat on the wooden coat stand. 'Good morning, girls,' she said, sitting down at her desk. The jewelled brooch pinned to her cream cardigan sparkled under the fluorescent light. Perhaps Mrs Walters wasn't quite as dull as Asha had thought.

The women fell silent, settling into the rhythm of the day. Working on files, serving tea, the day rattling on with the typewriters going at full pelt, the sharp, sooty scent of ink in the air – and though Asha whizzed through her work, every so often she thought of the night before at dinner. Sitting at the kitchen table, Vijay in the chair opposite and Jaya in her usual seat to the right. They listened as Jaya complained about Vikash, who shared their house, taking the last of the bread, and then talked about the letter she'd had from Mrs Goswami, grumbling about the snow in Canada. Asha did her best to look at Vijay only enough that Jaya wouldn't notice something was wrong. Luckily Vijay complied, focusing on Jaya as much as he could. Yet as Asha continued to type up her documents, unease prickled on her skin, because the way he behaved confirmed something once and for all: she hadn't imagined it.

Finally, five o'clock arrived and the typewriters stopped.

'Right, let's make a start!' Sinead jumped up, as though the turn of the minute hand had sprung her into action.

'Go and get the rest of them then, Penny.' Mrs Walters watched her go, then took out a Quality Street tin, opening the lid to reveal some forlorn lumps of pastry. 'I've made sausage rolls,' she announced, with more than a hint of pride. Asha usually left work straight away, but everyone would be staying behind for the office party.

The solicitors came out, looking a little dazed after a day in their stuffy offices. They huddled together in a corner, except for the trainee, Harry, who'd started a month ago. He walked over to Asha and Sinead as they stood by the desk with a huge bowl of salt and vinegar crisps on it.

'Do you want a sherry, Harry?' Sinead grinned.

'Leave off. I'm having beer,' he said, running his hand through his hair. 'You're not drinking, Asha?'

'Oh no, I'm fine.' In Uganda, alcohol was for the men, after hours and usually out of sight. She'd never got the taste for it and she wasn't sure now was the time to start.

'Look at her,' said Sinead, grinning as Mrs Walters tried to mingle with the solicitors, her cheeks pink from the sherry.

'This must be a bit of a change from India, hey, Asha?' said Harry.

'I wouldn't know, I've never been.'

'Good start, Harry,' said Sinead, pouring Blue Nun into a wine glass. 'Asha's from Africa.'

Harry shifted his weight from one foot to the other. 'Well, still a bit of a change from Africa? What's it like, anyway?'

Asha raised an eyebrow. 'Uganda?' She trailed off, not knowing where to start.

'Must have seen quite a few animals out there, hey?' Harry knocked back his drink and helped himself to another.

'Birds, I suppose, a few fruit bats,' said Asha, watching Sinead's eyes widen.

'Is that all?' he said. 'What about rhinos, did you have them?'

'Rhinos, gorillas, crocodiles, well, yes, those too. Didn't see any when I was at the shops in Kampala city centre,' Asha smiled. 'It's not all Tarzan and cannibals, you know.'

Sinead smiled. 'That's told you, Harry.'

Harry took a huge gulp of beer and flicked his hair again. 'So, you married, then, Asha?' he said, moving a little closer than necessary.

'Very married,' said Asha, a pang of guilt spreading across her chest.

Harry straightened his back and looked over at Sinead. She kept her eyes on her wine glass. 'I'm not married, you know that. But as far as you're concerned, I may as well be.'

Harry shrugged his shoulders. 'Suit yourself.' He took a handful of crisps and headed towards Penny, who was standing by the window looking as though she was considering jumping out.

'How are you finding it here, Asha, in the madhouse?' said Sinead.

'I like it.' There was a lot to be said for a simple day, a normal life, something to take her mind off the worries that still persisted. It almost felt like a holiday, after all those months in Uganda, cooped up in the house with the family, to do something that she'd chosen for herself, to be around people who knew nothing of the horrors she'd faced, whose biggest concern was whether they'd have to eat one of Mrs Walters' sausage rolls out of politeness.

'Yeah, we're not so bad, are we?' Sinead took a crisp. 'Actually, some of us might be going out next Friday, just to the pub or something. Why don't you come along?'

'Thank you,' said Asha, nodding. She wanted to go but thought of Jaya, on her own in the house, especially with Vijay working longer hours now.

'I didn't know you were married,' said Sinead, looking at

Asha's bare finger, the lack of a wedding ring. 'Or was that just a line you use as a safety guard?'

'I had to stop wearing jewellery in Uganda.' Asha stared at her finger. 'I should probably put it back on now, though.'

'Well, yes, if only to keep Harry away!'

'He's not so bad.' Asha looked back over at him. 'He seems OK.'

'Who wants OK, though, Asha?' Sinead crossed her arms as she leant against the desk. 'So what's your husband do, then?'

Asha took a breath and worked out the easiest way to tell her complicated story. 'He's not here in London,' she began, telling Sinead about how Pran had been stuck in Austria and how they'd only been married a short while before everything went wrong in Uganda.

'So you haven't seen your husband for, what, almost a year?' Sinead looked at her in disbelief.

Asha nodded. Though she'd known it had been a long time, hearing someone else say it out loud made it sound like it had happened to a stranger.

'After everything you've been through. All that time apart when you'd only just got married,' said Sinead, shaking her head. 'You must miss him terribly.'

Asha looked at her. That phrase: 'you must miss him'. As though it was a command. As though it was impossible to feel any other way.

29

Vijay

Vijay sat up from the sofa, pushing the tumble of hair away from his eyes. His neck was stiff; he tried to move it from side to side. He checked the clock on the mantelpiece. Seven o'clock. Why hadn't the alarm gone off? For weeks he'd been trying his best to keep out of the house as long as possible, hanging around the petrol station in the morning until Frank was ready to open up, staying out late with his friends from the barracks whenever he could. He pulled on a sweater, hoping Asha was already at work.

He got ready, but as he was about to go into the kitchen, he stopped. Asha was making chai at the stove, dressed in a burnt-orange dress, her hair pulled into a ponytail.

Asha turned her head towards him. Too late to turn back.

'Oh, it's you,' she said, her voice measured. A hint of panic in her eyes; clearly she was trying to work out how she was going to get out of the kitchen as quickly as she could.

'Is Ba around?' he said, hovering at the door and hoping Jaya would join them soon.

'She's praying upstairs.' Asha poured the chai into cups and set them next to a plate of toast. She hesitated. 'There's breakfast . . . if you want it.'

'Thanks,' said Vijay. He sat down, wondering how he'd manage to eat a thing with the awkwardness hanging in the air.

But they couldn't keep avoiding each other forever, he knew that.

She sat opposite him, gaze fixed on her plate.

They ate in silence for a few minutes but he couldn't take it any longer. He needed to say something. 'Look, Asha—'

'I think it's going to rain later. Better take an umbrella, don't you think?' She carried on chewing her toast quickly, looking down at the table.

'Maybe, I don't know. But listen—'

'I hope it's not going to be too rainy when Pran arrives. I can't believe he'll be here in a couple of weeks,' she said, as she stood up from the table.

He watched her as she tidied the stove, her back to him. He had to clear the air, try and make things normal between them again, or at least vaguely normal, before Pran arrived. Vijay's mouth went dry with guilt at the thought of him. How did things get so out of hand? He was about to say something but Asha got there before him.

'Pran will be right here with us, something good after all that stress we've been under.' A strained cheer in her voice. 'And of course, we'll all be busier once he arrives.'

'Yes, I guess so.'

'Not much time to sit around together.'

'No,' Vijay said quietly.

'It'll be so nice to have him back after all this time. Though it hardly feels like he and I have been apart, in a way.'

'No,' said Vijay.

She carried on, still facing away from him as she washed up, talking about the plans for Pran when he arrived, how she hoped he'd manage to get a job in a factory soon, how nice it would be to spend time with him.

It was plain to see: Asha had assumed her brother-in-law still wanted something to happen between them. But as he watched her by the window, dark hair shining in the light, there were two things that were clearer than ever to Vijay.

He loved Asha.

But he loved his brother more.

*

'It's so green, isn't it?' Marie asked Vijay. The evening air was still warm. They stood at the gates, looking out at Regent's Park. Marie wore layers of indigo and canary chiffon so long they swirled about her ankles. He'd offered to take her out as his way of paying her back for the job with her uncle Frank. Anything to take his mind off home, off Asha.

Marie walked ahead, twirling like a butterfly ready for flight. The spring blossom had made way for bright leaves on the trees, layers of green as far as the eye could see. He didn't have the heart to tell her that Uganda was just as green, vast hills covered in luscious grass, despite the fierce sun. He'd stopped telling people about that; it didn't match their visions of Africa. England was pretty, yes, but all a bit too neat and tidy: clean slices of nature, far too formal.

'We could go and visit the countryside one Sunday if you like, even greener out there.'

He looked at her. 'Maybe after my brother's settled in.'

'It'll be nice to have him back with you soon.'

Vijay looked at her, then nodded. He wanted Pran back with them, of course he did, but things had changed so much. He knew that his brother would want to take charge, like he'd done with the dukan, but life was different now for all of them. He couldn't imagine being cooped up in that small house together. How would he look his brother in the eye? Vijay and Asha would have to pretend everything was exactly the same. That same pang of guilt in his stomach returned every time he thought of her.

The sky turned indigo. He still hadn't got used to talking about ordinary things, like going out for a drink, instead of getting back for curfew, keeping yourself safe. Marie saw England as home. That ease in Marie's shoulders, the look of natural familiarity as she walked around her home city. He'd never thought about it in Uganda, but now he realized he'd never had that same ease, not really.

'You look like you're sucking on an old leather boot with that face.' Marie walked up to a parked car, cranked the wing mirror and slicked on some coral lipstick. She hurried back over to him and put her arm through his. 'Stop looking so maudlin. My mate's having a party. Wanna go?' Marie's long neck glowed in the light of the street lamp.

'All right,' Vijay shrugged.

They took the Tube to Kentish Town and arrived at a small block of flats. Marie stopped by the entrance.

'We're not going in?' said Vijay, bemused.

Marie lit another cigarette, wrapping her lips around the paper, smoke weaving its way out through the tip. 'Let's just wait here a moment.' She smiled at him, elegant wrist tipped back, holding the cigarette high in the air. Her smile an invitation, perhaps a dare?

The door opened and a couple spilled out, laughing, the sweet scent of hashish following them into the night air.

Marie grabbed the door handle before it closed. 'Come on,' she said.

He followed her along a dark corridor and up a communal staircase. The air was hot and thick with smoke now, muffled music getting louder with each step. They came to a green door covered in layers of old, chipped paint. Marie nudged it open.

Inside the flat, there was a narrow hallway with a mustard carpet and swirly brown fabric lampshade. Muted, buttery light shone on the people inside. Most didn't bother to look at Vijay or Marie, too busy talking, smoking or downing drinks from plastic cups or glass bottles, and dancing in the tiny sitting room. Others seemed more interested in what he was wearing than in his arm or his skin colour. There was no furniture nor carpets or lights here. The faint light from the hallway highlighted the black spaces where the floorboards were missing, like a huge gap-toothed grin. Marie led him on, moving to the music, hips swaying, through the crowd.

A shriek, so loud Vijay looked around the room to check someone hadn't been murdered. Marie spread her arms wide, running to a man on the far side of the room. 'Johnny!'

As far as Vijay could tell in the dim light, Johnny had long blond hair. He and Marie hugged each other.

'This is—' Marie began.

'Johnny, by any chance?' said Vijay. Johnny went on staring at Marie.

'And this is Vijay.'

'Veejay,' said Johnny, putting his arm around Marie. He smelt of Old Spice. Another reason to dislike him. 'You want a drink? They're over there.' He pointed towards a kitchen filled with dirty mugs and glasses, half-empty bottles of vodka and Lambrusco.

'All right, Johnny, we'll see you in a bit. Come on.' Marie took Vijay's hand as they walked through the room.

In the kitchen, Marie poured them both some vodka. 'Cheers,' she said, clinking her glass with his. They stepped out onto a balcony at the back of the flat. Her hair swirled around her jaw in the night breeze. In the distance, the lights of the other blocks glittered. They leant against the balcony edge as they talked.

'You've known Johnny long, then?' he said.

'Schoolmates.' She turned to face him. 'He can be a bit intense, I know.'

Intense was one word for him. Vijay changed the subject and they talked about Marie's family, Vijay's favourite music, the places they'd like to go if they had a bit of money.

Marie lit a joint. She took a drag, coral lipstick circling the tip, then handed it to him. He waited for the heavy haze to filter though his body.

'You don't mind?' he said.

'Mind what?'

'The way people look at us together?'

'Do you?'

Vijay shrugged. Strangers stared at him regardless of whether he had a pretty girl beside him.

'Not our fault if their lives are so boring that they have nothing better to do,' she smiled.

Vijay nodded. 'Their problem, not ours.'

'So how's it going at work? Uncle Frank not giving you hell, is he?'

'No, it's OK.' Hell was something he'd left behind, something that people like John back in Kampala were still dealing with. Frank and Woolfy were tricky, no doubt, but at least you knew where you were with them. 'People are people, like you said.'

They fell silent. The breeze was cool on his skin, the muffled music from the flat carried through the air. She moved closer and met his gaze. He pulled her to him, her curves against his body, the tang of lemon on her breath. Hoping to lose himself. He kissed her because she wasn't Asha, because she had nothing to do with Uganda and his past. He kissed her to forget it all.

30

Asha

Asha waited in Arrivals at Heathrow airport, Jaya and Vijay by her side.

Travellers burst through the doors, trolleys piled high with suitcases, some dazed and jet-lagged, others excited to find their loved ones in the crowd. Shrieks of joy, slaps on the back, a shout from a waddling toddler: 'Daddy!'

'Is that him?' Jaya said, standing on tiptoes to see beyond the mass of people.

'I don't think so,' said Vijay, leaning over the barrier.

For weeks, Asha had waited for the anticipation to kindle inside her, longed for excitement to build in her chest. It never came. Even now, standing in the airport, hoping that Jaya and the other eager families would somehow cast their spell on her too, there was nothing. Perhaps, after all the crushing terror, the grief that weighed heavy, the worry that churned in her stomach even now, perhaps there was nothing left for him.

Pran. There he was, feet shuffling, shoulders hunched, pushing a trolley carrying one small suitcase. He looked around with a hesitant smile. He picked up his pace. As he hugged Jaya tight, it made Asha ache for her own parents, to feel their embrace just once, instead of always consoling herself with Ba's airmail letters.

'Kemche?' Jaya's voice unsteady, tears on her cheeks.

'I'm good, Ba. It's so good to see you,' said Pran, as Jaya laid her hand on his cheek.

Pran turned towards Asha, eyes expectant yet uncertain. What would he make of her now? She brushed her new fringe away from her eyebrows, felt him taking her in, her skin paler than it had been in Uganda. He looked different too. His hair was longer, the waves curling around his neck, almost as long as Vijay's. Pran hated it that way, but then he'd had more important things to worry about, clear to see in all the weight he'd lost. They embraced briefly; anything more wouldn't be appropriate in public. Still nothing. Why no rush of joy, or relief, something?

He was dressed in a light cotton shirt, flared grey trousers. She handed him a checked jumper they'd bought for him to wear.

Pran greeted Vijay with a hug. 'Not been eating enough chips and fish, where's the rest of you gone?'

Vijay patted him on the back. 'I could say the same for you!' Vijay caught Asha's eye for a moment, but they both looked away quickly.

On the Tube home, Pran answered Jaya's many questions as best he could, explaining how he'd muddled along in Austria, struggling not only with the language but the food, having to rely on charity from the Red Cross, and a little manual labour here and there for Austrian people, who communicated by pointing and gesturing. Pran looked tired, his skin dull. Each time he glanced at Asha, she found her gaze settling elsewhere, on the seat opposite or the doors as they whooshed open and closed.

'But you were supposed to go to India, beta?' said Jaya.

'What was the point? There was no guarantee I'd get into India without a passport.'

'You couldn't stay in Uganda. Of course they would have taken you.' Jaya shook her head.

'Maybe. I wanted to take a chance in a country closer to all of you, not further away.'

'But when we left Uganda, we'd already agreed you'd go to Gujarat,' said Asha, shifting in her seat so that she could face him.

No answer.

'You knew you were going to go to Austria from the start? You planned it, all that time before we left, you knew what you were going to do?' said Asha. Another lie.

'I just didn't want to worry you all,' said Pran. 'I didn't know if it was going to work, what was the point in telling you?'

'Well,' Jaya patted his arm, 'you are here now. That is what matters.'

'What was it like when you left Uganda?' said Vijay. More people piled on at South Kensington. Further down the carriage, a woman tried to calm a screaming baby.

Pran sighed. 'There weren't many people around, it was getting difficult with the food shortages. Rice and salt ran out for a while. The streets were so quiet, it was like a ghost town.'

Asha felt a flash of guilt: others were still there, suffering, surviving as best they could. Or worse, like December. 'And what about getting to the airport?' she said, sharing a look with Jaya as she recalled their own journey out of the country. Pran had no idea what they'd been through, but there was no point in worrying him. 'How did you get out?'

'I took the government bus. They stopped us at the checkpoints. They beat up an old man when he refused to give them his wedding ring. He couldn't walk onto the plane without our help.' He paused for a moment and took a breath. 'I was fine, although like everyone else I was many shillings lighter by the time I got to the airport.'

They sat in silence for a while listening to the rickety Tube train making its way through the tunnels. Asha tried to catch hold of her thoughts. So much to make sense of. All the unsaid things between them. She felt the drum of the carriage rolling along the tracks beneath them. She sensed Pran's eyes on her again and looked down at the floor, self-conscious. She found herself catching her words, thinking about the right things to say to this man she'd married.

*

'This looks expensive,' Pran said, eyeing up the velvet seats. 'Is the ticket more expensive than other cinemas? Maybe we should have gone to one of those?'

Asha took in the twinkling chandelier above them, the sleek columns, the red velvet drapes across the front of the cinema screen.

'No, it's about the same as the other ones,' Asha said, recalling the simple decor of a cinema trip they'd been taken on during their time at the barracks. This building was much more opulent than any she'd set foot inside, in Kampala or London.

The usher showed them to their seats. 'Shall we get some ice cream?' Asha said.

Pran gave her a look. 'Shouldn't it be me asking you that?'

She paused. 'Well, if you're happy to go, I'll have a strawberry tub.'

Pran checked for the change in his pocket – money that Asha had counted out for him earlier. 'Will this be enough?'

She nodded. This was the first time that Pran and Asha had been alone since he'd arrived. They didn't share a bedroom because Vikash hadn't moved out from the spare room. While he looked for somewhere else to live, Asha and Jaya shared the second bedroom and Pran and Vijay slept downstairs in the sitting room.

It was Jaya who'd suggested Asha and Pran go out for the afternoon, presumably to help them get back to normality, whatever that looked like now. Why couldn't they settle back to the way they'd been before? Life would be so much simpler. Asha was relieved when Pran suggested watching a film, an excursion that wouldn't require much conversation, then felt guilty for being more interested in the swindling gangsters on screen than she was in spending time with her own husband.

Pran returned with two tubs of ice cream, already melting at the edges, the cardboard starting to sag from the moisture. They ate quickly and in silence.

When the film started, Asha struggled to concentrate, conscious of Pran's arm on the armrest, his elbow nudging hers. After a while, like a nervous teenager on a first date, his hand hovered over her own. But before so much as a finger could touch her, she'd already reached for her handbag. She put it on her lap, made a big show of opening it and rummaging for something she didn't need before snapping it closed and clutching it with both hands. It stayed there for the rest of the film.

During the intermission, the velvet curtains rustled as they were drawn across the screen. Pran went over to the smoking area, although the haze had already spread throughout the cinema. It took her back; everything did, his voice, his soapy-musky scent, his dark eyes, they all brought back memories. The night December was taken, when she'd found Pran with a cigarette on the veranda, not a scratch on him, while Vijay was lying there on the ground, blood pouring from his head. That strange look on Pran's face. And later, in bed, when he still couldn't explain himself properly. Her thoughts seemed to splinter into a million pieces, always trying to make sense of things. Yet she could barely look at him, let alone speak to him about it.

When the film finished and their eyes had adjusted to the daylight outside, they took the bus home. The conductor made his way from seat to seat. To pass the time, Asha pointed out the shops nearby; the post office, the grocer's, carrying on the kind of polite conversation that was usually reserved for acquaintances. But after a while, they ran out of things to say and the drone of the bus filled the silence. Pran turned towards her.

'I know it must have been hard for you here, Asha, without me.' Pran spoke in a hushed tone, even though it was unlikely that anyone around them could understand Gujarati. 'I know it's been difficult, all these months.'

'It's been difficult for both of us,' said Asha, because it felt like the right thing to say.

'I wished I'd been here with you, but at least you had Ba and Vijay,' he said, leaning in towards her.

She couldn't look at him, staring straight ahead. Uninvited thoughts of that moment in the park with Vijay.

'Things are going to get better now, I promise,' he said.

'I — we just need time, that's all.' Asha rang the bell and stood up before he had another chance to speak.

*

Vikash moved out of the house a week later, saying a cheerful goodbye and a thank you for Jaya's cooking – though he kept quiet when it came to Asha's. He'd taken down the posters of Arsenal football team – Vikash had decided to support them mostly out of convenience as the stadium was nearby, even though he couldn't afford to buy a ticket – and removed the bottles of Brut and containers of Brylcreem. Jaya replaced them with her jar of coconut oil and a photograph of

Motichand, staring into the distance, a long mara of dried flowers draped around the simple frame. Pran would join Asha in the main bedroom and Vijay would continue to sleep downstairs in the sitting room, pulling out bedding each night from a cardboard box that was kept in the corner.

When Asha and Pran had still slept in separate rooms, she had listened out for his footsteps walking across the hallway, slower than Vijay or Vikash's, or the creaky floorboard that only Pran seemed to walk over, or the running of water and the clank of the boiler as it kicked in when he was in the bathroom. She would wait in her own room until he'd gone and she could go downstairs to take off her make-up.

Now, she got into bed before he came up. Asha pretended to be asleep, wanting more time to get used to having him close by again. Pran climbed into bed, the mattress giving way under his weight. To her surprise, he stayed still, didn't try to move towards her. The darkness, the heft of his body, everything took her back to the checkpoint in Kampala, back to the soldier as he'd gripped her body and torn her clothes.

Asha edged to the farthest point of the bed until she was almost falling off, her breath shallow, heart fast. Pran turned and moved towards her.

'Don't, please, Pran.'

He paused, then whispered, 'I know it's been a long time. Let's—'

'Let's just lie here,' said Asha. 'Please.'

'Of course.' Pran turned onto his back, the insistent tick of the alarm clock the only sound in the room.

*

Asha looked forward to going to work more than ever, a chance to escape. She'd leave as early as she could and often got off the Tube a stop early, taking in the blue plaques that marked the historical landmarks around the city. She'd taken different routes to work so that she could collect them like a set of stamps. And all the while, she marvelled at living in a city that had not only the time but also the money to look back at the past, to commemorate it, to keep the past alive. She walked by the grand building where Dickens had his private apartments on Wellington Street, transported back to Sunday afternoons in Jinja reading *Oliver Twist*. She carried on, taking a walk through her education: Rudyard Kipling, Joseph Conrad and Sir Isaac Newton.

She took in the quiet, almost ghostly feel of London at this time of the morning, the stench of rotting rubbish, alcohol and urine, all the echoes of the night before mingling with the smell of baking bread and frying bacon in the little cafes along the street.

There was time to think on her walk to the office. The space in her head that had for so long been taken up with memories of gunfire or their many money worries gave way to thoughts of Pran. The longer they'd spent apart, the more difficult it had been to picture him in her mind. She remembered an old photograph one of her friends had shown her when they were teenagers. A pretty picture of the view from Kololo Hill, milky sunshine softening the magnolia trees, the white houses and terracotta rooftops. But years later, just before the expulsion was announced, she'd stood on that same hill herself and seen the truth: how the Asians' houses looked down at the Ugandans' houses below, and beyond them to the huge grey mound at the bottom, the landfill dump full of rubbish.

She knew then that the Kololo Hill in the photograph didn't really exist. And it was the same with Pran. In the short time she'd known him before they'd married, she'd captured a small glimpse of her husband as she thought he was. But it was only after all those months apart that a thought rose in her mind: would she have made the same decisions today?

She cast her mind back, remembering how she'd returned to her home in Jinja one afternoon after work to the sound of her father shouting in the sitting room. Papa shouted often, about anything and everything, that it was too hot or too windy or the way a customer had spoken to him that day. It was as though if he didn't shout every so often he might burst open. He sometimes shouted until he exhausted himself, sinking into a chair to catch his breath. But he yelled so often that it had lost all effect. And besides, Papa's loud voice came from a round face, his kind eyes filled with love.

Asha didn't hurry to the sitting room. She stood by the front door, waiting for her father to bark the story to her mother. The problem was, her Ba's calm manner only made her father shout even louder.

'Is this how things are now, Jayshri? How can she do this to us, heh?'

Even though it became apparent Papa had no intention of stopping, Asha decided to join them. He looked up at her from his armchair, opening his mouth to speak, then closed it again. He turned to Asha's mother, sitting in a chair opposite him.

Her Ba looked up. 'Asha, Papa was at the dukan today.' So it was some story about an annoying customer. Why was he so angry he couldn't even speak?

'Mr Prasad, you know, the one with the too-wide eyes?' said Ba, waving her hands in front of her own face. 'He came to the dukan today. And he said—'

'He said,' her father had found his voice again, clutching the armrests on his chair as he yelled, 'how nice it was to see my daughter out with her "special friend". The way he said it. So gleeful.'

Asha blinked at her father. She knew what was coming, but wanted to wait until it was confirmed.

'I told you we gave her too much freedom, Jayshri.' Her father rose to his feet, his voice rising with it. 'Didn't I tell you?'

Her Ba ignored him. 'Mr Prasad said you were seen with a boy. Just the two of you.'

'We set up all those introductions for you,' said Papa. 'We could have found you a nice boy. Why have you done this? Who is this boy?' He said the word 'boy' as though he'd smelt something bad on his shoes.

'He's just a friend, Papa. It's nothing to worry about.'

'Nothing to worry about? You were seen, Asha, a customer came and told me what my own daughter was up to behind my back, running around town with a boy and you say it's not bad?'

'Who is he, Asha?' said her Ba. Asha marvelled at how serene she seemed.

'His name's Pran,' she said.

'Pran?' said Papa, his brows unfurrowed. A Hindu first name: something to allay Papa's worries. His shoulders relaxed further when Asha told them Pran's last name, yes, he was a suitable caste. And finally, her father sat back in his chair with a sigh of relief when Asha confirmed that yes, he and his family were dukanwara just like them.

Asha endured a short lecture about how this wasn't how things were usually done and that they were only thinking of her reputation and how lucky for her they were liberal people, and that if they moved fast with a wedding it could all be explained away and there would be little for the community to gossip about.

She was carried along with all the plans, no time to think about whether any of it was what she wanted. Always assuming there'd be more time with Pran, to decide what she did want, get to know each other away from the prying eyes of parents and the community, time to think about all the little things she knew about him that she'd gathered together like trinkets, creating a version of him she was not sure existed. Was this all she had to base the rest of her life on?

It didn't matter, it was too late now.

Less than a week later, Pran and his family came to Jinja. Her mother gave her clear instructions: after a brief hello, Asha was to stay in the kitchen until the tea was served and then she could make her appearance. Even though the relationship hadn't started in the proper way, things would be done in the traditional manner now. And so Asha listened to the others' small talk and polite laughter in the sitting room until she was eventually summoned. She edged into the room holding a tray lined with teacups and a pile of saucers. All eyes on her. The teacups clattered as she walked; she kept watch over them to make sure they didn't spill. Downcast eyes, ridiculously playing the role of the timid bride. She held the tray out in front of each guest, finally coming to Pran. He looked up at her. As he reached out for the chai, he pressed down with the lightest touch, settling the jittery teacups.

The elders started making plans for a formal engagement and a wedding soon after, things decided without her. Forced to stay quiet, she fixed her gaze on a tiny thread along the hem of her mother's sari that had come loose, a bead hanging precariously from the cotton. She'd watched it tumble to the floor.

What would she have done if she had her time again? She'd have tried to stand up to Papa and her Ba, not let herself be swept up in it all, asked her Papa to give her more time, to wait, at least. It was easy to say now, of course. But how could she not think about all the things she'd do differently, now that she'd learnt that life was so fragile it could be taken away from you in a matter of days, how could you not wonder if the choices you'd made were the right ones?

*

Asha opened the old wooden door under the stairs, the smell of damp bricks seeping out into the air. 'You put the coins here.' She showed Pran the slot in the electricity meter. But today, instead of putting more money in, she emptied out a handful of large silver coins from it. 'We can use these for the shopping.'

Pran frowned. 'But won't we run out of electricity?'

'It's fine, plenty in there already. The meter's the safest place in the house to store money.' Asha stood up, pulled on her coat and grabbed the long black umbrella propped up in the corner.

She went outside and said hello to Mr Theodorou who was tending his flowers, hopped over puddles, ducked to avoid umbrellas, dodged a woman with a pram who rushed along the street with such determination she looked like she was trying to win a race, while Pran trailed along behind.

In Uganda, the rain was like a brief lovers' tiff: quick and swiftly forgotten, soaked up by the sun's rays in no time. English rain, on the other hand, lingered long after it had fallen, sulking on the pavement for hours on end.

Asha didn't turn towards the kids on the other side of the street as they called out as usual, 'Go back to your own country.'

She didn't bother looking at them; instead, she muttered, 'I can't,' under her breath and carried on walking. This was the quickest route to the shops, it wasn't as though she was going to take a different way just to avoid idiots like them. Pran turned his astonished gaze from the children to Asha as she carried on.

At the grocer's, Asha hurried, barely looking at the familiar cans, packages and cartons before she picked them up, while Pran tried to keep up, stepping out of the way of other customers, his brows furrowing as he tried to find a space to stand. He leant against a shelf stacked with Kellogg's Cornflakes and sent a couple of boxes tumbling to the ground; when he turned to pick them up, he nearly tripped up an elderly woman, her lips frozen into the shape of an 'O'.

He followed Asha outside. While the cars raced along the high street, she inspected and squeezed the vegetables that were piled up in little containers. Next, she grabbed a handful of little green globes that looked like tiny cabbages, puckered and wrinkled. 'What are they?'

'These taste good in shaak,' said Asha. She could tell from Pran's bemused face that he was wondering, just as she and Jaya had when they'd first seen Brussels sprouts, how anything so ugly could taste good, and how it was possible that there'd be anything left of them after they'd withered and wilted in a hot curry.

She knew that Pran would struggle to get used to all this, after the markets in Uganda, where the vendors laid out their wares on brightly coloured fabrics, the piles of pink marbled beans and ndizi freshly picked at dawn in the countryside, the rice and grains piled up in gunny sacks, the stench from the beef and goat and vegetables slowly turning in the heat, the hammering metal of the shoemakers, the choking smoke of the sigris, the sweet smell of peanut paste, the women sitting in a row as they pulled the wings off grasshoppers as though they were shelling peas, ready for frying. Asha remembered how once, when she was a little girl, she'd been waiting while her mother haggled over tomatoes and onions and seen something wriggling amongst the fresh produce, shades of pastel blue amongst the bright layers of greens: a small baby nestled in a cloth amongst the leafy vegetables.

On the way home from the grocer's, the rain started up again.

'Let's wait a few minutes, it might stop soon,' said Asha. They sought shelter under a shop awning. She tensed her shoulders as a raindrop that had managed to find a gap between her neck and collar trickled down her back. Next to them, an old woman huddled in the corner with her tartan shopping trolley, waiting for the clouds to clear.

When they got home, Asha shuffled the post that had arrived while they were out.

'Here, let me see,' Pran said, reaching towards her.

'They're just bills,' she said.

Pran took the letters and scanned the numbers. 'So much for rent?'

'We were lucky to get it for so little,' said Asha, more sharply than she'd intended. She walked into the kitchen and put the shopping down.

Pran paused at the kitchen door. 'I'm glad you were all together at least and Vijay could look after you.'

A mix of annoyance and guilt shot up Asha's spine. 'I can look after myself. So can your Ba.'

'Of course,' said Pran quietly, watching her put the things away. He paused, then said, 'Do you like it here?'

Asha shrugged her shoulders. 'It's better than where we were.'

'But does it make sense to you, the life here?'

Asha stopped what she was doing and looked at him in confusion.

'At least Uganda made sense to me,' said Pran.

'Sense?' Asha laughed. 'The madness and the murder made sense to you?'

'I mean, I understood it, how to get by and make a living.' Pran sat down at the table, head bowed.

'But they took your living away from you,' said Asha.

'You think we're safer here just because the people in power have white faces?'

'That has nothing to do with it, Pran. It *is* safer here.'

'But they could send us back any time they wanted.'

Asha sat down at the table opposite Pran and sighed. 'So the best solution is to go back to Uganda before the English tell us to leave too?'

'They don't want us here.'

She thought back to the help they'd received at the airport, Mrs Boswell at the barracks, Sinead at work. She looked at him, his face in despair. 'Don't talk like that.'

'What, Asha, you didn't notice those children? Telling us to get out of their country.'

'I noticed. The same way I noticed in Uganda when they shouted at us to go home too. "Wahindi *rudi* India", remember?'

Pran shook his head. 'But that's different. We were born there, they had no right to say those things in Uganda.'

'Really? The way so many of us carried on building our nice dukans and homes, treating servants like they were nothing? We should all admit it. We didn't really care, we never thought the problems of that country were anything to do with us. No wonder so many of them wanted us to go.' Asha leant forward. 'Anyway, at least here, we're not looking over our shoulder all the time.'

Pran peered at her. 'Nothing's ours.'

'Was it ever?'

'But in Uganda—'

'We're not in your precious Uganda now.' Asha stood up, chair scuttling across the lino floor. She opened the window, freezing air filling the kitchen. 'You hear that?'

Pran stared at her.

'Can you hear gunshots or screams? Can you smell the smoke from the rifles? We're not in your beautiful Uganda.' Asha laughed mockingly. 'Yes, things are strange and some people don't want us here, but at least we're safe. No chance of passing a dead body on the way to the airport. Or have you forgotten all those things when you think of your beloved Uganda?'

'I haven't forgotten. You know that.' Pran looked down at his hands.

'Why won't you let it go? Do you have to keep reminding me of everything we've lost?'

'But I don't belong here. I'm still Ugandan,' said Pran, his voice fraught. 'There's no space for me here.'

'I know the house is cramped, Pran, but—'

'I don't mean that. There's no space *for me*. I don't fit!'

'You have to make a space for yourself.' For the first time in ages, Asha felt an urge to walk over to him, ruffle his hair as she used to in the early days of their marriage, take his hand.

But Pran wasn't completely wrong. How would they deal with the growing space between them?

*

Asha came home from work, slipping off her shoes by the front door, keys clinking onto the hook in the hallway.

'How was work?' Pran came out from the sitting room, eager as a puppy dog.

'Oh, fine.' The bland exchange, now an everyday occurrence, began again, questions met with vague responses. Formality replaced intimacy.

She escaped to the bathroom to change out of her work clothes. Their day revolved around Asha's routine. Pran woke up when she rose for work, they ate dinner after she came home, and at the weekend they'd go to the launderette or the cinema together. In Kampala, life had revolved around others: the many social engagements at the temple, gurudwara or mosque for weddings and festivals, friends and families' homes. They'd longed for, they'd fought to carve out time to be together on their own.

But here in England, she spent her time trying to put distance between them. When Pran went into the sitting room, she went into the kitchen. If he went downstairs, she went upstairs. In bed, the awkward game continued, as she tried to sense the position of his body, deep in slumber, contorting herself into an 'S' shape to dodge his careless limbs. They'd played the opposite game in Kampala, seeking each other out in the dark, searching for bare skin, lips brushing lips.

As Asha changed out of her work clothes and put on a kameez and jeans, Jaya called her down, asking her to help her set the table. The others joined them when dinner was served.

'So at the moment, you all pay for different things?' Pran pushed the sorry-looking pile of aubergine stalks from the ringra nu shaak into the corner of his plate and helped himself to a pile of rice, followed by a ladle of daar.

'Yes, like I told you,' said Vijay. 'Asha pays the rent, I pay the bills, Ba pays for the shopping when she has a bit of money coming in from her cooking at the temple. Vikash's lodging money helped when he was here, too.'

'And the money and gold you got out of Uganda?' said Pran.

'There's not much of that,' said Asha, annoyed at the memory of Pran's own smuggling coming back to her again. 'Anyway, it's for an emergency.'

'But have you looked at all your outgoings together?' Pran took another rotli from the pile, glistening with ghee. 'Maybe there's ways you can save some money here and there?'

'We did that already.' A crackle of annoyance in Vijay's voice. 'We're managing.'

'Your brother is just trying to help, beta,' said Jaya.

'But he's not, is he? He's making things worse. We've done the best we can. It's not as if we've had it easy.'

'And you think I've had it easy, Vij?' said Pran.

'Yes, fine. But meddling in our plans isn't helping anyone. We got on the best we could.'

'Yes, and all I'm saying is—'

'Chup! Let's just eat now, talk about it later,' said Jaya, but neither of her sons listened.

'I'm just saying that we might be able to save a few pounds if we're more careful.' Pran stared at Vijay. 'Why don't I have a quick look?'

'Vijay's right,' Asha said. Jaya and Pran both glared at her with the same large brown eyes. She felt her cheeks flush as she sided with Vijay. 'We've got things under control. What we need is more money coming in.'

'It's not that easy,' Pran sighed. 'You know what the man at the factory said to me today? "Any more of you lot and we'll have enough to turn this place into England's biggest corner shop".'

'Forget them,' said Vijay. 'My friend at the jobcentre might be able to help you.'

'They're not the right kind of jobs,' said Pran. What he really meant was that jobs working in a factory or on a building site were beneath him. Why couldn't he forget his pride for once?

'They're all temporary, just until we can get back on our feet. And we might be able to get a business loan eventually, it's what Madhuben's husband from the barracks did. He's got his own shop now.' Asha poured out the chaas into bowls for everyone and then took a sip of the yoghurt drink. 'Just take a job, any job, that's all that matters right now.'

31

Jaya

The months passed. Though Jaya loved having Pran home, the bitter days and dark nights of winter felt longer than ever. Power cuts, electricity shortages, the working week squeezed into three days. Vijay talked of petrol coupons used to ration supplies. A strange new world, queues for bread and flour; daar and shaak cooked in the morning and kept in a thermos to eat for dinner; cards played by candlelight, huddling around the gas cooker in the kitchen to keep warm. At first, Jaya had quite liked it, the candles reminding her of the divas they'd lit each Divari, the flames glinting, the orbs of light in the darkness. But as it went on through January and February, through a winter that never seemed to end, it brought back other memories, of Motichand calling to her when he arrived home, December's laugh ringing out on the early-evening breeze. Thankfully, they were back to normal weeks again now, and somehow, Pran had even managed to hold onto his new job in a factory.

Jaya opened the front door, marvelling at the fact that no one had stolen the milk money. Every morning, the fat glass bottles sat neatly lined up on the doorstep. She took them into the kitchen, loving the satisfying way that the foil lid gave way underneath her thumb, then added it to the stack of other tiny metal saucers in the corner of the worktop. Mary, the little girl down the street, would come and collect them at the weekend, although how a piece of foil could be valuable enough for a charity collection, Jaya couldn't understand.

She boiled the milk, then whisked in the last of the remaining yoghurt. She left it in the sitting room – the warmest part of the house – with the temperamental electric heater on, waiting for it to turn into a new batch of yoghurt. It was a dry day, so Jaya wrapped herself in as many layers as she could and braced herself for the snap of the wind against her face. The garden was tiny but she tried to make the best of it. When they'd first arrived, she'd been annoyed at the weeds that had cheekily pushed themselves through the gaps in the paving, though she couldn't help but admire their determination to survive. In the borders, she tended to the few bedraggled shrubs that she was doing her best to keep alive. She'd even got Vijay to create a makeshift cover with an old umbrella attached to the fence, to hold off the worst of the heavy rain, but it had collapsed in a corner like a dead crow.

As she went over to try and fix it, she caught sight of a patch of earth, newly smoothed over with soil. It couldn't have been an animal; a cat wouldn't sweep so neatly after doing its business. She reached up to unhook the old pair of garden gloves from the back of the toilet door, then pushed the earth back with a stick. A plastic bag peeked out from the damp soil. She tore it open and found a yellow Tupperware box inside, *her* Tupperware box, then peeled open the lid to reveal a thin pile of £1 and £5 notes, the silver ink and greying paper like the sky above.

*

'Sit.' Jaya gestured towards the kitchen chair, waiting for Asha to take her place. She had had to wait an entire day to speak to her. Now she took her chance while Vijay and Pran were in the sitting room, listening to the Saturday evening news on the radio. Outside, snow had settled in the garden, gleaming ghostly white in the darkness.

'But I've just started the paratha,' said Asha, slapping another one into the frying pan.

'Do it in a minute, Asha, please.' Judging by the smell of burning, it was too late to save the paratha anyway. She couldn't help but glance at the steel plates that Asha had forgotten to pick up from the draining board, now watermarked, misty tears trailing down the sides.

Asha turned off the heat, wiped her hands on her apron and sat down.

'I found some money, buried in the garden in my Tupperware.' It sounded even more ridiculous saying the words out loud.

Asha said nothing. Most likely weighing up whether Jaya needed to have a lie-down.

'I already asked Vijay if it was his, and he said he didn't even know what Tupperware was, let alone where it was kept in the kitchen,' said Jaya. 'So I thought it was yours?' Jaya looked at Asha, hoping she could make sense of it.

'It's not mine,' said Asha, no hint of surprise in her voice.

'But that only leaves Pran.' Surely it wasn't his. Out of all of them, he was the most considered, measured, he wouldn't resort to doing things like this. Besides, he'd only been working a short while, barely earning enough to set aside.

Asha turned her gaze towards the window, then sighed. 'He's done it before.'

'What do you mean?'

Asha told Jaya about the money Pran had hidden in the yard before they left Uganda. 'He told me we'd go back and get it one day.'

'But then why is he burying more here?' said Jaya, running her finger along the edge of her thumbnail.

'Doesn't trust the banks here, I guess, not after what Amin did,' said Asha. She hesitated, looking at the kitchen floor. 'He asked me and Vijay for some, said he'd keep it safe for the family. I didn't think much of it at that time.'

'I'll have to speak to him. He can't go around hiding money in the ground,' said Jaya. And aside from that, how could anyone think about going back to Uganda after everything that had happened?

'No, wait. I don't think that's a good idea. He's—' She broke off.

'What is it? Tell me.'

'I don't think he's coping.'

Jaya felt disloyal, agreeing with Asha. She brushed it away instead. 'But he's got his job at the factory now.'

'It's not just work, though.'

'But we're all here, we're all together,' said Jaya. 'He should be looking forwards now.'

'It's the whole way of life here, it's tough for him.'

'How do you mean?' How could it be tougher than the life they'd left behind?

Asha sighed. 'We've been here for so long without him. We're settled, and he's only just found a job. And he's working for someone else – he hates that.'

'I should have helped him more,' said Jaya, guilt swelling in her chest. Her poor son, stuck between the only world he'd ever known and a future he didn't choose for himself. Of course he was trying to take control of his life, of course he was struggling. She should have known.

'It's not your fault,' said Asha. 'Give him some time. Pushing him right now might make it worse. If things don't get better, I'll talk to him.'

Jaya stood up. Asha mustn't see her tears. She stared out of the window. It had begun to snow again; the fat moon made the snowflakes glow so bright it looked like the stars were falling out of the sky.

*

In the coming days, Jaya sought comfort in her faith. She lit incense each morning and placed it on the only shelf in the bedroom that didn't wobble, next to her wooden murti statuettes of the Hindu gods.

The colourful, gold-leafed murtis she'd kept in the little shrine at home in Kampala had been far more ornate. Each morning, she'd walked in the pale light of dawn across the yard to the small room that was kept especially for her shrine, slipping her chumpul off outside, the leather sliding against her feet. The wooden structure that housed the shrine had been intricately carved by hand. There was a little nick in the front where December and Pran had knocked it against the wall when moving it into place. She'd sometimes run her finger along that ridge, jagged and rough, surrounded by sleek wood. It reminded Jaya that life wasn't perfect, that you had to accept the bad as well as the good. Ribbons of sandalwood smoke swirled out from the agarbatti she'd lit. She didn't particularly like the heavy, suffocating smell but it made her think of her own Ba, who had lit the same incense when Jaya was a small girl, in a little corner of their home, a world away from gilded statuettes or ornate frames.

Now, in her new home in England, Jaya took out her mara from the bedside table. She loved the smoothness of the beads, solid and firm beneath her fingertips, the sandy wood carved into perfect spheres. The curve of each bead nuzzled against the next on a never-ending loop of fuchsia thread. She held each bead in turn between her finger and thumb, whispering her mantras.

Faith kept her coming back each day but also habit, familiarity. It was one of the few things that was hers alone, something no one could take from her. Even if the temple was destroyed and the mara pulled apart, beads toppling across the floor, faith kept her coming back. And fear. If she was honest, she was frightened. If she didn't believe, fate might turn against her and her family, hurt them far worse than it had already. So Jaya believed on behalf of all of them, twirling the mara round and round on her fingers, day after day, to protect them from harm.

When she'd finished her prayers, she looked at the murtis and thought of her mother. How she'd told her the stories of Brahma, the creator of the universe; Vishnu, the protector; and Shiva, the destroyer. The idea of Shiva had terrified Jaya as a little girl. Even when her mother explained: 'He has to destroy, otherwise how else can life renew and transform again?'

'But what if he destroys our house, my school?' Jaya had asked.

'He does everything for a reason, beta. There's no need to be afraid.'

Now, she tried to take comfort in her mother's words: change was good, life could be rebuilt. She clung to those words as tightly as she clung to her mara. The family had to renew and transform; Pran would be all right again.

32

Asha

Asha picked the letter up from the doormat. She didn't recognize the handwriting on the white envelope, but it had a London stamp. She put it on the mantelpiece and waited for Pran to open it that evening.

'Who's it from?' said Asha. Most of the letters they opened were either bills or airmail letters from friends and family abroad.

'It's from Rakesh. He's here in London with his family,' Pran looked up at her.

'He's here?' Asha read the letter. Pran had lost touch with his old friend in the mess of expulsion. 'How did he get our address?'

Pran explained that Rakesh had somehow managed to get it through a mutual friend. When Pran replied, they received an invitation for the whole family to go for Sunday lunch.

Rakesh lived with his family in a block of flats near Ealing Common. They climbed a concrete staircase that reeked of urine and stale smoke, with walls covered in a mixture of posters telling people where to put the rubbish and handwritten scrawled messages. More graffiti met them as they reached the second floor. Here, the row of flats ran along an open balcony that looked down onto a playground where teenagers hung around, cramming themselves onto a climbing frame that was clearly meant for small children. A few doors along, a little girl with blonde bunches sat on a step, clutching a paper bag. She was picking out cherries, chewing each one and throwing the stones on the ground.

Laughter and the buzz of a radio came from inside the flat. Rakesh opened the door. 'Pranbhai! Kemche?'

Pran hugged him and smiled. He hadn't looked this happy since Asha saw him in Arrivals at Heathrow.

Rakesh looked different, as though he'd shrunk; the bulk of his tall frame had disappeared. He'd grown a beard, thick dark hair swirling along his jawline. Asha recalled the last time they'd seen each other and said goodbye, in the bright light of the temple, all praying for the same things, for safety and refuge. 'Come in, everyone. Jayamasi, it's so nice to see you.'

Jaya patted his arm as they went into a narrow hallway. To their left was a kitchen with just enough space for a cooker, two cupboards and a small refrigerator. Every surface was crammed with large bowls and plates covered in tea cloths, and saucepans and frying pans were piled on the hob. Three young women, including Rakesh's wife Sulekha, bustled about, washing and preparing and tidying, avoiding hips and elbows.

They all said hello to each other and Jaya found the one tiny space left on the worktop to put down a margarine tub carrying some *buteta vara* she'd fried that morning, filling the house with the scent of mustard seeds and turmeric. They followed Rakesh to the main room, painted a murky pea-green colour that gave the place a gloomy feel, despite the bright blue sky and haze of sun outside. Two men, one of whom Asha recognized as Rakesh's father, were nestled on a sofa that had been covered in an old cotton sari, the worn beige-and-brown velvet armrests peeping out from the corners, while two younger men sat on scuffed wooden stools. Rakesh's mother made herself comfortable on an armchair, hands meeting across her belly as she kept a watchful eye on the young women coming in and out of the kitchen, debating the best place to put this plate or that bowl. Four children ran around; they couldn't have been more than six or seven, singing nursery rhymes. It was as though everyone in the room was competing to see who could make the most noise. And yet, even though there was little room for Pran, Jaya, Asha and Vijay to stand, let alone sit, despite the fact that the room was hot and stuffy, Asha felt more at home than she had in months. The familiarity made her heart swell, reminding her of the many Sundays she'd visited friends and family, eating coconut sweetcorn, fried kachori and samosa, drinking sugar cane juice in the late-afternoon shade, talking until the crickets joined them in their chatter under the moonlight.

'*Challoh*, let's eat,' said Sulekha, refusing Asha's offer of help. 'Please, don't be shy.'

The food was unveiled: golden-brown daar na bhajia glistened in a large bowl; another full of *muttur bhat*, the turmeric-coloured rice studded with peas; fenugreek paratha; a peppery chicken curry; yoghurt spiced with cumin and a kachumber of sliced tomatoes, cucumber, onion and grated carrot. They'd somehow managed to get their hands on *halwo*; the flat slices of baked milk and sugar scattered with flaked almonds and pistachio were piled on a plate. The joy of doing things that everyone else did bubbled inside Asha. Gathering together with friends, eating delicious food, surrounded by laughter and noise and music: the sounds of an ordinary life.

They sat down on the carpet in the centre of the room while Rakesh shooed the kids away. He told them all how they'd got out of Uganda.

'And you managed to get a job quite easily?' said Pran.

'I'm not sure anything's easy here. But I managed to get a job in a department store. I help with the tailoring, like I used to in Uganda,' said Rakesh. 'But it's still tough, with all of us living here.'

'You live here together?' said Asha. Many Ugandan Asian families were living in cramped conditions, but there were at least twelve people in the room excluding Asha and her family. Sulekha had already told them there were only two bedrooms in the flat.

'My sister and brother-in-law have moved to another flat with their own family now,' said Rakesh, glancing at the two youngest children. 'But we live here with my parents and the kids. Sulekha and I sleep in here, the others take the two bedrooms.'

'And you've been here since you arrived?' Pran leant forward.

Sulekha served them glasses of water, a strand of curly hair falling loose from her bun. 'We were up north before, in an army barracks there for a while. Then we came to London, as we had a few friends here already. We would have got in touch sooner, but you know how things go. So much to think about. We're only just settling in.' Sulekha glanced at Rakesh with weary eyes. The strain must have taken its toll, the two of them responsible for three generations of their family.

'We thought we'd be able to move out by now, but with the money I get from my job it's not really enough,' said Rakesh. 'We're looking into some help from the government for my parents.'

'Not that they want to take it,' Sulekha said.

'Handouts are for poor people,' said Rakesh's father, who shifted in his seat on the sofa, putting his empty plate on the armrest.

No one had the heart to remind him that they *were* poor people now.

'It's a little easier for you, I suppose, as you're all working?' Rakesh said.

'It helps having more than one income. But it's still hard,' Pran replied.

Rakesh took a sip of water. 'You know some people are talking about going back.'

'To Uganda?' said Jaya.

'But the news reports have said things are just as bad. There's still a lot of fighting,' said Vijay.

'They're leaving Asians alone though, the ones who stayed behind, like the civil servants and the other skilled workers,' said Rakesh. 'And there were a few more who managed to stay after expulsion, the ones who hid themselves in the smaller towns away from the cities.'

'Wasn't everyone else supposed to leave, just like us?' said Jaya, recalling Amin's threat of expulsion camps for any stragglers.

'Somehow they managed to stay under the radar. And now there's bigger things to worry about than a few Asians hanging around. Some of the Asian businesses that were taken over have already collapsed.' Rakesh shrugged.

Pran stopped eating. 'How do you know all this?'

'I've got a cousin who stayed there, they get word out sometimes, through our relatives in Kenya.'

'So they're running businesses?' Vijay asked.

'I don't know about that. But they're managing to get some goods across the border, selling things on the black market. They're getting by, perhaps better than we are.' Rakesh and Sulekha shared a look. 'I'm thinking about it myself.'

'Returning?' said Pran.

'Just thinking about it,' Rakesh nodded. 'Not yet, I need to wait and see what happens out there. If things change.'

'But you'd all go back?' Asha was alarmed, they had young children to protect if nothing else.

'No, just me, at first. The family could stay with my brother-in-law and I'd save up some money.'

'It's so dangerous.' Jaya shook her head. She looked at Rakesh's dad with concern in her eyes but he was too busy picking at the crumbs on his plate, while his mum was dozing in her chair, purring like a cat.

'They're not as worried about the Asians since we were expelled. There's too few of us over there to be the enemy any more.' Rakesh lowered his voice, aware that the children were still hovering around. 'They're even asking Bangladesh and Pakistan to send people over, doctors, engineers. People who've never set foot in the country before. You think they'd go there if it was so bad? Amin's starting to realize he's made a mistake. And anyway, it's only a matter of time before they get rid of him, it must be. Others are always waiting in the wings.'

'So what would you do?' said Pran, mopping up the last of the chicken curry with a piece of paratha.

'I need to look into it, but my cousin said I might be able to help him. He has contacts in the government too, they might be able to help me get the papers together.'

'And it doesn't bother you, even after everything that happened to us?'

'Asha.' Pran gave her a look.

'It's OK,' said Rakesh, smiling. 'A lot of terrible things happened there, I know. But look at the life we have now.'

'But at least you're all safe here together, beta,' said Jaya.

'Things are already different over there. People stick together, some live in the temples and gurudwaras too,' said Rakesh. 'And besides, the ordinary Ugandans are still there, they had no choice but to stay.'

Jaya lowered her head. Asha guessed that she was thinking of December and his daughter.

Rakesh glanced at the children, who had come back into the room arguing with each other about a penny they'd found somewhere in the house. 'Anyway, enough talk of Uganda, please take some more food.'

They finished their meal, talking about simple things, their work, their homes, sweeping away thoughts of the danger and chaos Rakesh was considering going back to, but Asha couldn't shake it from her mind. Why was it that Rakesh's words relit the spark that had been missing from Pran's eyes for so long?

Later, Asha made a start on the dishes in the kitchen. Through the window, she saw the children running up and down the long balcony, playing with skipping ropes. Sulekha brought the last of the plates into the kitchen. 'There's still a lot of food left over. You'll have to take some.'

'I don't think I'll eat again for a week, I'm so full,' Asha smiled at her. Little glossy bubbles of washing-up liquid escaped from the bottle as she poured some onto a sponge. She stood back, taking care not to get any on her red kameez, and said, 'You really don't mind Rakesh going back?'

Sulekha piled up plates next to the sink and sighed. 'I'm not sure how much say I have in the matter.'

'But isn't it better for you all to stay together?' Asha wondered if she was going too far, pushing her like this.

'I don't know what Uganda's going to be like, but it's difficult enough here. Feeding and clothing everyone. But better to do that and live apart than go hungry living together.' Sulekha paused for a moment. 'One worry after another. The children stuck inside all winter. And those power cuts, the nights in the dark. We thought we'd left all that behind with the curfews.'

Asha couldn't help but feel relieved that she and Pran didn't have children to worry about, on top of everything else. It wasn't something they'd have to think about for quite a while. 'But power cuts are one thing, what about the danger?'

Sulekha shrugged her shoulders. 'We wouldn't take the children there until we were sure it was safe. But like Rakesh said, they seem to be leaving us Asians alone now. It's not perfect, I know, but Amin can't go on forever.'

Asha looked out of the window, across the sky streaked with feathery white clouds. Things did change, of course they did, just look at her marriage with Pran, look at her life now, so far from the one she'd imagined for herself years before. But putting your life at risk? She couldn't imagine it.

*

Throughout the next week, Pran seemed newly focused on life again, fixing the broken door handle in the kitchen, taking more of an interest in helping at the temple. At first, Asha daren't ask what had caused it, in case it broke the spell. But it was clear that lunch with Rakesh had raised his spirits.

'You seem better,' said Asha, as they lay in bed one night, the light from the street lamps seeping through the curtain fabric.

'Better? Didn't know I'd been sick in the first place.' Pran turned his head towards her.

She thought about the best way to phrase her next question. 'It just seemed like you were finding things a little tough? I don't know.'

Asha could make out the contour of his eyes, looking up at the ceiling. He paused before speaking. 'I guess I realized I need to get on with things, we've wasted so much time already.' He curled his arm under his head. 'Things are going to be different now.'

They fell silent, listening to the cars driving past the house.

'I can't believe Rakesh is thinking about going back,' she said, hoping he'd show little interest.

'He's finding it difficult, like we all are. You've heard the news about home. Inflation through the roof, food shortages. They've woken up and realized that we weren't the bad guys. It's an opportunity.'

'The opportunity to get killed?' It was crazy to go back, with Amin's thick fingers wrapped around the country's throat, as tight as ever.

'Things have changed.'

'You're not serious?'

'I don't know, we should think about it, though. I could try and get in through Kenya, maybe. I owe it to Papa to get our house back.'

Asha sat up, leaning on her arm, hair trailing across her shoulders. 'What are you talking about?'

'I need to finish what I started there.'

'But Pran—'

'All those times growing up, I saw the disappointment in Papa's face. He wanted to build something but he just didn't know how. I was turning things around before he died, I was going to give him everything he wanted. Why would I just give that up?'

'But you could start again here, you're young.'

'We belong in Uganda, building my Papa's business just like he wanted.'

'But I have a life here now, a job I like. It took everything I had to start again. I won't go back.'

'Look, I know how you feel.'

'You have no idea!'

'I know you can't imagine going back right now.'

'I can't imagine going back ever. Not ever.' She tried as hard as she could to keep her voice down; her heart drummed against her chest. 'You don't know what it was like.'

'I do know.' Pran tried to take her hand but she batted him away. His voice was tender. 'Asha, I do know. Vijay told me about what happened to you. The soldier.'

She sat upright, pulling her knees to her chest. 'He had no right to tell you.'

'He thought it might help. He could see . . . He could tell things weren't the same between us, after I arrived.'

What had Vijay told him exactly? What did Vijay even think he'd seen? It didn't matter now, Pran knew. And perhaps, in a way, it was a relief not to have to pretend any more, at least about that.

'Those salas, disgusting men.' Pran's voice shook. He reached out and put his hand on her cheek. 'I'm sorry,' he said.

She pulled away. 'They didn't—' She didn't know how to begin to explain. Anger all over again.

'I'm so sorry for all of this,' Pran whispered. 'This isn't what I wanted for us, any of it. I want to go back and change it all.' He reached out again. This time, she didn't stop him. She was so tired of the sadness wearing her down.

She didn't resist when he pulled her towards him. She didn't stop herself lying down next to him. She wanted to forget the memories of the soldier, his acrid breath, his hands on her limbs; she needed to crowd it all out with new memories. And so she kissed Pran, his forehead, his eyelids, his lips, searching for the people they had once been, following the arch of his back, kissing his palms, his neck, his shoulder, searching for a single trace of the life they'd left behind.

*

The morning sunlight woke them both up.

Pran gave her a sleepy smile. Asha kissed his dimples.

'It's good to have you back,' he said.

'I didn't go anywhere,' she said, although she knew what he meant. 'And I don't think you should go anywhere either.'

Pran stroked her shoulder, staring at the ceiling. 'Uganda? It's only something I'm thinking about.'

'Well, don't. For me. For all of us. Forget it.' Asha rested her head on his chest. She couldn't lose him again. She'd forgotten how good it felt to hold him, to feel the rise and fall of his breath next to her. 'I want you to stay here, please. Stay here. Don't forget what it was like.'

'They took all they could.'

'Did they, Pran? What about your life?'

'Nothing's going to happen.'

'You've already forgotten what happened with December?' she said, struggling to control her voice. 'I've never seen you like that.'

He turned his head. 'Like what?'

'That night the soldiers came to the house, when I came out of the bedroom. You seemed like you were in another world. Lost, I guess.'

'I was in shock.'

Asha stared at him. 'Something was wrong.' She thought she'd buried the memories away. It was only now, as she thought back to that evening, something unlocked inside her mind that she hadn't been able to reach before. The look on Pran's face that night reminded her of the first time he lied to her. 'Did something—'

'Why are you raking it all up again?'

'I just—'

'No!' Pran got up and opened the door. Though he whispered, it did nothing to hide the anger in his voice. 'No more talk about the expulsion, ever. I've had enough!'

Asha stayed where she was, feeling the sheets beside her

grow cold. The more she searched for the truth about what happened that night, the more confusing it seemed. Why hadn't they hurt him when they found December hiding away? She'd seen this evasiveness before, the way he'd made her feel paranoid about the dukan. One thing was certain: if Pran wouldn't give her the answers she was looking for, she'd find them another way.

33

Jaya

Jaya turned around as Vijay shot through the kitchen door. This was his new way of arriving when he was in a hurry, running from the hallway, sliding across the plastic runner into the kitchen in his socks. He'd misjudge it one day, fly across the kitchen floor and slam into the back door, it was inevitable. Vijay straightened up, brushing his hair out of his eyes. It was getting longer by the month, skimming his neck and constantly looking like it had never seen a comb, never straight, even minutes after he got ready in the morning.

She'd laid out an assortment of foods: paratha and chai for herself and Pran; Weetabix for Asha, which she ate like toast, spread with butter; fried eggs for Vijay.

'I was thinking, why don't we go for a day trip, have a picnic?' said Jaya, taking a sip of chai. She watched Pran as he broke off a piece of paratha and scooped up some mango chutney. Though he looked tired from the many hours he was working, he also seemed more content than he had in months.

'That's a good idea, maybe next month when the weather's warmer,' Asha said, taking care not to get food on her clothes, though it was her own fault for wearing a blouse with huge sleeves that ballooned at the bottom like aubergines.

'Maybe,' said Vijay quietly. 'But I might not be here then.'

Jaya looked over at him, though he seemed to be inspecting his fried eggs intently. 'Why not?'

'I'm thinking of travelling, going abroad.'

No one spoke. Vijay pretended not to have noticed and took a bite of his toast.

Pran snorted. 'You haven't travelled enough? You've found a country that doesn't want to throw you out – yet – and you already want to leave?'

'I don't understand, Vijay, where will you go?' said Jaya.

'I was thinking about India. You know, Papa talked about it all the time. I know more about England than the place where he was born. I'm not exactly sure yet.'

'You don't even have a plan?' said Pran.

'Where did plans get us back home?' Asha said, shifting in her seat.

Pran lowered his voice. 'That's not the same.'

'You can't leave, beta,' said Jaya. 'We only just got your bhai back.'

'It won't be for long, Ba.'

'And where are you going to get the money from?' Pran pushed his plate aside.

'I have a bit saved up, now Frank's paying me what I'm due at the petrol station, and I might work along the way. Besides, India's a lot cheaper than here,' Vijay mumbled. 'I don't understand why everyone's making such a big deal of it.'

'It would be nice to just run off whenever we wanted,' Pran sneered. 'No, you're not going.'

'It's not up to you,' Vijay laughed.

'Don't you realize how selfish you're being?' said Pran.

'Selfish? You'd know, wouldn't you?' said Vijay. 'All these months, I've been helping out. I just want to do one thing, one single thing for myself. What's wrong with that?'

'It's just a shock, beta,' said Jaya. She wasn't sure whether her heart could take any more pain.

'I know, but I'm not going anywhere just yet. I still need to save up for the ticket and everything.'

'We've lost so much and now you're going to go running off on some trip around the world. You can't wait to get away from me.' Jaya's voice was more forceful than she'd intended.

'No, it's not that, of course it's not,' Vijay said, his tone gentle. 'Might as well do this now, then I can come back, think seriously about going to university. I just want to have a little fun first, that's all.'

'Shame the rest of us don't have time for fun,' said Pran.

'Enough, Pran.' Jaya glared at him. The rest of breakfast was eaten quickly and in silence. Pran and Vijay got out of the kitchen as soon as they could.

Asha helped her clear up. She must have seen the concern in Jaya's face. 'He's very young, life stretching thousands of miles ahead of him,' she said.

'But he has seen how dangerous it is,' said Jaya.

'The entire world isn't like Uganda. Even Uganda wasn't always like that, don't forget. Be grateful that he can see beyond all that.'

Jaya stopped what she was doing, resting the cloth on the worktop. 'I've lost enough people to last a lifetime.'

'It's not forever.' Asha turned towards her.

'You make it sound so easy.'

'Maybe it would be good for him to get away from all of us, just for a little while.' Asha put the plates down by the sink, staring out of the window. 'Maybe you should let him go.'

Jaya looked at her. She knew why he wanted to go, he was so young, after all, with so much taken away from him. But could she let her family be split again?

Jaya clutched the coins in her palm, ready to pay for her ticket as she climbed on the bus with Pran. The woman in front wore a transparent plastic hat and Jaya could see her silver hair wrapped around lilac rollers. What was the point? At least with a sari chundri covering your head you couldn't see beneath it.

The bus was busy so they wobbled up the stairs and took a seat on the upper deck. Luckily, no one was smoking. The light reflected across the shiny ceiling and along the metal window frames. Outside, the criss-crossing telephone lines always seemed close to the top of the bus, as though they'd get caught up somehow. They rumbled along, past the rounded walls of Bounds Green station, past the bakeries and haberdasheries and fish and chip shops and onwards through the sun-dappled streets.

'We need to talk Vijay out of this crazy plan of his,' said Pran.

'I think it might be too late.' She mopped her forehead with a handkerchief; the air was uncomfortably warm.

'He's not thinking straight. Thinks he's invincible, he's acting like a child.'

Jaya gave a weary smile. 'He's older than I was when I went to Uganda.'

'That was different. You had Papa.'

'But I made the journey on my own.' For a moment, Jaya considered telling him how alone she'd been when she arrived in Kampala, but it wasn't their custom. They loved each other, yes, had lived in the same house for many years, yet their lives were unknown to each other in so many ways.

The bell sounded and the bus came to a stop outside Turnpike Lane station. She watched more people get on below. 'Still, I don't think he should go, not when we have all been apart for so long,' she said. 'And he says he doesn't need anything, doesn't even want money from us to help him.'

'That's the only good thing about all this, that he's not thinking about wasting the money we've been saving,' said Pran. 'We need it for when we go back.'

'Back?' Jaya clutched the seat in front.

'You heard Rakesh, he's going back. I could join him.'

Why was Pran clinging to Rakesh's stories like this? 'They won't let you in. And even if they did, aren't you scared about what could happen?'

'You sound like Asha now,' he said, shrugging his shoulders.

'She agrees with me?' Jaya huffed. 'At least someone sees sense.'

'If I have to struggle, I'd rather do it in Uganda than here.'

'We need to get on with our lives here now.' Jaya tried to keep her voice down, glad that the bus was busy, the people wrapped up in their own conversations. Of course she longed to go back too, but the things she missed most were no longer there. 'After all the things Amin did to us, how can you even consider it?'

'What he did, Ba, was to take everything from us. I was born a Ugandan Asian, I'm going to die a Ugandan Asian. Not here, in a country that doesn't want me.'

Jaya looked at him. She knew what it meant to be forced out of the country you called home; she'd always be Indian, even if she never set foot there again. Yet unlike Pran, she'd learnt to let other places into her heart, make them a part of her too. She reminded herself to whisper. Even if people couldn't understand what they were saying, it would be clear from the tones of their voices that something was wrong. 'Don't fill your heart with anger, Pran.'

'Aren't you angry too?'

'Of course I am!' Jaya took a long breath to calm herself.

'But why fight fate? We need to make the best of what we have and build something new.'

'No, Ba.' His voice curled with anger. 'I'm sick of people telling us what to do and where to go.'

'Chup!' Her grip on the seat in front of her turned her knuckles pale. 'Stop. I don't want to talk about this, not here. Leave it alone, Pran.'

They sat in silence for the rest of the journey. But after they got off the bus and began walking down the street, Jaya stopped abruptly.

She glared at Pran, still trying to settle her restless breath. 'That money is for our future. Here, in this country, in our new home. I'm not letting you go back there, Pran.'

'It's not the same now—'

'After everything we've been through, how can you put me through this? After all we suffered.'

'But Ba—'

'Your Papa's death.'

'Listen to me, Ba.'

'And December!'

Pran stopped speaking. He stepped back as though she'd slapped him with her own hand. Her chundri fell from her head but she carried on.

*

The primary school was a three-storey building with red bricks and a slate roof and glossy black gates. They walked inside, through hallways filled with paintings of line-drawn houses and families with too-large heads and purple hair, past the little hooks at waist height with a long, low bench underneath. The front of the parquet-floored main hall was now covered in old multi-coloured saris. The stage, framed by navy curtains, now housed murti statues of Ganesh and Vishnu, guarding various offerings of food. Rather than travel for hours to the nearest temple each week, the community had decided to create their own.

'Jayaben, kemche? How is everyone?' said Kamlaben. They'd kept in touch after they'd grown close in the barracks, and she'd put her cooking skills to good use, now catering for weddings and other occasions throughout North London. Jaya and her friend talked about working together on bigger events. As usual, Kamlaben had made various sweet treats, slabs of creamy barfi and bright orange swirls of jelebi. Her talcum-powdered skin puckered as she insisted, 'Take some home later, I made too much.' She gestured in the direction of the food. On her right hand there were three dots that formed a triangle; the traditional symbols that showed the village and caste to which Kamlaben belonged still remained years later. They pointed upwards towards her fingers, the colour of the tattoos more grey-blue than the green-blue they must have been when first applied decades before in India. And yet here she was, in a country where most people would have no idea what the symbols even meant.

While Pran joined the other men, Jaya followed her friend, who now wore her sari so high it rippled at the tops of her ankles: her defence against English puddles, whether it was raining or not. More people arrived and they settled down for the *bhajan*, sung beautifully by Kamlaben's niece.

Though Jaya sang along too, she found her thoughts wandered. She tried to think back to what it was like to be young, to have the kind of dreams that Vijay now had, but her youth had been so different from his. Every journey in her own life had been forced on her: to Uganda, to England.

How lucky Vijay was to be able to make his own decisions. She sang along with the temple hymns, the scent of incense and the sugary sweetmeats filling the hall. She didn't understand the Sanskrit words, but she'd been told the meaning by others. The girl on the stage sang about compassion for others, patience and kindness. Jaya glanced at Pran, singing serenely. Such a contrast with how he'd been earlier, so angry as he told her how they couldn't let Idi Amin get away with it, how he couldn't forget the past. It must take so much energy to cling onto anger like that, to grasp it so tightly that it made you blind to everything else around you.

Asha had told her to be grateful that Vijay didn't carry fear in his heart, despite everything that had happened. After all, he had so much to be angry about. She thought about how they'd found Vijay in a crumpled heap in the kitchen the night December was taken, the look of anger when he'd been unable to stop the soldier attacking Asha, the disappointment on his face when he'd come home, night after night, still desperate to be given a job by someone who would look past his arm and the things he couldn't do and focus on the many things he could. Yes, as the sun shone through the windows and the songs of forgiveness echoed around the room, Jaya knew what she had to do.

34

Asha

Outside, the day had cheered up; the grubby sky had mellowed to pale blue and the shade had retreated to the far corners of the garden.

Through the glazed back door, Asha could make out Vijay's silhouette, sitting on the doorstep. They'd managed to avoid being alone together since Pran had come back. Things weren't exactly the same between them, but now that Vijay was leaving for his trip, there was no point making things awkward. That time had passed; they'd both been under so much stress. It was a moment of madness that felt like a lifetime ago. And besides, Asha needed Vijay's help now.

She stepped outside. 'Nice day,' she said, wandering out towards the fading flowers in the far corner of the yard.

Vijay looked up at her in surprise. 'Yeah,' he said slowly.

'Best to make the most of good weather whenever we can.'

He nodded, a cautious look on his face. 'You finished your job applications? Pran said you were trying to get them done as quickly as possible.'

Asha was glad that he was making an effort with her too. 'Almost. I'll do some more later.'

'Don't you like the place you're working at the moment?'

'It's fine, but it's mainly dealing with wills and things like that. Those people aren't the ones who really need help.' Asha shrugged. She'd found a couple of new roles, one at Haringey Council helping in the housing office, a couple working with local charities. Sinead from the office said she'd have a look at them over a quick drink when they were finished. 'I should be grateful, I know. At least I have a decent job to go to each day.'

'No, I know what you mean. Doing something that you want, not just something thrown at you, right?' He held a bowl of Jaya's fruit salad in his hand. She'd chopped the strawberries and peaches so small the fruit looked like tiny gemstones floating in the condensed milk.

'And to do things differently, I suppose,' said Asha. 'I could have done more when I was back in Uganda.' Like others, she'd been so wrapped up in her own life back there, never thought about helping the people around her.

'Yeah, I think we could all have been better. Maybe things would've been different then,' Vijay said. 'Anyway, it looks like I've managed to upset both Pran and Ba. Two for the price of one!'

'It's just a bit of a shock for them, this whole trip idea,' Asha said. 'They'll come round.'

'Soon, I hope. Trying to get a decent price on the plane ticket, they're not cheap.'

'Never knew you were capable of doing something quite so interesting.' Asha smiled, but she immediately wished she hadn't said it. She wasn't ready to go back to bantering with him as though the moment in the park had never happened.

He put down his empty bowl and squinted up at her in the sunlight. 'My friend has an old Pentax he's going to let me have. I fixed it up, I can send you all photos. The temples, the places Ba and Papa grew up.'

'Do you think your Papa would have liked it here in England?' Asha tried to imagine Motichand here with them now, walking around the house. Too small, too neat, for his boisterous ways.

'I doubt it. Too much hard work and weak tea!' Although Vijay joked, his deep voice was infused with sadness. 'You'll look after her, won't you? Ba, I mean.'

'Of course, Pran will too. Don't worry about us.'

Vijay looked down at a crack in the paving stones. 'I don't know about Pran. His head's all over the place. All this talk about going back.'

Asha hesitated. 'I didn't think he was serious before.' The renewed bond between her and Pran was as fragile as a silk thread but he insisted on looking backwards when they should have been moving on. 'But he keeps telling me how we'll all change our minds about it too.'

'That's the thing with Pran,' Vijay sighed, 'he loves to take control.'

They fell silent, the cloying scent of next door's roses drifting in the breeze. She stared at a snail determinedly making its way along the garden fence, leaving a silver trail behind it. She turned back towards him.

'Does that still hurt?' she said, pointing at the light scar on his forehead where the soldiers had hit him.

'No. It's fine.' Vijay smiled. 'I forget it's there most of the time.'

Asha paused, wondering if she should say something. 'I've been thinking about that night.'

'With the soldiers?'

She nodded. 'I don't know. All of Pran's talk about going back, I suppose it's made me think about it again.'

Vijay sat forward, resting his elbows on his knees.

'There's this thing that keeps coming back to me.' Asha brushed away a strand of her hair. 'Do you remember much about it?' Her chance to find out the truth. She had to know, once and for all.

He paused for a moment. 'Well, I remember everything until they hit me. Then it gets a bit fuzzy.'

'Well, yes. But things could have been a lot worse, couldn't they?'

Vijay looked at her in surprise. 'You don't think December disappearing was bad?'

'No, oh sorry, that's not what I meant. It's just the soldiers didn't seem that angry with you and Pran, when they found out about December. I mean they didn't even touch Pran?'

'There was more booze running through their veins than blood by that point,' said Vijay. 'They weren't thinking straight.'

Asha shielded her eyes with her hand. 'It just seemed like a miracle that neither of you . . .' That night, the terror, that endless wait in the darkness with Jaya, all of it came back to her. Vijay was right, the soldiers were drunk, there was no point dragging up bad memories or trying to make sense of it. 'Anyway, enough about Uganda, I have plenty of that with Pran and his plans.' She started heading towards the kitchen door.

'It was strange, though.' Vijay's voice was low.

Asha stepped back and looked at him, his eyes sparkling in the light. 'What was?'

'I mean, I was pretty dazed when they hit me, but I heard the soldiers leave. I heard footsteps.'

'What's strange about that?'

Vijay looked down. 'The thing is, it was all so quiet. And the whole time, I don't remember hearing December, or Pran. I don't think so, anyway.'

Asha stared at him.

'I didn't really think about it at the time, no noise from either of them.' Vijay shrugged. 'There was so much going on.'

'How sure are you?'

'Well, I'd just been hit over the head by a man who'd drunk more alcohol than the rest of Uganda put together so . . .'

'So you might have blacked out?'

'Maybe. But I remember lying there for a long time. I don't know, it's hard to explain.'

She'd known, deep down. Vijay didn't need to explain any of it.

35

Vijay

Vijay had stayed out in the garden long after Asha had gone back inside, watching the sky turn dark blue as next door's children shrieked and weaved their way through the alleys behind the houses. He was glad he and Asha had had a chance to speak before he went; things had been so odd, particularly after Pran arrived. The uneasy feeling every time Pran mentioned how well they'd all stuck together in his absence, the awkward glances. That's why travelling would be the best thing for him. It would be good to get away from the family, create some memories of his own that weren't tainted. He wanted to make sure that Ba's early life and Papa's weren't forgotten. Yet even now, his excitement for his trip was dampened by guilt. Ba shouldn't have to worry about him, or about Pran and his talk of Uganda. How could Pran think about leaving his wife, his family, just when he'd got them back? Why couldn't he see how lucky he was? Just then, Vijay heard the scuttle of a chair in the kitchen. He got up and went back inside.

Jaya was sitting at the table, while Pran poured them both glasses of water.

'How is everyone? Is Kamlamasi well?' said Vijay, leaning against the door.

'Yes, beta, they are all well, you should have joined us.' Jaya looked up at him, her tone mellow. 'Although, of course, there will be lots of temples in India too.'

'In India?' Vijay looked up at her.

Pran turned around. 'Who cares? He's not going.'

'It's up to Vijay whether he goes.' Jaya spoke to him in the same tone she'd used when they were children, after they'd grazed their knees or caught a fever.

Pran loomed over the table. 'He belongs here with us.'

'Why are you talking about me as though I'm not even here, Pran? I can make my own decisions.'

'This is ridiculous. You don't even have a plan. You're going to waste your money.'

'Yes, that's right. My money, that I saved, even when you weren't working.' Vijay stopped himself.

'Go on, say it.' Pran stepped towards him, his voice getting louder. Jaya stood up and put her hand on his chest in an effort to calm him.

'I didn't mean it. I'm sorry,' said Vijay, shaking his head. He lowered his voice. 'But that money's mine. What's the problem?'

'The problem is, we're a family. We should stick together after everything we've been through.'

'What's going on?' said Asha, coming down the stairs. They must have woken her from her nap.

'The money isn't just yours, Vij, we need to plan for our future,' said Pran, ignoring her.

Vijay stood up straight, his back stiffening. 'Your future in Uganda? You're going to run away, leave the people you care about here, aren't you?'

'That's rich, coming from you.' Pran's mouth twisted into a sneer.

Jaya turned, her body mirroring Pran's. 'It's Vijay's decision.'

'But you said you didn't want him to go?' Pran looked down at her. 'Why've you changed your mind so suddenly?'

'Vijay is right, it's his life.'

'No, I'm the head of the family. You're not going.' Pran slammed his hand on the table.

'Head of the family?' Vijay stepped towards Pran. 'I'm so sorry, I must have missed that. And where were you all those months when we were alone, who was the head of the family then?'

'That was different!' Pran shouted.

Asha rushed over to Pran to pull him back, but he moved his arm away. 'Please, Pran, sit down.' She tried to get him to meet her gaze.

Vijay knew he should stop needling, it was making things worse, but why should Pran always take control?

'He has to stay here with you until it's safe enough for you to join me, Ba,' said Pran.

Jaya put her hand to his cheek. 'Please, stop talking about Uganda.'

Pran turned from Jaya to his wife. 'And Asha, too.'

Asha met Pran's gaze. 'I told you before, I'm never going back to Uganda.'

Pran threw his hands up in the air. 'Everything we've ever had is back there.'

'No, not everything,' said Jaya, placing her arm on his shoulder. 'We are here. What about us?'

'But what kind of life do you have?' Pran shook his head.

'A secure one,' said Asha.

Pran stared at each of them in turn, waiting for another answer, one that suited him better. But there was no answer for him, only silence.

*

'Well, at least I'll keep fit while I'm travelling, lifting this thing,' said Vijay, as he and Jaya did their best to fasten his backpack. He couldn't believe he was finally leaving; the past few weeks getting everything in order had dragged on and on.

'Are you sure you've got everything, beta?' she said.

'Yes, Ba, I told you. It hadn't changed on the fifth time of asking and it won't have changed on the tenth either.' Vijay smiled. 'I'll be fine. Don't worry.'

'And do you have space for the vara? That airline food is awful.'

Asha walked in, her light cobalt blouse rustling as she moved. 'Are you sure you don't want us to come to the airport with you?' she said.

'You're starting to sound like Ba now,' said Vijay.

'Sorry,' Asha said, looking sheepish.

'Right, I think I've got everything now.' He stood up, hoisting the backpack onto his shoulders. 'If I don't topple over before I get to the Tube station.'

'Take care.' Asha smiled at him and patted him on the shoulder. Her goodbye was still many times warmer than Pran's had been that morning. All he'd done before leaving for work was tell him to be careful in a low, grave voice.

Jaya's tears were already falling. 'You'll write as soon as you get there, won't you?' She hugged him tightly while he did his best not to fall on her with the weight of the bag behind him. He needed to remember her, all of her, her coconut scent, the softness of her arms.

He made his way to the Tube station and said goodbye to his new home. The city would wait for him.

When he got to the terminal at Heathrow, he walked over to the check-in desk and smiled.

'What took you so long?' Marie gave him a long kiss. 'Let's get out of here, shall we?'

36

Asha

Across the water, the buildings of the South Bank turned from pink to bronze in the late-afternoon light, as Asha and Pran walked through Victoria Embankment.

Asha pulled the collar of her wool coat around her neck. After so many months, the silence between them should have been comfortable by now, but in Asha's head, it was as obtrusive as the shrieks of the nearby children and the rumble of the cars. They followed the path, guided by the street lamps flicking on along the way.

'I meant to tell you, I've got an interview for that job at the council.' For the first time in ages, she felt the buzz of working towards something she'd chosen for herself.

'That's nice,' Pran said, trying to sound interested. From the way he looked at her, she knew what he was thinking. In his head, it was all temporary, their whole life in England. 'And you're sure about changing jobs?'

'I want to help people here. I can't do that in my current role.' She suddenly felt shy explaining herself to Pran, who was always so focused on saving money and being practical. All roads led back to Uganda.

He nodded.

They stopped at a bench near a stretch of grass and she took out a thermos of chai from her handbag. She unwrapped the sandwiches that Jaya had given them earlier: white bread, a little butter, a little green chilli chutney and some slices of cucumber, the fresh smell reminding her of Jinja's red earth after the rain.

'Actually, I forgot to tell you.' His voice was cool, casual. 'I bought my ticket to go back.' He looked out across the water as if it was nothing.

Asha turned towards him. 'And you forgot to tell me?'

'I've talked about it for a while.'

'But you've gone and booked it. Another thing you've kept from me?'

'It's not like that. Anyway, it's not a surprise, is it?'

'You said you were thinking about it. I didn't know you'd just go ahead without telling me.' The truth was, Asha had thought that she'd somehow still be able to talk him out of it. Too late now. 'So when are you leaving?'

'A few weeks' time. The quicker I get out there,' said Pran, 'the quicker I can get things settled.'

Settled for the rest of them to join him, he meant, though Pran knew by now not to bring that up. She was sick of talking about his plans for her. This was her time now.

'Talking of Uganda,' her voice was taut, 'I was thinking about December the other day.'

'Again? You and Ba, always talking about him. I might start getting jealous.' A thread of frustration ran through his voice.

She searched for clues in his eyes, dusk casting shadows across his face. 'That night he disappeared.'

'It's getting cold. Shall we go back?' He rubbed his hands together.

'Don't change the subject.'

'It's not that. I just worry about you, always focusing on the past.'

'Me? Isn't that what you're doing?' she said. 'We never talked about that night, not properly.'

He sighed. 'Do you enjoy reliving it all, Asha?'

'Stop it.'

'The soldiers took him. We never saw him again. Shall I get it printed on a card, so I don't have to keep repeating myself?'

'Vijay said he didn't hear a struggle.'

He laughed, openly bitter now. 'Vijay had been knocked against a wall, not sure he heard much of anything.'

'But he'd come around by then. When they left, all he heard was footsteps. He told me.'

He turned towards her. 'Talking behind my back now?'

'Vijay told me that there was no noise, no struggling, nothing.'

'The soldiers had guns. They'd already hit him, why make things worse?'

'But it doesn't make sense.' Asha tried to catch her breath. Always so hard to get the truth from him. 'Wouldn't December have made some noise? He must have been frightened.'

'I don't remember. Maybe he did and you just didn't hear. You were across the other side of the yard.'

'Wouldn't the soldiers have shouted when they found him, shouted at you for hiding him?' The breeze had picked up. She pushed a lock of hair from her face.

'They were drunk, Asha.'

'You're not telling me everything. I know it.'

'There is no "everything".'

'Tell me.' Asha stood up from the bench and loomed over him.

'Stop, Asha. People are staring.'

'*Muneh ke!* There's something else, I know it!' Asha's voice faded to a whisper as she took Pran's face in her hands, his stubble rough against her skin. 'I just need to know what really happened, please tell me.'

Pran looked down at the ground. 'I had no choice.'

'Choice about what?'

'It all happened so fast. I had to do something.'

'You're not making any sense.' She stepped back from him.

'December was in danger whatever happened. I had to do something.' Panic in his eyes. 'After the soldiers left, I went to check on December.'

'He was still there?' she said. Pran tried to take hold of Asha's hands but she pulled away.

'The soldiers were so drunk, they didn't bother to search properly. They'd opened the storeroom door, barely looked around and came out again. He'd been hiding in the far corner.' Pran's voice was so quiet that Asha had to step closer to hear him above the people around them and the screech of the trains on the bridge nearby. 'It was December who first suggested it, I swear.'

'The soldiers didn't take him?' She needed to say the words out loud.

Pran sighed. '"I'll leave in a moment," December said, "it's not safe for you all if I stay".'

'And you didn't try and stop him?' Her cheeks flushed. He made it sound so simple, as though December was heading off to the market for the day, not leaving forever, disappearing into the darkness.

'I should've tried. But the family was in danger. We were risking all our lives for his.' Pran looked down at his hands, rubbing one thumb across the other, over and over again. He waited for Asha to speak, but the words had piled up on her tongue.

Pran continued, 'I gave him some money and we waited until we were sure the soldiers had definitely gone.'

'You knew he was leaving and you didn't at least let your Ba say goodbye to him?'

'It was easier that way.'

'Easier for who, Pran? For you?'

'I was trying to keep you all safe.'

Asha looked at him. A tiny part of her understood why he'd done it, feeling that same grip of fear she'd felt that night when she'd seen the soldiers in the house, worrying what they'd do to Pran, to all of them. But why had he lied to her for so long?

'You never told me the truth.'

'What good would have it done?' His head still bowed. 'I feel guilty every day. Every time any of you mention his name.'

'But after everything I said, you promised you wouldn't lie to me again. We'd lost so much, I thought I could at least trust you, I could hold onto that if nothing else.' Sickness swelled in her stomach. He'd let her think she was foolish for doubting him. Lying to her face for months. Lying to everyone he loved.

He looked up at her. No words left.

She began to walk away from him, gathering pace.

Pran followed. 'Asha, wait.'

She couldn't look at him any longer. Couldn't bear to hear his voice. She carried on towards Embankment station, weaving through the people, past a flower seller who was packing up his things, the pavement dotted with withering petals.

Pran caught up with her. She shrugged his hand away and carried on walking. 'You dragged Vijay to the police station when he was hurt, you let your mother wait, holding out hope that you would bring him back.'

'But I gave December money, so he could get away. As much cash as I could.'

She stopped and turned sharply towards him. 'Money. Paper and ink. Your answer to everything. How would that have protected him? They would have found him and taken that too. Well done. You helped him live, what, an extra minute, maybe two?' Asha tried her best to control her voice. At least their speaking in Gujarati meant that passers-by couldn't understand what Pran had done. The shame of it.

Pran took her by the shoulders; she felt his breath on her. 'What do you think would have happened to us, Asha, if he'd stayed?' An elderly man paused to watch them, concern on his face.

She summoned a small smile to show there was nothing to worry about and turned back to her husband. 'But the soldiers had gone.'

'You don't know that. Some homes had been looted by the army two, three times, with the families still in the house. And you know what they do to the young women.' Asha looked away from him. 'Anyway I hadn't worked it all out, there was no guarantee we'd get him out.'

'It was all settled, that's what you said?'

'It was still risky. They might have stopped him before he got to the border. Every minute he stayed, we were in danger too.'

'You're making it sound like it was December's fault.' Asha threw her hands in the air. 'Their fault, not his. They wanted to kill him because of who he was. Don't you see?'

Pran's face was filled with confusion.

'He was just like you. Acholi or Indian, it's all the same. They hated us all because of who we were.'

Asha walked away from him. Pran knew better than to follow this time. She listened to children shrieking in delight, the laughter of young couples holding hands and embracing near the water's edge. She wanted to scream at them all to shut up.

Would it have been better not to know the truth, to bury his lies? He kept throwing it back in her face, how he'd only done it for the people he loved. She'd felt that terror, creeping beneath her skin, the danger. She'd felt that desire to protect, no matter what. But what he'd done. To lie to his own family. That was something else.

She carried on walking and found herself near the Royal Courts of Justice, ghostly in the dark, winding her way through ancient streets, the old buildings dripping with shadows. She hurried on, trying to flee her anger, her thoughts. On into the night she walked for hours, through the city.

She thought back to the day after the soldiers came, things that seemed so small, so insignificant at the time. That morning, she'd gone into the storeroom while Pran and Vijay had gone to speak to the army and find out what had happened to December. The folding bed was tucked away behind the large gunny sacks, the chalky smell of rice and flour still filled the air. More sacks were slumped in the far corner where December must have hidden away. But it was only now she remembered that his few belongings, his bag, were all gone. She'd not thought about it at the time, lost in confusion, about how odd it was that the soldiers would let him take his bag with him when they cared so little for human life.

And later, when she'd climbed into bed with Pran that evening, his sadness reflected in his eyes.

'What a day,' he'd said, stroking her hair.

'I can't believe he's gone,' said Asha, sheets hot beneath her. 'I know we agreed you wouldn't go and speak to the army again, but perhaps it's worth one last try?' She knew the answer but asked the question anyway, clinging on to hope.

'I don't think so. They were adamant today.' Pran looked up at the ceiling. 'I'm sorry, Asha.'

'I can't wait to get out of this place,' she said. 'I'm so sick of this danger hanging over us.'

'Those salas won't be able to control us much longer.' Pran

turned back towards her and trailed his thumb across her cheek. 'And perhaps . . .'

'Perhaps what?'

'Maybe it's for the best. One less thing threatening us.'

She lifted her head. 'Don't say that.'

'But you said it yourself, the danger hanging over us.'

'That's not what I meant.'

'What happened to December's awful.' He sighed. 'No one deserves that. But one good thing came out of this. We're safer now.'

Asha put her head back on the pillow. 'I can't think about that right now. All I can think about is the look on your Ba's face this morning.'

Pran hadn't responded, she recalled now, as she carried on through the streets of London. They'd both fallen silent.

By the time she got home, the house was dark. In their room, Pran was sitting on the bed with the lights off, completely still.

'I was worried about you,' he said quietly. He didn't look up.

Though he sat right there in front of her, she grieved for him, thinking of the man he used to be – or the man she thought he was.

'I needed to think and work it all out in my head.' She closed the door behind her.

'And have you?'

'There are more questions than answers.'

'So ask,' he said, voice flat.

'How were you going to get December out? If the soldiers hadn't come?'

'We talked about this,' he said. 'That wealthy family Vijay and I worked with.'

'And how were they going to help?'

Pran was silent.

'Well?'

'I asked them if they knew a way to help people get out.' He paused. 'But they said they couldn't help with things like that, not with the expulsion going on. Things were too dangerous.'

'So what were you going to do?'

Pran stared at her, shook his head in response.

'You didn't know, did you?' She knew the answer before he looked at her. Perhaps she'd even known back in Uganda, somewhere deep down.

'He didn't really have a chance at all,' Pran said.

'So you let him leave, like prey to be hunted.' She paused, then said, 'Wait. Did you tell that family about December?'

'I didn't tell them his name.'

'No, I mean did you tell them that you were hiding someone in the house?'

'Of course not.' Pran gave an empty laugh. 'I just said someone I knew needed help and they wanted to get a friend out of the country.'

'But they might have guessed that it was you, it was your house?'

'Don't be silly, Asha.'

'Even if they weren't sure, with the army hassling everyone they might have tipped off the soldiers. To keep them off their own backs.' She thought of all the people they knew who'd left silently in the night, worried about being betrayed.

'No, that's not possible.' He shook his head.

'How do you know, Pran?'

'They were just two drunk soldiers trying their luck.'

'The world was upside down. You can't be sure that the family weren't to blame.'

'If they'd been tipped off, the soldiers would have kept looking.' He looked up at her for the first time, his face in darkness except for the outline of his cheek, etched in weak light.

Anger twisted in her chest. She sat down on the other corner of the bed, her legs weak beneath her.

'I couldn't let anything happen to you,' said Pran.

'But you let it happen to December?'

She watched him, how small he seemed as he collapsed onto the bed.

'All I ever wanted was no secrets,' she said. 'To stick together, no matter what.'

She lay down next to him, neither touching the other. What use were words now? She couldn't change any of it. And leaving aside the past, what about all his obsessive plans to return, when all she was trying to do was build something from the remnants of their old life? Something that had been small, like a tiny crack in a windowpane, had grown between them, until it could all collapse into nothing.

Now what? It wasn't as though they could divorce, no one did that, not amongst the people they'd grown up with. The shame would tear her parents apart; Jaya too, who'd been there for her when no one else had been.

But how could Asha ignore all the lies he'd told, move on, pretend that they were just another ordinary couple? If they acted as if everything was normal, wouldn't she be a liar too?

37

Asha

Asha pinned her sari into place as best she could. Still so difficult, even after years of practice.

'Hurry up, Asha. We'll be late,' Pran called from the bottom of the stairs.

Asha rushed across the bedroom, nearly sending her pile of library books tumbling off the table. She wrapped herself in a blue saal to keep the cool weather out, and joined Pran and Jaya in the car. The Ford Cortina spluttered into life. Pran borrowed it from time to time from one of his friends at the factory, who'd bought it for next to nothing. A fact they were reminded of every time they turned the engine on.

'It worked straight away!' said Pran.

'That's a first.' Asha looked across at him.

'It's not so bad,' said Jaya.

'Exactly, it gets us where we need to go, right?' Pran said, tapping his hand against the dashboard as though he was petting a horse.

'Better than getting the bus, I suppose. I can't stay too late anyway.' She was meeting Sinead for a coffee and a catch-up tomorrow. Asha played with her sari chundri as they made their way down Bounds Green Road.

'Isn't that the sari I bought you?' Pran glanced at the fuchsia-pink silk, the gold-beaded embroidery.

Asha nodded. 'Just after we got married.'

Pran smiled. 'I thought so. I haven't seen you wear it before.'

'Not had the chance until now.'

They arrived at the wedding venue, a mahogany-panelled school hall in Enfield, the smell of wood polish mingling with the smoky sandalwood scent of agarbatti. The couple had already had a separate civil ceremony a couple of days before. The school hall was cheap to hire and served as a venue for the Hindu ceremony. The wedding had already started and the guests sat in rows facing the stage. The *mandwo* stood proudly on top, four carved wooden pillars, decorated here and there with whatever red plastic flowers they'd managed to get their hands on. Beneath it, the *maharaj* took the bride and groom through the rituals, while close family, including the bride's mother, Kamlaben, looked on. Asha watched as the couple under the mandwo gazed at each other and repeated the Sanskrit words after the maharaj. How beautiful the scene looked, how similar to her own wedding. And how different the new couple's lives would be from hers and Pran's.

As usual, the guests continued chattering, paying little attention to the wedding ceremony itself. 'If God had wanted us to stay quiet during a Hindu wedding, he'd have made it an hour shorter!' Motichand used to say. He would wriggle and fidget his way through. Asha watched Pran as he went to sit with some friends from temple.

After the ceremony, they took their place in the queue for food, the air filling with the sweet scent of basmati rice and the lemony tang of curry leaves. Young men stood behind the table serving *buteta nu shaak*, small pieces of potato glistening in the tomato sauce; puffed up rounds of golden-brown *puri*; sweet saffron-coloured pearls of bundhi, all piled up in the little compartments of the white plastic plates.

Jaya inspected it all. She'd helped Kamlaben the day before

with the food preparation, and was now bossing the servers about as she went along the line, telling them to serve bigger portions and complaining that the shaak wasn't hot enough.

'Look, Asha,' Jaya said, as they took their places along the trestle table. She gestured to Ramniklal and Hiraben, who were waving from the other end of the hall. They hurried over with their own plates of food, smiling all the way.

'Jayaben, how nice it is to see you.' Hiraben clutched Jaya's hand. 'And Asha, you look so well!' Jaya had written to Hiraben but they hadn't seen each other since their first few months in England.

Asha introduced Pran. Ramniklal and Hiraben shared their news, how they'd settled down in the Midlands. After both working at the local typewriter factory, they'd managed to secure a business loan and started a newsagent with a distant cousin of Ramniklal's.

'He wants it open seven days a week,' Hiraben rolled her eyes.

'We'd have holidays too,' Ramniklal protested.

'Five hours on a Sunday afternoon is not a holiday,' Hiraben smiled.

But though they both looked a little tired, their faces were full of a hope Asha hadn't seen at the barracks.

Asha told them about her new job, working in the housing office of the local council.

'And Vijaybhai?' said Hiraben, taking another spoonful of bundhi.

'He is still off roaming the world,' said Jaya, shaking her head in mock annoyance. 'But he says he'll be back soon, or at least that's what his last postcard told me.'

'Well, I hear you have plenty to keep you occupied, Jayaben, with your own little empire,' said Ramniklal, smiling. Jaya must have told him how she'd teamed up with Kamlaben, cooking at events. Pran had shown her how to keep her own accounts and she even put some money aside in a bank account each month.

Though Jaya spoke shyly, the pride in her eyes was clear to see. 'Oh, it's just a little bit here and there, *thoru thoru.*'

Asha looked at each of them as Jaya made plans for them to go and visit the couple, agreeing to stay over for a few nights. To relax and laugh and talk, free from the worry of being homeless and unemployed, seemed ridiculously indulgent, even now. But Asha loved the warmth of it, an intense happiness that filled her up.

'We heard a lot about you,' said Ramniklal, turning to Pran.

'Oh yes? Asha probably said I smoke too much?' Pran grinned.

Ramniklal looked awkwardly at Asha. 'No, sorry, I meant your Ba. She told us about you in her letters. Your difficulties getting into England.'

'Oh, I see,' said Pran, looking down at his plate.

'And you're going back to Uganda soon?' said Ramniklal.

'You're very brave.' Hiraben leant forward, resting her arm on the table.

'Oh, I don't know,' said Pran. 'Amin will be gone soon.'

'And the army?' Ramniklal's voice betrayed his concern.

Pran shrugged. 'It's fine. They're saying they want people to help them run the old dukans.'

'And Ashaben, you'll go too?' said Hiraben. It was plain to see on their friends' faces, that same confusion that Asha and Jaya had felt ever since Pran first brought up Uganda again.

She shook her head. 'I'll leave the hard work to Pran.'

'For now, at least,' said Pran, shifting in his seat. 'I'm going back next week.'

'I've tried to talk Pran out of it, but he insists. So stubborn,' Jaya's voice went quiet. 'I will stay here with Asha and Vikash, who used to live with us, said he could come back for a few months to help with the bills. Anyway, Vijay will arrive back soon enough.' As well as the postcards, Vijay had sent a few photographs taken on his old Pentax. Vast temples, Jaya and Motichand's family huddled together and smiling; each image had a date and a handwritten note from him. Jaya had put them all on the mantelpiece, tears of happiness and sadness in her eyes.

Later, the hall was cleared and the chairs moved to the edges of the room while the harmonium player and a *tabla* player set up.

'There's *garba*?' Jaya put her hands together.

'The bride loves dancing, apparently,' Hiraben said.

Asha joined Jaya and Hiraben. 'Too much for me,' said Ramniklal, taking a seat.

Pran went and sat with his friends to watch. Women and a few men formed a large circle and began the familiar dance, slow at first: a clap, a click, a clap, saris sweeping across the floor, moving around the room to the beat of the tabla and the deep melodies of the harmonium. The music getting faster with each round, the heavy timbre of the drumbeat vibrating through Asha's body.

She watched Jaya and Hiraben giggling as they left the line, their faces glistening with sweat, the music too fast for them. Asha carried on with the younger women, their faces gleeful, dizzier with each round, on and on, round and round, head spinning, hair coming loose from her bun, skin slick with moisture, willing herself on and on, round and round, until finally she stumbled out of the circle.

'You stayed so long, Ashaben.' Hiraben came over and nudged her. 'These young girls can keep dancing forever, heh, Jayaben? Remember those days?'

Asha tried to catch her breath.

'Here,' said Jaya, handing her a cup of water.

She gulped it down in one. 'I think I need some fresh air.'

Asha went outside round the back of the school, where hop-scotch games had been chalked into the playground in pastel pinks and mint green. In the sky, sunset began to give way to night.

A shiver ran up her neck.

Pran was already standing outside smoking, leaning against the wall. He turned towards her.

'I'll come back later,' she said, voice cool. No point in pretending now, there was no one else around. She turned back.

'Wait, stay a moment,' Pran called out.

She stopped, her back to him. 'What for?'

'To talk.'

'We've had plenty of time to talk.' She looked back at the past few weeks, how they'd gone over the same things again and again. In public, they pretended that nothing had changed because it was easier than dealing with Jaya's questions and worry.

'But I'm leaving soon,' said Pran.

'I know.' Asha turned towards him as he held his cigarette in the air. The muffled sound of wedding songs drifted outside, people singing about leaving home, making new families, happy new lives.

'I don't want to leave things like this between us.'

'It's too late for that.'

'You'll still join me later, though? You have to.'

'I have to?'

'I mean, if you don't, what will people say? What about Ba?'

'What would Ba think about what you did?' The breeze had picked up, rustling through the chiffon of her sari.

'You promised you wouldn't tell her.'

'Don't worry, I'm still keeping your secrets.' Asha laughed bitterly. Jaya had been through enough. Telling her the truth would break her into little pieces. It was the one thing they could both agree on. 'You go to your precious Uganda and leave her in peace. Leave us both in peace.'

'Don't talk like that, please. Don't you care what people think?'

She shrugged her shoulders. 'I'd rather deal with people saying things than go back to that hell.'

'You'll change your mind. We'll get everything back. Just give me some time.'

'Time to let you lie to me again? Or time waiting until you're killed out there?'

He kicked the sole of his shoe against the wall, whispering, but his voice was full of fury. 'Don't talk like that. I'm trying to help us . . .' He carried on talking but Asha was no longer listening. The words were the same wherever she was, Uganda, England. When it all came down to it, she didn't believe him any more. A strange calm settled in her chest as she turned away.

'Wait, Asha, wait. There's one more thing I need to ask you. Please.'

She stopped as she reached for the handle of the exit door, not bothering to turn back towards him. 'What?'

'What if I stayed? What if I didn't go to Uganda? If I stayed with you here. We'd be OK then, wouldn't we?'

Her hand remained on the door handle, knuckles red from the cold. She didn't turn back. Instead, she caught her reflection in the glass. She saw Pran behind her, eyes frantic, desperate as he called her name again. She looked beyond, to the people inside, to the flashes of colour, the sequins glinting like stars, everyone dancing and laughing together.

Asha pulled the door open and went inside.

Acknowledgements

Many people helped me to take this story from a vague idea in my mind to my debut novel.

A huge thank you to my agent, Jenny Savill, who understood exactly what I wanted to do with *Kololo Hill* and made my dream a reality. Thank you also to the Andrew Nurnberg Associates team who've championed this book throughout.

I'm indebted to the entire team at Picador; our first meeting felt like coming home. Your passion and dedication have shone through every step of the way. A special thank you to my brilliant editor, Ansa Khan Khattak, for your insightful comments and for sometimes knowing Jaya and her family better than I did. So many others have played a part in bringing *Kololo Hill* into the world including Chloe May whose hard work has pushed *Kololo Hill* through the editing stages and into print, Lucy Scholes who has designed a dream cover that I'm so proud to show off and Emma Bravo, Katie Bowden and Kate Green who have all tirelessly spread the word about my book. Thank you all.

Debi Alper and Emma Darwin, you are superwomen. The 'Self-Edit Your Novel' course helped make *Kololo Hill* what it is today.

I thought that I was entering an ordinary writing competition in 2018, but how wrong I was about the Bath Novel Award.

I'm honoured to be a part of your international community. Thank you to the BNA readers and, in particular, Caroline Ambrose, for helping me on my journey.

A huge thank you to Aki Schilz and Joe Sedgwick at The Literary Consultancy, Anjali Joseph at UEA, Spread the Word, Lorena Goldsmith and the DGA First Novel Prize, CBC Creative, Jericho Writers and the wonderful Andrew Wille. The ability to hear other authors' success stories at the London Writers' Cafe, Asian Writers' Festival and Riff Raff London events inspired me to keep going.

I wouldn't have written a word of this novel if it hadn't been for Deborah Andrew's early support. You pushed me to take risks and gave me the tools to write no matter what. Thank you for helping me to fall in love with writing again after twenty years away from the page.

The goodwill of the entire writing community is extraordinary, but I could never have dreamt of meeting friends like the #VWG. Your talents inspired me and your kindness nourished me when I needed it most, as well as keeping me entertained when I really should have been working on my book!

A number of early readers provided excellent feedback. Daniel Aubrey, whose enthusiastic support, talent for writing page-turners and selecting funny GIFs knows no bounds; and Lorna (Loarn) Paterson, kind, tireless and meticulous. You both cheered me on and showed endless patience while reading my many drafts. Thanks also to Sheena Meredith, Cathy Parmenter and Gill Perdue for taking the time to read later versions.

Thanks to my beautiful friends Finn, Hema, Lisa and Marina, who made me smile, celebrated my successes and kept me going through everything.

Finally, my love and thanks to my parents and grandparents, who made sacrifices in their lives so that I could have a world of opportunity in my own.

Author's Note

It's always interesting, explaining my family background. 'I'm British Asian, but my parents are East African Asians, my ancestors are from India.' Cue various explanations of how that came to be. My mum was born in Kenya, my dad in Tanzania, and I spent many family holidays enjoying the places where they'd grown up.

There was also a wider story, one that very few British people appeared to know about, unless they recalled the news reports from the early 1970s. The story of 80,000 Ugandan Asians expelled from their home. I'd often wondered what it would be like to leave everything you know and love behind, to start again. When children at school told me to 'go back to my own country', I spent a lot of time wondering where my 'own country' was. I would think hard about what my family would do, where they would go, and decades later I finally had the opportunity to explore those questions through my writing. This novel is inspired by real-life events. I have tried to be as authentic as possible in bringing that history to life, but *Kololo Hill* is, of course, primarily a work of fiction.

I used a variety of resources to research the Ugandan Asian experience. Yasmin Alibhai-Brown's wonderful *The Settler's Cookbook: A Memoir of Love, Migration and Food* gave me a window into colonial East Africa.

Immigrants Settling in the City: Ugandan Asians in Leicester by Valerie Barrett and *From Citizen to Refugee: Uganda Asians Come to Britain* by Mahmood Mamdani enabled me to understand what it must have been like for those trying to rebuild their lives in a new country. Hansard (Hansard.parliament.uk) helped me piece together the British government's response to Idi Amin's decree and the subsequent treatment of the refugees.

'Exiles: Ugandan Asians in the UK', an oral history project by the SOAS Centre for Migration and Diaspora Studies in collaboration with the Royal Commonwealth Society and the Council of Asian People (CAP), provided me with rare first-hand accounts of the Ugandan Asian expulsion. The BBC website and YouTube both gave me access to lots of archive material from the early 1970s, in both East Africa and Britain.

To better understand Vijay's experiences, I read *Defying Disability* by Mary Wilkinson and *Disability and the Welfare State in Britain* by Jameel Hampton. YouTube vloggers including Grace Mandeville provided an insight into life with an upper-arm disability.

I also spoke at length to my parents and wider family to get a feel for East Africa from an Indian point of view. I'll treasure the time I spent learning more about their own upbringings in Kenya and Tanzania, in the shadow of Idi Amin's atrocities across the border.

In May 2017, I visited Uganda as part of a research trip, to better understand what life might have been like for ordinary Ugandans. I understood instantly why people call this stunning country 'the pearl of Africa', as well as why it must have been so difficult to leave. The exact number of people who disappeared and were murdered by Idi Amin's government is unknown; estimates suggest it could have been up to 500,000. He was responsible for the deaths of many people from rival tribes as well as anyone who dissented or disagreed with him.

Although many Ugandan Asians were beaten, harassed or raped, the vast majority got out of the country alive.

While there were some Asians who were friendly with house boy and girls, as well as others who they knew socially, I've not come across any stories of Asians protecting Ugandans the way Jaya and her family help December. However, I came across an anecdotal account of an Asian family helping to hide tribesmen caught up in the Mau Mau revolt against the British in Kenya. I used this as inspiration to explore the key relationships in my story.

Writing a novel is tough, of course. But it was nothing compared to the life of my Nani, who as a teenager sailed for weeks across the ocean from India to Kenya with a baby, while the lights of the steamer ship were blacked out to protect them from the war raging across the world. Putting pen to paper, fingers to keyboard is not so extraordinary. Leaving one world behind to create a whole new one, sometimes twice over, that's truly remarkable.

I hope you enjoyed this book. If so, I'd be so grateful if you could leave a rating or review to help others discover *Kololo Hill* too.

www.neemashah.com